Look Out, Lancaster County

4-IN-1 STORY COLLECTION

WANDA E. BRUNSTETTER

ISBN 978-1-61626-256-3

All Pennsylvania Dutch words are taken from the *Revised Pennsylvania German Dictionary* found in Lancaster County, Pennsylvania.

Cover and chapter art illustrations by Richard Hoit.

For more information about Wanda E. Brunstetter, please access the author's website at the following Internet address: www.wandabrunstetter.com.

Published by Barbour Publishing, Inc., P.O. Box 719, Uhrichsville, Ohio 44683, www.barbourbooks.com

Our mission is to publish and distribute inspirational products offering exceptional value and biblical encouragement to the masses.

Printed in the United States of America.
Dickinson Press, Inc., Grand Rapids, MI 49512; D10002808

School's Out!

Dedication

To my son, Richard Jr., who had his share of fun
with lightning bugs when he was a boy.

And to my grandchildren: Richelle, Philip, and Ric,
who, like Rachel Yoder, enjoy doing many fun
things on their mini-farm.

Glossary

ach—oh
aldi—girlfriend
baremlich—terrible
bensel—silly child
bletsching—spanking
blicking—shelling
boppli—baby
bruder—brother
bussli—kitten
busslin—kittens
butzemann—scarecrow
daadihaus—grandfather's house
daed—dad
danki—thank you
dumm—dumb
dunner—thunder
fleh—fleas
galgedieb—scoundrel
gretzich—crabby
gut—good
jah—yes
kapp—cap
kinner—children
kischblich—silly
kotze—vomit
lecherlich—ridiculous
mamm—mom
maus—mouse
naerfich—nervous
rutschich—squirming
schnell—quickly
schweschder—sister
verhuddelt—confused
wedderleech—lightning
wunderbaar—wonderful

"Das Lob Lied"	"The Hymn of Praise"
Der Herr sie gedankt.	Thank the Lord.
Em Tom sei hutschle bin ich leedich.	I'm tired of Tom's neighing.
Gebscht uff?	Do you give up?
Guder mariye.	Good morning.
Immer druwwle eiyets.	Always trouble somewhere.
Kens devun hot's duh kenne.	Neither one could do it.

Introduction

The Amish are a group of people who, due to their religious beliefs, live a plain life without the use of many modern tools. Early Amish people lived in Europe, but many came to America in the 1700s so they could worship freely. More than 150,000 Amish now live in the United States and Canada.

The Old Order Amish wear plain clothes, much like the American pioneers used to wear. Because they believe electricity is too modern, they use kerosene, propane gas, coal, diesel fuel, and wood for heating their homes, cooking, and running their machinery and appliances. Telephones are not allowed inside their houses, but some Amish have phones in their shops, barns, or sheds outside the home. Most Amish use a horse and buggy for transportation, but they ride in cars with hired drivers to take longer trips and go places where they can't drive their buggies.

At one time, most Amish men farmed for a living, but now many work as blacksmiths, harness makers, carpenters, painters, and in other trades. Some Amish women earn money by selling eggs, fruits and vegetables, or handmade items such as dolls and quilts. Others work in gift shops, bakeries, or restaurants.

Many Amish children attend a one-room schoolhouse from grades one to eight. Once they leave school, they spend time learning a trade so they can get a job and earn money to support themselves and their families.

Most Amish do not hold their worship services in a church building. They have church every other week, and it's held in the home, shop, or barn of different church members. In order to keep their religious beliefs, the Amish have chosen to live separate, plain lives.

Chapter 1

The Unforgettable Picnic

Boom!

Rachel Yoder shivered when the thunder clapped. She didn't like storms, and she especially didn't want one this evening. She was tempted to bite off the end of a fingernail like she often did when she felt nervous, but she caught herself in time. Nail biting could make you sick if your hands were dirty, and it was a bad habit she needed to break. Her mom often said so.

Rachel poked her head through the flap at the back of her family's dark gray Amish buggy and was glad to see that it wasn't raining. Maybe the storm would pass them and be on its way. Today was Friday, and this evening's picnic was her family's way to celebrate the last day of the school year. She didn't want anything to spoil their fun.

A horn honked from behind, and Pap guided their horse to the side of the road. Rachel peeked out the flap again, this time sticking her head out so she could get a good look at the fancy cars going by. *Woosh!* A gust of wind came up as she leaned out to wave at a shiny blue convertible. *Zip!* Rachel gasped as the white *kapp* [cap] she wore on her head sailed into the air and landed near the edge of the road. "*Ach!* [Oh!] My kapp—it's gonna get run over!" she hollered.

"Rachel Yoder, you know better than to lean out the buggy like that," Pap scolded. "What if you had fallen?"

"Can I get my kapp?" she asked tearfully.

"No!" Mom shook her head. "You might get hit by a car."

As the blue convertible started to pass, Rachel saw surprise on the face of the blond woman riding in the passenger's seat. The car pulled over behind their buggy, and the woman got out. She picked up Rachel's kapp and brought it over to the stopped buggy. "I believe this blew out of your buggy," she said, handing the limp-looking kapp to Rachel's father.

"Thank you," Pap said. "It belongs to my daughter."

"Thank you," Rachel echoed as Pap handed the kapp to her.

Rachel's cheeks heated with embarrassment as she put the kapp on her head.

"Stay in your seat now, Rachel," Pap said. He waited until the car had passed; then he pulled back into traffic.

Jacob, who was eleven, two years older than Rachel, sat up and yawned. He had been asleep in the seat beside her. "Are we there? I'm hungry."

"No, Pap stopped to let some cars go by." Rachel was careful not to mention that her kapp had blown off when she'd leaned out of the buggy. She knew Jacob would have teased her about it.

Jacob wrinkled his forehead, and the skin around his blue eyes crinkled. "Noisy cars sometimes scare our horse as they whiz by."

Rachel had seen horses do all kinds of strange things when they got spooked. She felt sorry for the horses. Still, she thought it would be fun to ride in a fast car. She leaned close to Jacob and whispered, "I saw a shiny blue convertible."

He shrugged. "So?"

"I'd like to ride in a car like that one someday," Rachel said. It was a secret she'd told no one else.

Jacob looked at Rachel as if she didn't have a lick of sense. Of course, she knew her brother thought most things she said and did were kind of strange.

"Don't you ever get tired of riding in this closed-in buggy?" she asked.

" 'Course not. I like our buggy just fine," he said.

"If I ever get the chance to ride in a convertible and see how fast it goes, I'm gonna take it," she mumbled.

Jacob nudged Rachel's arm. "You'd best not let anyone hear you speak such foolishness. It's one thing to ride in a car when we need to hire a driver for a reason, like to go to the big city. But just riding in one so you can see how fast it goes would be seen as a prideful, selfish wish."

Rachel crossed her arms and turned her back to her brother. She decided to drop the subject, but she turned around again and glared at Jacob when their parents weren't looking. He didn't understand the way she felt. He hardly ever did, and neither did their older brother, Henry. But at least Henry didn't act like something was wrong with her, the way Jacob did.

Boom! Rachel shuddered again. "It better not rain and spoil our picnic," she said, hoping Jacob wouldn't notice her hands shaking.

He elbowed her in the ribs. "What's the matter? Are you afraid of a little *dunner* [thunder]?"

"It's not the thunder that makes me *naerfich* [nervous]," she said, elbowing him right back. "It's those horrible bolts of *wedderleech* [lightning] I'm worried about."

"We'll be okay. It's not even raining, so the storm will probably pass over us." Jacob leaned his head against the back of the seat and closed his eyes again.

Maybe if I think about something else I won't feel so nervous. Rachel glanced toward the front of the buggy, where her parents and older sister, Esther, sat chatting in the Pennsylvania Dutch language that Amish people often spoke.

"*Em Tom sei hutschble bin ich leedich* [I'm tired of Tom's neighing]," her father said.

Rachel clutched the folds in her dress. It worried her to hear Pap complaining about their horse Tom. Pap had just said, "I'm tired of Tom's neighing," and she wondered if he was planning to get rid of their old horse. Rachel couldn't bear the thought. Tom was a nice animal and had been their main buggy horse for many years. What was wrong with a little neighing? People talked whenever they wanted to say something. Shouldn't a horse be able to neigh whenever he felt like it?

Mom responded to Pap's comment, but another car whizzed past and drowned out her words. Rachel felt left out. She thought she should know if they planned to get rid of Tom.

"*Kens devun hot's duh kenne* [Neither one could do it]," Esther said.

Who was her sister talking about, and what couldn't they do? Rachel was about to ask, but Pap pulled onto the dirt road leading to the pond, and she craned her neck to see the water.

"Yea! We're here, and the storm's passed by, so we can have our picnic!" Jacob jumped out of the buggy and ran toward the pond.

Esther stepped down next. The small white kapp perched on the back of her brown hair was always neatly in place. Not like Rachel's head covering, which often came loose during playtime.

Rachel climbed out of the buggy and reached up to

touch her own kapp, to be sure it was still there. Mom often scolded her for not remembering to put it on when they went out in public.

Esther smiled. "It's a *wunderbaar gut* [wonderful good] evening for a picnic."

"*Jah* [Yes]," Mom said. "It *is* a wonderful good evening for a picnic. Too bad Henry didn't want to join us."

"He'd rather be with his *aldi* [girlfriend]." Jacob rolled his eyes so they looked like they were crossed, and he coughed a couple of times as though he were gagging.

"Any sixteen-year-old boy who has a girlfriend wants to be with her. Henry thinks he's in love. That's what some nineteen-year-old girls think, too." Pap gave his brown beard a tug as he winked at Esther.

Esther's cheeks turned pink. Even though it hadn't been officially announced yet, Esther's family knew that she planned to marry Rudy King in the fall.

Rachel leaned into the buggy and grabbed a patchwork quilt from under the backseat. She didn't want to hear all this mushy love talk or think about getting married. She felt the best part of life was playing in the creek near their home, climbing a tree, or lying in the grass, dreaming about the interesting things she saw whenever they visited one of the nearby towns in Lancaster County, Pennsylvania.

Esther followed Rachel to a spot near the pond, and the two of them spread the quilt on the grass. Jacob ran along the water's edge, throwing flat rocks and hollering every time he made a perfect ripple. Pap unhitched Tom and tied him to a tree. Then he took their ice chest from the back of the buggy. Mom carried the picnic basket, and the two of them headed toward the quilt.

"I'm never getting married," Rachel told her sister.

Esther smoothed the edges of the quilt. "You'll change your mind someday."

"Rachel's probably right. She'll never get married 'cause she's too much of a *boppli* [baby]," Jacob said, as he joined them by the quilt.

"I am not a baby!"

"Are so."

Rachel couldn't let her brother have the last word, so she jerked the straw hat off his sandy-blond head and flung it into the air. "Am not!"

"Hey!" Jacob raced after his hat and grabbed it when it landed near the edge of the pond.

"Settle down, you two." Pap placed the ice chest on the grass. "We came to celebrate school being out, not to see who can shout the loudest or stir up the most trouble."

"That's right," Mom agreed as she opened the wicker basket and removed plates, cups, napkins, and silverware. "Let's put our energy into eating this good food that Esther and I prepared."

Rachel flopped onto the quilt with a groan. "What about me? I did the *blicking* [shelling] of the peas for the salad."

"Do you want me to tell Mom how many you wasted by seeing if you could hit the goose's beak?" Jacob murmured quietly so their parents couldn't hear.

Rachel glared at him. She didn't think anyone had seen her. But the goose was always so mean to her, she couldn't resist the urge to *boing* a few peas at it.

Pap removed his hat and scooted over beside Rachel. "Shelling peas is important business."

Rachel smiled. At least someone appreciated her efforts. Her stomach rumbled as Esther opened the ice chest and set out the picnic food. Scents of golden brown fried chicken, tossed green salad with fresh peas, pickled beets, muffins with apple butter, and homemade root beer filled the air.

"It's surprising we had any root beer to bring on our picnic," Jacob said, nudging Rachel with his elbow. "If you'd dropped a few more jars the day Pap made the root beer, we wouldn't have any to drink."

Rachel frowned. She couldn't help it if she'd accidentally dropped two jars of root beer when she'd carried them to the cellar. They'd been slippery and didn't want to stay in her hands. Then she'd had a sticky mess to clean up.

"Clumsy butterfingers," Jacob taunted. "You're always making a mess."

"Am not."

"Are so."

"That's enough, you two," Mom said with a shake of her head.

Rachel settled back on the quilt. She couldn't wait to grab a drumstick and start eating. But first, all heads bowed for silent prayer. *Thank You, Lord, for this food and for the hands that prepared it,* she prayed. *Bless it to the needs of my body. Amen.*

When Pap cleared his throat, it signaled the end of prayer time. "Now let's eat until we're full!"

Mom passed the container of chicken to Rachel, and she reached for a drumstick. She added a spoonful of salad to her plate, two pickled beets, and a muffin. "Yum. Everything looks mighty gut." She was about to take a bite of the chicken, when Jacob smacked it right out of her hands. "Hey! That's mine!" she hollered.

"You want to eat that after a stinkbug's been on it?" he said, studying the leg.

"What?" Rachel eyed the chicken leg. Jacob was right. There was a fat old stinkbug on her piece of chicken.

Jacob smashed the bug with his thumb and handed it back to her. "Here you go."

A terrible odor drifted up to Rachel's nose. "Eww. . . that stinks! Why'd you do that, Jacob?"

He gave her a crooked grin. "Didn't figure you'd want to eat a stinkbug."

She put the chicken leg on the edge of her plate and pushed it away. "I'm not eating that stinky thing now."

Jacob snickered. "Jah, I'll bet that could make you real sick. You might even die from eating chicken that had a smelly bug like that on it."

"I'm not hungry now." Rachel folded her arms and frowned.

"Just take another piece of chicken and finish eating your meal," Mom said as she stared at Rachel over the top of her silver-framed glasses.

Pap looked over at Jacob and frowned. "You shouldn't be teasing your sister."

"Sorry," Jacob mumbled with his mouth full of muffin.

Rachel took another drumstick, and her stomach flip-flopped. What if she'd eaten that piece of chicken with the stinkbug on it? Could she have gotten sick? Her appetite was gone, but she knew if she didn't eat all her supper, she wouldn't get any dessert. She probably couldn't play after the meal, either. She bit into the fresh piece of chicken, trying not to think about the smelly stinkbug.

"I'm glad school's out," Jacob said. "I think we should have a picnic every night to celebrate."

Mom smiled. "We'll try to have several picnics this summer, but remember there's plenty of work to do. We women have a big garden to care for, and you'll help your *daed* [dad] and *bruder* [brother] in the fields."

"Right now I don't want to think about working." Jacob swiped a napkin across his face and jumped up. "I'm going to play in the pond."

"Don't get your clothes wet or muddy. I don't need dirty laundry to do when we get home," Mom said as

Jacob sprinted off in his bare feet.

"*Immer druwwle eiyets.* [Always trouble somewhere.]" Pap looked over at Mom and grinned.

"That's true, Levi," she responded. "There's always trouble somewhere. Especially when our two youngest children get so excited about summer that they start picking on each other."

Rachel didn't like the sound of that. She wasn't trouble—just curious, as her teacher would say.

She finished her dessert and scrambled to her feet. "I think I'll go wading, too."

Mom caught hold of Rachel's hand. "I hoped you and Esther would pick wild strawberries. Plenty are growing nearby, and they'd taste wunderbaar gut for breakfast tomorrow."

"Do I have to pick berries?" Rachel whined. "I want to play in the water."

"Do as your *mamm* [mom] asks." Pap's eyebrows furrowed, and Rachel knew he meant what he said.

Esther stood and smoothed the wrinkles from her long blue dress. She looked at Rachel and smiled. "I can pick the berries on my own."

While Rachel waited for her mother's reply, an irritating bee buzzed overhead.

"I guess it would be okay," Mom finally agreed.

Rachel swatted at the bee. Big mistake. A few seconds later, a burning pain shot from her finger all the way up her arm.

"Ach!" she cried, jumping up and down from the shock of the bee's sting. She shook her finger and waved her arm.

"Calm down," Pap instructed as he took a look at her hand. "Scoot over to the pond, take a little dirt and water, then pat the mud on the stinger. That should help draw it out."

Rachel dashed to the pond. She had wanted to go there, but not with a cruel bee stinger making her whole arm throb.

Near the water's edge, she found Jacob building a dam from mud, rocks, and twigs. His dark trousers, held up by tan suspenders, were rolled up to his knees.

He gets to have all the fun! Rachel thought. *It's not fair.*

She scooped some dirt into her hand and added several drops of water. When a muddy paste formed, she spread it on her sore finger. Soon the throbbing lessened, so Rachel decided to see if she could make a better dam than Jacob's.

She waded into the cool water and giggled as it splashed against her legs. The bottom was mushy and squished between her bare toes.

"You'd better watch out," Jacob warned. "Your dress is getting wet."

Rachel glanced down. Sure enough, the hem was dark from where the water had soaked through. "I wish I didn't have to wear long dresses all the time," she grumbled. "You're lucky to be a boy."

Jacob frowned as if Rachel had said something terrible. "You complain too much. Can't you be happy with the way things are?"

Rachel stuck her finger between her teeth and bit off the end of the nail, spitting it into the water. "Sometimes I wonder if I'm supposed to be Amish."

Her brother's eyebrows lifted. "You were *born* Amish."

"I know, but sometimes I feel—" Rachel stared into space. Way down inside, where she hid her deepest secrets, she wondered what it would be like if she could do some of the things the non-Amish children her people called "English" got to do. "Sometimes I wish I could wear pants and shirts like the English girls do," she said.

"Sisters! Who can figure 'em out?" Jacob pointed at Rachel. "Especially you, little *bensel* [silly child]."

"I am not a silly child. If anyone's silly, it's you." Rachel flicked some water in Jacob's direction, and the drops landed on his shirtsleeve, making little dark circles.

Her brother only chuckled as he kept building his mud dam.

Rachel plodded toward the shore and gathered a few more twigs. She would make her dam even bigger than Jacob's, and then he would see that she wasn't a bensel. "Now, what did I do with that twig I was going to use?" she muttered.

"It's in your hand, little bensel."

Rachel's face flushed. She was about to say something, when Mom called, "Rachel! Jacob! Come dry your feet. It's time to go."

Jacob cupped his hands around his mouth. "Coming!" he shouted.

When her brother hurried away, Rachel bent down, placed the twig and another clump of mud on the side of her dam, and stepped back to admire her work. Suddenly, her foot slipped on a slimy rock, and she stumbled. She swayed back and forth for a moment, then *splash!* Rachel landed facedown in the water.

She was still sputtering and trying to stand in the slippery mud when Pap reached her. He scooped her into his strong arms, and Rachel leaned against his shoulder. "I didn't mean to fall in the water," she sobbed.

"You should have come when your mamm called," Pap said harshly, as he tromped up the grassy bank and placed Rachel on the ground near the horse and buggy.

She stood dripping wet, with her teeth chattering. Her kapp had come off and hung around her neck by its narrow ties, and most of her hair had come loose from the bun at the back of her head. She didn't know whether to laugh or cry.

Jacob pointed at Rachel and howled. "Your hair's stickin' out in all directions. You look like a prickly blond porcupine."

"Do not!" Rachel snapped. She knew she might look

silly, but she didn't look like a prickly porcupine.

Mom wrapped the picnic quilt around Rachel's shoulders.

"I'm sorry, Mom." Rachel sniffed and swiped at the water dripping from her soggy hair onto her cheeks. She wiped her muddy face, arms, and legs on the quilt.

"Sorry is good, but if you'd come when you were called, you probably wouldn't have fallen into the water," Mom said crossly, looking at the muddy prints Rachel had left on the quilt. "When we get home, you'll have laundry to do."

Rachel frowned. She hadn't meant to get her clothes wet. Why should she have to wash them? After all, the quilt was an old one; that's why they'd taken it on the picnic.

"We'd better head for home," Pap said. He helped the women into the buggy, and Jacob scrambled in after them.

The ride home was not pleasant. Rachel's wet dress stuck to her skin like tape. Shifting on the hard seat, she felt a shiver tickle her spine, and she pulled the quilt tightly around her shoulders.

Jumbled thoughts skittered through Rachel's mind. Jacob thought she was silly, and she knew she'd caused trouble for her parents. She wondered if every day of summer would be as topsy-turvy as this picnic day. She decided she'd better steer clear of trouble!

Chapter 2

Afraid of the Dark

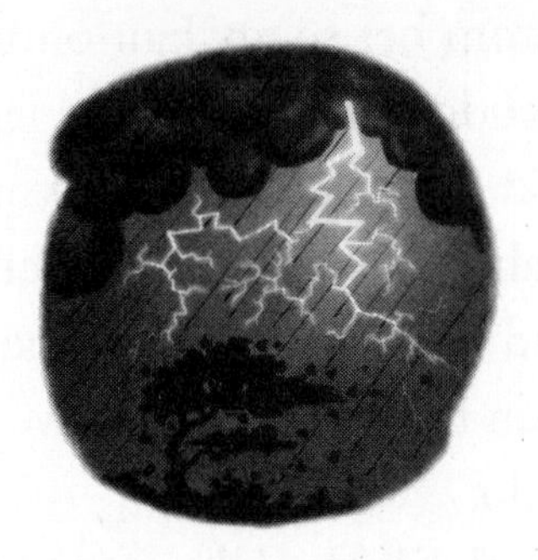

The sun was just beginning to show when Rachel came downstairs for breakfast the next morning. She knew her mother would be up early, getting ready to go to the Millers' house. Mom planned to help Anna Miller do some cleaning in preparation to host the biweekly Sunday worship service at the Millers' house in two days. Since Rachel was eager to call on their neighbors, she found it easier to get out of bed so early.

Rachel took an apple-crumb pie out of the refrigerator and placed it on the table. It was one of her favorite breakfast pies, and her stomach growled as she thought of how good it would taste.

"When breakfast is over, we'll need to hurry through our chores," Mom said. "Esther's already milking the cows. Henry and Pap are hitching the horse to our buggy, and I sent Jacob to the henhouse to gather eggs."

Rachel snickered. "Jacob always says that gathering eggs is women's work. He must be really *gretzich* [crabby] this morning."

"I don't care if Jacob is crabby. If he thinks only women can gather eggs, he's sorely mistaken. That kind of thinking is just plain foolish." Mom reached for the kettle of oatmeal sitting near the back of the stove. She pushed a wisp of pale blond hair away from her face, where it had worked its way out from under the kapp covering her bun.

Rachel had just finished setting the table when the rest of the family came into the kitchen. Everyone gathered around the table and bowed their heads for silent prayer. Rachel prayed that she would be allowed to have two pieces of apple-crumb pie and also that she'd have lots of fun at the Millers'.

By nine o'clock, breakfast was over, the kitchen had been cleaned, and Mom and Rachel had finished the rest of their chores. Satisfied and full after eating a bowl of oatmeal and two pieces of pie, Rachel followed Mom outside and climbed into their buggy. She felt certain that today would turn out better than yesterday.

"Are you sure you won't come with us to the Millers'?" Mom asked Esther, who stood in front of the buggy, stroking the horse's ear.

Esther shook her head and smiled sweetly. "Rudy is picking me up soon. We're going to the Hertzlers' place to look at some horses. He's thinking about buying a new one."

Mom nodded and handed Rachel her kapp. "I found this hanging on the wall peg in the kitchen. Were you planning to go without it, or were you daydreaming again?"

With a sigh, Rachel put the head covering in place. "Sorry, Mom. I forgot."

"You've been so forgetful lately," Mom said. "What seems to be the problem?"

Rachel shrugged. "I've got a lot on my mind." After all, school was out now, and she had lots of plans for her summer.

Mom gave Rachel a curious look but made no reply. She turned to wave at Esther and started the horse trotting down the lane leading to the main road.

"Sure was a nice picnic supper we had yesterday, jah?" Mom said as they rode along.

"Except for when I almost ate a stinkbug, got stung by a bee, and fell in the pond," Rachel mumbled.

Mom reached over to touch Rachel's hand. "The stinkbug wasn't such a big thing. The bee sting was an accident. And if you had come out of the water when you were called, you might not have fallen in."

"I was just trying to have a little fun."

"I know, but you must learn to listen. That will help you stay out of trouble."

Rachel nodded. "I've been wondering. . . ," she said, changing the subject.

"What's that?"

"Yesterday on the way to the pond, I heard Pap say something about Tom neighing too much."

"That horse seems to complain about everything these days," Mom said with a click of her tongue.

Rachel's forehead wrinkled with concern. Tom was getting old and couldn't do everything he used to do. Maybe he had a right to complain.

They soon turned onto a gravel driveway. Howard and Anna Miller's three-story house was even larger than the Yoders' home. The Miller family included six boys and four girls—so they needed lots of room. Two of the girls were already married and lived with their husbands on their own farms, but the rest of the Miller children still lived at home.

As soon as Rachel climbed down from the buggy, she spotted Anna Miller chopping weeds in the garden. Her plump figure was bent over a row of strawberry plants. Beside her stood six-year-old Katie. Nearby sat little Sarah's baby carriage. When Anna saw Rachel and her mother, she waved and set her garden hoe aside.

Mom and Anna greeted each other in the Pennsylvania Dutch language, while Rachel squatted next to the carriage so she could see the baby better. "Sarah sure is a pretty boppli," she said.

"Jah, we think she's a pretty baby, too," Anna replied with a smile.

For the next several minutes, Anna, Mom, Rachel,

and Katie admired the infant and made silly baby sounds.

"I expect we should get busy with the cleaning and baking," Mom finally said.

Anna nodded. "I appreciate you coming to help today, Miriam. Since the boppli came, I seem to be getting further behind on all my chores."

While Mom helped Anna clean house, Rachel looked after Katie and baby Sarah. She liked being in charge of the little ones. It made her feel important. Besides, Mom had promised Rachel some free time after lunch, and she looked forward to exploring the Millers' yard.

"Let's go look for the *busslin* [kittens] that my cat, Missy, had," Katie suggested.

She pointed to a little hole under the front porch. "They could be in there."

Rachel parked the baby carriage under the shade of a maple tree. Then she and Katie knelt and peered into the opening.

"I don't see any kittens," Rachel said as she stuck her hand inside the hole and felt all around. When she pulled her hand out again, she discovered a grasshopper perched on the end of her thumb.

Katie squealed and jumped away. "Eww! I don't like bugs!"

Rachel set the grasshopper in the flower bed. "I think bugs are okay as long as they're not on my food."

"Let's go see if the kittens are in the barn," Katie said, tugging Rachel's hand.

Rachel pushed the baby carriage down the dirt path. When she and Katie entered the barn, she parked the carriage near some bales of hay stacked by the door. Then Katie looked for the kittens inside an empty horse stall while Rachel climbed the hayloft to hunt for them there.

"Ahhhh!"

Rachel's heart lurched as she heard the shrill scream. She scrambled down the ladder. Katie stood on a bale of hay, trembling from head to toe. "What's wrong, Katie? Why are you standing up there?"

Katie pointed across the room. "*Maus* [Mouse]. I saw a maus."

Rachel could hardly believe anyone would be afraid of a little old mouse. She thought mice were cute. And mice didn't chase you around, nipping at your legs, the way their old goose sometimes did.

"The maus won't hurt you," she said, holding her hand out to Katie. "Come on, let's go outside and swing."

Katie nodded, and pushing the baby carriage, the two girls headed behind the barn. Rachel loved to swing—and it was hard for her to take turns. But while Katie swung, Rachel pushed Sarah in her carriage so she wouldn't fuss. Then when it was Rachel's turn to swing, Katie pushed her sister's carriage around in the grass.

At noon, the dinner bell rang. Rachel and Katie rushed into the house, where everyone took turns washing up at the sink. Finally each person was seated at the huge wooden table in the center of the Millers' kitchen. Howard Miller and his six sons ate quickly so they could get back to the fields to work more, but Rachel took her time eating. She enjoyed every bite of the tasty cold meats and cheeses, homemade bread, potato salad, canned applesauce, and chewy peanut butter cookies Anna had served for lunch. Anna and Mom had already begun to clear away the dishes when Rachel swallowed her last bite.

"I'm going to put my *kinner* [children] down for a nap so we can finish our cleaning without any interruptions," Anna said to Mom as she scooted Katie toward the stairs. "If there's time, maybe we can do some baking this afternoon."

Rachel was glad she didn't have to take a nap like the younger children. She helped her mother wash the dishes. When they had been dried and put away, she asked if she could go outside to play.

"Jah, but don't get into any trouble," Mom said, peering at Rachel over the top of her glasses.

"I won't. I promise."

As soon as Rachel opened the back door and stepped onto the porch, she noticed that the sky was filled with heavy, gray clouds. The air smelled like rain, and she drew in a deep breath. She slipped off her shoes, hopped down the porch steps, and skipped across the lawn.

Her first stop was Anna's flower garden. Rachel loved flowers, and she fought the urge to pick a few of the prettiest ones, since she hadn't asked for permission. Besides, too many bees landed on the flowers, and Rachel didn't want to get stung again.

Rachel headed down the path that led to the creek. Howard Miller's waterwheel squeaked as it turned, making the water ripple and gurgle. Rachel knew the wheel was important because it created some of the power used on the Millers' farm. Because electricity was considered worldly, the Amish in her area used other methods of energy that weren't so modern.

While Rachel tossed rocks into the creek, a gust of wind rustled the treetops, and a few drops of rain splashed to the ground. She shivered at first, worried she might be caught in a storm. Then she smiled. If it rained hard enough, there might be some mud puddles she could tromp through. Meanwhile, she would go play in the barn. She was only halfway to the barn when she saw Katie's cat, Missy, run out the open barn door, followed by four little gray and white kittens. *They must have been in there the whole time and we missed them,* she thought.

Rachel called to Missy, but the cat ignored her and kept running. Thunder boomed, and all five cats raced down the steps and through the open doorway of the underground root cellar. The wind blew so hard Rachel had to hold on to her kapp in order to keep it from blowing off her head.

She hurried after the cats. As she stumbled down the stairs and into the small, cold room, she shivered. Even with the door open, it was dark inside, and she didn't see any sign of Missy or her kittens.

Rachel blinked a couple of times. As her eyes adjusted to the darkness, she noticed wooden shelves fastened to the wall. They held glass jars filled with home-canned fruits and vegetables. Empty boxes sat on the concrete floor, waiting for the crops of potatoes, carrots, and other root vegetables the Millers would harvest later.

"Here, kitty, kitty," Rachel called. Neither Missy nor any of her kittens responded. Rachel only heard the howling wind and steady raindrops splattering on the steps outside the cellar door.

More thunder rumbled, followed by another gust of wind.

Bam! The cellar door slammed shut, and Rachel screamed as the darkness swallowed her.

Rachel wasn't afraid of much, but two things really frightened her—dark places and thunderstorms. She had taken a risk by coming into the dark cellar. Now she had to be brave and deal with both of the things that scared her most.

Rachel drew in a shaky breath, then inched her way forward. When her fingers touched the doorknob, she turned it and pushed the door. Nothing happened.

Leaning her weight against the heavy wooden door, Rachel pushed and pushed until she had no strength left in her arms. Her heart pounded like a woodpecker tapping on a tree. "I'm trapped! I'm afraid. . .and nobody knows I'm down here."

Rachel pressed her cheek to the door. "Someone, please help me!"

Plinkety plink. Plinkety plink. No answer except the rain hitting the door.

She stuck her finger in her mouth and gnawed off a fingernail. She tried to pray, but her words came out all jumbled. "Wh–what if they—" *Sniff.* "N–never find me?" *Sniff. Sniff.* "H–help me, Lord."

Rachel remembered hearing a minister at church once say that heaven has no dark places. That was a comforting thought, but it didn't help the situation she faced right now.

Something soft and furry rubbed against Rachel's ankle, and she knew it was one of Missy's kittens. She bent to pick it up, and the soft ball of fur purred when she lifted it to her face. Then it licked Rachel's nose with its rough, wet tongue.

Rachel dropped to her knees, and as she touched each lump of fur climbing into her lap, she realized that all four kittens and Missy were there.

She felt a little better knowing she wasn't alone, but she was still afraid. *There must be an oil lamp down here,* she thought. *I just need to find it.*

Rachel gently pushed the cats aside and stood shakily. She felt her way around the room until her hand touched something cold and hard. "It's a lantern!" she exclaimed. Her fingers moved up and down, back and forth along the shelf that held the lantern until she touched a book of matches. With a sigh of relief, she picked it up, struck a match, and lit the lantern. A warm glow spread throughout the tiny room, showing the shelves full of canning jars.

Rachel spotted a jar of pickled beets, and her stomach rumbled. It must be near suppertime. Would Mom go home without her? After all, she'd told Rachel to stay out of trouble, and here Rachel was now, in the middle of disaster.

"Maybe I should have a little snack—just in case," she murmured. "Anna probably won't miss a few beets from one jar, and I'm sure she wouldn't want me to starve to death."

Rachel picked up the old-fashioned glass jar, pulled the heavy wire off the top, and popped off the lid. She loved beets, especially when they were pickled with vinegar, sugar, and cinnamon. "Mmm. . .they smell so good." She poked two fingers inside, withdrew one spicy red beet, and popped it into her mouth. "Yum."

As Rachel started back across the room, a kitten darted in front of her, and she stumbled. The jar crashed to the floor, breaking the glass and splattering beets and sticky red juice everywhere. The juice even dotted the kittens' fur and Rachel's dress. "Ach, what have I done?" she moaned.

She knew beet juice stained clothes. Her mother wouldn't be happy about trying to get the red splotches out of Rachel's dress. She hoped the Millers wouldn't be upset about having a stained floor.

Suddenly, the room went dark again. Rachel had noticed that the oil was low in the lamp, but she didn't expect it to go out *this* soon. Rachel held very still, remembering that she wasn't wearing any shoes and that glass covered the floor.

Unsure of what else to do, Rachel carefully touched the floor to make sure no glass was in her way as she dropped to her knees. She prayed, "Dear God, You know I'm afraid of the dark, so would You please help me not cry?"

Just like before, the kittens and the mother cat hopped into Rachel's lap, which made her feel less afraid. She closed her eyes, leaned her head against the cellar door, and was soon fast asleep.

Chapter 3

A Wunderbaar Surprise

Rachel was dreaming about pickled beets, kittens, and shiny blue cars, when the cellar door jerked open, and she fell backward. She sat up, feeling dazed, and looked over her shoulder. She saw Howard Miller and his sons Jake and Martin, each holding a lantern.

"The little bensel got herself locked in the cellar." Jake chuckled and slapped his knee.

Rachel didn't see what was so funny, and she didn't like being called a silly child any more now than when Jacob had called her that. "What time is it?" she asked with a yawn. "How long have I been down here?"

"It's half past six," Howard answered. "Your mamm has been frantic with worry. She said she'd planned to head for home by five o'clock, but when she couldn't find you, she sent me and the boys out looking."

"I followed Missy and her busslin into the cellar. Then

the wind blew the door shut, and I couldn't open it again." Rachel bit her bottom lip to keep it from quivering. "I—I didn't know if anyone would ever find me."

"Aw, sure they would," Martin said with a snicker. "Come winter, when Mom needed some of her canned food, she would have headed straight to the cellar. What a surprise she would have found in here, too!"

Rachel knew Martin was only teasing, but she wasn't amused.

Jake sent a beam of light from his lantern all around the room and made a sweeping gesture with his other hand. "What's all this mess with the broken glass and the beet juice?"

"I—I was hungry, and I—" Rachel's voice broke, and she drew in a deep breath to get control of her emotions. "I know I shouldn't have taken the beets without asking, and I'm sorry about the mess. If you'll leave one of your lanterns here so I can see, I'll clean it up."

"Never mind, Rachel. I'll see that everything is taken care of later on." Howard patted Rachel's head. "I'm glad you've been found. Now we'd best get you back to the house so your mamm can quit worrying."

Rachel pointed to the kittens that lay curled in a ball next to their mother. "What about them? We can't leave Missy and her little busslin alone in the cellar."

"The door's open now, so they can leave whenever they want." Howard nodded at his sons. "Hurry to the house and tell Rachel's mother that we found her."

Jake and Martin took off on a run, and Howard scooped Rachel into his strong arms. She felt safe and secure and so relieved that she had been found. She was glad he'd been so nice about the mess she'd made.

Later that evening, after Rachel had bathed and changed into clean clothes, she sat with her family around the supper table, telling them how she had been trapped in the cellar. "And I only had the company of Missy and her four little busslin," she said at the end of the story.

Mom handed Rachel a glass of cold milk, and Pap passed her a basket of warm bread. "You had quite an ordeal today," he said. "Did you learn anything from it?"

Rachel nodded. "I'll never go into another root cellar without telling someone where I'm going." She didn't mention how scared she had been.

"God was watching over you today," Mom said, as she helped herself to some meatloaf and handed the platter to Esther.

"He was?" Rachel asked as she bit into a piece of bread.

"Sure," Mom replied. "God sent Missy and her busslin to be with you in the cellar."

"Was it dark in the cellar?" Esther asked as she passed the platter to Rachel.

"Most of the time it was." Rachel drank some of her milk. "I was worried that the kittens would be afraid of the dark, so I found an oil lamp and a book of matches. The cellar was well lit until the lamp ran out of oil."

"Like those furry critters needed any light," her oldest brother, Henry, put in.

Jacob snickered. "I'll bet Rachel was the real scaredy-cat."

Rachel wasn't about to tell her brothers how frightened she had been, but before she could say anything more, Pap gave Jacob a stern look. Rachel figured she would get one of those looks if she said anything unkind to her brother, so she crossed her eyes and wrinkled her nose at him when her parents weren't looking.

Jacob crossed his eyes and wrinkled his nose right back at her. Then he grabbed a hunk of meatloaf and popped a piece into his mouth.

"Did you get everything done at the Millers' today?" Esther asked, looking at Mom.

"We finished the cleaning," Mom said. "But when the rain started, I decided that Rachel and I should go home, so Anna and I never did any baking." She glanced over at Rachel. "When the wind started howling like crazy, I thought you would hurry back to the house."

Rachel said nothing. She just stared at the blob of spinach Pap had put on her plate. Then she reached for the bowl of mashed potatoes, added a scoop to her plate, and stirred the ugly, green, slimy-looking blob in with the potatoes. Spinach was her least favorite vegetable, and she hoped if she mixed it with the potatoes, the yucky stuff might go down a little easier.

"When the dunner and wedderleech started and you still didn't return to the house, I began to worry." Mom reached past Esther and patted Rachel's hand as Rachel was about to take a bite of her mashed potatoes. The spoon flipped out of her hand, and the gooey glob flew across the table and landed on Jacob's plate, spattering the blob of slimy spinach and potatoes all over the front of his shirt.

"Ugh!" Jacob scowled at Rachel. "You did that on purpose, Rachel-the-scaredy-cat, who's afraid of thunder and lightning."

"Did not."

"Did so."

"Did not."

"Did—"

"That's enough!" Pap clapped his hands, and Rachel and Jacob stopped arguing.

Rachel knew better than to act like this at the table, but Jacob made her so angry she could hardly control her temper. *I know God loves everyone,* she thought, *but I'm guessing Jacob tries the Lord's patience as much as he does mine.*

Mom pointed to the sink. "Jacob, you had better get that mess cleaned off your shirt before it leaves a stain. I've had enough dirty clothes to deal with for one day."

Rachel knew her mother was talking about the dress stained with beet juice that she had worn to the Millers'. She figured no matter how much Mom scrubbed that dress, the ugly red stains would probably never come out.

Jacob glared at Rachel and pushed away from the table with a groan. He marched across the room, opened the cupboard door under the sink, and dumped Rachel's potato-spinach mess into the garbage can. Then he wet a dishrag and started rubbing the front of his shirt real hard.

Mom passed the bowl of spinach to Esther, who handed it to Rachel.

Rachel knew she would be in trouble if she didn't take some, so she dipped the spoon in and plucked out a tiny piece, placing it on the edge of her plate.

Mom clicked her tongue, and Pap raised his dark, bushy eyebrows. Rachel added a little larger piece and felt relieved when Pap nodded and said, "Jah, okay."

"How did the Millers know where to look for you?" Henry asked, as Rachel held her nose, popped the spinach into her mouth, and washed it down with a gulp of milk.

"Howard sent two of his boys to look down by the creek," Mom said before Rachel could reply. "Two of his sons went to their neighbor's place to see if Rachel had gone there, while Jake, Martin, and Howard searched their own farm. When they had looked in all the obvious places, Howard decided to try the root cellar. I'm glad they found you before we got the whole neighborhood in an uproar."

Rachel sighed, remembering how scared she had been during most of the ordeal. "I'm glad he thought to look there. I wondered if I would ever get out of that terrible place."

Just as Jacob was about to sit down again, someone knocked on the back door. "I'll get it!" Jacob raced across the room and flung the door open.

Esther's boyfriend, Rudy, entered the kitchen. He carried a wicker basket draped with a piece of green cloth. "Sorry to disturb your supper," he said, glancing at the table.

"That's all right. Would you like to join us?" Mom asked.

"No, thanks. I stopped at the Millers' place this evening to drop off benches for our church service on Sunday. Howard asked me to deliver this special surprise to Rachel." He smiled and stepped toward the table, holding the basket in front of him.

Pap nodded at Rachel. "Why don't you see what it is?"

Rachel didn't have to be asked twice. She loved surprises.

Rudy handed her the basket, and when she lifted the cloth, she gasped. "Oh, it's one of Missy's busslin!" She stroked the kitten's head. "I'm going to call you Cuddles."

Esther's eyebrows rose. "Cuddles?"

Rachel nodded. "All of the busslin were so cuddly when they kept me company in the cold, dark cellar."

"Howard told me about your ordeal. He said you seemed worried about the kittens," Rudy said. "He wanted you to have one of them, and this is the *bussli* he chose for you."

The gray and white kitten, with a speck of red beet juice still on one paw, nestled against Rachel's arm and purred. Rachel leaned over and nuzzled its wet nose. "Can I keep her?" she asked, looking at Mom and then at Pap.

Mom smiled. "If it's all right with your daed, it's fine by me."

Pap tugged on the end of his beard. "I suppose it'll be okay, but you must promise to take care of it."

"And the bussli will sleep in the barn with all the other animals," Mom quickly added.

Rachel placed the kitten on the floor and ran to the table to give Mom and Pap a hug and a kiss on the cheek. "This is such a wunderbaar surprise! I promise I'll take good care of Cuddles."

Jacob groaned and shook his head. "What a dumb name for a cat."

Rachel hurried back to the kitten and lifted it into her arms. "It's not dumb. You're just saying that because you're jealous."

"Am not. You should name it Trouble since that's all you ever get into."

Rachel didn't feel like arguing with Jacob anymore. And she didn't want to think of the trouble she'd caused that day for her mother and the Millers. She felt happy to be holding one of the sweet little bundles of fur that had snuggled in her lap and kept her company while she was trapped in the cellar.

Chapter 4

Egg Yolks and Hopping Frogs

Rachel carefully opened her eyes. She squinted at the ray of sunlight streaming through a tiny hole in the dark shade covering her bedroom window. It was time to get up and do her morning chores. Then she and her family would go to the three-hour church service at Howard and Anna Miller's house.

Rachel yawned and sat up. Swinging her legs over the side of the bed, she stood and hurried to the other side of the room. The dress and apron she usually wore to do her chores hung on a wall peg near her dressing table. She took them down and quickly dressed.

When Rachel entered the kitchen, she saw her mother standing at the counter, cutting a shoofly pie into equal pieces. "Hurry and do your chores," Mom said. "We don't want to be late for church." She handed Rachel a wicker basket. "Be sure to go out to the chicken coop first. I'm scrambling eggs for breakfast and need a few more."

Rachel grabbed the basket and rushed out of the house. She paused at the barn door, tempted to play with Cuddles, who had been made to sleep in the barn because that's where Mom thought animals belonged. Rachel peeked in and saw Cuddles sleeping on a bale of hay, so she hurried on to the chicken coop, knowing she could play with the kitten later.

Inside the chicken coop, Rachel found four empty nests and six more with hens sitting in them. She hoped there were eggs under those hens, because she didn't want to return to the house empty-handed.

Rachel placed the basket on the floor and picked up the first chicken. *Bawk! Bawk!* The red hen fussed, but Rachel didn't give in. She had a job to do, and she planned to get it done.

Three eggs were in that nest, so Rachel leaned down and placed them inside the basket.

Bawk! Bawk! The hen hopped into the basket and fluffed up her feathers like she belonged there.

"That is not your nest," Rachel scolded, nudging the chicken with the toe of her sneaker. Usually Rachel came out to the coop in her bare feet, but she'd had a bath last night and didn't want to get anything grimy or slimy between her toes.

With another blaring squawk, the hen hopped out of the basket and waddled to the other side of the coop.

Rachel hurried down the line, removing each hen from its nest and filling her basket with their bulky brown eggs. When she was done, she left the coop and headed across the yard toward the house.

Rachel had only gone as far as the clothesline when she noticed a couple of fat green frogs hopping along the edge of the grass near the garden.

If I could take the two of them with me, I could race them after church, she thought.

Rachel set the basket of eggs on the ground and ran to the barn for a small box. When she returned, the frogs were gone. She walked up and down the garden rows and finally found them under the leaves of a strawberry plant.

Rachel dropped to her knees, inched forward, and reached out her hand. One frog hopped to the left. The other frog hopped to the right. She gritted her teeth, determined to catch both of those leaping frogs.

Rachel crawled slowly until she spotted one of the frogs again. She lifted her hand, held her breath—then, quick as wink, she grabbed it. The other frog hopped out of the garden, so Rachel hurried and put the first frog in the box. Then she snapped the cardboard flaps down fast. Next, Rachel followed the second frog as it hopped across the grass and into one of Mom's flower beds. It took her three tries to catch it, as the frog hopped away every time her hand came near, but she finally captured the critter and put it in the box along with its friend.

Rachel ran to the buggy, which had already been hitched to old Tom. She opened the back door and slipped the box under the backseat.

Remembering the eggs she'd been sent to gather, Rachel rushed back to the spot where she had left the basket. She bent over to pick it up and had taken only a few steps when she heard a shrill, *Honk! Honk!*

Rachel whirled around and gasped when she saw Clara the goose heading straight for her. Rachel knew it wasn't right to hate any animal, but she certainly didn't like Clara—at all. And Clara didn't like her. Any time Clara saw Rachel, she made a beeline for her. If Clara caught up with Rachel, she'd nip at Rachel, a goose's way of biting. Goose bites, Rachel had learned, hurt very much.

"Shoo! Shoo!" Rachel cried. She clung to the basket with one hand and waved her other hand at the honking bird, but Clara kept coming.

Rachel screamed and ran for the house as fast as she could. She was almost to the porch when she felt Clara's *nip! nip!* on the backs of her legs.

"Ouch!" Tears stung Rachel's eyes as she tried to hop out of the goose's reach. She grabbed the railing and pulled herself forward. Missing the first step, she tripped and fell.

When Rachel picked herself up she noticed the basket of eggs. "Oh, no, they're all broken, and now I'm a mess!" Runny, yellow yolks mixed with pieces of shell and the slimy white part of the eggs clung to the front of her apron. She whirled around, prepared to give Clara the chase of her life, but the goose was gone.

"Always trouble somewhere," Rachel grumbled, as she trudged into the house. She wasn't looking forward to telling her mother that they would have no more eggs for breakfast.

To Rachel's surprise, Mom didn't scold her about the broken eggs. She only said, "I told your daed he should get rid of that mean old goose. One of these days, she'll end up in my stewing pot." Then Mom said she would just use the eggs she already had and might fix a batch of oatmeal to go with them.

"Guess I'd better go upstairs and change into my church dress," Rachel said.

Mom nodded. "I'll need to tend those wounds the goose put on your legs, too."

"I can do it." Rachel felt better now that she was safely away from Clara.

An hour later, the Yoder family pulled into the Millers' yard. Rachel noticed several other Amish buggies lined up next to Howard Miller's barn. She leaned close to Jacob and whispered, "I hope Cousin Mary is here today. I can't wait to tell her about Cuddles."

Jacob tugged on Rachel's sleeve. "I still say that's a dumb name for a cat."

She jerked her arm away. "And I say it's not." She hardly noticed that their buggy had stopped.

"It's a bensel name!" Jacob taunted.

"You're a bensel!" Rachel accused, her voice rising.

"Rachel!" Pap's voice interrupted the squabble.

Rachel looked at her parents' horrified faces. Then she realized Pap had parked their buggy next to Bishop Wagler's buggy. Bishop Wagler was the head minister of their church, and she always felt a little nervous when he was around.

The bishop had stepped to their buggy to greet Pap, and she wondered if he'd heard her and Jacob arguing. He pulled his fingers through the ends of his long, gray beard and greeted Pap in Pennsylvania Dutch.

Pap turned to respond to him and climbed down from the buggy, but Mom sat there, frowning at Rachel. Rachel gulped. She knew Mom felt misbehaving in public was one of the worst things a child could do. To behave badly in front of the minister was even worse.

"You're going to get it now!" Jacob whispered to her as they climbed out of the buggy.

"But you started it!" she hissed at him.

"Um-hmm." Rachel heard her mother clear her voice as a warning.

As soon as Pap had unhitched the horse and put it in the Millers' corral with the other horses, he, Henry, and Jacob joined other men and boys under a leafy maple tree. Mom and Esther joined the women, who stood on the front porch visiting. Rachel grabbed her frog box and hurried to look for her cousin. By the time she found Mary standing near the barn, she had no time to tell Mary about the frog race. Most of the people were moving indoors so church could begin.

Rachel put the box with the frogs on the Millers' porch, next to the kitchen. Then she hurried into the living room to sit on a long wooden bench on the women's side of the room. Mom and Esther sat near Mary's mother, Irma, and Rachel and Mary sat on a bench ahead of them with some other girls their age. Pap, Henry, and Jacob took their seats on the men's side of the room.

Deacon Byler passed out the hymnals. While the congregation sang, the bishop and the other two ministers left the room. Rachel knew they always left the service during this time to discuss church business and decide who would preach the first sermon. Rachel hoped Bishop Wagler hadn't heard her and Jacob arguing, and she worried that Mom would punish her when they got home. Of course, Jacob had been in on the argument, so he should be punished, too.

Rachel shot a glance at her mother. Mom smiled and sang with all her heart. Tears threatened to squeeze from Rachel's eyes. If the bishop said anything to Mom or Pap about how disagreeable Rachel was, Rachel knew her parents would feel a terrible shame.

She didn't know any other children who seemed to get into as much trouble as she did!

When the church leaders returned, the singing

ended. Rachel leaned close to Mary and whispered, "I have some news to tell you."

"Really, what is it?"

"I got a special surprise Friday night. And that's not all. Today I brought along a couple of—"

"Um-hmm." Rachel heard Mom quietly clearing her throat.

When Rachel looked over her shoulder, she saw Mom put a finger to her lips and give Rachel a stern look over the top of her glasses. "Shh. . ."

Rachel knew she was expected to be quiet during church, but it was so hard to sit still and not talk. She was already in trouble for squabbling with Jacob in front of the bishop, so she knew she'd better do as Mom said.

Halfway through the service, Anna Miller slipped out of the room. She quickly returned with a platter of dried apple pieces. She gave some to the children so they could sit through the rest of the service without getting too hungry.

Rachel ate hers eagerly, thinking about the noon meal and the time of fellowship afterward. She had just finished the last bite when she heard a strange noise.

Ribbet! Ribbet!

Rachel looked down. *Oh, no!* One of the frogs leaped along the floor under the bench in front of her. She held her breath, praying no one would notice. She hoped the frog might hop toward her so she could capture it.

The sermon had just ended, and the people were about to sing a closing hymn, when the frog jumped with all its might. It landed in the lap of Sarah King, an elderly woman sitting directly in front of Rachel.

"Ahhhh!" Sarah screeched. She jumped off her bench, knocking the frog to the floor. It sat dazed for a moment. Then it hopped in one direction and then another.

Jacob jumped up and dashed across the aisle. He tried to capture the frog, but the sly old critter kept hopping away. Martin Miller joined the chase as shrieks and hollers came from all sides of the room. But the frog continued to jump, and the boys, wearing determined expressions, kept darting after it.

Rachel gasped when the frog landed in ten-year-old Elsie Byler's lap. Elsie screamed and jumped up. Everyone sitting on her bench jumped up, too.

Jacob raced across the room, took a flying leap, missed the frog, and knocked over the bench.

Ribbet! Ribbet! The frog leaped again; this time Jacob grabbed it, but it leaped out of his hands and landed on seven-year-old Aaron King's shoulder. Then before anyone could move, it hopped down the boy's shirt.

Aaron hollered and raced around the room as if he'd been stung by a bee. Aaron's mother reached out as her son ran by. She pulled the back of his shirt out of his trousers. The frog sailed through the air, landing near the front door.

Rachel held her breath and gnawed on a fingernail as Bishop Wagler moved to the front door, grasped the handle, and jerked it open. As though the frog knew who was in charge, it jumped right out the door. Jacob and Martin put the bench back in place. Everyone sat down, and the singing started again as if nothing unusual had happened.

When church ended, the men and boys put their black felt hats on their heads and filed out of the house. Next, the younger girls left. The women and older girls went to the kitchen to prepare the meal. Rachel started for the door, but Mom grasped her hand. "Do you know anything about that frog?" she asked, staring hard at Rachel.

Rachel nodded. She bit her lips so she wouldn't smile. Now that it was over, she realized it had been funny to see the frog land in Sarah King's and Elsie Byler's laps and down Aaron King's shirt. But she was sure her mother didn't share those feelings.

"Sorry, Mom," Rachel said. "I wanted to have a frog race this afternoon, and I didn't think the frogs would get out of the box."

"Frogs?" Mom repeated.

Ribbet! Ribbet!

Mom turned to look at the box sitting on the utility porch. "How many more frogs did you bring, Rachel?"

"Just one." Rachel hurried to the box and picked it up. "I'll take this outside right away."

Mom nodded. "We'll talk about this little escapade when we get home." As Mom turned and walked away, Rachel heard her mutter, "Always trouble somewhere!"

Rachel tried to think of some way to get out of punishment, but she figured nothing would help her this time. She had been lucky to get off without a *bletsching* [spanking] this morning after she'd ruined the eggs. And she was certainly fortunate that the frogs had apparently made her mother forget about Bishop Wagler hearing her ugly words.

"You brought the frogs, didn't you?" Mary asked when Rachel stepped outside.

Rachel nodded. "I thought it would be fun to have a race with them after church."

"Are you in big trouble? Do you think you'll get a spanking?" Mary asked.

"Maybe. Or I might have extra chores to do." Rachel set the box on the ground, lifted the lid, and watched frog number two hop away.

Mary flopped onto the grass under a willow tree. Rachel dropped beside her. "It would be nice to have church out here where it's cooler, don't you think?" her cousin asked.

"Jah, and those benches can get pretty hard after a while," Rachel agreed.

"I know, but we couldn't have church outside during the winter."

Rachel snatched a blade of grass and bit off the end.

At least it was better than chewing her nails. "You'll never guess what I got Friday night," she said, thinking a different subject would make her feel better.

"What?"

"Guess."

"Did your mamm make you a new dress?"

Rachel shook her head. "She probably won't do that until right before school starts again."

Mary's pale eyebrows wiggled together, and she rubbed her chin. "Hmm. . . Did you get some licorice? I know that's your favorite candy."

"That's not it, either. *Gebscht uff*? [Do you give up?]"

Her cousin nodded. "Jah, I give up. What did you get?"

"A bussli."

"That's great. Now our two cats can play together," Mary said excitedly. "Where did you get the kitten? What's its name?"

Rachel explained about being trapped in the Millers' root cellar and how Missy and her kittens had kept her company. She told Mary that Rudy had brought Cuddles over as a surprise gift from Howard Miller.

"You must have been scared down there in that cellar," Mary said, her eyes opening wide.

Rachel was about to tell her how horrible it had been, but the girls were called to join the women for their noon meal.

Rachel sat between her mother and sister at a long

picnic table. Mary sat across from Rachel, between her own mother and sister. The meal included hot bean soup, ham-and-cheese sandwiches, and lots of cold milk to drink. For dessert, Anna Miller served apple and cherry pie. Rachel ate until she couldn't take another bite. Then she patted her stomach and looked at the clear, blue sky. The sun felt warm against her face, and for the moment she forgot about the mean goose, broken eggs, and hopping frogs that had nearly ruined her day. She sighed as clouds covered the warm sun. As hard as she tried to steer clear of trouble, trouble always seemed to find her.

Just then, a drop of water splattered on Rachel's nose. It was followed by another and another. "Oh no, it's starting to rain!" she moaned.

What was the use of school being out if it was going to rain all summer? Rachel sighed. Even the weather was causing trouble in her life!

Chapter 5

Where Is Summer?

Flinging the back door open wide, Rachel rushed into the kitchen. "It's raining again! Can you believe it, Mom? How many more days of rain are we gonna have?" She stood inside the door, dripping wet and frowning. Ever since the frog episode during church, she'd had extra chores to do, and doing them in the rain wasn't much fun.

Mom was cutting quilting material at the kitchen table, but she looked at Rachel and smiled. "Rain is good for the garden, and the crops in the fields need it, as well."

"But, Mom, where is summer? All we've had for a couple of weeks now is rain, rain, rain."

"Sunshine will come again soon," her mother answered. "Now, you're dripping water all over my clean floor, and if you don't get out of that wet dress soon, you'll likely catch a cold."

Rachel shrugged and headed for the stairs. What was the use in complaining to Mom? No one in her family seemed to understand how she felt about anything. Rachel wondered if her mother ever remembered what it was like to be young.

When Rachel entered her room, she found Cuddles lying at the foot of her bed. She hurried across the room and shook her finger in the kitten's face. "You know what Mom would say if she caught you napping on my bed. She doesn't want you in the house, much less up on the furniture. And you'd get me in big trouble."

Rachel stroked the kitten's soft, silky head. "Guess I can't really blame you for sneaking in. The weather's too awful to be doing anything but sleeping on a soft, warm bed."

Cuddles responded with a lazy stretch and a faint *meow*. Then she began to purr.

Rachel slipped out of her wet clothes and into a clean dress and hurried to the window. Pressing her nose against the glass, she groaned. "Sure wish I could be at the creek today instead of cooped up in this stuffy old house. It's supposed to be summer, and I'm bored. There must be something fun I can do."

The kitten's loud purr turned to a soft rumble, but she didn't open her eyes.

A knock sounded on Rachel's bedroom door, and she called out, "Come in!"

The door squeaked open, and Jacob poked his head inside. "Mom went out to the barn to check on the calf that was born yesterday. She wants you to help Esther start supper." When he spotted Cuddles on Rachel's bed, he shook his head and said, "You'd better put that cat outside. You know Mom doesn't like—"

"I know, I know," Rachel interrupted. "But it's raining, and it's not fair to make my sweet little bussli stay outdoors in this awful weather." She sat on the bed beside Cuddles, just in case her brother decided to haul the kitten outside.

"Aw, you're silly. Animals don't mind the rain," Jacob said with a grunt.

"They do so," Rachel argued. "The cows always head straight for the barn whenever it rains. Even the chickens have the good sense to stay in their coop until the sun comes out."

Jacob waved his hand like he was shooing away a pesky fly. "Well, if Mom catches that cat on your bed, you'll be in big trouble."

"You're not going to tell, are you?" Rachel figured she had enough problems with the extra chores she'd been assigned.

"Naw, but you'd better hurry and get downstairs before Mom comes back inside and wonders why you're not helping Esther."

"*Danki* [Thank you], Jacob."

"You're welcome."

Rachel was a bit surprised that Jacob was being so nice. It seemed like he usually liked to see her get in trouble. She stroked Cuddles's paw and headed downstairs to help her sister.

The rain continued all that week, and Rachel complained about it almost every day. "If summer doesn't get here soon, it'll be over. Then school will start again, and I won't have had any fun at all," she announced during supper one evening.

"Summer will come. It always does," Pap said from his place at the head of the table. "The rain's put us behind in our fieldwork, but we should still be glad for it. It could be the only rain we'll have all summer."

"I hope it is. This awful weather has kept me from playing outdoors." Rachel pointed to the container sitting near Esther. "Pass the pickles, please."

"If you want something fun to do, maybe you should put on your thinking cap and come up with something you will enjoy." Esther pointed to Rachel's plate. "And you already have two pickles."

Rachel frowned. She didn't even remember taking the pickles. Maybe that was because she was so upset over the rain.

"If you're bored, you can come to the barn and help me brush the horses," said Henry. "I think that's fun, and you're always pestering me to let you help."

"*Humph!* You always tell me that brushing horses

is men's work." Rachel bit into one of her pickles and puckered her lips. She liked the tangy flavor of garlic and dill, but it made the edges of her mouth pull together.

"It *is* men's work," Henry answered with a wink. "But just this once, I might let you help."

Rachel shrugged her shoulders. "I'll think about it."

"Maybe you'd like to help me do some quilting. I find that to be enjoyable," Mom said, forking another piece of ham onto her plate.

Rachel shook her head. "I'd probably end up pricking my finger with the needle, like I usually do whenever I try to sew."

"I've got an idea," Esther said. "Why don't the two of us do some baking? We can make one of your favorites—banana chocolate chip cookies."

Rachel pushed her chair away from the table and began to clear her dishes. "I'm not really in the mood for baking, either."

"Well, young lady, it seems as if all you want to do is grumble and complain. So after you wash the dishes, I think it might be a good idea if you head on up to bed," Pap said firmly. "Maybe if you sleep off this bad mood, you'll wake up happier in the morning."

"Jah, you go around looking like you've been sucking on a slice of dill pickle," Jacob put in.

Rachel thought about the verse of scripture from Proverbs 17:22 that Pap had read to them one evening before bed. It said: "A cheerful heart is good medicine, but a crushed spirit dries up the bones." She knew the Bible verse didn't actually mean her bones would dry up if she wasn't happy, but she got the point just the same.

"I'll help Esther make cookies," she said as she ran water into the kitchen sink.

"And no more complaining?" Pap asked.

She shook her head.

"*Der Herr sie gedankt* [Thank the Lord]," Mom whispered. "Jah, thank the Lord."

When Rachel finished the dishes, she helped her sister set out the items they would need for the cookies.

"Why don't you mix the dry ingredients?" Esther suggested. "I'll beat the eggs and mix all of the wet ingredients."

Rachel frowned. "How come you get to do the fun part? Why can't I beat the eggs?"

Esther handed Rachel a large bowl and the eggbeater. "You can mix whatever part of the cookie batter you want."

Rachel thanked her sister and went to the refrigerator to get out two eggs. When she cracked the first one into the bowl, a piece of eggshell fell in, as well. "Who said making cookies was fun?" she grumbled as she stuck her fingers into the gooey egg whites and pulled out the shell.

"You said you wanted to beat the eggs," Esther reminded. "Would you rather I do that part while you mix the dry ingredients?"

Rachel nodded and slid over to the other side of the counter, where Esther had already placed a sack of flour and a can of shortening.

"Don't forget the baking powder and salt," her sister said. "They're still in the cupboard."

Rachel slid a wooden stool to the cupboard and climbed up. "Whoa!" She almost lost her balance but kept herself from falling by grabbing the handle on the cupboard door.

"Are you okay?" Esther asked. "Would you like me to do that for you?"

"I'm fine." Rachel reached into the cupboard for the box of salt and leaned down to set it on the counter. *Let's see now. Does the recipe call for baking powder or soda?* She squinted at the spice containers and boxes of other baking ingredients. *I probably should ask Esther, but then she might think I'm* dumm [dumb] *and don't know anything.*

Rachel grabbed the box of baking soda and placed it beside the salt. Then she reached for a package of white sugar and climbed down.

When the ingredients were all mixed and the cookies were put in the oven, Rachel could hardly wait to get a bite. They smelled so good! Finally it was time to grab a pot holder and take the first batch of cookies out of the oven. Rachel waited until they had cooled before she ate one. "Something is wrong with these cookies," she said, wrinkling her nose. "Maybe the banana you put in wasn't ripe enough, Esther."

"I'm sure it was." Esther lifted a cookie from the cooling rack and took a bite. "Eww. . .these do taste funny. How much sugar did you put in, Rachel?"

"Half a cup, I think."

Esther shook her head. "You were supposed to use one full cup, so that's why the cookies aren't sweet enough."

"Oh. Guess I got *verhuddelt* [confused]. It seems I get confused a lot lately."

"The cookies aren't puffed up the way they should be, either. How much baking powder did you use?" her sister asked.

"I. . .uh. . .thought I was supposed to use baking *soda*."

"The ingredients for the cookies are right there on top of Mom's recipe file," Esther said, pointing to the small metal box on the cupboard. "It seems that you didn't follow the directions for the dry ingredients."

"Trouble again," Rachel mumbled. "Maybe I should have helped Henry with the horses instead of trying to make cookies." She hung her head. "I guess I'm nothing but trouble. I can't seem to do anything right these days."

"You just need to pay more attention to what you're doing," Esther said, giving Rachel a hug. "We can add more sugar and some baking powder to the rest of the cookie dough. Would you like to mix them in?"

Rachel shook her head. "No, thanks. I think I'll go

to my room and get ready for bed." Rachel ran out of the kitchen and dashed up the stairs.

When Rachel entered her room, she flopped onto the bed. As she lay there feeling sorry for herself, she studied the cracks in the ceiling. They reminded her of a jigsaw puzzle. She hoped Mom wouldn't find out about the cookies. She didn't want to get into trouble for wasting food.

Boom! A crash of thunder reminded her of the whole reason she'd been inside messing up cookies anyway.

"I hope summer will hurry up and get here," she muttered. "It will be my birthday soon, and it won't be any fun if we have to eat supper in the house that night." Mom had told Rachel that they might have a picnic in the backyard for her birthday.

Rachel licked her lips as she thought about juicy, plump hot dogs roasting over the coals of Pap's barbecue pit. She could almost taste Mom's tangy potato salad and smell the spicy pickled beets.

"Sure hope I get some fun gifts this year," she murmured. She hoped for a skateboard and had even dropped a few hints to her family.

Suddenly, an idea popped into Rachel's mind, and she sprang to her feet. "If I had enough money, I could buy my own skateboard. I probably won't get one for my birthday anyway. It seems like I always get gifts that are practical instead of fun."

Rachel rushed to her dresser and jerked open the top

drawer. She pulled out a small, blue bank shaped like a pig and held it over her bed, shaking the contents until all the money fell onto her patchwork quilt. She counted out six dollars and fifty cents. The skateboard she had seen at Kauffman's Store cost fifteen dollars, so she would need another eight and a half dollars to buy it.

Rachel tapped her finger against her chin. "I wonder how I can earn the rest of the money before my birthday gets here. Maybe I could sell something to Noah Kauffman. Lots of tourists look in his store for Amish-made items, so I might be able to make something they would like."

Rachel dropped the coins back into the bank. "I'm sure I can come up with a few things to sell before our next trip to town." She flopped onto the bed and stroked Cuddles, who had found her way into Rachel's room once again. "With a skateboard, I could sail up and down the sidewalks in town, the way I've seen so many other kinner do. Maybe I could even ride it to and from school every day. Then I would get there quicker, and I'd be home earlier, too." She patted the top of her kitten's silky head. "And it would give me more time to spend with you, my furry little friend."

Cuddles licked the end of Rachel's finger with her small, pink tongue.

"A skateboard wouldn't be nearly as exciting as riding in a car, but it would be faster than walking." Rachel pressed her face close to the kitten's nose. "I still want to go for a ride in a fancy, fast car someday, but until then, a skateboard will have to do."

Cuddles gave Rachel another sandpapery kiss, this time on her nose.

"Maybe you'd like to go for a ride on my new skateboard. Would you like that, Cuddles? Would you, girl?"

The kitten was falling asleep, for her eyes had closed, and her only response now was a soft, gentle purr. Rachel felt sleepy, too. She nestled against her pillow, dreaming about soaring with Cuddles on a shiny new skateboard.

Chapter 6

Fireflies and Secrets

By the end of June, the rain finally stopped. Sunshine and warmer weather took over, so Rachel could spend more time outdoors. She played with Cuddles, climbed her favorite tree, and waded in the creek. She plodded back and forth in the cool water now, trying not to get the edge of her long, blue dress wet.

As Rachel stepped carefully across some slippery rocks, she thought about her kitten and how much she loved her. She thought about the tasty apple pie she'd had for breakfast that morning. And she thought about her birthday and wondered what gifts she might get.

Two weeks earlier, she and Esther had gone to town to buy groceries. She had taken some of the pet rocks she'd painted to Kauffman's Store. Noah Kauffman had said they were nice. He especially liked the ones she had made to look like ladybugs. He'd taken the rocks on consignment, which meant if he sold any, Rachel would get half of the money and he would get the other half. She hoped that by the time they went to town again all the rocks would have been sold. Then she could buy the green and silver skateboard she had put on layaway with her piggy bank money.

"Rachel! Come up to the house, *schnell* [quickly]," Mom called.

Rachel shielded her eyes from the glare of the sun and squinted. She saw Mom standing on the back porch, with her hands cupped around her mouth, and wondered why she wanted her to come quickly.

"Rachel! Schnell!"

"I'm coming, Mom." Rachel plodded out of the creek, remembering the last time she hadn't come when Mom had called. No way was she doing laundry again!

Up in the yard, Rachel found Pap lighting the barbecue, while Henry and Jacob moved the picnic table under the shade of a maple tree. "Are we having a picnic?" she asked her oldest brother.

Henry nodded. "Mom and Esther are in the kitchen getting everything ready, so you'd better hurry inside to help."

Rachel bounded up the stairs. She loved picnics!

A short time later, the Yoders gathered around the picnic table. After their silent prayer, Mom passed the food. They had grilled hot dogs, tangy potato salad, spicy pickled beets, maple-flavored baked beans, and plenty of Pap's icy-cold, homemade root beer.

Rachel had second helpings of everything. By the time she'd finished eating, she could hardly breathe. "Yum. Everything tasted wunderbaar," she said, licking her fingers.

"You do have a napkin," Mom said, shaking her head.

Rachel glanced at the wadded napkin in her lap. It was a lot more fun to lick your fingers than to wipe them on a plain old napkin. Still, she didn't want to risk getting in trouble with Mom, so she blotted her lips on one corner of the napkin and said, "May I please have the empty beet jar?"

Mom gave Rachel a curious look over the top of her glasses. "Whatever for?"

"I want to catch fireflies."

Her mother shrugged and handed Rachel the jar. "You'd better rinse it out well, or those poor little bugs might turn purple."

"I will, Mom." Rachel ran into the house to rinse the jar in the sink. A short time later, she returned with the clean jar in one hand and her kitten tucked under her arm. "Cuddles and I are going to take a nap," she said as she passed Esther, who sat on the porch swing, reading a book. "We got up extra early this morning. Could you wake me when the fireflies start to shine?"

"I would, but Rudy's coming to take me for a drive. He wants to see how well his new horse pulls the buggy."

"I'll ask someone else then." Rachel had only taken a

few steps when Esther called out to her.

"You're not going to kill those poor fireflies, are you?"

Rachel shook her head. " 'Course not. I just want to give myself some light when I go to bed tonight."

"Ah, I see." Esther left the swing and joined Rachel on the step. "Are you afraid of the dark?"

"Maybe. . ." Rachel really didn't want to answer Esther's question.

"Why don't you use a flashlight?"

"The batteries went dead the last time I tried that."

Esther shrugged. "I hope the fireflies work out for you then."

Cuddles meowed as Rachel headed across the yard. She leaned down and kissed the kitten on the nose. She noticed Mom and Pap walking by the garden, and decided it would be best not to bother them. Then she passed by the picnic table and spotted Jacob and Henry playing a game of checkers. She stopped and tapped Jacob on the shoulder.

"What do you want, Rachel?" he asked, as he took two of Henry's checkers.

"Cuddles and I are gonna rest awhile. Will you wake me when the fireflies start to rise and shine?"

"Jah, sure," Jacob mumbled.

"Danki." Rachel wandered to the tallest maple tree in their yard and sat on the grass. She set the empty jar down, placed Cuddles across her chest, and leaned against the tree trunk. She felt so tired, and Cuddles's gentle purring soon put her to sleep.

Whoo-hoo! Whoo-hoo! Whoo-hoo! Rachel's eyes popped open. She could barely see the great horned owl that looked down at her from a branch in the tree. She sat up quickly and glanced around the yard, wondering how long she had been asleep. It was almost dark, and Rachel could see the fireflies as they fluttered up from the grass.

"Why didn't somebody wake me?" She set Cuddles on the ground, reached for the glass jar, and scrambled to her feet.

Rachel was about to chase the fireflies when she heard voices. She noticed that Henry and Jacob were still at the picnic table. They weren't playing checkers, but their heads were close together.

"This needs to be kept secret," Henry said quietly. Rachel stopped and listened closely, but she could barely hear him. "We can't tell anyone, okay?"

Jacob nodded. "I won't say a word. I promise."

Secrets? Promises? What was going on? Rachel hurried to the picnic table and nudged Jacob's arm. "What were you and Henry talking about?"

Jacob looked at his older brother, and Henry shook his head. Then Jacob looked back at Rachel and said, "We weren't talkin' about much at all."

"But you said something about a secret," she persisted. "What kind of secret are you keeping?"

Henry tweaked the end of Rachel's nose. "You'll find

out soon enough, snoopy sister."

"I'm not snoopy. I just—"

"Say, why aren't you out there catching lightning bugs?" Jacob asked, changing the subject. "I thought that's why you wanted the empty jar."

Rachel pointed to her brother and frowned. "Because someone forgot to wake me, and they're *fireflies* not *lightning bugs*."

"Jah, well, I've heard 'em called *lightning bugs*," Jacob said. "Only a bensel would call them *fireflies*."

Henry snickered. "I guess they get the name *lightning bug* because the light on their stomach flashes off and on."

"That's right. Put several of those critters inside a jar, and you'll have enough light to read by." Jacob poked Rachel's arm. "Since you're awake now, don't you think you'd better get busy and capture those *lightning bugs* before it's time to go to bed?"

"Well, if you won't tell me your secret, I guess I will try to see how many *fireflies* I can catch." No way would Rachel call them lightning bugs just because Jacob said that's what they were. She hurried away, and when she came to a spot in the grass where several fireflies had risen, she dropped to her knees. A few minutes later, Rachel had the jar filled with dancing, glowing bugs.

Lights on. Lights off. Lights on. The insects' shimmering stomachs twinkled and lit up the whole jar.

"This is perfect. Now when Mom tells me to put out

the oil lamp by my bed, I can still read." Rachel smiled.

Inside the house, Rachel found Mom and Pap playing Scrabble. "I was about to call you," Mom said, nodding at Rachel. "It's time for you to get ready for bed."

Rachel didn't argue. Since she had her jar of lights, this was one time she didn't mind going to bed. She hugged Mom and Pap and gave each a kiss on the cheek. Then she said good night and scampered up the stairs.

Rachel set the jar of fireflies on the small table by her bed and opened the window. She was glad there was a tall maple tree growing outside her window. That gave Cuddles a way to get inside. Then she undressed and slipped into her long, cotton nightgown. Next she headed for the bathroom to wash her face and brush her teeth.

A few minutes later, Rachel returned to her room and knelt by her bed to say her prayers. "Heavenly Father, bless everyone in my family, and let the angels surround my bed as I sleep through the night. Amen."

She picked up her favorite book, turned down the oil lamp, shut the window, and crawled into bed next to an already-sleeping Cuddles.

Rachel held the book close to the jar, but to her surprise, no light came from it. She tapped on the side of the glass. Still nothing. No twinkling lights. Not a single one.

"What's going on?" Rachel set the book aside and grasped the lid on the jar. She twisted the lid off and peered inside. "Hmm. . .maybe they've fallen asleep." She jiggled the jar this way and that. "Wake up you sleepy fireflies, and give me some light."

Suddenly, the room began to glow, as tiny, shimmering fireflies flittered toward the ceiling. Some flew to the left. Some soared to the right. Some drifted down and landed on Rachel's stomach.

"I'm all lit up!" She jumped out of bed, and some of the fireflies went with her. Reaching out with one hand, and then quickly with the other, she ran around the room, chasing the fireflies and laughing so hard her sides ached.

Cuddles woke up and joined the chase, leaping into the air and swatting at the fireflies with her paws.

"What's all the ruckus about?" Mom said as she burst into Rachel's room. She stopped just inside the door. "Oh, Rachel, what have you done?"

"The fireflies quit glowing, so I opened the jar lid, and then—"

"We've got to get them out of here," Mom said as she clapped her hands together.

"Please, don't hurt any of them," Rachel pleaded. "I'll try to get every bug back into the jar."

"And how do you plan to get them back in that jar?"

Rachel thought a minute. Mom was probably right. It would be hard to capture all those bugs. An idea popped into Rachel's head. She rushed across the room, pulled up the window shade, and opened the window as wide as it would go. The cool evening breeze blew in, lifting Rachel's long hair so it fell against her face. A few seconds later, little bugs blinking off and on sailed out her window and into the night sky.

Rachel lit the oil lamp and looked around the room. "I think they're all gone."

"So it would seem." Mom moved past Rachel and shut the window. "Now into bed with you. From now on, there will be no more critters in this room." She bent over and picked up Rachel's cat, who sat in front of the window, meowing for all she was worth. "And that includes busslin with *fleh* [fleas]!"

"I'm sure Cuddles doesn't have fleas, and she likes it here with me."

Mom shook her head. "The kitten belongs in the barn, not in your room."

"If Cuddles had a flea collar, then could she come inside?"

Mom tapped her chin as she tipped her head. "We'll see." She left the bedroom, carrying Cuddles and muttering, "Immer druwwle eiyets."

Rachel crawled back into bed with a grunt. Such a day this had turned out to be. There were secrets no one wanted her to know, bugs that wouldn't shine when they should, and now Cuddles had been taken back to the barn with no promise of ever being allowed in Rachel's room.

Rachel felt lonely without her kitten and a bit

nervous because the room was so dark again. To help her feel less afraid, she sang one of her favorite church songs, "*Das Lob Lied*," which was "The Hymn of Praise." It reminded her to praise God, even when things weren't going the way she wanted them to.

"Have a good night, Lord," she whispered as her eyes drifted shut. "I'll talk to You in the morning. And please help me stay out of trouble."

Chapter 7

Birthday Surprises

On the day before Rachel's birthday, she and Esther went to town so Esther could get some fabric she needed for her wedding dress. Rachel asked to go to Kauffman's to see if any of her painted rocks had sold.

"Sure," Esther agreed. "After we finish our errands, I'll take you out for a late breakfast." She tapped Rachel on the shoulder. "In the meantime, I'm going to the quilt shop across the street to look at some material. I'll be back for you in half an hour."

"Okay." Rachel hurried into the store, full of excitement. *If all my rocks have sold, I might be able to take my new skateboard home today,* Rachel thought as she headed to the display case to see the green and silver skateboard that would soon be hers. She skidded to a stop. The skateboard was gone. The case only displayed a pair of roller skates, a baseball glove, and a few jump ropes. *He's sold it! Noah Kauffman sold my skateboard.* Tears filled Rachel's eyes, and she bit her bottom lip, struggling not to cry.

When Noah finished waiting on a customer, he walked up to Rachel and said, "Good morning, Rachel. Have you come to collect your money for the painted rocks I've sold?"

She sighed. Money? What good was money if she couldn't have the skateboard?

"All your rocks are gone, and I have your consignment money waiting," he said with a smile.

"But the skateboard I wanted to buy is gone."

Noah nodded. "The one you put on layaway, right?"

"You said you'd keep it until I had enough money, but it's not there anymore."

"It's still in the store. I keep my layaways in the back room," Mr. Kauffman said.

"Am I ever glad to hear that!" Rachel exclaimed.

"Should we take care of the money matter now?"

"Jah, please."

"Your part of the profit is five dollars."

Rachel's smile quickly turned to a frown. "Is that all?"

Noah nodded. "I charged one dollar for each of your rocks, and your half for ten rocks is five dollars."

"But that's not nearly enough for the skateboard."

"Do you have any more painted rocks to sell?" he asked. "The tourists seem to like them. Especially the ones you painted to look like ladybugs and turtles."

Rachel shook her head. "I would need to paint more, and since my birthday is tomorrow, I had hoped to get the skateboard today."

"I'm sorry, Rachel," Noah said. "I guess it will have to be a late birthday present."

With her head down and her shoulders slumped, Rachel walked away. She would wait for Esther outside. If she stayed in the store, she would only think about the wonderful, shiny skateboard she wouldn't be riding on her birthday.

As Rachel waited on the sidewalk, she stood with her arms folded, watching plain horse and buggies and shiny, fast cars pass on the street. When she spotted an English boy riding a skateboard on the sidewalk, she felt worse.

It's not fair that I can't have my new skateboard today, she thought. *If I can't find the time to paint any more rocks, I may never have enough money to get the skateboard off layaway.*

Rachel closed her eyes and tried to think about something else—anything to get her mind off the skateboard she wouldn't have in time for her birthday.

When Rachel heard someone clear their throat, she opened her eyes. It was Esther coming to take her to breakfast. At least that was something to smile about.

A short time later, Rachel and Esther sat in a booth at the restaurant. "What would you like to order?" their waitress asked, looking at Esther.

Esther smiled at the young English woman. "I think I'll have a blueberry waffle and a cup of hot tea." She glanced over at Rachel. "Would you like to place your own order, or would you rather I do it for you?"

"I can do it." Rachel looked up at the waitress and said, "I'd like my waffle to be strawberry, please. Oh, and I would also like to have a glass of grape fruit juice."

The waitress raised her dark eyebrows and flipped her ponytail with one hand. "Are you sure that's the kind of juice you want?"

Rachel nodded. Of course she was sure. She wouldn't have ordered it if she wasn't sure.

The waitress shrugged, wrote Rachel's order on her tablet, and walked away.

While they waited for their meal, Rachel asked Esther, "Did you get the material you wanted for your wedding dress?"

Esther smiled. "I found just the right shade of blue. I also bought the white material I'll need to make the apron." She nodded at Rachel. "How about you? Did you buy anything at Kauffman's Store?"

Rachel shook her head. "Not really." She was tempted to tell her sister about the skateboard she had put on layaway but decided it would be best not to mention it right now. Esther might think Rachel was selfish for wanting to buy her own birthday present. Besides, she didn't have the skateboard and might never own it if she couldn't earn enough money. "I'm sure glad we haven't had any more rain lately," she said, changing the subject.

Esther glanced out the window. "This day has started off warm, so a nice rain shower would be very gut."

Rachel was about to argue the point when their waitress arrived with Esther's tea and a glass of strange-looking juice for Rachel. Instead of purple, like grape juice should be, it was yellow.

Rachel reached for the glass and sipped. "Ugh! This isn't sweet like grape fruit juice."

"It's what you ordered," the waitress said.

Rachel shook her head. "No, I—"

"You said you wanted a glass of grapefruit juice, and that's what I brought you. I'll be right back with your breakfast." The waitress walked away before Rachel could say anything more.

Rachel frowned and puckered her lips.

"What's wrong?" Esther asked, leaning toward Rachel. "Don't you like grapefruit juice?"

"I—I thought I had ordered grape juice, not this sour-tasting stuff." She lifted her glass and wrinkled her nose. "Do I have to drink this?"

"What do you think Mom or Pap would say about that?"

"They'd probably say it would be wasteful not to drink it."

Esther reached across the table and picked up Rachel's glass. "Then I shall drink it for you, and you can order the right kind of juice this time."

Rachel breathed a sigh of relief. "Danki, Esther." She hated to cause trouble, but she was sure glad she didn't have to drink it!

Her sister smiled. "You are most welcome."

Rachel awoke the next morning, knowing that today was her tenth birthday and that the one thing she wanted most still sat in the back of Kauffman's Store. Maybe after she finished her chores for the day, she could paint more rocks for consignment. However, she still wouldn't get the skateboard today.

When Rachel entered the kitchen, she found her mother standing near the cupboard.

"*Guder mariye* [Good morning]. Happy birthday," said Mom.

"Good morning. Where is everyone?" Rachel asked.

"Pap, Henry, and Jacob are outside doing their chores. Esther went somewhere with Rudy, and they'll eat breakfast out." Mom nodded toward the cupboard across the room. "Would you please get out the maple syrup? I've fixed some buttermilk pancakes this morning, and they're keeping warm in the oven."

Rachel went to the cupboard and took the syrup down from the shelf.

"If you will please set the table, we can eat as soon as the men come inside," Mom said as she took some butter from the refrigerator.

Rachel hurried to get the dishes and silverware out. She had just placed the glasses on the table when the back door creaked open. Henry and Jacob clomped into the kitchen.

"Pap will be right in," Henry told Mom as he went to the sink to wash his hands. When he finished, he turned to Rachel and said, "Happy birthday, sister."

Rachel noticed that Jacob held his arms behind his back, like he might be hiding something. She craned her neck to see what it was, but he kept turning this way and that to block her view. "Can I open my gifts before we eat?" Rachel asked.

"Gifts? Who said anything about gifts?" Pap said as he stepped into the kitchen.

Rachel giggled. "I think you're teasing me. Jacob and Henry must have a gift because they look guilty, and Jacob's hiding something behind his back."

Pap chuckled, causing his beard to jiggle up and down. "So, who wants to go first?"

"We will." Jacob held his hands in front of him, revealing a homemade wooden skateboard with shiny chrome wheels. "Henry and I have been working on this for weeks."

Rachel's mouth dropped open. "Is—is this the secret you were whispering about the other night?"

Henry nodded, and Jacob grinned.

"I—I hardly know what to say," she stammered.

"We knew you wanted a skateboard," Jacob said,

handing it to her.

"Jah, you've dropped plenty of hints," Henry put in.

"I know, but I didn't think I would ever get one, so I—" Rachel's voice trailed off. How could she tell her brothers that she had put her own skateboard on layaway? The homemade skateboard wasn't nearly as beautiful as the green and silver one at Kauffman's Store, but she knew it would hurt her brothers' feelings if she refused their gift. So Rachel took the skateboard and smiled. "Danki, Jacob. Danki, Henry."

"You're welcome," they both said.

Rachel wondered what she would do with two skateboards if she went ahead and bought the skateboard at Kauffman's. Should she tell Noah to take the fancy one off layaway and then spend her money on something else? *I'll figure that out later,* she decided. *Right now I just want to enjoy my birthday.*

"Now it's my turn," Mom said as she headed across the room to her sewing cabinet. She removed a small basket and handed it to Rachel.

Rachel set the skateboard on the floor and opened the lid of the basket. Inside were some pins, needles, thread, scissors, and several small pieces of material.

"I thought it was time you had your own sewing basket," Mom said.

Rachel didn't like to sew. She would much rather be outside playing with Cuddles, climbing a tree, or wading in the creek. But she didn't want to hurt her mother's feelings, so she smiled and said, "Danki, Mom."

Mom smiled and nodded, then she nudged Pap's arm with her elbow. "It's your turn, Levi."

Pap opened the front of his shirt and pulled out a small package wrapped in brown paper. He handed it to Rachel and winked. "This is just for fun."

Rachel opened Pap's present. Inside, she found a bag of licorice and a large metal ring with a handle on one end. "Licorice is my favorite candy," she said with a grin.

Pap nodded. "Jah, I know. It's my favorite, too."

Rachel picked up the metal ring. "What's this, Pap?"

"It's a bubble blower. You just need a bowl full of soapy water with a squirt of glycerin added. Then you'll be all set. With this special ring, you can make bigger bubbles than you ever imagined."

Rachel gave her father a hug. "I guess I will."

"You've received some nice birthday gifts," Mom said, "but I think we should eat now." She opened the oven and removed the baking dish filled with pancakes, and everyone gathered around the table.

"Let's pray, and then we'll eat," Pap said with a nod.

Rachel enjoyed every bite of the delicious buttermilk pancakes Mom had made. When they finished their meal and Rachel had helped clean the kitchen, she decided to try out the bubble maker Pap had made for her.

She stepped onto the back porch and sat on the top step. She set the pan of soapy water Mom had fixed next to her and dipped the metal wand into it. When she pulled the wand out and waved it in the breeze, she was surprised to see a huge bubble. It blew lazily across the yard. Rachel laughed, then quickly made more bubbles. Cuddles, who had been lying beside Rachel, sprang to her feet and jumped off the porch. The kitten dashed into the yard after the colorful bubbles, but just as her paw touched a bubble, it popped and disappeared.

"You *kischblich* [silly] bussli! Here are some more bubbles for you to chase." Rachel waved the wand again and again, laughing each time Cuddles thought she could catch the shiny, see-through balls.

"It looks as though you're having fun. Mind if I join you?"

Rachel turned and looked up at Pap, who stood behind her. She had been so busy playing that she hadn't heard him come out the door. "You want to blow some bubbles?" she asked.

"If you don't mind sharing the wand." Pap sat on the step beside her.

"Of course I don't mind." Rachel handed the metal ring to her father, and he dipped it into the soapy water. Instead of waving the wand as she had done, he blew gently on it. A fat bubble formed. As it started to leave the ring, Pap blew again, causing a second bubble to form and stick to the first one. He blew one more time, and a third bubble stuck to the first two. Then he waved the ring slightly, and the three bubbles, still held together, sailed across the yard.

Rachel clapped her hands. "Oh, Pap, you've made a triple! I've made doubles with my plastic bubble blower before, but I've never made a triple!"

"Look at all the different colors—pink, purple, blue, yellow, and green." Pap seemed almost as excited as Rachel. The twinkle in his clear blue eyes let her know he was having a good time.

"The colorful bubbles remind me of a rainbow," she said.

He nodded. "That's right, and the rainbow reminds me that the world God made is full of beauty."

"Like all the pretty flowers in Mom's garden," Rachel said dreamily. "Each one is full of beautiful colors."

Rachel noticed a faraway look in Pap's eyes as he stared across the yard. "I've enjoyed looking at flowers ever since I was a boy. My older brothers often teased me about it, though," he said with a wink.

Rachel reached over and grabbed her father's hand, squeezing it. So far her birthday had gone better than she'd expected.

Chapter 8

Skateboard Troubles

Rachel was eager to try out her new skateboard, so after Pap and her brothers headed to the fields to work, she put her new bubble wand in her room and took the skateboard outside. Mom had forbidden Rachel to ride on the paved road in front of their farm, saying it was too dangerous. So Rachel knew she would have to find another place to try it out. The graveled driveway was out of the question because the wheels would never roll smoothly over the rocks. The grass had too many bumps, so that wouldn't do. The wooden floor in the barn might work, though.

Holding the skateboard under one arm and calling Cuddles to follow, Rachel headed for the barn.

As soon as she stepped through the door, she realized that the barn was definitely big enough for skateboarding. Unfortunately, most of the floor was covered with bales of hay piled on it.

Rachel groaned and flopped onto one of the bales to think. Maybe she could move the hay out of the way to create a path for skateboarding. However, that seemed like a lot of trouble, and she probably couldn't move the heavy bales alone. "There must be somewhere I can try out the skateboard Henry and Jacob worked so hard to make for my birthday."

Finally an idea popped into her head. She jumped up, grabbed the skateboard, and dashed out of the barn. She looked around the yard and spotted Mom hanging laundry on the clothesline. If she hurried, she thought she could make it to the house without being seen.

Rachel scampered to the back door, slipped inside, and scurried up the stairs with Cuddles on her heels. She screeched to a stop in the hallway and studied the long wooden floor. It had been freshly polished and looked like the perfect place to try her skateboard. Cuddles stopped, too, only she curled up in a corner and quickly fell asleep.

Rachel stood at one end of the hall and placed the skateboard on the floor. She had watched other children in town ride their skateboards up and down the sidewalks, so she knew how to stand. Put one foot on the board, the other one on the ground, and push off. It looked easy enough.

Rachel soon discovered that keeping her balance was the hardest part. It wasn't easy to hold her body upright and move forward at the same time. Soon after she had pushed off, the skateboard sailed down the hallway, and she swayed back and forth like a tree branch in the wind. "This is so much fun!"

In spite of the trouble Rachel had remaining upright, she enjoyed the ride, although it didn't seem nearly long enough. By the time she had made four trips up and back, she was able to keep her balance fairly well.

"Look at me, Cuddles," she called to her sleeping cat. "I'm having such a good time!"

Cuddles opened one eye and replied with a *meow*. Then she curled her paws under her head and settled back down.

"That's okay," Rachel said. "You go ahead and sleep while I have all the fun. I'll take you for a ride on my skateboard some other time."

Rachel was about to start down the hall again, when a shrill voice called out, "Rachel Yoder, what are you doing?"

Rachel whirled around so fast, she lost control of the skateboard. It sailed across the floor, and Rachel fell hard, landing on both knees. "Ouch! Ouch!"

Mom rushed up the stairs to Rachel. "Are you hurt?"

"Jah, my knees are bleeding."

"And see here what you've done." Mom pointed to a hole near the hem of Rachel's dress.

Rachel wiggled on the floor, trying not to cry. "I—I

didn't do it on purpose."

"Calm down," Mom said softly as she examined Rachel's knees. "I can't help if you don't stay still."

"If I'd been wearing pants like English girls get to wear, I probably wouldn't have gotten hurt," Rachel complained.

"There will be no more of that kind of talk," Mom said crossly. "Now stop with the *rutschich* [squirming] and let me take a closer look at the damage you've done."

"I can't help it if I'm squirming." Rachel sniffed. "My knees hurt awfully."

"You brought this trouble on yourself. You know better than to ride your skateboard in the house." Mom pointed to the hardwood floor. "Now look at what you've done to my freshly polished floor."

Rachel hadn't noticed all the ugly streaks her skateboard had left. She felt sad because she knew she had marred Mom's clean floor. "I'm sorry," she cried as tears seeped under her lashes and splashed onto her cheeks. Her knees hurt, and she felt so ashamed that she didn't even care if Jacob heard about this and called her a crybaby.

"Sorry is good, but you must learn a lesson," Mom said, shaking her head. "You need to start thinking about what you're doing and stay out of trouble. As soon as we clean and bandage your knees, you will have to scrub and repolish the floor. And then you may try out your new sewing kit on the hole you put in your dress."

The last thing Rachel wanted to do was mend her dress, but she knew better than to argue with Mom—especially after she had messed up the shiny, clean floor. She glanced at Cuddles, who was still asleep in the corner of the hall. It was a good thing the kitten hadn't been on the skateboard with her when she fell. It was bad enough that she had injured her knees. She wouldn't have wanted Cuddles to get hurt, too.

Mom helped Rachel to her feet. "No more skateboarding in the house. Do you understand?"

Rachel nodded and stared at the floor. "Where can I skate?"

"I don't know where would be a good place, but I think trying to balance on a silly old skateboard is just asking for trouble."

"A lot of kinner have them. I've seen many of the English kinner ride skateboards in town."

Mom frowned. "You know, Rachel, some folks believe other people's bread tastes better than their own."

Rachel knew that Mom meant it wasn't good to always want the things others had. But was it really so wrong for her to want a skateboard?

Mom pointed to Cuddles. "You know the cat's not supposed to be in the house."

"Sorry," Rachel mumbled.

After Mom cleaned up Rachel's knees and bandaged them, Rachel spent the next hour cleaning and polishing the hallway floor. By the time she had finished, she wondered if having a skateboard was worth so much trouble.

Esther and Rudy showed up while Rachel sat at the kitchen table, mending her dress. "Sorry I wasn't here to wish you a happy birthday this morning," Esther said before she leaned over Rachel's chair and kissed the top of her head.

Rudy placed a large paper sack on the table. "It's my fault your sister was gone so long. We hired a driver to take us to Lancaster so we could do some shopping."

Rachel shrugged. It really didn't matter that her big sister hadn't been there when she opened her presents this morning. She didn't even care that Esther hadn't given her anything. Rachel's day was ruined the moment she'd fallen off the skateboard and discovered that she'd marred Mom's floor.

Esther looked around the room. "Where's the rest of the family?"

"Mom's upstairs, checking the hallway floor I just polished. Pap, Henry, and Jacob are working in the fields." Rachel set her sewing aside and stood.

"Why did you polish the hallway floor?" her sister asked. "I thought Mom did that yesterday."

Rachel nodded. "She did, but I scuffed it with my new skateboard."

"Skateboard?" Rudy's dark eyebrows drew together, and he glanced at Esther with a strange look on his face.

"Jah," Rachel explained. "I couldn't find anyplace to skate on it, so I tried the hallway upstairs."

Esther pointed to the paper sack Rudy had placed on the table. "You may as well open this, Rachel, because you'll probably want to take it back right away."

Rachel peered inside the sack and gasped. "Another skateboard?"

Esther nodded. "I knew you'd wanted one for a long time."

"We stopped at a toy store in Lancaster this morning and bought it," Rudy added.

Rachel just stood there, too stunned to utter a word. Finally, she began to laugh. She laughed and laughed until tears rolled down her cheeks and her sides ached.

"Do you think this is funny?" Esther tipped her head and gave Rachel a curious look.

Rachel hiccupped on another chuckle. "It *is* funny. I woke up this morning owning one half a skateboard, and now I own two more!"

Rudy's eyebrows lifted high on his forehead. "Huh?"

"I didn't think anyone would buy me a skateboard for my birthday," Rachel explained. "So a few weeks ago I put one on layaway at Kauffman's."

"You did?" Esther touched Rachel's shoulder.

"Jah, but I didn't have enough money to get the skateboard off layaway. Then this morning, Jacob and Henry gave me a wooden skateboard they had made for my birthday. Now, you and Rudy have just given me—"

"Another skateboard," Esther said, finishing Rachel's sentence. "Oh, little sister, that *is* funny!"

"I haven't told anyone else in the family about the skateboard I planned to buy myself," Rachel said in a whisper. "I didn't want to hurt Jacob's and Henry's feelings, because they must have worked hard on the one they made." She leaned over and touched her sore knees. "And now the skateboard they gave me has caused so much trouble, I almost wish I didn't have any!"

"Today was a day for learning lessons, wasn't it, sister?" asked Esther.

"Jah," Rachel replied with a nod.

"Say, I have an idea. Why don't you return the skateboard we gave you and use the money you get back to buy something else?" Rudy suggested.

"That probably would be best. And I'll cancel my layaway on the other skateboard." Rachel drew in a quick breath and released it with a huff. "Now if I can just find a good place to ride the one skateboard I'm going to keep."

"How about the barn?" Rudy asked. "There should be plenty of room in there for you to skateboard."

Rachel shook her head. "I already thought of that, but too many bales of hay are stacked in the barn."

Rudy smiled. "I don't think that's a problem. I'll go to the fields and see your daed. If he says it's okay, I'll move some of the bales out of the way so you'll have enough room to skateboard."

"That's a wunderbaar idea," Esther said excitedly. "And I'll help Rudy move them."

Rachel gave Esther and Rudy both a hug. She had gotten a new skateboard, would soon have a place to ride it, and tonight they would probably have a barbecue supper. This had turned out to be a pretty good birthday after all.

Chapter 9

Dunner and Wedderleech

Rachel looked forward to sharing a meal with her family at Uncle Ben and Aunt Irma's home. Uncle Ben was Pap's older brother. Mary was Uncle Ben and Aunt Irma's youngest daughter—and Rachel's favorite cousin. She hoped that after supper she and Mary would have time to play on the swing hanging from the rafters in the barn.

"Sure wish I could have brought Cuddles along," Rachel said from her seat in the back of the buggy. "She would have enjoyed playing with Mary's cat, Stripes."

"Maybe some other time, Rachel," Mom called over her shoulder. "After your kitten gets used to riding in the buggy."

"That was disgusting when you brought that critter along on a ride last time, and she threw up." Jacob wrinkled his nose. "Just thinking about *kotze* [vomit] is enough to make my stomach flip-flop. Your cat is as much trouble as you are!"

"Let's have no more of that talk," Pap scolded. "We don't need to ruin our appetites."

"That's right," Henry agreed. "Cousin Abe told me his daed's fixing homemade ice cream for dessert, and I hope to eat at least two bowls."

"Me, too," Jacob agreed. "I might even have three bowls."

"What a pig," Rachel mumbled. "Oink, oink."

Jacob poked her on the arm. "Look who's talking. The last time Mom made ginger cookies, you ate half a dozen before I finished one."

"Did not."

"Did so."

"Did not."

Esther turned in her seat and put her finger to her lips.

Rachel knew her sister wasn't trying to be bossy. She probably didn't want Rachel or Jacob to get in trouble this evening.

Not that Jacob would get in trouble, Rachel thought. *I'm the only one who gets in trouble around here!*

So for the rest of the ride, Rachel remained quiet, watching the scenery and dreaming about riding in a fast car with the top down.

Soon they were pulling into Uncle Ben's place, and before long, everyone had found seats at the picnic tables in the backyard. Rachel sat beside Mary and her older sister, Nancy. Jacob sat between his cousins Abe and Sam. Henry and Esther sat at the table with the grown-ups.

Besides barbecued hot dogs and burgers, the families could choose from coleslaw, cucumber slices, cherry tomatoes, macaroni salad, potato chips, and ice-cold lemonade.

"God is good. Let us thank Him for what He gives to us," Uncle Ben said before all bowed their heads for silent prayer.

The meal was tasty, and everyone seemed happy. After the meal, Rachel and Mary were about to walk to the barn, when a cloud burst open and rain began to fall.

"Looks like we might be in for another summer storm," Pap said.

"We'd better clear this table quickly." Mom grabbed empty dishes, and everyone else did the same.

"Even though it's raining, we can still go to the barn," Mary said as she and Rachel raced for the house with their hands full of empty bowls. When everything had been cleared away, the girls headed for the barn.

Boom! Crack! Thunder clapped, and lightning zigzagged across the sky. Rachel shuddered. She only feared a few things, and lightning was one of them.

"Come on, let's run!" Mary grabbed Rachel's hand and pulled her across the yard.

"I hope the rain stops soon," Rachel panted as the girls entered the barn. "We had enough rain when summer first began."

"Think how nice and fresh the air smells after it rains." Mary scampered up to the hayloft, and Rachel followed. If the storm got any worse, she didn't want to be alone.

"Sure wish I didn't have to wear this dress," she complained. "It would be a lot easier to climb if I could wear trousers like Jacob."

Mary grunted. "You wouldn't really want to dress like a boy, would you?"

Rachel shrugged. "Have you ever wondered how God dresses?"

Her cousin smiled. "Maybe He wears all the love everyone gives Him."

"You might be right." Rachel looked around the hayloft. "Say, where's your cat? I thought Stripes liked to sleep up here."

Mary flopped onto a pile of straw. "He does, but if he isn't tired, he could be most anywhere."

"He wouldn't be outside when it's raining, would he?"

"Probably not. He might be here somewhere, trying to catch a mouse." Mary tugged Rachel's hand. "Have a seat, and we can talk while we listen to the rain hit the roof."

Thunder boomed again, and Rachel trembled. "Maybe we should go back to the house."

"Aw, come on. Don't be so naerfich. We'll be fine."

"I'm not nervous. I'm just a little bit afraid." With a gusty sigh, Rachel sank to her knees beside her cousin.

"What is it about the rain that makes you so scared?" Mary asked.

"It's not the rain, it's the dunner and wedderleech I don't like," Rachel replied.

Mary lifted her hands toward the ceiling. "God made the thunder and lightning, so why be afraid?"

"I know the dunner won't hurt me. It just sounds bad when it echoes through the sky." Rachel plucked up a piece of straw and twirled it around her fingers as she fought the urge to bite off a nail. "It's the wedderleech that worries me."

"How come?"

Rachel frowned. "Pap told us the other day that he heard about a man who had been struck by lightning."

Mary's eyes grew wide. "Did he—"

"No, the man didn't die, but he had burns on his body, and all of his hair turned white." Rachel touched the side of her head. "I don't know what I would do if my blond hair suddenly turned white."

"Rachel! Mary! Where are you?" The voice interrupted the conversation.

"We're up here, Nancy," Mary called to her sister.

"The ice cream is ready, and Mama sent me to get you."

"Okay, we're coming." Mary and Rachel stood and brushed the hay stubbles from their dresses. They carefully went down the ladder and hurried out of the barn.

In the house, the girls and their families gathered around Aunt Irma's kitchen table, eating creamy homemade ice cream with chocolate topping and fresh strawberries.

Then Pap pushed his chair away from the table and stood. "This has been a most enjoyable evening, but I think it's time for us to go home. The rain isn't letting up, and it's getting dark."

"Do you have to go so soon?" Mary asked with a groan. "I wanted to take Rachel to my room and show her the doll I'm making."

"You can show her some other time," Mary's father said.

Everyone said good-bye, and as Pap hitched up the horse, the rain pelted the ground even harder.

By the time Rachel's family had pulled onto the highway, lightning filled the night sky. Thunderous roars shook their buggy.

Rachel shivered as she thought about the day she had been trapped in the Millers' root cellar. It had been thundering and lightning then, too.

Esther reached under her seat and grabbed a quilt, which she wrapped around Rachel's shoulders.

"Danki," Rachel said gratefully. She hoped the warmth of the quilt would help her stop shivering.

"Isn't the storm exciting?" Jacob shouted in her ear.

She shook her head. "I don't think so. And don't holler. It makes me more nervous."

"Aw, you're just an old scaredy-cat. You've always been that way, but it's been worse since you got locked in the Millers' cellar."

Rachel didn't understand why her brother chose a time like this to tease. Bad storms were no laughing matter. She looked at him and squinted her eyes. "Maybe someone should lock you in a cellar, and then we'll see how brave you are!"

Mom turned in her seat at the front of the buggy and looked sternly at both of them over the top of her glasses. "Your daed's having a hard enough time trying to control the horse in this awful weather. He doesn't need you two yelling."

"Sorry," Rachel and Jacob said at the same time.

Pap guided the horse off the main road and onto the graveled driveway leading to their farm, but suddenly, he pulled on the reins. "Whoa, there! Hold steady, boy!"

"What's wrong?" Mom asked.

Pap pointed to the left. "Fire! Our barn is on fire!"

Rachel looked out the rain-streaked window. Sure enough, thick smoke bellowed from their barn, and angry red flames shot high into the sky.

"It must have been struck by the lightning!" Pap hollered. He smacked the reins hard, and for the first time in a long while, old Tom galloped up the driveway. When they reached the yard, Pap stopped the horse and said to Mom, "You'd better drive over to the Johnsons' place, Miriam, and ask them to phone the fire department. Then head to the Millers' and let them know that we could use their help." Pap jumped down from the buggy. Henry, Jacob, and Esther did the same. Rachel just sat there, watching helplessly as her family raced for the buckets sitting near the outside pump.

Mom slid into the driver's seat and reached for the reins. Then she turned to Rachel. "You can either get out and help fill buckets with water or ride with me."

Rachel blinked several times, fighting back tears. "I'll stay and help." She climbed down from the buggy and watched Mom speed out of the yard.

Rachel's legs felt heavy as she stumbled toward the water pump.

The fire burned fast, and Rachel's heart nearly stopped beating when she saw Pap and Henry race into the barn. She breathed a sigh of relief when they returned, leading several animals safely out. Rain and ashes from the fire covered the men's faces. Even Esther, who stood at the pump, filling buckets and handing them to Pap and her brothers, looked a mess.

Rachel noticed that the rain had tapered off. *Why, when we need heavy rain to help stop the fire?* she wondered.

"It's not helping!" Henry gasped as he grabbed another bucket and threw it at the burning flames. "What are we going to do, Pap?"

"Rachel, don't just stand there. Help fill some buckets, schnell!" Pap shouted.

Rachel forced herself to stop shaking and dashed to the pump. The buckets were heavy, and she struggled against the howling wind whipping the hem of her dress. The choking smoke burned Rachel's eyes, and tears stung her hot cheeks. Pap's barn was important. He kept all the animals there, as well as the alfalfa hay he raised to sell. He couldn't lose it. He just couldn't.

Soon the yard was full of neighbors, both Amish and English. Everyone worked hard, dumping buckets of cold water onto the angry, burning flames.

The wind grew stronger, and the fire spread quickly throughout the barn. The fire trucks still hadn't arrived.

Rachel gasped when old Tom trotted into the yard with no buggy and no Mom. Should she tell Pap or let him keep working? She didn't want to worry him, but if something had happened to Mom— Even though Rachel felt she caused a lot of trouble for her mother and that Mom often punished her, Rachel loved her mother very much.

Finally, Pap signaled the men to stop, and Rachel stood with the others and watched Pap's barn burn to the ground. The fire trucks arrived at last, but it was too late.

Rachel stepped up to her father, ready to tell him that old Tom had returned without Mom, when another buggy pulled into the yard. Anna Miller got out, and so did Rachel's mother.

"Mom! Where have you been?" Rachel shouted.

"What happened to our buggy?"

"Old Tom broke away when we tried to put him in the Millers' barn," Mom explained. "He seemed so jittery on the drive over that I decided to leave him there and ride back in Anna's buggy."

"I'm glad you're all right," Rachel said, hugging her mother.

Mom nodded and patted Rachel's head. "I'm fine, but I see our barn didn't do so well." She reached for Pap's hand as he stepped beside her. "Did you get all the animals out, Levi?"

"Jah," he mumbled. "I believe so."

"It will be okay," Mom whispered. "We'll ask our friends and neighbors to help us rebuild."

"I've helped others rebuild." Pap slowly shook his head. "But in all the years we've been married, this is the first barn I have ever lost."

"When trouble comes, we must not be too proud to ask for help," Mom said with a catch in her voice.

Pap nodded. "You're right, Miriam. I will ask."

Rachel wished she could do or say something to make Pap feel better. At least he'd been able to get the animals out. That was a good thing.

Then sudden panic struck Rachel. *Cuddles! Where is Cuddles?* Had her sweet little bussli been in the barn when it caught fire?

Rachel cupped her hands around her mouth and hollered, "Has anyone seen my kitten?"

Chapter 10

Barn Raising

Pap, Henry, Jacob, and several Amish men who lived nearby spent the next few days cleaning up the mess from the burned-out barn.

On Friday, when Rachel came downstairs to help with breakfast, first she opened the back door and called for Cuddles. Rachel called for Cuddles many times every day, but the kitten was still missing. Rachel only saw a yard full of Amish men and boys who'd come to help raise the new barn. Mom had said probably a hundred or more would help, and Rachel was sure at least that many had arrived already.

"I guess Pap will have plenty of help today," she said to Esther, who had just finished setting the table.

Her sister nodded. "Even many of our English neighbors have come to help. All the men will be busy today preparing the planks, panels, rafters, and beams that will make up Pap's new barn."

"Since the table's already set, what would you like me to do?" Rachel asked, stepping to the counter where her mother stood cracking eggs into a bowl.

"I could use a few more eggs, so why don't you run out to the chicken coop and see how many you can find?"

Rachel frowned. "Oh, Mom, do I have to? You know the trouble I have when I try to gather eggs."

"Just watch what you're doing, and I'm sure you'll be fine." Mom nudged Rachel toward the door.

With a weary sigh, Rachel trudged across the yard toward the chicken coop. She was relieved when everything went okay and she found six plump eggs. None of the hens gave her a bit of trouble, either.

She headed back across the lawn but almost tripped on some boards that were to be used on the barn. She grunted and moved on until Frank Johnson, one of their English neighbors, asked if she would bring him a drink of water.

Rachel set the basket of eggs on one of the wooden tables and hurried to the pump. She grabbed a paper cup from the stack sitting there, filled it with water, and took it to Mr. Johnson.

He smiled and took a drink. "That hit the spot. Thanks."

"You're welcome." Rachel rushed back to the table where she had left the basket, only to discover that it was gone. "Have you seen my basket of eggs?" she asked

Jacob when he walked by carrying a hammer and a can of nails.

He shook his head and kept walking.

Rachel questioned several other people, but no one had seen the eggs.

"Always trouble somewhere," she muttered as she headed to the house.

"How'd it go in the chicken coop?" Mom asked when Rachel entered the kitchen empty-handed. "Didn't you get any eggs?"

"I collected six." Rachel grunted. "But I set the basket on one of the tables so I could get Frank Johnson a cup of water, and when I got back, the basket was gone."

Mom's pale eyebrows lifted, and she peered at Rachel over the top of her glasses. "Where did it go?"

"I have no idea." Rachel moved toward her mother. "I told you I didn't want to collect the eggs."

"There has to be some explanation. Did you ask the men if they had seen the basket?"

Rachel nodded. "Nobody knew anything about it. Now the eggs are missing, and so is my cat."

"I'm sure Cuddles is just hiding someplace," Mom said with a shake of her head. "But someone must know what happened to the basket of eggs. Baskets don't jump off the table and walk away by themselves."

"I–I'll go back outside and look again." Rachel was beginning to believe that *she* was the trouble. Maybe she had set the basket somewhere else and didn't remember doing it. She had been kind of forgetful this summer.

"That's okay. I'll make do with the eggs I already have," her mother said. "Our menfolk ate earlier, so everyone's had breakfast except you, me, and Esther."

Rachel glanced around the kitchen. "Where is Esther? She was here when I went to the chicken coop. I hope my *schweschder* [sister] isn't missing now, too."

"Your sister isn't missing. She just went outside to say hello to Rudy."

"That's good." Rachel moved to the sink to wash her hands. "At least I know I'm not to blame for Cuddles being missing."

Mom made no comment. She just placed a frying pan on the stove and started cooking the eggs she already had.

A few minutes later, the back door opened, and Esther stepped into the kitchen, carrying a wicker basket.

"Where'd you find that?" Rachel asked.

"Outside on one of the tables."

"Which one?"

"The table closest to where the new barn's going to be." Esther set the basket near Mom.

"I didn't put it on that table. I'm sure I set the basket on the table nearest the pump. Someone must have moved it." Rachel squinted. "I wonder if Jacob—"

"It's not important," Mom said, waving her hand. "We have our eggs now, and that's all that matters."

Rachel grunted. If Jacob had taken the eggs, he

should be punished. But Mom probably didn't even care. Rachel felt that she always got scolded for the things she did, and Jacob got away with everything.

By noon, the skeleton of the barn had begun to take shape, rising high above the ground. The Pennsylvania Dutch language drifted up from the work site as men and boys pounded nails, cut boards, and fit them securely in place.

Rachel joined Mom, Esther, and several other women in the kitchen while they prepared lunch for the workers. The tables were filled with meatloaf sandwiches, several kinds of salad, pickles, olives, potato chips, and plenty of iced tea, water, and lemonade. For dessert, they could enjoy gingerbread and a variety of cookies. Since the weather was still warm, everyone ate outside at the tables. During the meal, the men even took time to visit and tell jokes. Even when disaster struck, whether it was big or little, Rachel was learning, you kept going and made the best of things.

"Say, where's your straw hat?" Jacob asked Pap as he selected another slice of gingerbread.

Pap grabbed a couple of peanut butter cookies and said, "I took it off when I washed up at the pump. It must be over there still."

"Not anymore." Jacob pointed to one of the beams overhead. "Look there, Pap. Someone nailed your hat to the new barn!"

Pap tipped his head and squinted against the glare of the sun. A huge smile crept across his bearded face. "All right now—who's the *galgedieb* [scoundrel]?"

A few Amish boys sitting nearby snickered, but nobody said who the scoundrel was. For once Rachel was glad she hadn't done anything wrong.

"That's all right. My head was getting too warm anyway." Pap glanced at Rachel and winked. Then he chuckled.

Rachel gritted her teeth as she helped clear away the dishes. Maybe Jacob hadn't moved her basket of eggs. It was probably those same teasing boys who had nailed Pap's hat to the barn. She was tempted to scold them, but Mom called her to join the women and girls at the picnic tables.

When the meal was over, Rachel and Mary hurried to the creek. They sat under a willow tree, and Rachel leaned against the tree trunk.

"Sure is nice to see how many folks have come to help build your daed's new barn," Mary said.

Rachel nodded. "I know Pap appreciates it, but it doesn't seem fair that we lost the barn."

"I heard my daed say the other day that trouble can make us stronger and teaches us to call on God."

Rachel groaned. "I've been calling on Him ever since the fire, but I don't think He's listening."

"What's wrong?" Mary asked.

"I'm worried about my kitten."

Mary frowned. "Where is Cuddles? I haven't seen her today."

"The last time I saw her was the morning before the barn burned down." Rachel bit her bottom lip to keep it from trembling. Thinking about her kitten made her feel so sad. "What if Cuddles was trapped inside the barn when it caught fire?"

Mary gasped. "That would be *baremlich* [terrible]."

Rachel nodded. "It would be worse than terrible."

"Should we go look for her?"

"I've looked and called for her every day, but there's no sign of Cuddles anywhere." Rachel's eyes burned with tears, and she blinked to keep them from spilling over. "I don't believe she's ever coming back. I think I've lost her for good."

Mary held Rachel's hand and gently squeezed it. "Don't say that. I'll help you search for the bussli. Maybe she's someplace you haven't already looked."

"Jah, maybe so."

Rachel and Mary spent the rest of the afternoon looking for Cuddles, but they couldn't find her. They finally decided to give up and go to the house for cookies and milk.

Shortly before suppertime, the workers went home. Many promised to return the next day to help Pap put the final touches on his new barn.

Rachel asked her mother if Mary could spend the night.

Mom looked over at her sister-in-law. "What do you think about that idea?"

Aunt Irma nodded. "Jah, sure. It's fine with me."

Rachel hugged her cousin, and the two of them jumped up and down. Rachel thought having her cousin spend the night might help her forget about her missing kitten. At least it would keep her too busy to think about it so much.

"Calm down, Mary," Aunt Irma said with a click of her tongue. "You be sure and help Rachel with her chores."

Mary nodded. "I will, Mama."

The girls stood on the porch, watching as the last buggy pulled out of the Yoders' yard. Then they ran into the house, giggling.

That evening after they'd eaten supper and all the dishes had been washed, dried, and put away, Mom turned to the girls and said, "You'd best take a bath before you head upstairs to bed."

"Oh, Mom," Rachel groaned. "We're not that dirty."

"I just washed your bedsheets, and I don't want any filthy little bodies soiling them tonight."

Rachel knew she wouldn't win this argument, so she trudged down the hallway toward the bathroom, with Mary right behind her.

When the girls awoke the following morning, the men were already hard at work. The piercing sound of hammers and saws echoed through Rachel's open window.

Mary yawned and pulled the sheet over her head. "It can't be time to get up already."

Rachel opened one eye and squinted at the sun streaming in through the crack of the dark window shade. "I'm afraid the sun is almost over the barn already. I guess we should have gone to bed a little earlier last night."

"We'd better hurry and get dressed," Mary said as she swung her legs over the side of the bed. "Your mamm and Esther will need our help."

The girls entered the kitchen just as a knock sounded on the back door. Mom opened it, and Jake Miller entered, carrying Rachel's kitten in his arms.

"Cuddles!" Rachel cried. She raced to Jake, and he handed her the squirming animal. "Where have you been, you silly bussli?"

"I found her over at our place this morning, playing in the flower beds with Missy and her other busslin," Jake said.

"Do you think she got scared when the storm blew in and headed back to the place where she was born?" Rachel's mother asked.

Jake nodded. "That's what my daed believes happened. The cat's probably been there the whole time, and we didn't see her until today."

Tears welled in Rachel's eyes as relief washed over her like a spring rain. "Danki for bringing Cuddles back to me, Jake."

"You're welcome."

She kissed the tip of the kitten's nose. "At least you knew what to do when trouble came. Welcome home, my furry little friend."

Chapter 11

Out to Pasture

Rachel's eyes felt heavy, and she leaned her head against the seat in the back of their buggy. They had been to the public auction so Pap could buy some things he needed for the new barn. Now it seemed to be taking them forever to get home.

"Why are we stopping again?" Jacob complained.

Rachel opened one eye and looked at him. "Ask Pap. He's the driver."

"It must be our stupid horse," her brother said, wrinkling his nose. "Every couple of miles old Tom stops in the road. When he does decide to go, he plods along like a turtle. That horse isn't worth much anymore. I think we should get rid of him."

Rachel sat up straight. "No way! Tom may be a little slow, but he's a good horse. It wouldn't be right for Pap to sell him."

Jacob nudged her arm. "The old horse will probably end up at the glue factory. Jah, that's where Pap should take him, all right."

Rachel's mouth dropped open. "How can you say that? Turning our trusty horse into a pile of glue would be terrible!"

"Oh, don't let Jacob rile you," said Henry, who sat in the seat ahead of them reading a book. "More than likely Pap will just put old Tom out to pasture."

Rachel tapped Henry on the shoulder. "Out to pasture? What does that mean?"

"It means that since the horse isn't good for anything, he'll be put in the empty fields to spend the rest of his days alone," Jacob said before Henry could answer.

"But that's not true," Rachel argued. "Tom is good for lots of things."

Jacob snorted. "Name one."

Rachel rested her chin in the palm of her hand. "Let me see. . . ."

"You can't think of anything, can you?"

"Give me a minute, and I'll come up with something." Rachel squeezed her eyes shut and thought hard. A few minutes later, her eyes snapped open. "I've got one."

"What is it?"

"Tom is good for petting because he's nice and tame and doesn't bite."

"Being good to pet doesn't make him useful to Pap."

"Well, he's useful to me." Rachel pouted. "I love old Tom, and if he's put out to pasture, then I'm going with him!"

Jacob shook his head and muttered something about Rachel being *lecherlich* [ridiculous].

I'm not ridiculous, Rachel thought. *You're just mean!*

She closed her eyes again and tried to relax, but she could only think about their poor buggy horse and what might happen to him. By the time they got home, she decided to talk with Pap.

Rachel waited until everyone else had left the buggy and headed for the house. Then she hopped down and sprinted around to where Pap was unhitching the horse.

"Can I speak to you a minute?" she asked, stepping beside him.

"Jah, sure. What's on your mind?"

"It's about old Tom."

Pap's eyes narrowed. "That horse has been nothing but trouble for me these days. He's through pulling our buggy."

"Oh, but, Pap—"

"I mean it, Rachel. Old Tom gets tired and either walks too slow or stops in the middle of the road whenever he wants. I'm afraid he's finished."

Tears filled Rachel's eyes, blurring her vision. "You—you mean you're going to sell him to the glue factory?"

Pap tipped his head and looked at Rachel as if she

had lost her mind. "Where did you ever get that idea?"

She sniffed and reached out to pat the horse's neck. "Jacob said you might sell him to the glue factory."

"You should know I'd never do that." Pap stroked the end of Tom's nose, and the horse nuzzled his hand. "I'm going to put this old fellow out to pasture."

"No, Pap, please don't do that," Rachel pleaded. "Tom wouldn't like being out there all alone."

"He won't be alone," Pap said as he led the horse toward the barn. "My workhorses will be in the pasture with Tom when they're not helping me and the boys in the fields. And Sam, my other buggy horse, will join them sometimes, too."

Rachel followed Pap and Tom into the barn. "So putting the horse out to pasture isn't a bad thing?"

Pap shook his head. "It just means he'll take life a little easier from now on."

"You mean like Grandma and Grandpa Yoder who live in the *daadihaus* [grandfather's house] next door to Uncle Ben and Aunt Irma's?"

"That's right. Grandma and Grandpa can't do all the things they used to, and they're not expected to work as hard anymore." Pap smiled. "Since they live in the grandfather's house next to your uncle Ben, they're never lonely, and someone is always close by to care for their needs."

Rachel sat on a bale of hay while Pap removed the dirt and sweat from old Tom with a currycomb and brush. "How soon do you plan to put the horse out to pasture?" she asked.

Pap gave the horse's flanks a gentle pat. "Probably tomorrow morning."

"And he'll stay there and never be allowed in the barn again?"

Pap shook his head. "He'll be out in the pasture during the day and spend his nights in here, same as always."

"Hmm. . ." Rachel decided she would think of some way to make Tom's retirement days more pleasant. She thought about Grandma and Grandpa, too, and how she wanted to do something special to let them know how much she loved them.

The following day, Rachel asked Mom if she could have an apple and some carrots to take out to the pasture and give to old Tom. Mom said it was okay, so a few minutes later Rachel hurried out the back door, carrying a plastic bag with some carrots and an apple inside. When she reached the pasture, she found Tom lying under a tree near the fence. The old horse got up and wandered over to greet her as soon as she called his name.

"Are you lonely, boy?" Rachel asked, climbing the fence and seating herself on the top rail so she could pet the horse.

Tom neighed in response and nudged Rachel's hand.

"I brought you a treat," she said, holding a carrot out to him.

Tom chomped it hungrily and nudged her hand again.

"Okay, okay. Don't be in such a hurry," she said with a chuckle.

After Tom had finished the second carrot, she reached into the bag and offered him the apple. "Now this is your dessert."

Tom crunched the apple, snorted, and let out a loud *neigh!* Then he bumped Rachel's hand again with his warm nose.

"I don't have anything else for you," she said. "If you're still hungry, you'll have to eat some grass. That's why it's here, you know."

Tom twitched his nose and shook his head as if he were telling Rachel he didn't want more grass.

"I've got to go see Grandpa and Grandma Yoder now, but I'll be back tomorrow." She patted the horse's head and was about to climb down when *thud!* The fence shook, pitching Rachel forward.

"Agh!" Off the fence she flew, landing with a *splat* in the horses' watering trough.

Rachel pulled herself up, coughing and spitting water out of her mouth. One of their big billy goats stood on the other side of the fence, shaking its head and baaing so loud that Rachel had to cover her ears.

"Shoo! Shoo! Get on back to the goat pen!" Rachel hollered, waving her hands. "Thanks to you butting the fence, I lost my balance and fell in the water trough."

The goat let out another loud *baa* and ran off.

Rachel crawled out of the trough, wrung the water from her dress, and climbed back over the fence. "Always trouble somewhere," she grumbled as she headed for the house.

Later, dressed in clean, dry clothes, Rachel got Mom's permission to pick a few flowers to take to Grandma. She had painted a rock for Grandpa and put it inside a canvas bag that she set on the porch while she picked flowers.

After Rachel had a bouquet of pretty pink flowers in one hand, she picked up her canvas bag. She was about to head out when she spotted Cuddles sitting inside one of Pap's old work boots on the porch. "You silly bussli," she said with a laugh. "What are you doing in there?"

Cuddles looked at Rachel and meowed.

"Are you stuck? Do you need help getting out?" Rachel set the flowers and the canvas bag on the porch step and bent over. She lifted Cuddles by the scruff of her neck, then set the kitten on the porch. "There, now. That's better, isn't it?"

Cuddles jumped back into the boot with another *meow!*

Rachel shook her finger in the kitten's face. "I don't have time to play your silly games. I'm going to see Grandma and Grandpa Yoder now." She plucked Cuddles out of the boot for a second time and set her on the porch.

The kitten leaped into the boot again and stared at Rachel, as if to say, "I dare you to make me move."

Rachel grabbed her canvas bag and the flowers and then stepped off the porch. "You can stay there the rest of the day, for all I care." She headed around the side of the house and stopped to look at a grasshopper sitting on the sidewalk. Suddenly, Cuddles dashed around the corner of the house and pounced on her bare foot. "What's gotten into you today, Cuddles?"

The kitten rolled onto her back and pawed at the air, like she did whenever she wanted Rachel to scratch her stomach.

Rachel stepped around the cat. "Not now, Cuddles. I need to get these flowers over to Grandma before they wilt." She stuck her foot out and nudged the cat a little, but Cuddles leaped up and swiped Rachel's leg with her paw.

Rachel jumped back. "Ouch! Your claws are sharp, and you should be ashamed of yourself for being so mean." Of course, Rachel knew her kitten wasn't really being mean. Cuddles just wanted to play, so she was doing everything possible to get Rachel's attention.

"You seem to find trouble as easily as I do, little bussli. But you don't mean to, and I still love you," Rachel said, patting the kitten's soft fur. "I'm your mother now, and I guess moms always love their babies no matter how much trouble they get into."

Rachel stopped and thought about what she'd just

said. She felt terrible whenever she got into trouble with Mom. She was always a little afraid Mom would stop loving her because she caused so many problems. But maybe Mom wasn't any more upset with her than she was with Cuddles.

"I love you no matter what," Rachel told Cuddles. "And I guess Mom loves me, even when I make mistakes."

Cuddles purred and licked the scratch marks she had left on Rachel's leg.

Rachel smiled. "I accept your apology, and if you'd like to go with me to Grandma and Grandpa's house, I'd be happy to have your company."

The kitten meowed and purred louder. Rachel and Cuddles set out on foot, but instead of walking along the road all the way, Rachel decided to take the shortcut through the woods. About halfway there, she spotted some pretty yellow wildflowers blooming near a leafy bush. She picked a few to go with the pink flowers from Mom's garden.

Rachel figured it would be best not to put Cuddles on the ground, because the curious kitten would probably see something that interested her and run off. So she put Cuddles inside her canvas satchel. Then Rachel squatted and picked wildflowers. When she had enough to make a nice bouquet, she removed Cuddles from the satchel and was on her way again.

Soon they were walking up the driveway to

Grandma and Grandpa Yoder's house. Because the house was next to Uncle Ben and Aunt Irma's place, Rachel found her cousin Mary in the yard, playing with Stripes.

"What a surprise!" Mary said with a friendly wave. "I didn't know you were coming over today. Did you bring Cuddles so our cats can play together?"

"Actually, I came to see Grandma and Grandpa." Rachel lifted the bouquet she held in one hand. Then she placed Cuddles on the ground. "Maybe the cats can play while I do that."

"Do you want me to watch the cats, or should I go to Grandma and Grandpa's house with you?" Mary asked.

"Maybe it would be best if you stayed with the cats. That way, Cuddles won't be as likely to get into trouble or run off." Rachel scratched a spot on her arm, wondering why it felt so itchy all of a sudden.

"Okay. I'll see you later then." Mary plunked down on the grass between the two cats, and Rachel headed for the daadihaus.

I hope they're not napping, Rachel thought when she knocked on the door and got no response. She set the flowers on the porch swing and was about to leave, when the door opened and Grandma stuck her head out. "Rachel, what a surprise! Are your folks here with you?"

"No, I walked over by myself. Well, my cat is with me, but she's out in the yard playing with Stripes."

Rachel reached for the flowers and handed them to Grandma. "These are for you."

Grandma smiled, and her blue eyes seemed to sparkle more than usual. "How thoughtful of you. Danki, Rachel."

"You're welcome." Rachel reached inside the satchel and removed the painted rock. "This is for Grandpa. I painted it to look like a turtle, because Grandpa likes turtles."

"I'm sure he will be pleased to have this one." Grandma opened the door wider. "Come inside. I made gingerbread this morning. So if you have the time, maybe you can visit while you eat a piece of the bread and drink a glass of cold milk."

"I'd like that." As Rachel entered Grandma's kitchen, a warm, fuzzy feeling came over her. She was glad she had decided to visit her grandparents.

Rachel thought about the Bible verse from 1 John 4:11 that Pap had read to the family a few nights earlier, "Dear friends, since God so loved us, we also ought to love one another."

She liked doing something nice for people. It made her feel happy that she had let Grandma, Grandpa, and even old Tom know how much she loved them. And it made her feel even happier to realize just as she loved Cuddles no matter what, her mother also loved her, even when trouble seemed to find her.

Chapter 12

A New Friend

The afternoon sun beat down on Rachel's head as she trudged wearily across the alfalfa field, carrying a jug of cold tea Mom had asked her to take to the men. To keep her mind off the terrible heat, Rachel let her thoughts wander.

First she thought about the itchy rash on her arm. The morning after she had visited her grandparents, Rachel had discovered the rash and shown it to her mother. "That's poison ivy," Mom had said, clicking her tongue. "How'd you get into that?" Rachel told Mom about picking the wildflowers on the way to Grandma and Grandpa's place. The flowers had been growing near a leafy bush that must have been poison ivy. Mom had put lotion on Rachel's arm and given her a pill to stop the itching, but that had been three days ago, and it still bothered her.

Rachel decided she had better concentrate on something else, because thinking about the rash only made it itch worse.

She thought about the trip she and Pap had made to Lancaster earlier in the week. They'd gone to the toy store so she could return the skateboard Esther and Rudy had given her. Then they'd made a visit to Kauffman's Store, and she'd asked Noah Kauffman to take the green and silver skateboard off layaway and put it back on the shelf so he could sell it to someone else. It had been hard to give up the two shiny skateboards, but she already had one skateboard. Even though the homemade skateboard wasn't nearly as nice as the store-bought ones, she liked it better because her brothers had made it. Rachel had used most of the money she'd gotten back to buy paint and brushes so she could make more pet rocks. She'd also bought a bag of licorice, a drawing tablet, several puzzles, and a flea collar for Cuddles. The kitten was allowed in the house once in a while now, but Mom still didn't want Cuddles to be on Rachel's bed.

Suddenly Cuddles darted between Rachel's legs, causing her to stumble and nearly drop the jug of iced tea. "Cuddles!" she exclaimed. "What are you doing out here?"

The cat looked up at Rachel and let out a pathetic *meow*.

Rachel shook her head. "I can't pick you up. I've got

my hands full trying to carry this big jug."

Cuddles trotted beside Rachel through the tall grass. A few minutes later, Rachel spotted Pap, Henry, and Jacob loading mounds of hay onto their wagon. "I brought you something cold to drink," she called.

Pap stopped working and wiped his sweaty forehead with the back of his arm. "You're just in time. I'm thirsty and ready for a little break."

"Me, too," Henry and Jacob agreed.

Rachel handed the jug to Pap. "You'd better go first, because if I give it to Jacob or Henry they might not leave any!" As Pap lifted the jug to his lips, she added, "I forgot to bring paper cups. Sorry about that."

"It's okay," he said with a wink. "I think we can manage." He tilted his head back and poured the cool tea into his mouth. Some of it missed and trickled into his beard, and that made him chuckle. Then Pap handed the jug over to Henry. Then Jacob drank from the jug, too.

"Will you give me and Cuddles a ride back to the house on the wagon?" Rachel asked her father.

"Hop in the back. We're almost ready to take this load of alfalfa to the barn," he replied. "Then we can get ready to go to market."

Rachel knew Pap was talking about the outdoor market that was being held on the other side of town.

Rachel bent, scooped her kitten into her arms, and climbed into the wagon. She played with Cuddles while the rest of the bales were loaded.

When they were finally ready to go, Jacob climbed in the back with Rachel, while Pap and Henry sat up front. Then Pap started the horses moving through the field toward home.

"Why'd you bring that flea-bitten cat with you?" Jacob asked.

"Cuddles followed me into the field, and I haven't seen any fleh since I bought a flea collar for her."

Jacob pulled a couple pieces of hay from a pile, leaned over, and stuck them behind Rachel's ears. "Now you look like a *butzemann* [scarecrow]," he said.

Rachel grabbed the hay and tossed it on the wagon floor. "I'm not a scarecrow, and I'm getting tired of you teasing me, Jacob Yoder."

He winked. "Don't you know that's what brothers are for?"

She folded her arms and frowned. "I'm glad you think so."

"I can't wait to go to the market," Jacob said. He leaned closer to Rachel and whispered, "Say, do you have any birthday money left?"

"Maybe. Why?"

He wiggled his eyebrows. "Thought you could treat me to an ice-cream cone or a root-beer float."

"Why should I when you tease me so?"

"Aw, come on little bensel. You know I'm only funning with you." Jacob grinned. "I'll be nice if you promise to buy me some ice cream."

Rachel rubbed her nose against the kitten's soft fur. "Maybe I will, and maybe I won't!"

When the Yoders arrived at the market a couple of hours later, Rachel was surprised to see the parking lot filled with cars and buggies. People seemed to be walking everywhere.

She climbed out of the buggy as soon as Pap halted the horse. "Is it all right if I walk around and look at some things by myself?" she asked her mother.

"I'd rather you stay with one of us," Mom replied. "It's not good for a young girl to be in a crowd of people by herself."

"She can walk with me," Jacob said with a twinkle in his eye.

Rachel figured her brother only said that because he hoped she would buy him some ice cream. "I'll think about it," she muttered.

"What did you say, Rachel?" Pap asked.

"It was nothing important." She looked up at her father and smiled. "What time should we be back at the buggy?"

"Why don't we meet here at five o'clock?" Mom suggested. "Then we can get a bite to eat on the way home."

"Sounds good to me." Jacob grabbed Rachel's hand and tugged it. "Let's get going, little sister."

As Rachel and Jacob walked away, Rachel spotted an English girl who looked to be about her age. The girl wore blue jeans and a pink T-shirt, and her blond hair was in a ponytail. She held a small, white dog.

"What a cute puppy!" Rachel exclaimed. "What's its name?"

"Bundles. I named him that because he's a bundle of fur. Do you want to pet him?"

Rachel stroked the dog's soft, floppy ears with one hand while Jacob tugged on her other hand and insisted, "Let's go."

Rachel ignored her brother and smiled at the English girl. "I have a kitten named Cuddles, and she's real soft, too."

The girl grinned at Rachel. "My name's Sherry Anderson. What's yours?"

"Rachel Yoder."

"It's nice to meet you, Rachel. Would you like to hold Bundles?"

Rachel nodded, and Jacob elbowed her in the ribs. "I thought we were going for ice cream."

"I never said that. Getting some ice cream was your idea." Rachel took Bundles from Sherry, and she giggled when the pup licked her chin.

"I think he likes you," Sherry said.

"Rachel, are you coming or not?"

Rachel knew Jacob was irritated, because a muscle in his cheek twitched when he squinted his eyes. She reached inside her purse and pulled out two dollars. "I'll stay here and visit with Sherry, and you can go get some ice cream by yourself. How's that sound?"

Jacob hesitated, but then he took the money and hurried off.

"I was about to take Bundles for a walk," Sherry said. "Would you like to come along?"

Rachel made sure Jacob was out of sight. Then she nodded. "I'd like that."

Sherry hooked a leash to her puppy's collar and placed him on the ground. When Bundles tugged on the leash and struggled to run ahead, Rachel figured he might be as eager to go for a walk as she was.

The girls and Bundles moved away from the crowd and headed across the parking lot.

"Sure is a hot day," Sherry commented. "Makes me want to go for a swim."

Rachel smiled. "I like to wade in the creek behind our house when the weather is hot and sticky."

"Another way I cool off is when I go for a ride in my brother's convertible," Sherry said.

Rachel's heart flip-flopped. "Convertible? He has a car with a top he can put down?"

Sherry nodded.

"I've never ridden in a convertible."

"You haven't?"

"No, just our neighbor's van whenever Pap hires him to take us somewhere we can't go in our buggy." Rachel swatted at a fly that seemed determined to land on her nose and tried not to scratch the patch of poison ivy on her arm. "I've always wondered what it would be like to ride in a car with the top down. Does your brother's car go real fast?"

Sherry nodded. "Sometimes. . .when we're on the highway."

Rachel was about to comment, when an English woman tapped her on the shoulder. "Would you mind posing for a picture, little girl?" She lifted her camera and pointed it at Rachel, but Rachel turned her head.

"I only want to snap a couple of shots," the woman insisted.

"I'm sorry, but no," Rachel mumbled.

"Are you sure? I'll pay you a dollar."

Rachel stared at the ground as she thought. *It would be nice to earn a dollar. And I wouldn't have to do anything except pose for a picture to get it.*

She looked at the woman and started to shake her head, when her new friend spoke up. "You can take my picture." Sherry flipped her ponytail, tipped her head, and presented a cheesy smile.

"Humph!" The woman turned and walked away.

"I think that lady must have a fly up her nose," Sherry said.

Rachel giggled. "Thanks for sticking up for me."

"Sure, no problem. I know that the Amish don't like to have their pictures taken."

Rachel wondered what Jacob would have done if he had been there. *Probably would have teased me and said, "Who'd want to take* your *picture, little butzemann?"*

Rachel's thoughts were interrupted when a deep voice called from across the parking lot, "Hey, Sherry. Mom just called on my cell phone, and she wants us to come home."

Sherry looked over at Rachel and stuck out her lower lip. "That's my brother, Dave. I guess it's time for me to go."

"Maybe we'll meet again sometime."

Sherry nodded. "I hope so."

As Rachel started across the parking lot toward their buggy, she smiled, thinking about how nice it was to have met someone new. Maybe sometime in the future, she and Sherry would see each other again. And maybe one day, Rachel might get the chance to ride in a shiny blue convertible.

When Rachel reached their buggy, she realized that none of her family had arrived yet, so she climbed into the back, stretched out on the seat, and closed her eyes. It was time to daydream.

Rachel imagined herself riding in a blue convertible with her new friend, Sherry. Sherry's brother drove the car. Bundles and Cuddles sat in the backseat between Rachel and Sherry. The wind whipped the narrow ties of Rachel's kapp as the car whizzed down the highway.

Rachel felt her body sway, first to one side, then

to the other, and her eyes snapped open. She sat up and looked out the window. She wasn't riding in a convertible at all. The buggy was moving! She glanced up front to see who was driving but saw no one in the driver's seat.

Rachel realized that Sam, the horse that had taken old Tom's place, must have broken loose from the hitching rail. Now he was galloping across the parking lot. The buggy passed a group of cars, bouncing up and down, weaving this way and that. Rachel screamed when it nearly scraped the side of a green van.

"Whoa, there! Whoa, Sam!" she shouted, but the horse kept running.

I need to get to the front of the buggy and grab those reins! Rachel thought.

She tried to stand up, but the buggy jerked again, and she fell to the floor.

Rachel crawled to the front seat on her hands and knees. She grabbed the back of the seat and started to climb over it. Suddenly, the horse darted to the left, tossing Rachel to the floor again.

"Help!" she screamed as tears rolled down her cheeks. She knew she couldn't do this alone. She really was in trouble now!

"I'm coming, Rachel! Hang on!"

With the racket of the runaway buggy, Rachel barely heard Jacob's voice. She pulled herself up again and looked out the side window. She saw Jacob running beside the buggy. He waved one hand and held an ice-cream cone in the other.

"Help me, Jacob!" Rachel cried.

Jacob tossed the ice-cream cone to the ground and raced past Rachel's window. "Whoa, there! Steady, boy!" he called to the horse.

Rachel's heartbeat pounded with the rhythm of the horse's hooves. "Dear God," she prayed as she clung to the seat, "please help my brother catch the horse!"

Suddenly the buggy lurched to a screeching halt. Jacob stuck his head through the doorway on the driver's side. He waited a moment, panting.

"I grabbed the horse's bridle and stopped him," he explained, still trying to catch his breath. "I'll lead him back to the hitching rail, so sit tight until I say it's safe to get out."

"Okay," Rachel said in a quavering voice.

When the buggy finally quit moving, Jacob came around to the back and helped Rachel down. "Are you all right?"

Rachel nodded. She could tell her brother was concerned, because his forehead was wrinkled and his eyebrows were drawn together. Ever since school had let out for the summer, Jacob had been teasing her. But now she knew how much her brother really cared. He'd proven that by coming to her rescue, and she was glad for his help.

"I didn't do anything silly, Jacob," she cried. The

words tumbled out of her mouth so fast she didn't even know what she was saying. "I was waiting for everyone in the buggy and fell asleep. I don't know how Sam got loose, but I woke up and he was running. I couldn't stop him."

Rachel threw her arms around Jacob. "Danki. Danki for saving my life."

"You're welcome," he said, patting Rachel on the back. "I knew you didn't cause Sam to run away. I tease you about being silly, but I know you are pretty smart for a girl your age."

Jacob seemed embarrassed and ready to change the subject. He looked at his empty hands. "I had my root beer float and was bringing you an ice-cream cone, but I threw it away so I could stop the horse."

She grinned at him, feeling happier than she had all summer. "That's okay. Knowing that you care about me is better than any old ice-cream cone."

"Of course I care. I'm your brother. I'll always love you and try to help whenever you're in trouble."

"I love you, too." Rachel hugged Jacob again.

"Maybe after supper, Pap will buy us all ice cream," he said with a lopsided grin.

She nodded and smiled. In spite of all her troubles, this summer had turned out to be pretty good, and the best thing was learning that Jacob didn't think she was a bensel. Not really. He did love her after all.

Back to School

Dedication

To my daughter, Lorine, a *wunderbaar* [wonderful] schoolteacher. And to my granddaughters, Jinell, Madolynne, and Rebekah, who enjoy doing many fun things at their country school.

Glossary

ab im kopp—go crazy
ach—oh
aldi—girlfriend
baremlich—terrible
bauchweh—stomachache
bensel—silly child
bletsching—spanking
boppli—baby
bopplin—babies
bruder—brother
daed—dad
daer—door
danki—thank you
dummkopp—dunce
dummle—hurry
ekelhaft—disgusting
fingerneggel—fingernails
galgedieb—scoundrel
grank—sick
kapp—cap
kinner—children
jah—yes
mamm—mom
maus—mouse
meis—mice
Mondaag—Monday
naerfich—nervous
nixnutzich—naughty
pescht—pest
rutschich—squirming
schnell—quickly
schtinkich—smelly
sei—hogs
uffgschafft—excited
wunderbaar—wonderful

Gern gschehne.	You are welcome.
Guder mariye.	Good morning.
Raus mit!	Out with it!
Sis mir iwwel.	I am sick at my stomach.
Was in der welt?	What in all the world?
Wie geht's?	How are you?

Chapter 1

First-Day Troubles

"Where's my sneaker? I can't find my other sneaker!" Rachel Yoder glanced down at her feet. On her left foot she wore a black and white sneaker, but her right foot was bare. *I can't go to school with only one shoe!*

Rachel dropped to her knees and peered under the sofa. No sneaker there; just a red checker piece from Pap's favorite game.

She crawled across the room to Mom's rocking chair and peeked underneath. Nope. Just the ball of blue yarn Rachel sometimes used when she played with her kitten, Cuddles. *Where could that sneaker be?*

Rachel had found one sneaker by her bed when she'd gotten up but couldn't find the other sneaker in her room. She grunted. "If that sneaker's not upstairs in my bedroom and it isn't down here in the living room, then where is it?"

She snapped her fingers. Maybe someone had hidden her sneaker so Rachel would be late for the first day of school. That wasn't something Henry, her sixteen-year-old brother, would do. But Jacob, who was almost twelve and liked to tease, might have taken it.

Rachel scrambled to her feet, stubbing her bare toe on the rocking chair. "Ouch! Ouch! Ouch!"

Hopping on one foot, she limped to the stairs and hollered, "Jacob Yoder! Did you take my sneaker?"

Jacob peeked around the banister at the top of the stairs and wrinkled his nose. "What would I want with your *schtinkich* [smelly] old sneaker?"

"It is *not* smelly!" Rachel frowned. "And I can't go to school today with only one shoe on my foot."

Rachel's mother poked her head through the kitchen doorway. "Then you'd better plan to go barefooted, because if you and Jacob don't leave soon, you'll be late for the first day of school."

"Not if I ride my skateboard. Then I can get there in half the time."

As Mom stepped into the hallway, her silver-framed glasses slipped to the end of her nose. "No skateboard, Rachel! It's much too dangerous for you to ride that thing to school."

"I'll stay on the shoulder of the road, I promise."

Mom shook her head. "Absolutely not. You and Jacob will walk to school, same as you've always done—with or without your shoes."

Rachel stared down at her feet, her right foot bare with the aching toe, and the left foot clad in a black and white sneaker.

This isn't good. Not good at all. She wished she had asked for a bicycle for her birthday instead of a skateboard. But she was sure her parents would have said no. Rachel had seen English children ride bikes to school, but none of the Amish *kinner* [children] she knew owned bikes. Even if she did own a bike, Mom probably wouldn't let her ride it to school.

Mom, and everyone else in the family, treats me like a boppli [baby], Rachel thought.

"If you can't find your other sneaker, why don't you wear your church shoes?" Jacob suggested as he tromped down the stairs in new black boots Pap had bought him.

Rachel looked at her mother.

"*Jah* [yes], sure," Mom said with a nod. "Hurry to your room and put them on. Be sure to fix your *kapp* [cap], too, because it's on crooked," she called as Rachel dashed up the stairs.

"Always trouble somewhere," Rachel mumbled, straightening the small white covering perched on her head.

Rachel hurried to her bedroom closet. She usually kept her black leather church shoes on a wooden bench underneath her dresses. She bent to get them and discovered they both were missing.

Rachel blinked and scratched the side of her head.

"*Was in der welt*? [What in the world?] Now where have my church shoes gone?"

Rachel looked around the closet but only found a box of small rocks she planned to paint so they looked like ladybugs, a stack of games and puzzles, and the wooden skateboard Jacob and Henry had made for her birthday. She gazed at the skateboard longingly, wishing she could ride it to school.

With a frustrated sigh, Rachel ran to her bed. She dropped to her knees and peered underneath, but no church shoes were under her bed. She just saw the same dust balls she'd seen when she'd looked for her sneaker, and an old faceless doll with one missing arm.

Rachel clambered to her feet and raced to her dresser. She pulled open each drawer and rummaged through the sweaters, socks, and underwear. No sneaker or church shoes there, either.

"I don't need this kind of trouble," Rachel wailed as she banged the bottom drawer shut.

"Rachel! Jacob's ready to leave for school, so you'd better hurry," Mom called from downstairs.

"I can't find my church shoes!" Rachel shouted in return.

"Then you'd best go barefooted."

Rachel sucked in her lower lip. She couldn't walk to school in her bare feet. Her toe still hurt from where she'd stubbed it. Besides, too many pebbles lined the shoulder of the road between their house and the one-room schoolhouse. She thumped the side of her head. "Think, Rachel. Where did you put your shoes last Sunday after church?"

She took a seat on the edge of the bed and closed her eyes. *Let's see now. . .* She remembered coming to her room to change out of her Sunday dress. Then she'd taken off her shoes and—

Rachel jumped up and raced out of the room. "I know where my church shoes are!" she hollered, taking the stairs two at a time.

"You'd better slow down or you'll slip and fall," Mom scolded, shaking her finger at Rachel.

"You said I'd be late for school if I didn't hurry. I know where my church shoes are, so I need to get them right now!" Rachel hurried past Mom and nearly bumped into Jacob, who had just stepped out of the kitchen with his lunchbox in his hand.

"I'm heading out now, so if you're not ready to go, then you can walk by yourself," he said with a frown.

She placed her hands on her hips and scowled. "Go ahead. I don't need you to walk with me anyway!"

"I would prefer that you walk together," Mom said as she joined them near the back door. "There's safety in numbers, you know."

Jacob tapped the toe of his boot against the hardwood floor. "Then hurry up, Rachel. Time's a-wasting."

"I need my church shoes. I remember putting them in the utility room last Sunday so I wouldn't forget to polish them before our next preaching service." Rachel darted into the utility room and halted in front of Pap's wooden shoe-shining box. There sat one of her good shoes—but only one. The other one was not there.

"Oh, no," she groaned. "Not another missing shoe."

Rachel grabbed the shoe and ran back to her brother. "Jacob, did you take one of my church shoes?"

"Right." He snickered. "Like I would want one of your schtinkich shoes."

"My shoes are not smelly, and if you're playing a trick on me—"

Mom held up her hand to quiet Rachel and then faced Jacob. "Do you have your sister's church shoe?"

He shook his head. "'Course not. Why would I take her dumb old shoe?"

"You don't have time to look for it now," Mom said, glancing at the battery-operated clock on the wall. "Rachel, it looks like you have no choice but to go to school in your bare feet today."

"I've got a better idea." Rachel dropped to the floor, slipped the church shoe on her right foot, and stood. "Now I have one shoe on each foot."

Mom clicked her tongue against the roof of her mouth. "But the shoes don't match, Rachel."

"I don't care. At least my feet won't hurt on the walk to school."

Jacob nudged Rachel's arm with his elbow. "You're such a *bensel* [silly child]."

She pushed his elbow away and grabbed her lunchbox from the counter. "I am not a silly child!"

"Think what you like, but don't complain to me if the kinner at school make fun of you today." Jacob snickered and headed out the door. "Everyone will probably think you're a little bensel."

Rachel figured Jacob would probably say things to irritate her all the way to school; but to her surprise, he walked a few feet ahead of her and never said a word. That was fine with Rachel. She'd rather daydream than talk to her brother anyway.

As Rachel continued to walk toward the Amish schoolhouse, her mind wandered. She thought about the skateboard she wished she could ride to school. She pictured Cuddles, her sweet little kitten, and thought about how much fun they had playing together. Then Rachel spotted a fancy red car speeding down the road, and she thought about how wonderful it would feel to go for a ride in a fast-moving car with the top down. Rachel figured she'd probably never get to ride in a convertible, but it was fun to think about sitting in the passenger's seat with the wind blowing the ties on her kapp, and her stomach jiggling up and down as the car bounced over the bumps in the road.

By the time Rachel and Jacob arrived at the schoolhouse, she'd forgotten all about her missing shoes—until a dark-haired Amish boy who looked to be about her age stepped onto the porch at the same time she did and pointed to her feet. "Say, how come you're wearing two different shoes?"

Rachel frowned. She didn't even know this boy, so why should she answer his question? Besides, he smelled funny—kind of like the fresh cloves of garlic Mom used when she made savory stew.

"Who are you?" she asked, sucking in her breath as she stepped backward.

He smiled, revealing deep dimples in his cheeks. "I'm Orlie Troyer. My family moved here from Indiana last week. What's your name? And why are you wearing shoes that don't match?"

"My name's Rachel Yoder." She stared at her feet. "I couldn't find both of my sneakers this morning, and I could only find one church shoe, so I wore one of each."

Orlie snickered. "Only a bensel would wear two different shoes."

Rachel stared into Orlie's chocolate-colored eyes and gritted her teeth. "I am not a silly child, and I can wear whatever shoes I want!" She released her breath in one long puff of air and took another step back.

"Ha! I say anyone who wears shoes that don't match has to be a bensel," he taunted.

Rachel gripped the handle of her lunchbox so hard, her fingers numbed. It was bad enough that she'd had to put up with Jacob's teasing. She didn't need anyone else bothering her today.

Orlie shifted from one foot to the other and stared

at Rachel with a big grin on his face. It made her feel like a fly caught in a spider's web. "How old are you, Rachel?" he asked.

"I turned ten this summer."

His smile widened. "I turned ten last February."

"That's nice." Rachel tried to push past Orlie, but he stood with his arms folded and his legs slightly spread, blocking the schoolhouse door.

"Are you in a hurry to get inside?" he asked in a teasing tone.

"As a matter of fact, I am."

"Not me. I don't like school so much." He wrinkled his nose. "Fact is, I'll be glad when I graduate eighth grade and can work for my *daed* [dad] in the blacksmith shop he's planning to open soon."

Rachel grunted. Orlie was short and thin. She didn't think he would have enough strength to do the hard work of a blacksmith, but she kept her opinion to herself.

When Orlie finally stepped away from the door, Rachel pushed past him. But *bam!* She tripped on a loose shoelace and fell flat on her face.

"Ugh!" She pulled herself to her feet, feeling the heat of embarrassment flood her cheeks.

Orlie held his sides and howled. "That's what happens when you don't tie your shoes. Maybe you should have come to school in your bare feet!"

Rachel jerked open the schoolhouse door.

Hope I don't have to sit near him today! she thought, glowering.

The schoolteacher, Elizabeth Miller, greeted Rachel inside the door. "*Guder mariye* [Good morning], Rachel." When Elizabeth smiled, her blue eyes twinkled like fireflies.

"Good morning." Rachel was glad to have such a kind young woman as her schoolteacher. Elizabeth was a pretty woman with golden hair. She'd taught at the Amish one-room schoolhouse for two years, and Rachel had never heard her say an unkind word to any pupils, whom the Amish referred to as "scholars."

Soon everyone was sitting behind desks. Rachel knew Elizabeth might rearrange the seats, but for now, she was happy to be seated at a desk across the aisle from her cousin Mary.

"How come you're wearing two different shoes?" Mary whispered, pointing at Rachel's feet.

Rachel grimaced. She was beginning to think wearing the mismatched shoes was a bad idea. "I'll tell you later."

Teacher Elizabeth tapped her desk with a ruler, and everyone got quiet. "Good morning, boys and girls."

"Good morning, Elizabeth," the scholars said in unison.

"We have a new boy in our school this year. His name is Orlie Troyer. He recently moved here to Pennsylvania from the state of Indiana." The teacher smiled at Orlie. "I hope everyone will make him feel welcome."

All heads turned toward Orlie, whom Rachel soon discovered had taken a seat at the desk directly behind her. Orlie grinned and nodded at Rachel. She turned back around. *I hope Teacher moves that fellow to a different desk.*

Elizabeth opened her Bible and read from 1 Corinthians 13:11: "'When I was a child, I talked like a child, I thought like a child, I reasoned like a child.'"

Rachel cringed. Jacob thought she was a silly child for wearing mismatched shoes, and so did Orlie. Did God think she was a silly child, too?

She shook her head. No, she knew she was a child of the King, and that meant she wasn't silly in God's eyes.

After the scripture reading, the scholars stood by their desks and repeated the Lord's Prayer. After the prayer, everyone filed to the front of the room and stood in rows according to their ages. Then they sang a few songs in German, the language Amish children spoke at home. Orlie, who was in the third grade, just like Rachel, had somehow managed to stand right beside her. He kept staring at her, and every time he opened his mouth, the smell of garlic drifted to Rachel's nose.

Rachel leaned away, but Orlie moved closer. Was he trying to pester her? Did he dislike her so much that he wanted to make her miserable?

Rachel was relieved when the singing time was over and she could return to her seat. At least with Orlie sitting behind her, she couldn't smell his breath so much.

Teacher Elizabeth wrote the math lessons for grades three to eight on the blackboard. Then she and her sixteen-year-old helper, Sharon Smucker, worked with the first and second graders, who needed to learn the English language better. When the clock on the wall behind the teacher's desk said ten o'clock, Elizabeth dismissed the scholars for morning recess.

Eager to be outside and away from Orlie, Rachel hurried to the swings with Mary.

"That new boy is sure a *pescht* [pest]," Rachel said, glancing over at Orlie, who stood across the schoolyard talking to Jacob and some of the other boys. She bit off a piece of her fingernail and spit it to the ground.

Mary wrinkled her nose. "That's so gross. Why do you have to do that to your *fingerneggel* [fingernails], Rachel?"

"I only chew my fingernails when I'm nervous or upset. That Orlie has me upset," Rachel explained.

"So, why do you think Orlie's a pest?" Mary asked.

"He made fun of me because I'm wearing two different shoes."

Mary giggled and pointed to Rachel's feet. "That is pretty strange."

"Can I help it if I couldn't find matching shoes this morning?" When Rachel looked across the yard, she noticed that Orlie was staring at her instead of talking to the other boys. "He's doing it again."

"Doing what?"

"He's staring at me, just like he was doing before school started."

"Maybe he likes you."

"He doesn't even know me." Rachel shrugged. "Besides, I don't like him."

"Why not?"

"Because he likes to tease and stare at me." Rachel wrinkled her nose and made a choking sound. "He smells like garlic, too."

Mary nudged Rachel's elbow. "Didn't you hear what the bishop said during church last Sunday?"

"What was that?" Rachel had been daydreaming during part of the service and had missed hearing most of the bishop's sermon, so she wasn't sure what Mary meant.

"He said we're supposed to love everyone. Even those who are dirty or smell bad."

"That's easy for you to say. You didn't have to stand beside Orlie during singing. He's not sitting behind you, either." Rachel grabbed the chain on her swing, pushed off with one foot, and spun around until the ground began to whirl. "I'm flying," she hollered, leaning her head way back. "I feel like a bird soaring up in the sky."

"The ties on your kapp are flying, too," Mary said. "If you're not careful, you'll lose it."

Rachel ignored her cousin and continued to spin. But suddenly, her stomach churned. She climbed off the swing as the teacher called them inside, and she could barely stand.

Rachel took a couple of shaky steps, stumbled backward, and held her stomach. "*Ach* [Oh], I don't feel so good."

"What's wrong?" Mary asked, reaching for Rachel's hand.

Rachel pulled back. "I—I think I'm gonna be sick." She turned and dashed for the outhouse.

When Rachel stepped out of the outhouse several minutes later, Orlie stood right outside the door, as though he'd been waiting for her. "Your face looks kind of green, Rachel. Are you *grank* [sick]?"

Rachel clenched her fingers so hard they ached. "I'm not sick. Just got dizzy from too much twirling on the swings, and I—I lost my breakfast."

"You should know better than to spin like that, little bensel," Orlie said, shaking his head. "Didn't your *mamm* [mom] teach you anything?"

"My mom's taught me plenty, and I am *not* a silly child!"

"My mom's taught me plenty, and I am *not* a silly child," Orlie repeated with a grin.

"It's not polite to mimic," she said.

Orlie shook his head. "It's not polite to mimic."

"Then stop doing it."

"Then stop doing it."

Rachel was tempted to say something more, but she figured Orlie would just copy her if she did. So she hurried to the schoolhouse and took a seat behind her desk. This day couldn't be over soon enough as far as she was concerned. She'd had enough first-day troubles!

Chapter 2

Lunchbox Surprise

I don't feel like going to school today. Can I please stay home?" Rachel asked her mother when she entered the kitchen the following morning.

Mom turned from the stove, where she was frying bacon. "Are you grank?"

Rachel shook her head. "I'm not sick, but I—"

"If you're not grank, then you'll go to school, same as always."

"But, Mom, Orlie will be there, and he'll probably tease me again."

"Who's Orlie?"

"He's a new boy at school. His family moved here from Indiana," Jacob said as he came into the kitchen.

"I see. Son, have you finished your chores?" Mom asked, turning back to the stove.

"Jah, but Henry and Pap are still doing theirs, and Esther's milking the cows. Pap said to tell you they'd be in for breakfast in about ten minutes." Jacob hung his straw hat on a wall peg near the door and went to the sink to wash his hands.

"The bacon and eggs should be done by then, so that will work out fine and dandy," Mom called over her shoulder.

Rachel sighed. Didn't anyone care about her problem with Orlie?

Mom looked at Jacob. "Would you please set some juice out?"

Jacob pointed to himself. "Who, me?"

She nodded. "Jah, I was talking to you."

"Okay." He dried his hands on a towel and headed to the refrigerator.

Mom nodded at Rachel. "I'd like you to set the table."

"I was just about to." Rachel pulled a stool to the cupboard. Then she climbed up and removed six plates and six glasses, which she placed on the counter. As she opened the silverware drawer, she decided to bring up the subject of Orlie Troyer again. "Orlie made fun of me yesterday, just because I was wearing two different shoes."

"Well, you can wear matching ones today," Mom said, "since soon after you left for school yesterday I found both of your shoes out in the barn. I figure that mischievous cat of yours must have hauled them there, because I discovered her playing with the sneaker."

Rachel frowned. She knew Mom didn't like Cuddles to be in the house, and now that she thought the cat had taken Rachel's shoes, Rachel hoped Mom wouldn't say Cuddles couldn't come inside anymore.

"I don't think Cuddles could have taken them," Rachel said. "She's just a kitten. I don't think she's strong enough. And I think they're too big for her to carry."

"That cat is big for a kitten, though," Mom pointed out. "She might have dragged the shoes out there by the laces."

"Even if it was Cuddles, she didn't hurt my shoes," Rachel said. "She probably wanted something of mine to keep her company."

"Puh!" Mom waved the spatula like she was batting a fly. "That cat's been nothing but trouble since the Millers gave her to you."

Rachel didn't think her kitten had been a bit of trouble. In her opinion, Cuddles was a nice little kitten, who had kept Rachel company and helped her not to feel so scared when she'd been locked in their neighbor's cellar. But there was no use saying all that to Mom. What really mattered was how Rachel was going to get out of going to school.

She hurried to put the dishes, glasses, and silverware on the table, then moved over beside her mother. "I'm done setting the table now. Do you need my help with anything else?"

"You can scramble some eggs while Jacob pours the juice."

Jacob grunted. "I think I should have stayed in the

barn and helped Pap and Henry with their chores."

Mom squinted her blue eyes as she glared at Jacob. "What was that?"

"Nothing, Mom," Jacob mumbled. He picked up the pitcher of juice and poured some into the first glass, while Rachel went to the refrigerator and took out a carton of eggs. She'd just finished mixing them in a bowl, when she decided to bring up the subject of Orlie again.

"Orlie teased me when I threw up after twirling on the swings yesterday. He mimicked me, too, and kept staring and whispering to me all day."

"He probably has a crush on you, sister," Jacob said before Mom could respond. "Boys tease when they're trying to impress a girl."

"He doesn't have a crush on me, and he certainly doesn't impress me!" Rachel's forehead wrinkled, and she fought the urge to bite a fingernail. "I don't like him much, either."

"That's not nice to say, Rachel," Mom said with a click of her tongue. "If you give the boy a chance, you might find that he's quite likeable."

"I doubt it," Rachel said with a huff. "Besides, Orlie's a pescht, and his breath smells funny—like he gargled with garlic juice."

Mom's glasses slipped to the end of her nose as she pursed her lips. "The Bible says we are to love everyone, Rachel."

"It's hard to love someone who's making your life miserable."

"God wants us to love even our enemies."

"I could like Orlie better if he didn't tease me, stare at me, or smell like garlic." As though Rachel's fingers had a mind of their own, one of them slipped right between her teeth.

"No nail biting, Rachel," Mom scolded.

"Biting your nails is a disgusting habit," Jacob put in.

Rachel pulled her finger out of her mouth and held her hands tightly against her sides. She felt more nervous today than any other time she could remember. She dreaded what Orlie might do to tease her. She'd always liked going to school—until Orlie Troyer had come and ruined it all.

"Can't I stay home from school just this once?" she begged, ignoring Jacob's nail-biting comment. He was no better than Orlie Troyer. Jacob just wanted to upset her.

Mom shook her head so hard the ties on her kapp swished from side to side. "You may stay home only when you're sick. Is that clear?"

Rachel nodded and sighed deeply as she reached for the stack of napkins in the center of the table. She realized she wouldn't get her way on this, so she could only hope and pray that Orlie wouldn't bother her again today.

When Rachel entered the schoolyard with Jacob later that morning, she noticed Mary playing on one of the teeter-totters with some other girls. Rachel was about to join Mary, when Orlie stepped out from behind a bush, blocking her path. "I see you're wearing matching sneakers today," he said, smirking and pointing at her feet.

She merely shrugged and fought the temptation to plug her nose as the strong aroma of garlic greeted her yet again.

Orlie stared at her with a peculiar look on his face, and Rachel felt like a bug about to be squashed. "Can I ask you something, Orlie?" she questioned.

He nodded. "Jah, sure. Ask me anything you like."

"What did you have for breakfast this morning?"

"Eggs, sausage, and biscuits. Why?"

Rachel fidgeted with the ties on her kapp as she shifted her weight from one foot to the other. Should she ask why his breath smelled so bad, or would that make him tease her more? "Well, I was wondering—"

"Well, I was wondering—" Orlie mimicked. He tipped his head to one side, and a chunk of dark hair fell across his forehead. "What were you wondering, Rachel?"

She drew in a deep breath. "Did you have anything with garlic on it?"

Orlie's face turned red as a pickled beet. "My mamm gives me a clove of garlic to eat every morning. She says it's to keep me from getting a cold." He shuffled his feet and glanced around as though he were worried someone might hear. "When we lived in Indiana, I got sick a lot and missed many days of school. Mom didn't want me to miss school this year."

Rachel stifled a giggle. She figured the garlic remedy probably worked pretty well, because with breath that bad, nobody would want to get close to Orlie. So he sure couldn't get any cold germs from anyone!

"You're not gonna tell anyone I eat a hunk of garlic for breakfast every day, are you?"

Rachel shook her head. No need for that. Anyone coming near Orlie would know he'd eaten a good dose of garlic. No wonder Pap called garlic "the stinking rose." Phew! She could hardly stand the disgusting odor.

The school bell rang, and Rachel felt a sense of relief. With Orlie sitting behind her, she wasn't close enough to him to smell his horrid breath. Unless she turned around, of course, which she had no intention of doing on purpose.

"Good morning, boys and girls," Rachel's teacher said with a smile as the scholars took their seats.

"Good morning, Elizabeth," the children said in unison.

Elizabeth opened her Bible. "Today I'll be reading from Mark 12:30 and 31. 'Love the Lord your God with all your heart and with all your soul and with all your mind and with all your strength. The second is this: "Love your neighbor as yourself." There is no commandment greater than these.' "

Rachel reflected on those verses. She thought loving God with her whole heart, soul, mind, and strength was easy enough, because God was a loving God who cared for His people and deserved everyone's love in return. Loving her neighbors wasn't too hard, either, since Rachel liked most of the folks who lived near them.

Then she thought of Orlie and frowned. Orlie wasn't so easy to love, however; but maybe she didn't have to, since he wasn't a close neighbor. Of course, Mom had reminded her this morning that the Bible said everyone should love even their enemies. Orlie wasn't exactly an enemy. So, if he wasn't Rachel's neighbor and he wasn't her enemy, maybe she didn't have to love him at all. Maybe the best thing to do was to pretend Orlie didn't exist. Yes, that's what she would do.

Rachel felt someone tap her on the shoulder. "*Psst*. . . Rachel, didn't you hear the teacher?"

Rachel sat there, determined to ignore Orlie.

Tap. Tap. He thumped harder this time.

Rachel whirled around. "What do you want?"

"It's time to stand and recite the Lord's Prayer."

Rachel turned back around and realized everyone else in the room was standing—and staring at her! She quickly jumped to her feet. So much for her plan to ignore Orlie Troyer.

The rest of the morning went fairly well, but at noon, when Rachel sat on the porch to eat her lunch, she discovered an unwanted surprise. Inside her lunchbox was a tuna fish sandwich with a hunk of wilted lettuce.

"Yuck! I don't like tuna," Rachel moaned. She thought tuna was disgusting, and it made her feel funny bowing her head to say a silent prayer of thanks for something she wasn't even thankful to eat. She closed her eyes. "Please God, no more tuna," she whispered out loud to let Him know how serious she was.

Orlie plopped down beside Rachel and tapped her on the shoulder just as she finished praying. "What'd you say?"

She grunted and slid to the edge of the porch, hoping he would take the hint and find somewhere else to sit. "Nothing."

"Yes, you did. You said something about tuna."

Rachel figured she may as well tell Orlie what she was upset about or he'd probably keep bothering her. "I asked my mamm for a peanut butter and jelly sandwich today, and she gave me tuna instead."

His eyebrows lifted a little. "You don't like tuna?"

"No way! It's oily and fishy and tastes really gross."

"No way! It's oily and fishy and tastes really gross."

Rachel ground her teeth together and stared at him. "Stop mimicking me."

"I like tuna just fine. For that matter, there's not much I don't like in the way of food," Orlie said with a nod.

Rachel didn't comment on Orlie's last statement; she just sat there trying to think of what to do with the disappointing sandwich she held in her hand and wishing Orlie would sit with the boys out on the lawn.

"'Course there's some things not related to food that I don't like," Orlie continued. "Want to know what they are?"

"Not really. Why don't you just eat your lunch and leave me alone?"

"I don't like buzzing bees, stinky pigs, dogs that bite, or smelly cow manure," he said, as if he hadn't heard Rachel's request. "And I don't care much for dirty little mice, either."

Rachel rolled her eyes skyward. Then she glanced around to make sure no one was watching. She was in luck. Everyone seemed busy eating their own lunches, and no one was looking Rachel's way. Since Teacher Elizabeth had brought her lunch outside and was sitting on a quilt under the maple tree, Rachel figured she could sneak back into the schoolhouse unnoticed. She grabbed the sandwich, hurried across the porch, pulled open the door, and dashed to the garbage can. With only a slight hesitation, she dropped the sandwich in and headed back outside to finish eating her lunch.

Since Orlie was still sitting on the porch, Rachel decided to take her lunchbox and sit on the grass near Mary. Unfortunately, Orlie followed and flopped down beside her. She looked the other way, and her stomach rumbled as she stared at her lunchbox. She only had a thermos of milk and one apple left. At this rate, she would starve to death before supper time.

"Want half of my sandwich?" Orlie offered. "It's bologna and cheese."

"No thanks," she said with a shake of her head. No way was she going to eat anything of Orlie's. It might have garlic on it.

Chapter 3

Dinky

I'm sure glad this is Saturday and there's no school," Rachel said as she climbed the stairs from the basement and followed her sister into the kitchen. Pap, Henry, and Jacob were working in the fields, and Mom had gone to Grandpa and Grandma Yoder's place soon after breakfast to help Grandma clean her house.

Esther set down the wooden box she'd brought up from the basement and turned to face Rachel. "You don't like school this year? You've always liked it before."

"I like school just fine. I *don't* like Orlie Troyer."

"He's that new boy at school, right?"

"Right. And Orlie's a real pain—always teasing, staring at me, mimicking things I say, and blowing his garlic breath right in my face." Rachel wrinkled her nose and tapped the side of her head. "It's enough to make me go *ab im kopp* [go crazy]."

Esther chuckled. "Oh, Rachel, how you do exaggerate. I'm sure nothing that boy could ever do or say would make you go crazy."

Rachel shrugged. Esther could think whatever she wanted; she wasn't the one who had to put up with Orlie's irritating behavior. "There's another reason I don't like school this year."

"Oh? What's that?"

"I have to walk with Jacob every day, and he complains because I walk too slow," Rachel said. "I wish I could ride a bike to school, like some English kinner get to do."

"Some folks believe other people's bread tastes better than their own," Esther said.

Rachel nodded. "Mom has told me that more than once."

"It's true. We shouldn't waste time wanting things others own. We should be happy with what we have."

Rachel tried to be satisfied, but sometimes it wasn't so easy. "Even if Mom and Pap did let me have a bike, Mom would probably say I'm too young to ride it to school." She shook her head and groaned. "Why does everyone treat me like a baby?"

Esther patted Rachel's arm. "Being the youngest member of the family must be hard."

Rachel nodded. "If Mom had another boppli, I wouldn't be the baby of the family anymore. Maybe then Mom and Pap would realize I'm grown up and would let me do more things."

"Jah, maybe so, but since Mom hasn't had any *bopplin* [babies] since you were born, she probably won't have any now." Esther rubbed a spot on her lower back. "Whew! That box was heavier than I thought. Guess I should have asked Pap or one of the boys to haul it up from the basement for me before they headed out to the fields."

"I could have helped you with it," Rachel pointed out. Sometimes she felt her older sister treated her like a baby, too. Just because Rachel was only ten years old didn't mean she wasn't strong or couldn't help with certain things. At least she should be allowed to try.

"You can help me now." Esther motioned to the box sitting near her feet. "I want to check these good dishes over thoroughly for any cracks or chips; and then we need to wash them so they'll be ready in plenty of time for my wedding on the first Thursday of November."

Rachel sighed. November seemed like a long time off, especially since she had to go to school every day between now and then. And she had to face that teasing, smelly-breath Orlie Troyer.

"Are you sighing because you don't want to help me?" Esther asked, reaching for the box.

"Oh, no. I'm happy to help," Rachel was quick to say. "I was just thinking that your wedding seems like a long time from now. I wish it could get here sooner."

"It's only two months away, and we have a lot to

do, so I'm sure the time will go quickly. If Mom hadn't gone to help Grandma clean her house this morning, she'd be here now, helping me." Esther smiled. "So I really appreciate your help, little sister."

Rachel pulled her shoulders back and stood as tall as she could. It was nice to be appreciated. "I'm sure I can do whatever Mom would have done."

"Jah, I'm sure you can." Esther dropped to her knees by the box. "Now first we open the box and take out the dishes."

"Okay." Rachel knelt beside her sister and fought the urge to rip the box open herself. She knew it would be better to let Esther do that, since the dishes were Mom's best china and would be used at Esther and Rudy's wedding.

Esther's hands shook like leaves fluttering in the breeze as she slowly lifted the lid. "I'm so *uffgschafft* [excited] I can barely make my fingers work."

Rachel didn't see why her sister was so excited about opening a box of old dishes, but she didn't say anything. She didn't want to hurt Esther's feelings.

When Esther lifted the lid, Rachel saw a row of delicate white china cups with little pink roses. Esther smiled slightly as she removed each one and set it carefully on the floor by the box. The layer under the cups held plates, and when Esther reached inside to remove the first one, the shredded paper surrounding the dishes moved a little. At first, Rachel thought it shifted from the movement of the plate, but when a little gray blob with beady eyes poked its head out of the paper, she knew what had happened.

"Ach! It's a *maus* [mouse]! It's a maus!" Esther hollered, jumping to her feet. "That's so *ekelhaft* [disgusting]!"

"It's not disgusting. It's only a baby mouse that must have found its way in through here."

Rachel pointed to a small hole in the side of the box. She reached inside and picked up another plate, and the whole box seemed to move. Five little gray mice scurried about, ducking their heads in and out, and pushing shreds of paper in every direction.

Esther let out an ear-piercing screech and hopped onto the closest chair. Her eyes looked like they were ready to pop right out of her head, and her face was as white as a pail of goat's milk.

Rachel could hardly keep from laughing at her silly sister. "Want me to catch the mice and take them outside?" she asked.

"Jah, sure. If you think you can."

"Of course I can." Rachel had a way with animals, and she certainly wasn't afraid of a little old mouse, so she marched to the pantry and pulled out a paper sack. Then she hurried back to the box and reached inside. She felt brave and grown-up. One by one, she picked up the baby mice and placed them carefully into the sack.

"It's safe for you to get off that chair now," she said, trying not to smile at her sister's anxious expression.

Esther clung to the chair like she feared for her life. "H–how do you know there aren't more creepy mice inside that box?"

"Well, let me see." Rachel slipped her hand into the box again, while she hung on to the sack with the other hand. She dug around one side and then the other, dipping her fingers up and down and all through the shreds of paper. "Nothing is in here now except for more dishes."

One of Esther's brows rose to a jaunty angle. "Are—are you sure?"

"I'm very sure," Rachel replied with a nod. "But if you're scared, then you can wait until I come back to the house. Then we can take the rest of the dishes out together."

Esther lifted her chin and frowned at Rachel. "I am not scared. I just don't like mice. I especially don't like the idea of their dirty little feet climbing all over my good wedding dishes."

I just don't like mice. I just don't like mice. Rachel remembered hearing similar words the other day at school. But who had said them? Who had told her they didn't like mice? She squeezed her eyes shut and tried to remember, but nothing came to mind. Oh well, she guessed it wasn't important. She needed to get the baby mice outside so Esther could climb down from that chair.

"I'll be back soon," Rachel announced.

"Jah, okay."

As Rachel opened the back door and stepped onto the porch with the bag full of mice, for some reason an image of Orlie Troyer popped into her mind. Thanks to Orlie, Rachel didn't like going to school anymore, and that wasn't fair. Well, she wasn't one to give up easily. If she could find a way to get Orlie to quit bothering her, she would do it. If she could only find something Orlie didn't like and tease him with it, maybe he'd finally leave her alone.

The bag in Rachel's hand vibrated as the mice skittered inside.

"That's it!" she shouted. "Orlie's the one who said he didn't like mice!"

A smile spread across Rachel's face. She decided she would turn four of the baby mice loose in the field behind their house, but she had other plans for mouse number five.

Rachel trudged across the yard, climbed over the fence, stopped to pet the old horse Pap had put out to pasture, and headed for the cornfield. When she got there, she opened the sack and released four of the mice. "Good-bye little *meis* [mice]. Have a good life."

She crossed the pasture, gave old Tom another pat, climbed over the fence, and headed for the barn. There she found some coffee cans in a cupboard under her father's workbench. Pap liked to save the cans to store his nails and other things. Rachel figured since her father had several empty cans, he wouldn't miss just one. She placed the paper sack that held the baby mouse onto the workbench, then wadded up a clean rag she'd found in one of the workbench drawers and put it on the bottom of the can. Then she took a screwdriver and poked a few holes in the plastic lid of the can.

"All right, little maus, in you go." Rachel opened the sack, removed the mouse, and placed it inside the can. "This will be your new home until Monday morning," she said with a satisfied smile. "And from now on your name will be Dinky."

The little gray mouse wiggled its whiskers at her as she put the lid on the can.

Suddenly Cuddles scampered across the floor and stopped at Rachel's feet. The kitten stared at Rachel with sad eyes, meowing for all she was worth.

Rachel felt bad because she hadn't spent much time with Cuddles lately, so she sat on a bale of hay, placed the coffee can beside her, and lifted Cuddles into her arms. "Hey, there, sweet kitten, have you missed me?"

Cuddles uttered a pathetic *meow*, then she licked Rachel's nose with her sandpapery tongue.

Rachel giggled. "That tickles."

Cuddles snuggled against Rachel and began to purr. Rachel closed her eyes. The kitten's warm body and her purring felt so good that Rachel knew she could easily fall asleep. She opened her eyes, determined not to give in to the sleepy feeling, and sat there stroking Cuddles behind her ears.

Suddenly, Cuddles's nose twitched, and her ears perked up. *Meow!* She leaped off Rachel's lap and landed near the coffee can that held Dinky captive.

"Oh no, you don't," Rachel scolded when Cuddles sniffed the lid of the can and swiped at it. "That mouse is going to be my pet, and he's got a job to do at school on Monday morning." She picked up the can and rushed out of the barn.

Quickly, she made her way to the house and slipped inside the front door, so Esther wouldn't hear her from the kitchen. Then, as quietly as she could, she tiptoed up the stairs and went straight to her room. She scurried to her bed, dropped to her knees, and slid the coffee can as far underneath the bed as she could. She'd give Dinky food later so he'd have plenty of energy for his mission on Monday morning.

Rachel glanced at the clock by her bed and realized she'd been gone quite awhile. Esther probably wondered what was taking her so long, so she needed to hurry and get back to the kitchen.

Esther stood at the sink, washing the wedding dishes. "What took you so long?" she asked. "I was beginning to wonder if you were ever coming back."

"Sorry. On my way out to the cornfield, I stopped to say hello to old Tom; and then on the way back to the house, I spent a few minutes in the barn with my kitten." Rachel wasn't about to tell her sister about Dinky. If Esther knew, she'd probably tell Mom and

Pap about Rachel's plans.

Esther flicked a soapy bubble at Rachel. "I started washing the dishes without you."

Rachel grabbed a clean towel from the drawer near the sink and reached for a china cup. "I'm here now, so I'll dry the dishes."

Esther smiled. *"Danki.* [Thank you.]"

"You're welcome."

As Rachel dried each dish, she carefully set it on the counter. The last thing she wanted to do was to break one of Esther's wedding dishes. Mom would scold her for sure if that happened. Esther probably would, too.

When they finished with the dishes, Esther told Rachel, "I've been thinking. . ."

"What have you been thinking?"

"You mentioned earlier how much you dislike walking to school with Jacob."

Rachel nodded. "That's true."

"Why don't you see if Mom will let you wait at the end of our driveway until some of the other scholars go by? Then you can walk with them."

"I suppose I could, but Jacob would probably tag along, and he'd still badger me about walking too slow," Rachel answered. "Then the others would probably make fun of me, too."

Esther pulled Rachel to her side and hugged her. "I know it's hard being a child, but someday, when you're grown and married with kinner of your own, you'll realize your school days weren't so bad after all."

Rachel shook her head. "That won't happen, because I'm never getting married. Not ever!"

Chapter 4

A Hard Lesson

On Monday morning, after Rachel ate breakfast, she hurried to help Mom and Esther do the dishes; then she turned toward the stairs leading to her room.

"Where are you going, Rachel?" Mom called to her. "You don't want to be late for school."

"I just need to get something from my bedroom," Rachel explained. She scampered up the stairs before Mom could say anything else. When she entered her room a few seconds later, she rushed to her dresser and pulled open the bottom drawer. She took out a large matchbox with several tiny holes along the top. Next, she went over to her bed, got down on her hands and knees, and pulled out Dinky's coffee can.

Rachel opened the lid and lifted Dinky out by his tail. Then she placed him in the matchbox. She couldn't hide a coffee can at school, but she knew she could easily hide a matchbox. Dinky looked happy and plump, because Rachel had taken good care of him, feeding him bits of cheese and cracker covered in peanut butter.

With a satisfied smile, Rachel rushed back to her dresser and grabbed a sweater from the same drawer where she'd hidden the matchbox. She wrapped the sweater around the matchbox, tucked it under her arm, and headed downstairs.

When Rachel entered the kitchen, she spotted Esther sweeping the floor. Mom stood at the counter making a peanut butter and jelly sandwich. *At least it's not tuna this time,* thought Rachel.

"Jacob's outside waiting for you," Mom said. She slipped the sandwich into a plastic bag and placed it inside Rachel's lunchbox. Then she tipped her head to one side and stared at Rachel. "What's with the sweater this morning?"

"In case I get cold," Rachel said. She grabbed the lunchbox off the counter and ran to the door, hoping Mom wouldn't ask more questions.

"I don't see how you could possibly get cold," Esther said. "It's been so warm the last few days; I can't imagine why you'd need a sweater."

Rachel shrugged. "That may be true, but fall is almost here. You never know when the weather might turn chilly."

Mom and Esther exchanged glances, but neither of them said a word. Rachel breathed a sigh of relief and hurried out the door.

Jacob stood on the porch, tapping his foot. "Well, it's about time. Are you trying to make us late for school?" he asked with a scowl.

She shook her head. "We won't be late, unless you dillydally."

"Jah, right. You're always the one who walks too slow. I don't stop to look at every bug and flower along the way like you do."

"Do not."

"Do so."

Rachel clamped her lips together so she wouldn't say anything more. She was in no mood to argue with Jacob. She only wanted to get Dinky safely to school so she could teach Orlie his first—and hopefully best—lesson of the day.

At school, Rachel slipped into the classroom while the other children were still playing in the schoolyard. She was relieved to see that Teacher Elizabeth was busy writing something on the blackboard. Rachel tiptoed to Orlie's desk. She took the matchbox out of the folds of her sweater, lifted the lid on his desk, and placed it inside, where Orlie was sure to find it when he reached for his school supplies.

Rachel scooted out the front door and joined Mary on the swings.

"You're not going to throw up again, I hope," Mary said, wrinkling her nose, as her lips scrunched together.

Rachel shook her head. "I've learned my lesson

about twirling on the swings."

"That's good to hear, because you looked green in the face when you came out of the outhouse that day, and I was worried about you."

"I've never gotten sick at school before," Rachel said. She pulled hard at the chains on the swing. "And I hope I never do again."

"Me neither. It's not fun to be grank."

"The only good part of being sick is that you get to stay home from school." Rachel pumped her legs to get the swing moving faster.

"Why would you want to stay home?" Mary asked. "Last year you liked school."

"That was true, until Orlie Troyer moved here and made my life so miserable."

Mary clicked her tongue, the way Mom often did. "He only bothers you because he knows he can."

"What's that mean?"

"It means, if you ignored him, he'd probably leave you alone. When a boy knows that his teasing bothers a girl, he does it more."

Rachel let her cousin's words roll around in her head awhile. Maybe Mary was right. If she didn't let Orlie know she was upset by the things he said and did, maybe he would leave her alone. "But it's too late for that," she mumbled when the school bell jangled. Orlie was about to get a big surprise.

Mary halted her swing. "Too late for what?"

"Oh, nothing." Rachel jumped off her swing. Then she hurried into the school. She knew if she was late, Orlie would probably tease her about that, too.

He deserves that little present I left him this morning! she thought. Finding a mouse in his desk might make him think twice about bothering her. And if that didn't work, she would ignore him, as Mary suggested.

Rachel glanced at Orlie as she passed his desk. He nodded and gave her a lopsided grin. She looked away quickly and slipped into her seat.

Teacher Elizabeth started the morning by reading Luke 6:31. "'Do to others as you would have them do to you.'"

Rachel's cheeks burned. Would she want someone to put something she was afraid of in her desk? No, of course not. A pang of regret shot through her. She gripped the sides of her desk, wishing she could run out the door. Maybe Orlie wouldn't see the matchbox. Then she could take it out of his desk during recess.

Rachel forced herself to stand beside her desk and recite the Lord's Prayer with the other scholars. But all she could think about was her naughty deed. She wondered if she'd get in much trouble.

A nudge in Rachel's back pushed her thoughts aside. "We're supposed to go up front so we can sing," Orlie said.

Rachel plodded to the front of the room with the others and moved her lips as though she were singing.

I wonder if Orlie will know I'm the one who put the mouse inside his desk. She poked a fingernail between her teeth and nibbled until it broke. *He'll probably tell the teacher on me.*

After the singing, the scholars returned to their seats. Rachel's insides quivered as she sank into the chair behind her desk, fretting about what would happen when Orlie discovered the mouse.

Orlie passed Rachel's desk and wiggled his eyebrows. Rachel turned and watched as he flopped into his seat with a silly grin. He lifted the lid on his desk. Rachel's heart nearly stopped beating as she waited for him to see the matchbox she had placed there. But to her surprise, it wasn't a matchbox Orlie took out of the desk; it was his math book and some paper.

Maybe he didn't see the matchbox. Maybe I can still get it.

Rachel reached into her own desk to get her arithmetic book, but before she had a chance to open it, Teacher Elizabeth let out a shrill scream and hopped onto her chair.

"Ach! Ach! There's a maus on my desk!"

Rachel noticed the matchbox sitting on one corner of Teacher's desk. Why hadn't she noticed it before, and how did it get there?

Dinky poked his tiny head over a stack of papers. He darted around the desk a few times, hopped into the open drawer of Elizabeth's desk, jumped back out, and skittered down the side of the desk.

Thud! As Dinky landed on the floor, the room filled with screams and screeches. A few girls leaped onto their chairs. Some boys sat at their desks, pointing at the mouse and laughing until tears ran down their cheeks. A few others joined Rachel in the chase to catch the mouse.

"Open the *daer* [door] and maybe it'll run outside," Mary suggested.

"No, don't open that door!" Rachel hollered. She saw Dinky scurry under Mary's chair.

"If it comes my way I'll smash it," David Esh, the boy who sat in front of Mary, hollered.

"You'd better not kill my pet maus!" Rachel could have bitten her tongue. She hadn't meant to admit that Dinky was hers. Now everyone would think *she* had put the mouse on Teacher Elizabeth's desk.

Elizabeth stepped down from her chair just as Rachel scooped Dinky into her hands. "Rachel Yoder, is that your maus?"

Rachel nodded slowly. "Jah."

"Did you bring it to school to scare me?"

"No, Elizabeth."

"Then why was it in a matchbox? And why was it sitting on my desk?"

"Well, I—" Rachel shuffled her feet and stared at the floor.

"*Raus mit*—out with it!" Elizabeth's face was getting

redder. Rachel knew she needed to say something to calm her teacher.

"I didn't bring Dinky—I mean the maus—to school to scare you, and I don't know how it got on your desk," she said.

"Well, it didn't get there by itself, now, did it?"

"No, Teacher."

"Put that mouse outside right now," Elizabeth demanded. "Then you'll need to sit down and do your math. You'll stay after school today to clean the chalkboard and do extra lessons."

Rachel felt sick. Dinky had become like a pet to her. If she let him go outside, she would never see him again. She didn't know how that matchbox got on Elizabeth's desk, but she figured Orlie must have had something to do with it. He'd probably found it in his desk and put it on the teacher's desk during the time of singing. Most likely he'd done it to get Rachel in trouble. Rachel disliked Orlie all the more. To make things worse, Jacob would have to stay late to walk her home. Then Mom and Pap would learn she'd taken a mouse to school, and that would spell trouble.

With a heavy heart, Rachel opened the schoolhouse door, plodded down the steps, and set Dinky on the ground. "Good-bye, little friend. I hope you have a good, long life."

When Rachel returned to her seat, Orlie leaned over her shoulder and whispered, "Why'd you do it, Rachel?

Why'd you put that maus in my desk?"

"You—you knew?"

"Jah, and I think it was a dirty trick."

Rachel sat with her arms folded. She could only think about losing Dinky and the punishment she'd get at home.

Guess that's what I get for trying to get even with Orlie, Rachel thought. *I should have just ignored him, like Mary said.*

Rachel decided to memorize Luke 6:31: "Do to others as you would have them do to you."

Chapter 5

Hurry-Up Cake

For the next several weeks, Rachel tried to stay out of trouble. She'd avoided Orlie so she wouldn't be tempted to do anything to him that she wouldn't want him to do to her. She also didn't want to do extra chores again. That had been her punishment for the mouse incident. She knew she'd been fortunate to escape a trip to the woodshed for a *bletsching* [spanking].

One Saturday morning Rachel looked at her calendar and realized it was Jacob's birthday.

"Oh, no," she moaned. "I forgot his birthday." Rachel and Jacob didn't always get along, but he was still her brother. She wanted to do something special to wish him a happy birthday.

Rachel rushed down the stairs and into the kitchen. Seeing her mother in the room, she quickly stepped up to her and whispered, "Where's Jacob?"

"He's outside doing chores, along with your daed

and older *bruder* [brother]." Mom nodded toward the basement door. "Esther went down to get the gift she hid for Jacob, and I asked her to bring up some canned peaches to go with our breakfast."

"I'm glad Jacob's not here."

Mom's glasses had slipped to the middle of her nose. She pushed them back in place and turned toward the stove. "Why are you whispering, Rachel?"

"I wanted to be sure Jacob didn't hear me."

"I just told you, he's outside doing chores."

Rachel felt the heat of embarrassment creep up the back of her neck. Mom must think she was hard of hearing, or a real *dummkopp* [dunce]. "I just realized today's Jacob's birthday," she explained. "I don't have anything to give him, so I was hoping I could make something he might like to eat."

Mom opened the drawer at the bottom of the stove and reached for the frying pan. "Jacob has a sweet tooth, so why don't you bake him a cake?"

"Is there enough time?"

"There might be if you make a hurry-up cake. That mixes and bakes faster than most other cakes."

"That's a great idea!" Rachel scurried to the cupboard where Mom kept baking supplies. "What exactly do I need?"

"Let's see now. . . . The recipe calls for cake flour, baking powder, sugar, salt, vanilla, butter, milk, and eggs." Mom called out the ingredients so fast that

Rachel could barely keep up. She rushed to the cupboard, then to the refrigerator to get everything she would need. She was tempted to ask her mother to repeat the list. But she didn't want Mom to think she was a little girl who couldn't remember anything.

"The directions for making the cake are in my recipe box," Mom said, as she plucked several brown eggs from the carton Rachel had just placed on the cupboard. "I'll need some of these for the French toast I'm making. That's one of Jacob's favorite breakfast foods."

Rachel nodded, even though she knew Jacob liked most food. He even liked tuna sandwiches and spinach, both of which Rachel could do nicely without.

"Be sure you mix the eggs and butter first. Then add the dry ingredients and milk alternately. Next, put in the vanilla and beat hard, and then pour the batter into two greased and floured cake pans. I'll heat the oven while you're doing that," Mom said.

Rachel's head felt as if it were spinning like a top. So much information rolled around. But she did her best to remember Mom's instructions. She was setting everything on the cupboard, when Esther entered the room. She had a large paper sack in one hand and a jar of peaches in the other hand.

"Where's the birthday boy?" she asked, handing Mom the peaches. Then she placed the sack on one end of the counter. "I figured Jacob would be in here looking for his birthday presents already."

"He's still doing chores with your daed and Henry." Mom motioned to Rachel. "Your sister's in a hurry to get a cake baked before Jacob comes in, so maybe you can help her."

Esther started toward Rachel, but Rachel shook her head. "If this is my gift to Jacob, then I need to make it myself," she explained.

"Okay, but let me know if you need anything." Esther opened one of the cupboard doors and removed a stack of plates. "I have to set the table anyway."

Rachel got out the recipe box and removed the card for hurry-up cake; then she quickly measured out the ingredients and put them in a large bowl. She hoped she hadn't forgotten anything, and that she'd put in the right amounts. The last thing she needed was for her cake to flop. Then Jacob and Henry would tease her.

"Watch out, Rachel, you're spilling flour all over the floor." Mom groaned. "I mopped in here after supper last night, and now you're making a mess."

"Sorry. I'll clean it up."

Rachel scurried to the utility closet to get the broom. She was on her way back when *phlumph!* She slipped in the spilled flour. The broom flew out of Rachel's hands, and she landed with a *thud* on the floor.

"Rachel, are you okay?" Mom and Esther asked at the same time. They hurried to Rachel's side.

"I'm all right." Rachel clambered to her feet, her face

heating with embarrassment. Why was it that every time she tried to do something that might prove she was growing up, she made a mess of things?

"If you're going to finish Jacob's cake before he comes inside, you'd better get it in the oven and let me clean the floor," Esther said, bending to pick up the broom.

Rachel didn't argue. She hurried to the counter and poured the cake batter into two cake pans, while Esther swept the floor and Mom followed with a wet mop. Then Rachel carried the pans of cake batter across the room. She placed them in the oven. When that was done, she collapsed into the nearest chair. She didn't know how Mom and Esther did so much baking—mixing the hurry-up cake together made her tired. At least now, if Jacob came into the kitchen before the cake was done, she could tell him that his birthday present was in the oven.

"The table is set, Mom," Esther said a few minutes later. "What else would you like me to do?"

"You can open the jar of peaches and put it on the table."

"Okay." Esther tapped Rachel on the shoulder as she neared the table. "How are things at school these days? Are you getting along better with that new boy?"

Rachel wrinkled her nose. "School would be better for me if Orlie moved back to Indiana."

"Rachel," Mom scolded. "Orlie and his family have

as much right to live in Pennsylvania as we do."

"I wouldn't mind him being here so much if he didn't tease me, and if his breath smelled better."

"You don't mind the horses, and their breath doesn't always smell sweet," Esther said. She placed the jar of peaches on the table and opened the lid.

Rachel couldn't deny that fact. Just the other day, when she'd gone out to the pasture to visit old Tom, he'd blown his hot, smelly breath right in her face. "What you said about the horses' breath is true," she admitted, "but the horses—and none of our other animals—say mean things or stare at me in peculiar ways."

Mom set the frying pan on the gas stove and turned on the burner. "When I met Orlie and his folks at church, I thought he seemed like a nice boy."

Rachel folded her arms and frowned. "You don't know him like I do."

"Be that as it may, he's still a child of God, and you should be kind to him."

Rachel thought about the day she had tried to scare Orlie with the mouse. She wondered if her plan backfired because she'd been trying to get even. Maybe if she did something nice to Orlie for a change, he would leave her alone.

If any of Jacob's cake is left Monday morning, I'll take a piece to school for Orlie, she decided. *A hunk of yummy cake might sweeten Orlie's breath, too.*

Ding! Rachel jumped out of her chair when the

timer on the stove sounded. "It's done! I've got to take Jacob's hurry-up cake out of the oven, let it cool, and frost it before he comes in."

Rachel grabbed two pot holders from a drawer near the stove. *Whoosh!* The heat roared at her as she opened the oven door. She carefully pulled out the cake pans. The cake layers looked a little browner than they should have. But they smelled good, and she thought that was a good sign. She walked carefully across the room and set the pans inside the refrigerator to cool them quicker. Then Rachel hurried to make strawberry icing.

By the time Rachel had mixed the icing, the cake pieces felt cool enough to frost. She took the cake out of the refrigerator. Still no Jacob. *He must not have finished his chores yet.* She picked up a cake pan and turned it upside down over a serving platter. It didn't budge. She tapped on the bottom of the pan with her hand. Nothing happened.

"Something's wrong with this cake," Rachel complained to her mother. "It won't come out of the pan."

"Try slipping a butter knife around the edges and see if that helps," Mom said.

Rachel did as her mother suggested, but the cake still wouldn't come loose. She tried the other pan. It wouldn't come out either. "Always trouble somewhere," she grumbled.

Esther stepped to Rachel's side. "Did you grease and flour the pans before you poured the batter in?"

Rachel squinted as she tried to remember what she had done. "Was I supposed to grease and flour them?"

"I told you to," Mom said. "When I gave you the instructions, I said to be sure you grease and flour the pans. It said so on the recipe card, too."

Rachel groaned. "I must have missed that part."

Just then, the back door opened, and Jacob stepped into the room, followed by Pap and Henry.

"Happy birthday, Jacob," Esther said, handing him the paper sack she had set on the counter when she'd first come up from the basement.

"What's this?" Jacob asked, smiling at Esther.

Esther nudged his arm playfully. "It's your birthday present, silly."

Jacob's smile broadened as he peered in the sack. "Wow, a new baseball mitt! I've been hoping for one." He hugged Esther. "Danki, sister."

Esther smiled, and Rachel frowned. The hurry-up cake she'd made, that was stuck in the pans, was a stupid gift compared to what Esther had given Jacob. She wished she could hide the cake so Jacob wouldn't see it.

Pap went to the storage closet and opened the door. Then he pulled out a fishing pole and handed it to Jacob. "This is from your mamm and me."

Jacob set the mitt on the counter and cradled the fishing pole in his arms like a mother would hold her baby. "Danki, Pap. Danki, Mom. I've been wanting a new one of these, too."

"*Gern gschehne*—you are welcome," they said together.

"Now it's my turn," Henry announced. He pulled a wooden yo-yo from his jacket pocket and handed it to Jacob. "I made this for you. Happy birthday, bruder."

"It's real nice." Jacob rubbed his hand over the shiny wood, then he slipped the loop of string over his finger, flicked his wrist, and bounced the yo-yo up and down. "Works real well, too. Danki, Henry."

"Gern gschehne," Henry replied with a smile.

Everyone looked at Rachel as if waiting to see what she had for Jacob. She groaned and pointed to the cake pans sitting on the counter near the stove. "My present's over there, but sorry to say, I can't get either one of the cake layers out of their pans."

Jacob's eyebrows lifted high as he examined the cakes. "You baked me a cake?"

Rachel nodded. "I tried to, and since I wanted to get it done before you came in from doing your chores, I made a hurry-up cake. Only thing is, I got in such a hurry, I forgot to grease and flour the pans." Rachel motioned to the bowl of strawberry icing, and her chin trembled slightly. "Now I have a bowl of icing I can't use, two halves of a cake I can't get out of the pans, and nothing to give you for your birthday." She hoped she wasn't going to cry, because she figured Jacob would make a big deal out of it if she did.

However, instead of making fun of her cake mess, Jacob grabbed a knife from the silverware drawer. He scooped up a glob of strawberry icing and slathered it on half of the cake. "Nothin' says we can't eat it right out of the pan," he said, reaching back in the drawer for a fork.

Pap grabbed a fork, too, and so did Henry. Mom stopped them. "With a little help from my spatula, I'm sure I can get the cake layers out of their pans." She nodded at the stove. "I'm making Jacob's favorite this morning—French toast. So no cake until we've had our breakfast."

"Oh, all right," Jacob sighed, even though he was grinning. "I guess I can wait that long to sample some of Rachel's good-smelling cake." He thumped Rachel on the back. "Danki, sister. I appreciate it."

Rachel thought Jacob was only trying to make her feel better, but at least he hadn't said anything mean about her messed-up cake. Next year, she would try to remember to do something really special for his birthday. Maybe she would make him a painted rock. Rachel was pretty good at painting rocks to look like various animals, even if she did say so herself. At least those didn't have to be mixed, baked, or floured!

Chapter 6

Surprise *Mondaag* [Monday]

As Rachel walked to school on Monday morning, her stomach quivered like it was filled with a team of fluttering butterflies flying in different directions. She carried a hunk of Jacob's birthday cake in her lunchbox. She planned to give it to Orlie during lunch today and hoped he would be surprised. She also hoped the gift might make him quit pestering her.

Jacob nudged Rachel's arm. "How come you're dawdling this morning? You're slower than a turtle walking uphill."

"Am not."

"Are so."

"I am not walking like a turtle, Jacob."

Jacob grunted. "Jah, you are. Your name ought to be Rachel Yoder, the Slowpoke Turtle, and if you don't walk faster, we'll be late for school." He poked her arm again. "Why do you always drag your feet every Mondaag morning?"

"I don't always walk slow on Monday mornings." Rachel kicked a small stone with the toe of her sneaker. "If you're worried about being late, go on ahead. Don't let me hold you back."

Jacob stopped walking and turned to face her. "You know I can't do that. Mom would be madder than a hornet trapped in a jar of honey if I let you walk to school alone."

Rachel knew Jacob was right. When Jacob graduated from school after eighth grade, then what would Mom do? Maybe by then she would think Rachel was old enough to go to school without a babysitter. Maybe by then she would realize that Rachel was growing up and could walk alone.

As a bright yellow school bus rumbled past, Jacob grabbed Rachel's hand and pulled her farther to the shoulder of the road. Rachel looked at the English children staring out their windows. She wondered if she were English and attended one of their public schools, if she'd have to put up with anyone mean like Orlie Troyer. She supposed there were boys like Orlie in every school, but that didn't make it any easier to think about facing him again this morning.

Jacob nudged Rachel again.

"What?"

"That hurry-up cake you made for my birthday on Saturday tasted pretty good, even if Mom did have to dig it out of the pan."

Rachel wasn't sure if that was supposed to be a compliment or if Jacob was teasing her again, but she decided not to make an issue of it. "Danki," she muttered, quickening her pace.

"Now you're walking too fast," Jacob complained. "Can't you find a happy medium?"

Rachel just kept on walking. Her brother was obviously looking for an argument this morning.

By the time Rachel and Jacob entered the schoolhouse, the butterflies in Rachel's stomach quieted. However, at noontime, Rachel's butterflies returned when her teacher announced that it was time for the scholars to eat their lunches. Should she give Orlie the piece of cake or forget about the idea? What if he didn't like hurry-up cake with strawberry icing? What if her gift didn't make him stop picking on her?

She drew in a deep breath and hurried over to the shelf where the lunchboxes were kept. Orlie was already outside, sitting in his usual spot on the front porch. He looked at Rachel and wiggled his eyebrows. "Got any tuna sandwiches in your lunchbox today?" he asked with a silly grin.

Rachel shook her head. "I packed my own lunch this morning. I made a peanut butter and jelly sandwich."

He smacked his lips. "Peanut butter's pretty tasty, but I like tuna better."

Rachel wrinkled her nose in disgust. "I—uh—brought you something for dessert," she said, sitting beside him.

Orlie leaned toward Rachel. His breath tickled her neck, and she smelled the pungent aroma of garlic. She held her breath as she reached into her lunchbox for the cake and handed it to him.

His eyebrows lifted. "What's this?"

"It's some of my brother's birthday cake, and I baked it myself."

As Orlie pulled the lid off the container, his eyebrows rose higher. "This cake sure looks strange. How come it's shaped so funny?"

"It stuck to the pan and we had to dig it out." Rachel paused and licked her lips. "But it tastes okay, so it's safe to eat."

"My mamm bakes lots of cakes, and none of 'em has ever looked like this." Orlie puckered his lips and made an *oink-oink-oink* sound. "This looks like something that should have been fed to the hogs. Maybe you should take some baking lessons from my mamm."

Rachel clamped her lips together. *That's what I get for trying to be nice.* Giving Orlie a gift hadn't stopped him from saying unkind things to her. In fact, it seemed to have made things worse. She shouldn't have bothered bringing Orlie a gift. He sure didn't deserve one—especially when he'd acted so ungrateful and had said mean things about her baking skills.

Orlie continued to stare at the cake as he wrinkled his nose, like it smelled bad. Maybe it was his own dreadful breath he was smelling.

Feeling like a balloon that had been popped with a pin, Rachel said, "If you don't want it, then just throw it away."

"If you don't want it, then just throw it away," he repeated.

Rachel was about to say something more, when Jacob and two other boys, Nate and Samuel, walked by. Nate stopped in front of them. "How come you're sittin' with her?" he asked, pointing at Rachel.

Orlie shrugged and his ears turned bright red.

"Maybe she's his *aldi* [girlfriend]." Samuel snickered. "Orlie likes Rachel," he said in a singsong voice. "Orlie likes Rachel, and she's his aldi."

"No, I'm not Orlie's girlfriend!" Rachel scooted quickly away from Orlie and reached into her lunchbox to retrieve the peanut butter and jelly sandwich she'd made. She took one bite, then dropped it back into the lunchbox. Her appetite was gone.

After lunch, Rachel's teacher clapped her hands and asked for the class's attention. "Judging from the way many of you chose several books to read the last time the bookmobile visited our school, I thought it would be fun to have each of you in grades three to six write a story."

Rachel's cousin raised her hand.

"Yes, Mary?"

"What kind of story?"

Elizabeth tapped her pencil against her chin. "Well, let's see now. . . . I think it should be a made-up story, but you can base it on a real person or some kind of true happening."

Orlie's hand shot up.

"What is it, Orlie?"

"Should it be about someone living or dead?"

"Either," the teacher replied. "Just make sure you change things enough so the story is fiction and not something that actually happened."

"Oh, okay."

Elizabeth tapped her pencil on her desk. "You can spend the next hour writing the story, and then we'll do something else that should be both fun and interesting."

Rachel wasn't excited about writing a story. She wished she could draw a picture instead, but she knew better than to disobey the teacher, so she set right to work on her story about the most unusual person she'd ever met.

Some time later, Elizabeth clapped her hands together again and said, "Time's up. Now you will each read what you've written. Rachel, would you like to go first?"

Rachel knew her teacher's question wasn't really a question. It was a direct command for Rachel to get out of her seat, walk to the front of the class, and read the story she'd written. She took a deep breath and swallowed hard, hoping she wouldn't throw up. If she'd known she would be expected to read her story in front of everyone, she would have written something else.

Slowly, Rachel stood. Her legs felt like bags of rocks had been tied to them as she walked to the front of the room carrying her notebook in her shaking hands.

Elizabeth smiled. "Go ahead, Rachel."

Rachel fought the temptation to bite off a fingernail and licked her lips instead. "Once there was a horse named Otis." She paused and cleared her throat. "Otis was an unusual horse because he smelled like a stinking rose and liked to eat weird things. Most horses eat hay, oats, and corn, but not Otis—he liked to eat tuna sandwiches and garlic cloves."

As Rachel continued with her story, her cheeks became hotter. Did Orlie realize her story was about him? Did the teacher and the whole class know that, too? Rachel finished the story by saying, "So, if you ever meet a horse that smells like a stinking rose and likes to eat weird food, you'll know it was Otis."

Rachel rushed back to her seat. She wished she could dash for the door and run all the way home. She didn't know what had possessed her to write such a story. Had it been her way of getting even with Orlie for saying mean things about her cake?

She grimaced. *I thought I was done with trying to get even. I thought I had decided to try and be nice to Orlie.* She reflected on the verse from Luke 6:31: "Do to others as you would have them do to you." *I wouldn't want someone to write a story about me and say bad things—not even a made-up story.*

"That was an interesting story, Rachel." Elizabeth's forehead wrinkled. Then she nodded at Orlie. "Now it's your turn, Orlie."

As Orlie passed Rachel's desk, he gave her a sidelong glance. She noticed how red his ears were, and she wondered if it was because of her story or if he felt nervous about reading his own story in front of the class.

Orlie shifted from one foot to the other, and his hands shook as he held on to his piece of paper.

"Go ahead, Orlie, we're waiting," Elizabeth prompted.

He cleared his throat and began. "Rosie the Raccoon had a problem." He paused and cleared his throat two more times. "Rosie's problem was that she didn't know how to bake. In fact, she baked a cake once that stuck to the pan and looked like pig food."

Rachel's ears burned, and she gripped the sides of her desk so hard her knuckles turned white. *Orlie wrote that story about me! Rosie the Raccoon didn't bake a cake that stuck to the pan. I did!* She glanced around the room. *I wonder if everyone knows.*

"Not being able to bake wasn't Rosie's only problem," Orlie said. "She was a picky eater who threw away her tuna fish sandwich when she thought no one was looking."

He continued with his story, telling how Rosie got

dizzy one day when she was twirling on a tree branch. Then she got sick and threw up.

Rachel clenched her teeth. *He'll be sorry. Orlie doesn't deserve for me to be nice to him.*

On the way home from school, Rachel felt so sorry for herself that she wasn't watching her steps and tripped on a rock. *Plop!* She fell and skinned both knees. "Ouch! That really hurts," she whimpered.

Instead of offering sympathy, Jacob scolded her for not paying attention to where she was going and accused her of daydreaming.

"I was not daydreaming," she argued.

Jacob snickered. "You were probably thinking about that story Orlie read." He pointed at Rachel. "It was about you, wasn't it? What was your name? Rosie the Raccoon?"

She grunted but didn't say anything. Nothing Rachel could say would make her feel better anyway. She just wanted to get home, clean her knees, and take a nap. That is, if Mom didn't have too many chores waiting for her to do.

When they arrived home a short time later, Jacob headed straight for the barn, and Rachel trudged wearily toward the house. She had just stepped onto the porch, when she noticed two of Mom's potted plants had been tipped over. Dirt was everywhere, and the plant stems were broken. She suspected her kitten had caused the mess, because Cuddles lay on the porch next to one of the pots, licking her dirty paws. Mom stood nearby, tapping her foot and clicking her tongue.

"Bad kitten!" Rachel scolded, shaking her finger in front of Cuddles's nose. "My whole Mondaag's gone bad, and now I come home to this?"

"What happened that made your Monday go bad?" Mom asked, looking concerned.

"More trouble with Orlie during school, and then I fell on the way home and skinned my knees." Rachel motioned to the overturned pot. "I'll change out of my school clothes and clean up this mess as soon as I've put some bandages on my knees."

"Would you like me to take a look at your knees?" Mom asked with a worried frown.

Rachel shook her head. "They're not so bad. I'll be all right." Rachel hurried up the stairs before her mother could ask any more questions. She figured if Mom knew the details of her horrible day, she would give her a lecture, and Rachel might even be given more chores to do.

By the time Rachel had bandaged her sore knees, changed out of her school clothes, and cleaned up the mess Cuddles had made on the porch, she was exhausted. Mom said Rachel could play until it was time to start supper, but Rachel was too tired to play. She decided to sit on the porch and blow bubbles with the metal wand Pap had given her for her birthday.

"At least nobody gave me a crumbly old cake that stuck to the pan and looked like it should have been fed to the *sei* [hogs]," Rachel grumbled, as she stared at the pan of soapy water sitting beside her on the porch.

"What was that about hogs?"

Rachel looked up and saw an elderly Amish man walking across the grass, carrying a black suitcase. He wore dark trousers held up by suspenders, a light blue shirt, and a straw hat. He walked with a slight limp, and his hair and beard were mostly gray.

He lifted his hand and waved. "*Wie geht's*—how are you?"

Rachel squinted against the glare of the sun as she stared at him.

The man stepped onto the porch and grinned at her. "Don't you know who I am, Rachel?"

"Grandpa Schrock?"

He nodded and sat beside her on the step. "Surprised to see me, are you?"

"Oh, jah. We didn't expect you'd be making the trip from Ohio until it was almost time for Esther's wedding."

"Thought I'd come to Pennsylvania a little sooner and surprise you." Grandpa patted Rachel's arm. "That will give me more time to spend with you and the family."

Rachel nodded. Grandpa Schrock's last visit had been a lot of fun. Rachel had been two years younger then, but she could still remember Grandpa sitting on the porch swing, sharing his bag of peanuts as he told her stories. Since he'd arrived almost a month before Esther's wedding, she figured they would have lots of time to do fun things together.

Mom stepped onto the porch with a curious look on her face. "I thought I heard voices, but I figured your daed and Henry were still in the fields, so—"

Grandpa turned toward her, and Mom's face broke into a huge smile. "Oh, Papa, what a surprise! Where did you come from?"

"Ohio. Where do you think?" he asked with a deep chuckle.

"Ach, you're such a tease." Mom and Grandpa hugged each other. Then Mom reached under her glasses to wipe away her tears. "We didn't expect you until the end of October, since Esther isn't getting married until the first Thursday of November."

"I decided to come early and surprise you. When my bus pulled into the station in Lancaster, I spotted one of your English neighbors and asked him to give me a ride over here." He hugged her again. "Are you glad to see me, daughter?"

Mom nodded. "Oh, jah, I'm always glad to see my daed."

Seeing the joy on her mother's face and knowing Grandpa would be with them for a whole month made Rachel smile, too. Maybe today wasn't such a bad Mondaag after all.

Chapter 7

More Surprises

For a little girl whose sister is getting married in a few days, you sure look sad," Grandpa said as he sat beside Rachel at the breakfast table one morning in late October. "Are you going to miss your big sister when she moves out of the house?"

Rachel glanced at Esther, who sat across from her. "I will miss my sister, but I'll miss you, too, Grandpa." For several days, Rachel had been thinking about the day Grandpa would return to Ohio, and how she wished he didn't have to go.

Grandpa's bushy, gray eyebrows lifted as he glanced at Pap and Mom. "Didn't either of you tell her my surprise?"

Mom shook her head. "We figured we should let you do the telling."

"Tell me what, Grandpa?" Rachel asked, leaning closer to him. "What surprise do you have?"

"I won't return to Ohio after Esther and Rudy's wedding."

Rachel's mouth dropped open. "You won't?"

"Nope. Your folks have invited me to live here. If you have no objections, I'll stay here for good."

Rachel thought this was such a wonderful surprise that she could hardly stay in her seat! Over the last few weeks, she and Grandpa had only spent a little time together. Now, with him staying permanently, they would have plenty of time together. They could do so many fun things—blow bubbles with Rachel's new wand, drive to the pond in one of Pap's buggies, take long walks to the stream, and tease Cuddles with string. Even having to put up with Orlie wouldn't seem as bad, because every day after school Grandpa would be waiting for Rachel at home.

Rachel reached over and took Grandpa's hand. "I'm real glad you're staying."

He grinned and squeezed her fingers. "Jah, me, too."

When Rachel arrived at school that morning, she received yet another surprise. A plump, red apple sat in the middle of her desk. She picked it up and turned to Mary. "Did you bring me this?"

Mary shook her head. "It was there when I came into the room."

Rachel opened the lid on her desk and placed the apple inside. She figured she would eat it at lunchtime.

Sometime later, Teacher Elizabeth announced that

it was time for lunch, and Rachel hurried to get her lunchbox. Since it was raining outside, everyone sat at their desks to eat their lunches.

As the rain beat against the schoolhouse windows, Rachel ate her peanut butter and jelly sandwich, followed by two chunky chocolate chip cookies. She washed them down with her thermos of milk. She was about to put her lunchbox away, when she remembered the plump red apple.

Rachel pulled the apple out of her desk and savored the first bite. *Umm. . .this is so sweet and juicy.*

"How's that apple taste?" Orlie asked, tapping Rachel on the shoulder.

She turned around. "It's good."

He grinned at her and blinked a couple of times. "I picked it from one of our apple trees this morning."

Rachel's mouth dropped open. A stream of apple juice dribbled down her chin. "You—you put the apple on my desk?"

"That's right. I put it on your desk early this morning, before you got to school."

"Why?"

"I wanted to surprise you."

Rachel was surprised, all right. Especially since Orlie hadn't said a word to her for several weeks. She hadn't spoken to him either. In fact, ever since the day Rachel and Orlie had written those fiction stories about each other, neither had said more than a few words to one another. It was better that way, Rachel decided—better for her, at least.

Rachel stared at the tasty apple. She'd never expected to get anything from Orlie—at least nothing nice. Maybe he was tired of making her life miserable and had decided to make amends. Maybe he wasn't such a bad fellow after all.

"Danki," she murmured.

"You're welcome." Orlie leaned forward a bit, and Rachel leaned backward—in case his mother had given him some garlic to eat again this morning. "I hear that your sister's gettin' married soon," he said.

"That's right. This Thursday."

He grinned. "Guess I'll see you there, 'cause my family and I have been invited to the wedding."

A sense of dread crept up Rachel's spine. Then she looked at the apple in her hand and decided having Orlie at the wedding might not be so bad. At least he was being nice now. It wasn't like she'd have to hang around him all day. *Crunch.* She took another bite of the apple. It sure was tasty.

Rachel bit into it again, only this time she felt something rubbery and slimy touch her lips. She wrinkled her nose and spit the piece of apple into her hand. "That is so ekelhaft!"

"What's so disgusting?"

"This!" Rachel's hand shook as she held it out so Orlie could see what she had almost eaten.

Orlie's eyebrows arched upwards. "Ach, there was a little critter in that apple."

Rachel gritted her teeth. "You gave me a wormy apple on purpose, didn't you?"

He shook his head. "How could I know a worm was inside?"

Rachel turned the apple over and studied it closely. Sure enough, she saw a small wormhole near the stem. How could she have been so stupid? She should have looked the apple over thoroughly before taking a bite. She should have known Orlie wouldn't have given her anything nice. He'd probably given her the wormy apple just to be mean.

She plunked the apple on Orlie's desk. "You are *uninvited* to Esther's wedding!"

He looked stunned. "Why?"

"Anyone who would give someone a wormy apple shouldn't be allowed to attend anyone's wedding."

"But, but. . .I—I didn't know. . . ."

"Humph! And I suppose you didn't know who you were writing about when you wrote that goofy story about Rosie the Raccoon?"

Orlie shrugged. "Knew it about as well as you knew who Otis the Horse was supposed to be."

Rachel whirled around and closed her lunchbox with a *snap*. Learning that Grandpa would be staying in Pennsylvania had been a good morning surprise. But receiving a wormy apple and hearing that Orlie planned to attend Esther's wedding were two afternoon surprises she could have done without!

As Rachel climbed out of bed on Thursday morning, excitement filled her soul. She'd spent several days helping Mom and Esther clean the house for Esther's wedding. Yesterday, many of their Amish friends had come to help, too. It had been a lot of work, but the house was now spotless, and everything was ready for the wedding.

Rachel skipped across the room in her bare feet, smiling. She wouldn't have to go to school today. All of the children who'd been invited to the wedding would also be excused. Not Orlie, though. He'd be sitting at his desk with plenty of work to do, because Rachel had uninvited him to her sister's wedding after he'd given her that wormy apple.

"It serves him right for being so mean," she muttered as she pulled her bottom dresser drawer open. Orlie needed to be taught a lesson, and Rachel hoped by missing Esther's wedding, he might learn that he couldn't go around teasing all the time without suffering the consequences of his actions.

Rachel picked up the small package wrapped in white tissue paper that she'd placed in her drawer. Then she tiptoed across the hall to Esther's bedroom.

"Come in," Esther called when Rachel knocked on the door.

Rachel stepped into the room and spotted Esther standing by her window. "Guder mariye, bride-to-be."

Esther turned to face Rachel. "Good morning. What do you have in your hands?"

"It's a wedding present for you," Rachel said, handing the package to her sister. "I made it myself."

Esther placed the gift on the bed, removed the wrapping, and lifted out a white hankie with a lacy edge. In one corner, Rachel had embroidered the letters E.K.—which would be Esther's initials after she married Rudy King.

"What a nice surprise," Esther said, hugging Rachel. "Danki so much."

"You're welcome." Rachel was pleased that her sister liked the gift. It had been a labor of love, since Rachel didn't like to sew much.

Esther motioned toward her door. "I guess we'd better go help Mom with breakfast now. Today's my big day, and I wouldn't want to be late for my own wedding."

Rachel giggled and followed her sister.

Downstairs, Mom scurried around the kitchen with a spatula in her hand. She halted and gave Esther a kiss on the cheek. "How's the bride feeling on this fine fall morning?"

Esther smiled, her cheeks turning pink as a rose. "I'm a bit *naerfich* [nervous], so you'd better give me something to do that will help settle my nerves."

Mom nudged Esther toward the table. "While I cook some oatmeal, you can help Rachel set the table."

"Okay, Mom." Esther's hands shook as she pulled paper napkins out of the basket in the center of the table.

"Why are you so nervous, sister?" Rachel asked. "You're shaking like a maple tree on a windy day."

"I'm nervous about marrying Rudy today."

"Then don't get married. Stay here with us."

"I love Rudy and want to marry him." Esther smiled. "Guess I'm really more excited than nervous."

"Every bride has a right to be nervous on her wedding day," Mom put in.

Rachel watched Esther place the napkins around the table, where each family member would sit. "I still don't see why Esther wants to get married," she said as she set spoons and knives on top of each napkin. "I'm never getting married. . .not ever!"

Mom chuckled. "You'll change your mind someday. Just wait and see."

At eight thirty sharp, more than one hundred guests filled the house to witness the marriage of Esther Yoder and Rudy King. Men and women sat on backless wooden benches in separate sections of the room, just as they did during their regular church services. After everyone was seated, Rudy's brother-in-law, Michael, announced the first song from the hymnbook called the *Ausbund*. On the third line of the song, the ministers stood and left the room. Rachel knew they were going upstairs to a room that had been prepared for them on the second floor. Rudy and Esther followed so they could receive counsel and words of encouragement before the ceremony. While they sang the second song, Rachel saw Orlie Troyer sitting across the room with some other boys.

She clenched her fingers into tight little balls in her lap. *What's he doing here? I told Orlie he was uninvited to Esther's wedding.*

Rachel spotted Orlie's mother sitting on the women's side, with Orlie's little sisters, Becky and Malinda. On the men's side, Orlie's father sat with Orlie's older brothers, Isaac, Jonas, and James, who were in their teens and had already finished school.

She sighed. *I guess if Orlie's family came today, they would expect him to be here, too. He probably never even told his folks I said he couldn't come. Sure hope he doesn't do anything to ruin my sister's wedding.*

Rachel's attention was drawn to the front of the room again when Esther and Rudy returned to their seats. The ministers entered a short time later, and Herman Lapp, one of the ministers, delivered the first sermon. Then came a time of silent prayer before the longer sermon, given by Bishop Wagler.

Rachel fidgeted on her bench. She wondered how much longer the ceremony would last. She thought about what she would say to Orlie after the wedding service.

When the bishop finally finished his sermon, he cleared his throat and said, "We have two people who have agreed to enter the state of matrimony, Rudy King and Esther Yoder." He paused and looked at the congregation. "If any here has objection, he now has the opportunity to make it known."

The room was so quiet Rachel thought she could have heard a feather fall to the floor. Surely no one would try and stop Esther and Rudy from getting married.

Bishop Wagler had just opened his mouth to speak again, when a streak of gray and white darted across the room.

Rachel gasped. "Oh, no. . .it's Cuddles, and she's after a maus!"

The cat zipped this way and that, swatting her paw every time she came near the mouse. The mouse zoomed under a bench on the men's side of the room. Grandpa reached down, trying to catch it in his hands. *Zip! Zip!* The mouse darted away, escaping not only Grandpa, but every other man who tried to capture it. Walter Troyer, Orlie's father, tried to stomp the poor mouse with his boot, but the tiny critter escaped to the women's side of the room.

"Ach, get away from me!" Anna Miller shouted, as the mouse ran across her shoes. Anna and the ladies near her screamed and jumped onto their bench.

Cuddles leaped into the air and landed in Sarah

King's lap. The elderly woman, who was Rudy's grandmother, turned white as snow and nearly fainted. Rachel's mother reached over to steady the poor woman.

"Everyone, please calm down!" Bishop Wagler shouted over the high-pitched screams. "Please take your seats and let the wedding continue."

Rachel knew the wedding couldn't continue until either the cat or the mouse had been caught. She did the only thing she could think to do—she jumped off her bench and chased after Cuddles. Round the room they went—the mouse going one way, the cat following, and Rachel right on its tail. Several men shouted directions.

Suddenly Orlie joined the chase. He dove for the mouse but missed. The critter darted right up Deacon Byler's leg.

Rachel gasped and grabbed her kitten as it scooted past. At least one problem was solved. She was about to haul Cuddles out the door when the mouse skittered up the deacon's chest, pitter-patted across his shoulders, and darted down his other pant leg.

The deacon grunted, and Orlie made another dive for the mouse. This time he grabbed it by the tail. The men nodded. The women sighed. Rachel just stood there, shaking her head. She figured Orlie had only tried to capture the mouse so he would look good in everyone's eyes.

He probably brought the mouse into the house in the first place, Rachel thought. *He probably just wanted to play another trick on me.*

As Rachel went out the door with Cuddles in her arms, she mumbled, "I wish Orlie Troyer would move back to Indiana."

Chapter 8

Misadventures

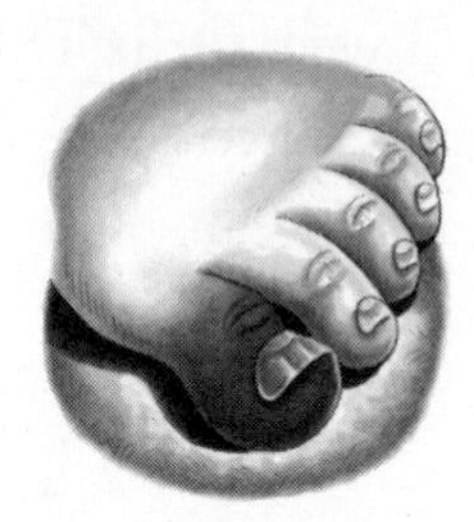

Rachel kicked a small stone with the toe of her sneaker as she headed to the chicken coop. She felt fretful, but not because of her chores. She dreaded going to school the day after Esther's wedding and facing Orlie again.

Rachel had been scolded by both Mom and Pap because her cat had disrupted the wedding. After Cuddles and the mouse had been put outside, the rest of the ceremony had been fine. Rachel had tried to explain that the cat had probably entered with guests who came into the house, but Pap had been quick to remind her that Cuddles should have been locked in the basement during the wedding.

As far as Rachel was concerned, the whole episode had been Orlie's fault. She was sure he'd brought the mouse into the house in order to cause an uproar.

Rachel entered the chicken coop and held her nose. She didn't want to be in this smelly building any longer than she had to. She opened the bag of grain, scooped some out with a dipper, and filled each feeding tray. Next it was time to give the chickens water.

Rachel picked up a watering dish and stepped out of the coop. Then she rinsed out the container, filled it with fresh water, and hurried back across the yard.

Squawk! Squawk! Rachel had just stepped back into the coop, when a chicken flapped its wings and flew up in her face. As Rachel tried to shoo the chicken away, the dish flipped out of her hand, and water went everywhere. "Oh, no. Now I have to start all over," she moaned.

Rachel had only taken a few steps toward the door, when her foot slipped on the slimy, wet floor. "*Umph!*" She landed hard. Clucking chickens flew everywhere, bumping into Rachel, pecking at each other, and sending feathers flying in every direction.

"Always trouble somewhere," Rachel grumbled.

She scrambled to her feet and stared at her rumpled, wet dress. Now she would have to change clothes before school.

Rachel went back outside to fill the watering dish, only this time she carefully screwed on the lid.

When Rachel was heading back to the house, she heard a horse whinny. Maybe she had enough time to say hello to old Tom.

Rachel scampered to the fence separating their yard from the pasture. "Come on, Tom. Come and get your nose rubbed."

Nee–eee. Tom pawed at the ground.

Rachel climbed onto the fence and leaned over, extending her hand. "Come over to me, boy. I can't reach you from here."

Nee–ee! Nee–ee! The horse continued to paw at the ground.

"What's the matter with you, Tom?" Rachel waited to see what Tom would do, but he wouldn't budge.

Grunting, Rachel lifted one leg and eased herself over the fence. Once her feet touched the ground, she moved over to stand beside the horse. "Easy, boy. Easy, now," she said, reaching out to touch Tom.

He bent his head and nuzzled her hand.

"Sorry, but I don't have a treat for you this morning. Guess I should have brought a sugar cube or an apple for you, huh?"

Tom whinnied and bounced his head up and down, as though agreeing with her.

A field mouse scampered through the grass at Rachel's feet, reminding her of the mouse at Esther's wedding. Her fingers curled into her palms until they dug into her flesh. *Orlie should be punished for doing that, and for giving me that wormy apple the other day, too.*

"Guess I'd better get back to the house now," Rachel said, giving Tom another pat. "I'll come visit you again soon."

Suddenly, the mean old goose that sometimes chased Rachel waddled up to Tom, squawking and pecking at the horse's legs. Tom flicked his ears, sidestepped, and kicked his back leg out at the goose. The goose flapped her wings and screeched. When Tom's foot came down, it landed right on the toe of Rachel's sneaker. She squealed and jumped out of Tom's way. So much for doing her good deed for the day.

"Every time I try to do something nice, things go bad," she muttered as she limped away.

By the time Rachel got back to the house, her foot hurt so bad she could barely stand.

"What's wrong, Rachel?" Mom asked when Rachel hopped into the kitchen. "Did you hurt yourself in the chicken coop?"

Rachel shook her head as tears filled her eyes. She had been able to keep from crying until she saw the look of sympathy on Mom's face. Now she wanted to dissolve into a puddle of tears. "I—I went out to the pasture to see Tom, then the crazy old goose came along and—"

"Did that cantankerous critter attack you like she did this summer? Because if she did, I'll have your daed put her down."

"The goose didn't attack me. She was after old Tom." Rachel hobbled to a chair at the table. "Tom kicked out at her, and his foot landed on my toe." She sniffed. "It hurts something awful."

Mom knelt in front of Rachel and removed the sneaker and black stocking on Rachel's right foot.

Rachel gasped when she saw how terrible her big toe looked. Not only was it swollen, but it was purple. "No wonder it hurts so bad," she whimpered. "Do—do you think it's broken?"

Mom's glasses had slipped to the middle of her nose. She pushed them back in place as she studied Rachel's toe. "It could be, but we can't do much for a broken toe. We'll need to put ice on it. And you'll need to stay off that foot for a few days."

Rachel's mood brightened. "Does that mean I don't have to go to school today?"

Mom nodded. "Since this is Friday, you'll have the weekend to rest your toe. You should feel up to going to school by Monday."

Rachel didn't like the pain shooting from her toe all the way up her leg. But if it meant missing school today, she was glad it had happened. She'd avoid seeing Orlie. She could also lie on the sofa all day with her foot propped on pillows and read her favorite book.

Mom rose to her feet. "Your daed's still doing chores with Grandpa and the boys. I'll have him carry you upstairs to your room as soon as he comes in."

"Can't I lie on the sofa in the living room?"

Mom's forehead wrinkled. "Oh, I don't know, Rachel. Jacob will be at school, but everyone else will be busy all day getting rid of the mess from yesterday. And we still have to clean the living room."

"I won't be in the way, I promise."

Mom shook her head. "I think it would be best if you stay in your room."

Rachel didn't argue. She was so glad to stay home from school that it really didn't matter where she spent the day.

Rachel reclined on her bed with her foot propped on two thick pillows and an ice bag resting on her toe. She thought about all the fun things she wished she could be doing. Even helping Mom, Pap, Grandpa, Esther, and Rudy clean the house would be better than lying alone with nothing to do but stare at the ceiling. She couldn't even play with Cuddles, because after what had happened yesterday, Mom had banned Rachel's cat from the house until further notice.

Rachel glanced at the clock on the table by her bed. She wondered what her classmates were doing right now. *Probably spelling,* she thought with regret. Spelling was Rachel's favorite subject. She always did well whenever she had a spelling test.

"How are things going?" Mom asked, poking her head into Rachel's room.

Rachel shrugged. "I'm bored. I don't have anything to do. I wish I could be downstairs with everyone else."

"Maybe later, after we finish cleaning." Mom lifted the ice bag from Rachel's toe and squinted. "Looks like the swelling's going down, but you need to stay off that foot for the rest of the day." She turned toward the door.

"I'll refill your ice bag."

"Danki."

Several minutes later, Mom returned. Besides the ice bag, she held the small sewing kit she'd given Rachel for her birthday. "Since you're bored, I thought you could do some mending for me."

Mom placed the sewing kit on the table by Rachel's bed and handed her one of Pap's socks with a hole in it.

Rachel frowned as she laid the sock beside her on the bed. "Oh, Mom. . .do I have to?"

Mom nodded and headed across the room, calling over her shoulder, "Pap will carry you down when it's time for lunch."

The door clicked shut, and Rachel sighed. She didn't care much for sewing, because she still couldn't sew a straight seam. Well, maybe it didn't matter how well she sewed, since no one would see the mended hole in Pap's sock.

Rachel reached for her sewing kit, threaded the needle, tied a knot, and picked up the sock. In and out, in and out, the needle went, until the hole finally disappeared. Her stitching was uneven and thicker in some parts than others, but at least she'd finished the job. Now she only needed to cut the thread and tie a knot. She picked up the scissors and held the sock up where she could see the tiny thread. *Snip.* "Rats! I missed." She tried once more. *Snip.* She missed again.

"What's wrong with me?" Rachel wailed. "Can't I do

anything right today?" She leaned closer and lifted the scissors for the third time. *Snip.* The thread still clung to the needle, but a piece of white ribbon lay in her lap.

Rachel reached up and touched the ties on her kapp. One tie was shorter than the other. "Oh, no! Now what have I done? I never should have gone to visit old Tom this morning." She flopped onto her pillow and thought about her horrible day. If only she'd returned to the house after feeding and watering the chickens, she wouldn't have gotten her toe stepped on. She would be in school right now, not sitting here looking at the tie she had cut by mistake. Even putting up with Orlie's teasing might have been better than sewing alone in her room. This was not a good day!

Chapter 9

Woolly Worm

"How's your toe feel today?" Grandpa asked as he took a seat on the porch beside Rachel on Sunday afternoon. Today was an off Sunday from church, so Rachel's parents had gone with Jacob and Henry to call on Grandpa and Grandma Yoder. Grandpa Schrock didn't want to go, and Rachel had decided to stay home with him.

"It's a little better now," Rachel said, removing her slipper and lifting her foot.

Grandpa leaned forward and squinted. "Hmm . . .still looks kind of purple, but the swelling's gone down. Think you'll be ready to go to school tomorrow?"

She shrugged. "My foot will be ready, but I'm not sure I will."

"Why?"

"I'm not looking forward to seeing Orlie again."

"He's that boy in your class who teases you, right?"

Rachel nodded.

Grandpa pursed his lips. "It seems you might do best to ignore the fellow."

"I've tried that and it doesn't work. Orlie keeps doing things to annoy me."

"Have you prayed about it, Rachel?" Grandpa asked, placing his hand on her shoulder.

She shook her head slowly, ashamed to admit that she hadn't prayed. She'd been so angry with Orlie she hadn't thought to pray about the matter.

Grandpa gently squeezed her shoulder. "When I was a boy my mamm always told me that prayer was the key to each new day and the lock for every night. There isn't much of anything that shouldn't be given to God in prayer."

"I guess you're right," Rachel said. "I'll try to remember to pray about Orlie."

Grandpa smiled. "Good girl." He meandered across the porch and plucked something off the wooden rail. "Well, well. . .what do you know?"

"What is it, Grandpa?"

"It's a woolly worm," he said, extending his hand out to her. "I used to see a lot of these in Holmes County, Ohio."

Rachel shrugged. "What's so special about a woolly worm? It's just an orange and black fuzzy caterpillar."

"Oh, no, Rachel. . .there's more to woolly worms than their color." Grandpa sat in the wicker chair again and closed his hand, trapping the woolly worm inside.

"Like what?" she asked.

"I was thinking about the woolly races."

Rachel tipped her head to one side. "Woolly races? What are those?"

"The woolly races involve a contest that's held in October during Charm Days." Grandpa uncurled his fingers and let the woolly worm creep around in his hand. "As many as eighty kinner take part in a contest to see whose woolly worm can be the first to make it to the top of a heavy piece of string." He chuckled, and Rachel noticed a twinkle in his blue eyes. "It's truly funny to see those youngsters clap, blow, whistle, and sing, trying to get their woolly worms up that string."

Feeling excitement zip up her spine, Rachel jumped out of the chair. "Got any ideas where I could find more woolly worms?"

"I might. Why?"

"I could take them to school and have a contest during recess."

Grandpa nodded and rose to his feet. "Sounds like a good idea to me." He faced Rachel, his expression becoming serious. "You'll have to abide by one important rule, though."

"What rule is that?"

"No touching the worm with your hands to make him move up the string."

Rachel nodded as her excitement grew. "I'll make sure everyone who takes part in the race knows that rule."

"I have something fun planned for recess this morning," Rachel said to Jacob as they headed for school on Monday morning.

"Oh, yeah? What?"

"I'm going to have a woolly worm race."

"A what?"

"A woolly worm race. Yesterday Grandpa told me about a contest that involves racing woolly worms. He helped me find a bunch of woolly caterpillars, and I've got eleven of them right here," Rachel said, lifting her lunchbox.

Jacob wrinkled his nose. "You put caterpillars in your lunchbox?"

She nodded.

"I hope you don't plan to eat them, Rachel."

"Of course not, silly. I'm going to have a woolly worm race during recess. The ten woolly worms the other kids will race are inside a cottage cheese carton in my lunchbox." She grinned. "I put Speedy in a yogurt cup by himself."

"Speedy?"

"That's right. Since Speedy's the fastest caterpillar we found, I've decided to race him."

Jacob rolled his eyes and shook his head. "What a bensel you are, little sister."

Rachel didn't bother to argue. She figured Jacob was probably jealous because he hadn't thought to have a woolly worm race at school. He'd see soon enough how much fun racing woolly worms could be.

When they entered the schoolyard, Rachel felt more and more excited. She and Grandpa had spent several hours searching for woolly worms. They'd looked under piles of leaves, in the compost heap behind Mom's vegetable garden, and behind a tree's bark. They'd even found a couple of worms by the side of the road. Rachel was sure the school children would enjoy the woolly worm race. Since she'd practiced the day before with Speedy, she was sure she would win.

At the school, Rachel opened her lunchbox. She placed the cottage cheese and yogurt containers on the floor under her desk. That way the woolly worms would have more air to breath through the tiny holes she'd poked in the lids. Teacher Elizabeth didn't seem to notice what Rachel was doing, as she was busy writing the math lesson on the blackboard.

"I brought something fun with me this morning," Rachel whispered when Mary sat down across from her.

Mary leaned over as far as she could. "What is it?"

"You'll find out at recess."

Mary shrugged and turned to face the front of the class, where Elizabeth stood with a Bible in her hands. Rachel barely listened as their teacher read from God's Word. She could only think about Speedy and the race she was sure he would win for her. It was hard to concentrate on the lesson after the time of prayer and singing. At recess time, Rachel reached under her desk, grabbed both containers, and bounded from the room.

"May I have your attention, everyone?" she shouted as she stood in the middle of the schoolyard.

A few girls and Orlie came over to see what Rachel wanted. Most of the boys, including Jacob, ignored her and kept playing.

"What's up, Rachel?" Mary asked, scrunching her nose.

"Are you planning to eat lunch early today?" Orlie laughed and pointed to the cottage cheese and yogurt containers in her hands. "Do you want us to watch you eat it, huh?"

She scowled. "What I have inside these containers is much better than cottage cheese or yogurt."

"What do you have?" Aaron King asked. "Is it something to eat?"

Rachel shook her head. "It's woolly worms. I brought them so we can have a contest."

"What kind of contest?" Phoebe Wagler, the bishop's granddaughter, wanted to know.

"It's a race to see whose woolly worm will reach the top of the string first."

Orlie's eyebrows furrowed. "What string? I don't see any string." He turned to face Mary. "Do you see any string?"

Mary shook her head, then looked at Rachel with questioning eyes. "What string are you talking about?"

"This." Rachel reached into her jacket pocket and

pulled out a ball of heavy string. "We can cut it into long pieces. Then we'll tie one end to the top fence rail and the other end to the bottom rail. We'll each set our woolly worm on the string and see which one gets to the top first."

"But I don't have a woolly worm," Aaron said with a frown.

"Me neither," Mary put in.

Rachel lifted the cottage cheese carton. "They're right here. You can take your pick."

"What's inside the yogurt cup?" Orlie asked.

"That's Speedy. . .my woolly worm."

"Speedy, huh?" Orlie slowly shook his head. "I'll bet I can make any worm in that cottage cheese carton beat yours anytime."

"Bet you can't."

"Bet I can."

"Bet you can't."

"Bet I—"

Her cousin Mary stepped between them. "You're wasting time arguing. Just race the worms and see who wins."

"Good idea." Rachel marched across the schoolyard to the fence. With a few quick snips of the scissors she'd put in her pocket, she cut several pieces of string.

"Who wants to pick a worm?" she asked, opening the cottage cheese container.

Aaron jumped up and down. "I do! I do!"

"Me, too," Mary echoed.

"I'll take one," Phoebe said with a nod.

Soon, several other children had chosen a woolly worm to race.

"How about you, Orlie?" Rachel asked. "Aren't you going to pick one?"

He nodded. "Jah, sure. I was just waiting for everyone else to choose so you didn't think I'd gotten the best one, that's all."

Rachel opened the lid on the yogurt container. "As far as I'm concerned, Speedy's the best. He's fast! You'll see."

"Jah, well, I'll bet my worm can beat him." Orlie reached into the container and plucked out a fat woolly worm. "This critter's name is Tiger. He's gonna beat every woolly worm here."

"We'll see about that." Rachel held up her hand. "Now, the rules are this: You can clap, sing, whistle, or blow on your worm to get him to move. But you can't touch him with your hands."

Everyone nodded in agreement.

"Okay, now, let's tie those strings to the fence and start the race!"

A few minutes later, ten children had lined up along the fence with woolly worms. Many of the scholars who had shown no interest in the contest now watched on the sidelines.

"Want me to signal when to start?" Jacob asked, stepping up to Rachel.

She shrugged. "Someone has to, so it may as well be you."

"All right then." Jacob cupped his hands around his mouth and breathed deeply. "One. . .two. . .three. . .go!"

Rachel put Speedy at the bottom of her string, tipped her head, and blew on his furry little body. "Go, Speedy. Get up that string, and be quick about it."

Mary clapped her hands and hollered, "*Dummle* [Hurry], slowpoke. Hurry now, please."

Aaron King sang a silly song to try and get his worm to move. "Woolly, woolly, ding-dong-ding; woolly, woolly, you make me sing. Woolly, woolly, now do your thing; woolly, woolly, I'll soon be king."

Rachel's worm was halfway up the string when she heard several children shouting and clapping. "Go, Tiger, go! *Schnell*—quickly!"

She stopped blowing on Speedy to glance at Orlie and almost gagged. He had his mouth open and was nudging the woolly worm with his tongue.

Rachel wrinkled her nose. "That's so disgusting. Besides, you're cheating, Orlie."

"Am not," he said in a muffled voice. His tongue was still out. He sounded like a baby trying to talk. "You said no touching with your hands, not your tongue."

He glanced at her out of the corner of his eye.

Rachel wasn't sure if Orlie's worm was crawling so fast because Orlie was coaxing it with his tongue, or if the woolly worm moved along quickly in order to get away from Orlie's garlic breath. Rachel leaned over and blew so hard on Speedy that he nearly fell off the string. "I'm going to win this race, and I'll do it fair and square!" she shouted.

"That's what you think." Orlie wore a satisfied smile as he prompted his worm with the end of his pointy tongue.

The children clapped and hollered—some cheered for Rachel, and others shouted for Orlie's woolly to win. Rachel was so busy blowing on Speedy and watching Tiger that she didn't even notice how the other children's worms were doing. Not until Aaron sang out, "My woolly won! My woolly won! We made it to the top. Jah, we're done!"

Rachel looked and her mouth dropped open. Sure enough, his woolly had reached the top of the string, two inches ahead of Rachel's, and at least one inch in front of Orlie's. "But—but I was sure my woolly would win," she mumbled.

"Oh, how sad." Orlie pretended to wipe tears from his eyes. Rachel gritted her teeth.

Everyone cheered, and Aaron bowed. "What's my prize for winning this woolly worm race?"

Everyone looked at Rachel. Her forehead wrinkled. She'd been so busy planning the race and thinking she would win that she hadn't even thought of a prize. "Well, I—"

"How about some chocolate chip cookies?" Elizabeth asked. She stepped up to Aaron and touched the top of his head.

His dark eyes widened, and he licked his lips. "You got some, Teacher?"

Elizabeth smiled. "Sure do. I brought chocolate chip cookies as a treat for the class today. Since your woolly won, I think I'll give you a few extra." She smiled at Rachel. "The woolly worm race was a good idea. How about if we do it again some other time?"

Rachel nodded. The race hadn't gone quite the way she'd wanted, but everyone seemed to enjoy it. Even though Speedy hadn't reached the top of the string first, at least Orlie and his pointy red tongue hadn't won.

Chapter 10

Substitute Teacher

When Rachel entered the schoolhouse one Friday morning, she was surprised to see Aaron King's aunt, Lovina, sitting at the teacher's desk. Lovina was a tall, thin woman who had never married. She still lived at home with her elderly parents. She had dark brown hair and almond-shaped eyes that were also brown. Rachel knew Lovina could be very stern. She wondered what Lovina was doing at the teacher's desk, and where Elizabeth was.

"Good morning, boys and girls," Lovina said after everyone sat down. "I'll be your teacher for the next several weeks."

Rachel's mouth dropped open. No, this couldn't be. She didn't want a substitute teacher.

When Lovina opened her Bible for the morning reading, Rachel raised her hand.

"What is it, Rachel?"

"Where's Elizabeth?"

"Her grandmother in Tennessee is ill. So Elizabeth has gone to help out." Lovina leaned slightly forward, with her elbows resting on the desk. "I'll be teaching your class until she gets back, sometime after Christmas."

Christmas? Rachel couldn't believe Elizabeth would be gone that long. What about the Christmas program? Would that be canceled if Elizabeth was still in Tennessee? Rachel felt badly that her teacher's grandmother was sick, but she wondered why Sharon Smucker, Elizabeth's helper, couldn't teach the class in her absence. However, she didn't ask the question. No point in saying something that might upset Lovina.

Rachel looked at Mary to get her reaction, but Mary gazed straight ahead.

Rachel sighed. She hoped Elizabeth's grandma would get well very soon, so Elizabeth could return to Pennsylvania before Christmas.

Rachel felt a tap on her shoulder, and she turned around. "Little bensel, didn't you hear what the teacher said?" Orlie asked, wiggling his eyebrows.

"I—I guess not. What'd she say?"

"We're supposed to stand and recite the Lord's Prayer."

"Oh." Rachel pushed her chair back and stood. She had not only missed hearing the Bible reading, but she hadn't even heard Lovina announce that it was time to recite their morning prayer.

Rachel had a hard time concentrating on the prayer. It was even harder to keep her mind on the songs after that. It didn't help that Orlie stood beside her, blowing garlic breath in her face. Finally the scholars returned to their seats.

"This morning, before we begin our lessons," the teacher said with a nod, "I want to give everyone their parts for the Christmas play next month."

Rachel thought about the program the scholars always put on for their families shortly before Christmas. Last year, she had recited a poem. The year before that she'd sung a song with some other children. She wondered what her part in the program would be this year. She hoped she would be given something easy to say.

"Since Elizabeth won't be here, I'll be in charge of the program this year," the substitute teacher said. "We'll have some singing, recitations, and a few of you will act out the Nativity scene. The play I have written includes parts for Mary, Joseph, five shepherds, and two angels."

"What about the baby Jesus?" Lovina's nephew Aaron hollered without raising his hand. "Won't there be a part for Him, too?"

"We won't use a real baby," Lovina said, shaking her head. "And from now on, please raise your hand if you have a question."

Aaron's face turned cherry red and he slunk low in his seat. Rachel was glad she wasn't the one getting in trouble with the teacher or being embarrassed in front of the class. She'd had enough of that in the last few months.

Phoebe Byler lifted her hand.

Lovina nodded at Phoebe. "Yes?"

"How about using a faceless doll to play Baby Jesus' part?" Phoebe suggested. "I've got an old doll we can use."

"I have one, too!" Becky Esh shouted. She covered her mouth with her hand. "Oops. . .sorry for not raising my hand, Teacher."

Lovina nodded, and a smile tugged at the corners of her mouth. "We can talk about that later. Right now I want to assign your parts. Then, after lunch, we'll begin practicing for the program."

She walked to the blackboard, picked up a piece of chalk, and wrote the words "CHRISTMAS PROGRAM" in capital letters. "If you don't see your name on the blackboard, that means you'll either have a poem to recite or you'll be part of the group that will sing a few songs."

Rachel watched with interest as Lovina wrote "Angels" on the board. Under that, she listed: "Phoebe Byler, Mary Yoder." Next, Lovina wrote "Shepherds," followed by five names: "Jacob Yoder, Aaron King, Harvey Esh, Abner Clemmons, and Noah Stoltzfus."

Jacob will be happy to get the part of a shepherd, Rachel

thought. She looked across the room and noticed that he was smiling. *He likes petting Grandpa Yoder's sheep. Maybe he'll be allowed to bring a sheep to the program so the play will seem more realistic.*

Rachel felt a nudge in her back, and she turned sharply. "Quit poking me, Orlie," she said through clenched teeth.

"Looks like we'll be workin' together," he said, pointing to the blackboard.

Rachel looked at the chalkboard and nearly choked. The word "Mary" was written there, with Rachel's name underneath. But even worse was what was written beside that. It said: "Joseph," by the name "Orlie Troyer."

Rachel slunk farther down in her seat than Aaron had. Playing the part of Mary with Orlie as Joseph was the worst thing she could imagine. She had to figure a way out of it quickly. She raised her hand and waved it.

Lovina nodded at Rachel. "Yes?"

"Can't I do a recitation like I did last year? I'll even write my own poem if that would help."

Lovina shook her head. "I chose the parts based on who I thought would fit the roles best, and I picked you to play Mary."

"Oh, but my cousin's name is Mary, so shouldn't she be the one to play the part of baby Jesus' mother?"

Lovina took a seat behind her desk. "I've made my decision on who gets what parts. Now it's time to begin lessons, so please open your books."

Rachel went through the rest of the morning feeling as if she had a bale of hay sitting on top of her head. She couldn't play the part of Mary in the Christmas program! Not with Orlie as Joseph! Orlie didn't like her; that was clear as glass. And she didn't care for him, either.

Rachel had seen other Christmas programs where the Nativity scene was acted out, so she knew what would be required of her in the role of Mary. She would have to sit on a stool behind a small wooden manager, and Joseph would be expected to stand right beside her. Just the thought of practicing every day with Orlie and sitting beside him during the program twisted Rachel's stomach in knots.

Maybe I could let old Tom step on my toe again, she thought as she returned to the schoolhouse after lunch recess. *Then my foot would be too sore to come to school.* She shook her head. That wouldn't work. When Mom heard that Rachel had been given the part of Mary, she would probably drive her to school in one of Pap's buggies every day, just so she could be there to practice, sore toe or not.

Rachel tapped her chin with the end of her pencil as she pondered the predicament she was in. If she prayed real hard, maybe Elizabeth's grandma would get well soon. Then Elizabeth could return to teaching school before the program. Surely Elizabeth would let Rachel out of being Mary. Or maybe Rachel could figure out some way to get exposed to the chicken pox or measles the week of the program. Then she'd be home sick in bed that day, not sitting beside Orlie in front of everyone she knew, feeling nervous about the possibility of forgetting her lines. What if Orlie decided to play a trick on her during the program? Why, the kids in class would make fun of her for weeks.

"All right now, scholars," Lovina announced. "I'm going to separate you into groups in order to practice for the Christmas program." She pointed to Mary and then to Phoebe. "You two angels can practice over there." She motioned to the left side of the room, and when Phoebe and Mary stood, Lovina handed them each a slip of paper. "Here are your lines, girls. They aren't hard, so you should be able to memorize them easily."

Next, she pointed to Jacob and the other shepherds. She instructed them to take their parts and practice at the back of the room.

Finally, Lovina nodded at Rachel and Orlie. "You two can practice your lines over there." She motioned to the corner of the room where the woodstove sat.

Rachel forced herself to walk to the teacher's desk. She took the slips of paper with hers and Orlie's parts and plodded across the room. She stared at the stove, wishing she could open the door and toss the paper into the burning flames. She figured that probably wouldn't do any good. The determined substitute would probably print another set of lines for Rachel and Orlie.

Orlie sauntered over to stand by Rachel, wearing a smug expression. "It'll be fun to have the best parts in the Christmas program, won't it?"

Fun for you maybe, because you can make my life miserable. Rachel plastered a smile on her face. For her, playing the part of Mary would be sheer torture.

As Rachel walked home from school that afternoon, she could only think about how awful it was to have a substitute teacher and how miserable she felt knowing Orlie would play Joseph. Throughout their practice time, Orlie had made wisecracks and messed up his lines just to confuse Rachel. While walking home, she usually enjoyed listening to the birds in the trees, looking for unusual shrubs, and watching the cars zip past. Not today.

"Why do you look so disagreeable?" Jacob asked, punching Rachel's arm. "You look like you've been sucking on sour grapes."

"I'm not happy about playing Mary in the Christmas program."

"Why?"

"Do you really have to ask?" Rachel groaned. "Orlie's playing Joseph, and you know Orlie and I don't get along."

"Maybe that's because you don't try hard enough to like him."

"I've tried every way I know to be nice to that ornery fellow. He always does something to get me riled," she answered.

"I'm sure that's why he does it." Jacob jabbed Rachel again. "I still think Orlie has a crush on you."

"He does not."

"Does so."

Rachel started to run. "Does not!" she called over her shoulder.

"Hey, wait! You know you're not supposed to walk home alone."

"I'm not walking; I'm running."

By the time Rachel reached home, she was panting, but she felt a little better about things. Maybe it was because she'd gotten her adrenaline pumping. Teacher Elizabeth had said once that exercise was healthy. She said it could help relieve stress because exercise released pain-killing hormones called "endorphins."

Maybe on the day of the Christmas program, I'll run to the schoolhouse, Rachel thought. *Then I'll have plenty of endorphins and won't feel so nervous.*

Chapter 11
Unexpected News

The sweet smell of sausage cooking on the stove drew Rachel into the kitchen one Monday morning in late November. "I'm so hungry I could eat a whole hog," she told her mother, who was cracking eggs into a bowl. "Will breakfast be ready soon?"

Mom nodded.

Rachel stepped close to the stove and sniffed the sausage links in the iron skillet. "Umm. . .those sure smell wunderbaar. Don't you just love the taste of sausage, Mom?"

Mom let out a feeble cry, covered her mouth with her hand, and darted out the back door.

Rachel stared after her mother and shook her head. "Now that's sure strange. I wonder what Mom's problem could be?"

A few minutes later, Jacob entered the kitchen, carrying an armload of kindling. "Mom's on the porch.

She said to ask you to watch the sausage cooking on the stove," he said. He dropped wood into the box beside the woodstove they used for heat during the winter months.

"Why do I have to do it? Isn't Mom coming back to finish cooking breakfast?"

"I think she's got a *bauchweh* [stomachache]."

"Mom's got a stomachache?" Rachel asked, feeling sudden concern.

Jacob shrugged. "I think so. She was holding her stomach, and her face looked almost as white as that snow coming down."

Rachel's eyes widened. "It's snowing?"

"Sure is."

Rachel rushed to the window and peeked through the frosty glass. Sure enough, big flakes dropped from the sky like fluffy cotton. "Oh, boy, maybe it will snow so hard we won't have to go to school today," she exclaimed. Then she remembered what Jacob had said about Mom having a stomachache, and her concerns returned. "I hope Mom's not getting the achy bones flu. She hardly ever gets sick."

Jacob nodded and pointed to the stove, where the sausage sizzled. "You'd better tend to those, don't you think?"

"Jah, sure." Rachel raced over to the stove, flipped the sausage links over with a fork, and turned to Jacob again. "Shouldn't you go back outside and check on

Mom? Or do you want to watch the sausage while I see if she's okay?"

Jacob grunted. "I'll check on Mom. If I tried to cook, I'd probably end up burning the sausage." He hurried out the door.

"Sure hope Mom's not sick." Rachel sighed and scrambled the eggs her mother had broken into a bowl. Then she poured them into an empty frying pan near the stove.

Mom returned to the kitchen a few minutes later, but her face looked pale. She walked across the room shakily.

"Jacob says you have a stomachache, and you don't look well, Mom," Rachel said. "Maybe it would be a good idea if you went back to bed."

"No need for that." Mom smiled and shook her head. "What's ailing me is nothing to worry about, daughter. *Sis mir iwwel.* [I am sick at my stomach.]"

Rachel's eyes widened. "You're sick at the stomach?"

"Jah. I felt like I could throw up while I was fixing breakfast, so I ran outside." Mom pulled out a chair at the table and dropped into it. "I'm in the family way, that's all."

Rachel gasped. She had heard others say "in the family way" and knew it meant that someone was going to have a baby. But she never expected her mother to be in the family way. "Mom, are—are you sure?"

Mom nodded. "I'm quite sure. I've had four bopplin,

so I think I know when I'm going to have another."

Rachel shook her head. "But—but Mom, at your age, I—I mean, I thought you were done having babies."

Mom crooked one eyebrow, and her glasses slipped to the end of her nose. "Are you saying I'm too old to have a boppli?"

Rachel flushed with embarrassment. "Sorry, Mom. I didn't mean it to sound that way. I don't think you're old. It's just that. . .well, I'm ten years old. I'm too old to have a baby sister, don't you think?"

"Whether you're too old or not, next summer, you'll be a big sister." Mom chuckled and patted her stomach. "And don't get used to the idea that you might have a baby sister. It could be a boy, you know."

Rachel thought of their neighbor, Anna Miller, who had ten children. One was still a baby. Anna always looked tired and always had so much to do. If Mom had a baby to care for, she'd be tired and busy, too. She probably wouldn't have time for Rachel anymore.

"I've had the morning sickness for a few weeks, but today was the worst." Mom reached for Rachel's hand. "Can I count on you to be my big helper?"

Rachel nodded. Maybe now, Mom and everyone else in the family would see her as a grown-up who should be allowed to do things she couldn't do before.

When Rachel arrived at school that morning, she noticed several boys having a snowball fight. With an enthusiastic yelp, Jacob joined them. Rachel went to find her cousin. She discovered Mary playing on the swings. She sat in the swing beside Mary and began to pump her legs to get the swing moving fast.

"Were you surprised to see the snow this morning?" Mary asked, catching snowflakes on her tongue.

"Jah, but I had an even bigger surprise than that." Rachel grunted. "In fact, it was news I never expected—not in a million years."

"Oh? What?"

"My mamm's going to have a boppli sometime this summer."

Mary's eyes grew wide. "Is that true, or are you teasing?"

"Of course it's true. Do you think I would make something up like that?"

"I—I guess not." Mary stopped swinging and faced Rachel. "You know what this means, don't you?"

"Jah," Rachel said, as she slowed her swing. "It means a lot more work for me. That's what it means."

"I suppose it will. But that's not what I was going to say."

"What then?"

"You'll no longer be the boppli in your family."

Rachel nodded. "That's right, I won't. And when the baby comes, I hope Mom, Pap, and everyone else will stop treating me like I'm a little girl."

"You are still a girl," Mary reminded. "But since the

baby will be smaller, maybe your family will treat you like you're more grown up in some ways."

"I hope that's how it goes." Rachel frowned. "I'm worried about Mom."

"How come?"

"She's been feeling sick to her stomach. This morning when she was fixing breakfast, she almost threw up."

Mary slowly shook her head. "Sorry to hear that. Feeling like you could throw up is *baremlich* [terrible]."

"I know it's terrible," Rachel agreed. "I've never liked being sick. If having a baby means getting sick, it's just one more reason why I'll never get married."

Mary poked Rachel's arm. "You say that, but I bet when you meet the right fellow, you'll change your mind about getting married and becoming a mamm."

"Humph!" Rachel folded her arms. "All the boys I know like to tease and make my life miserable. It's not likely I'll ever marry any of them."

"As my mamm often says, 'One never knows what the future holds.' "

Rachel opened her mouth to reply, but *splat!* A snowball landed on her head.

"All right, who's the *galgedieb* [scoundrel] who did that?" she shouted. A trickle of melting snow dribbled down her nose and onto her chin.

"There's your scoundrel," Mary said, pointing to Orlie Troyer. He stood a few feet away with a guilty look on his face. "He looks like a *nixnutzich* [naughty] child."

"He *is* a naughty child." Rachel gritted her teeth. "I may have to be Orlie's wife in our Christmas play, but I don't have to put up with this!" She jumped off the swing, packed a handful of snow, and hurled it at him.

The snowball landed on the ground. Orlie doubled over with laughter, which fueled Rachel's anger. She grabbed more snow and started after Orlie. She figured if she got close enough her aim would be better. *Swish!* This time the snowball barely brushed Orlie's jacket.

Orlie snickered. "You missed me! You missed me! So now you gotta kiss me!"

"That's what you think, Orlie Troyer! I'll never kiss you or any other boy!" Rachel started for the schoolhouse. She'd only taken a few steps, when she slipped and fell flat on her face in the snow. She bit her lip to keep from crying.

Laughing, Orlie ambled across the schoolyard and reached for her hand. "Here, let me help you up, little bensel."

Ignoring his offer, Rachel scrambled to her feet and brushed the snow off her clothes. She trudged up the schoolhouse stairs, mumbling, "I am not a silly child. I wish I'd never met Orlie Troyer!"

Chapter 12

A Little Secret

Stop *rutschich* [squirming]," Mom said. She turned in her seat at the front of the buggy and shook her finger at Rachel. "You're moving around so much that the whole carriage is shaking."

"I feel naerfich." Rachel stuck a fingernail between her teeth and bit off the end. She wished she could have run to the schoolhouse. But no, Pap insisted she ride in the buggy with the family. Now she would be a nervous wreck all through the program because she hadn't gotten her endorphins working.

Jacob nudged her in the ribs with his bony elbow. "You worry too much, you know that, little bensel?"

"I do not," she said, elbowing him back. "And stop calling me a silly child!"

"You don't have anything to worry about," Pap said from the driver's seat. "You've been in plenty of Christmas programs, and have always done just fine."

"This one's different," Rachel wailed. "I'm playing Jesus' mother."

"Playing the role of Mary and saying a few lines shouldn't be much different than reciting a poem or singing." Henry reached over from the seat behind Rachel where he sat with Grandpa Schrock. He patted Rachel's shoulder.

Grandpa quickly added, "They're right, Rachel. You'll do fine today. You'll see."

Rachel didn't reply. She just folded her arms and stared out the window at the falling snow. Her family didn't understand the real reason for her fears. She knew she'd sit by Orlie the whole time, smelling his garlic breath. She knew he'd be waiting for her to mess up. He'd probably laugh louder than anyone else when she forgot her lines.

Rachel glanced at the small gift on the seat beside her. Last week Lovina had asked the children to draw names for a gift exchange that would take place right after the Christmas program. Rachel had been disappointed to have drawn Orlie's name. She'd decided she would buy him a box of peppermints to freshen his breath. It was too bad he couldn't open it and suck on a couple of mints before the program started.

Rachel squeezed her eyes shut, as a tremor of nervousness shot through her stomach. *Dear God,* she prayed, *if You'll help me get through this program without making a fool of myself, I promise to keep my room clean and do whatever my parents ask.*

When they entered the schoolhouse, Mom commented on the lacy cut-out stars the scholars had put on the windows. Grandpa mentioned the detailed winter scene a couple of the older children had drawn on the blackboard with colored chalk.

Rachel nodded. "We've worked on the decorations for several weeks."

"Everything looks nice," Pap said. "I'm sure this will be one of the best programs yet."

Rachel wasn't so sure about that. She didn't see how her part of the program could be any good.

Other families began to arrive, and soon there was a huge pile of coats, hats, shawls, and outer black bonnets lying on the enclosed front porch floor of the schoolhouse. Inside, adults and children doubled up in the seats. The children who had parts in the program scurried behind the curtain at the front of the room.

Rachel's palms turned sweaty, and her knees began to knock as she listened to children recite their poems and perform short skits. When it was time for the Christmas story to be read from the Bible, Rachel, Orlie, the angels, and the shepherds took their places in front of the curtain.

Rachel sat on a stool near the wooden manger with a faceless doll inside. Orlie took his place beside her, staring at the doll. The angels stood to one side with their arms outstretched. Jacob and the other shepherds knelt in front of the manger. Lovina had said no when Jacob had offered to bring one of Grandpa Yoder's lambs to the program.

Dorothy Kauffman, an eighth-grade girl, read the Christmas story from Luke 2, while Mary, Joseph, the angels, and shepherds remained in place. That was easy. Rachel was good at sitting.

When the scripture had been read, the Bible characters came to action. Phoebe and Mary stepped forward and recited a poem: "We are two little angels who have a story to tell—it's about baby Jesus, whom we know so well. Jesus, God's Son, came to Earth as a little child; He was born in a stable so meek and mild."

The girls stepped back in place. Next the shepherds spoke their lines. "Baby Jesus, so tiny and dear, placed in a manger with animals near," they said in voices loud and clear. "Baby Jesus, the Son of God, was visited by shepherds with staff and rod."

Earlier, Rachel had spotted Pap, Grandpa, Henry, Rudy, and Grandpa Yoder near the back of the room. Mom, Esther, and Grandma Yoder sat in chairs behind some of the desks. Rachel noticed the smiles on their faces. They were pleased that Jacob had done so well.

Next, wearing a big grin, Orlie spoke his lines: "Jesus had a manger bed, with only some straw under His head. Jesus didn't cry or fuss one bit; though a bed made of straw just wasn't fit. Jesus, our Savior, came to

Earth; He was born in a stable, such a lowly birth."

Orlie had said his lines perfectly. Rachel noticed that his mother, father, little sisters, and older brothers had smiles on their faces.

Now it was Rachel's turn. She opened her mouth to speak but couldn't seem to find her voice.

Orlie nudged her arm once, then twice.

Rachel pushed his hand aside and swallowed hard. Still, nothing came from her lips.

"Rachel, what's the matter? You're supposed to say your lines," Orlie whispered, bending near her ear.

Rachel nodded, licked her dry lips, and tried again. "Mary—uh—Mary thanked God with a—" She paused and glanced at the audience. Everyone looked at Rachel with eager expressions, which only made her feel more nervous.

She cleared her throat. Oh, how she wanted to bite off a fingernail, but it wouldn't look right for Jesus' mother to do something like that. So to keep her hands still, Rachel sat on them.

"Go on, Rachel," Orlie prompted quietly. "Say the rest of your lines."

Rachel began again. "Mary—uh—thanked God with a prayer of pays. . .I—I mean, a prayer of plays." Several people snickered. Rachel wished there were hole in the floor so she could crawl into it. Instead, she sat up straight, looked right into the audience and said, "I meant to say, Mary thanked God with a prayer of praise."

Mom smiled at Rachel, and Pap nodded. Feeling a little more confident, Rachel opened her mouth to say the rest of her lines. Suddenly her mind went blank. What came next? She tried to think, but jumbled thoughts whirled around in her brain like the clothes in Mom's wringer washing machine.

Teacher Lovina, who stood at the side of the room, raised her eyebrows and stared at Rachel. *Thump. Thump. Thump.* She tapped her foot.

She probably thinks I'm a real dummkopp, Rachel thought. *And right now, I feel like a dunce.* The other scholars had done well; she didn't understand why she couldn't do the same.

"Everyone's waiting for you to say the rest of your lines," Orlie whispered.

"I know," she said through clenched teeth.

"Then say them."

"Uh—Mary was blessed in—in so many ways," Rachel began. She paused again, trying to think of what came next, but her mind seemed to be completely empty. She squeezed her fingers into the palms of her sweaty hands. *Think, Rachel, think. What comes next?*

Mom leaned slightly forward with a worried expression. The rest of Rachel's family shook their heads as if they couldn't believe she'd forgotten her lines.

Suddenly, Orlie bent and placed his hand on the faceless doll's head. "Mary loved God and praised Him from her whole heart," he said with a quick nod. "She was thankful for Jesus right from the start."

Orlie straightened and gave Rachel's shoulder a squeeze. She exhaled a sigh of relief. She could hardly believe he had come to her rescue. Orlie had said the rest of her lines as if he was supposed to have said them.

That was something a good friend would have done, not an enemy. Maybe Orlie wasn't Rachel's enemy after all. Maybe he even liked her just a bit.

Rachel felt guilty for all the things she'd thought and said about him. Now she wished she had bought something better than a box of mints to give Orlie for his Christmas present.

Lovina stepped forward and led the scholars and their parents in several Christmas songs. Then it was time for refreshments and opening gifts.

Rachel waited near Mary while their substitute teacher called off names and handed out the presents. She wished she could find a way to snatch the package that held the box of mints and hide it from Orlie. But that would mean he wouldn't have a gift, which wouldn't seem right, either.

"Rachel Yoder, here's your gift," Lovina announced.

Rachel stepped forward and took the package. She placed it on her desk, tore off the paper, and opened the box. Inside were two glass jars—one filled with peanut butter and the other filled with strawberry jam. She picked up the card inside and read it out loud.

"So you never have to eat
tuna sandwiches again.

Your friend always,
Orlie Troyer."

Tears stung Rachel's eyes. She blinked a couple of times to keep them from spilling onto her cheeks. Orlie thought of her as his friend. He proved that by helping Rachel when she forgot her lines.

"Orlie Troyer, this one's for you," Lovina said, extending Rachel's gift to Orlie.

Rachel wished she had prayed about her situation with Orlie, as Grandpa had suggested. But she had been too busy thinking up ways to get even. Now she wished she could hide. Orlie was already opening the gift. She held her breath as he lifted the box of mints and read the card she'd included. Then he walked up to Rachel and gave her a big grin. "Danki, Rachel. Maybe these mints will take the horrible taste out of my mouth when my mamm gives me garlic for breakfast."

Rachel giggled and lifted the jars of peanut butter and jelly. "I like what you gave me, too."

"Glad to hear it."

Rachel shuffled her feet and fought the urge to bite off a nail. This time she was nervous for a different reason. "I—I was wondering. . ."

"What's that?"

"Why have you been so mean to me since you moved here? Especially since your card says you're my friend."

He looked stunned. "You think I've been mean?"

Rachel nodded. "You've teased and made fun of me. That's being mean, wouldn't you say?"

Orlie's cheeks turned red as a cherry. "I—I was just trying to get your attention."

"Why?"

The color in his cheeks deepened. "Because I—I like you, Rachel."

Rachel was shocked. She bit her lower lip as she looked away. Boys sure had a funny way of showing they liked a girl.

"Sorry if I made you mad," he whispered.

Rachel touched his arm. "I'm sorry for being mean to you, too."

She pulled her hand quickly away, realizing she'd just touched a boy. "Say, Orlie, I was wondering. . ."

"What's that?"

"When's your birthday?"

"February twenty-fifth. Why do you ask?"

"I might give you one of my painted rocks as a present. Or maybe I'll make a hurry-up cake for your birthday." She giggled. "I have two months to practice, so maybe it won't turn out so bad."

He thumped her on the arm. "Does that mean we're friends?"

"Jah," Rachel said with a nod. Then she whispered, "Just don't tell anyone, okay?"

"No, of course not. It'll be our little secret."

Recipe for Rachel's Hurry-Up Cake

1½ cups cake flour (do not substitute)
2 teaspoons baking powder
1 cup sugar
¼ teaspoon salt
2 eggs
¼ cup butter, softened
1 cup milk
1 teaspoon vanilla

Preheat oven to 325 degrees. In a mixing bowl, mix cake flour with baking powder, sugar, and salt. In separate bowl, mix eggs and softened butter. Add dry ingredients and milk alternately to egg and butter mixture. Add vanilla and beat hard for 3 minutes. Pour into 2 greased and floured 8-inch layer cake pans and bake for 5 minutes. Raise oven heat to 350 degrees and bake for another 30 minutes. Cool, remove from pans, then frost with strawberry icing.

Strawberry Icing:
4 tablespoons (or more) strawberries, mashed
3 cups confectioners (powdered) sugar
⅓ cup butter, softened

Blend butter and powdered sugar together in bowl. Stir in mashed strawberries, adding enough to make a creamy frosting. Spread on cooled cake.

Out of Control

Dedication

To the students and teachers at the Honeybrook School in Topeka, Indiana. Thanks for letting me visit with you!

Glossary

ach—oh
aldi—girlfriend
appeditlich—delicious
baremlich—terrible
bauchweh—stomachache
bensel—silly child
blappermaul—blabbermouth
bletsching—spanking
boppli—baby
bruder—brother
buwe—boy
daed—dad
danki—thank you
dappich—clumsy
dumm—dumb
ekelhaft—disgusting
grank—sick
guder mariye—good morning
gut—good
hund—dog
jah—yes
kapp—cap
kinner—children
koppweh—headache
kumme—come
maedel—girl
mamm—mom
maus—mouse
melassich—molasses
mupsich—stupid
retschbeddi—tattletale
schmaert—smart
schnee—snow
schneeballe—snowball
schnell—quickly
schweschder—sister
ungeduldich—impatient
verhuddelt—mixed up
wasserpareble—chicken pox
wunderbaar—wonderful

Halt ei, sell geht zu weit!—Stop, that's going too far!
Sis nau futsch!—It's all ruined now!
Dummel dich net!—Take your time, don't hurry!
Gern gschehne.—You are welcome.

Chapter 1

Sledding Troubles

W*oosh*. . . *Woosh*. . . The wind whistled under the eaves of the house, rattling Rachel Yoder's bedroom window.

Thump-thumpety-thump! Rachel's heart pounded inside her chest. She shivered and pulled the quilt under her chin. She had thought she was getting less afraid of storms. But it was hard to be brave in a dark room with the wind making strange noises. What if the windows broke? What if the tree outside her bedroom window toppled and crashed onto the house?

Rachel closed her eyes and prayed, "Dear God, protect this house and all of us in it. Help me not be afraid."

Rachel drew in a deep breath. She felt a bit calmer, and her heart wasn't beating so fast. Maybe now she could sleep.

Tap-tap. Tap-tap.

Rachel's heart raced again. She tipped her head toward the window and listened. *Tap-tap. Tap-tap.* Was someone knocking on the glass? Had they climbed the tree outside her window? Were they trying to enter her room?

My imagination is just playing tricks on me. The wind is just blowing a tree branch against the window.

Screech. . . Screech. . . The new sound reminded Rachel of fingernails on a blackboard.

There's no reason to be afraid, she told herself. *God is watching over me.*

Rachel pushed the quilt aside, turned on the flashlight she kept by her bed, and plodded across the chilly wood floor. She lifted the dark green window shade and pressed her forehead against the cold glass.

Screech. . . Screech. Tap-tap. . .tap-tap.

Rachel gasped when she saw a small pink paw flopped against the window.

"Cuddles!"

She quickly opened the window, and a gust of cold wind swept into the room. "You silly kitten! What are you doing in that tree on such a cold, snowy night?"

Cuddles's pathetic *meow* was drowned out by the wooshing wind.

Snowflakes swirled into the room. Rachel picked up the cat and shut the window. "Poor Cuddles," she whispered against the cat's frosty head. "Did you get locked out of the barn?"

Cuddles meowed again and licked Rachel's chin with her sandpaper tongue.

Rachel giggled. "You're sure getting heavy, Cuddles. Before long you'll be a full-grown cat."

Meow!

"Do you want to sleep with me tonight?"

Meow! Meow! Cuddles pushed her paws against Rachel's chest and purred.

"You're getting me all wet!" Rachel felt the cold dampness through her nightgown and shivered. She plucked a small blanket from the doll cradle Pap had made her last Christmas. Then she wrapped Cuddles in the blanket and placed her at the foot of the bed.

Rachel was about to crawl back in bed, when Cuddles wriggled free from the blanket, leaped into the air, and landed on Rachel's pillow. The cat purred as she kneaded the pillow, first with one paw and then the other.

"Stop that!" Rachel scolded. "You're getting my pillow wet!" She picked up the cat, wrapped her in the doll blanket again, and placed her back on the end of the bed. "Now go to sleep, and I'll see you in the morning."

Rachel crawled into bed and pulled the quilt under her chin. The howling wind didn't bother her nearly so much now that Cuddles was near. She closed her eyes and was almost asleep when she heard *screech. . .screech. . .*

Her eyes popped open and she sat straight up.

Cuddles was scratching a bedpost.

"Don't do that! You'll mark up my bed." Rachel pushed the covers aside and climbed out of bed. She wrapped Cuddles in the doll blanket and placed her at the end of the bed. "Now go to sleep."

Rachel was about to climb into bed again, when Cuddles sprang off the bed, slid across the floor, and bit into the shoelaces from one of Rachel's shoes. She flipped her head from side to side. *Bump. . .bump. . . bump. . .*the shoe thudded against the hardwood floor.

"*Shh. . .* If you're not careful, you'll wake Mom and Pap." Rachel grabbed the shoe and put it in her closet. Then she picked up Cuddles and put her on the bed. "If you make me get up again, I'll put you back outside."

Meow! Cuddles tipped her head and looked at Rachel as if to say, *"I'll be good. Please, don't put me in the cold."*

"All right then." Sighing, Rachel got into bed, pulled the quilt up to her chin, and closed her eyes. She listened for several minutes, but all was quiet. Cuddles must have finally gone to sleep.

When Rachel woke up the next morning, she rushed to the window and lifted the shade. The wind had stopped howling and the snow had quit falling. A perfect day for sledding!

Rachel thought about her new friend, Orlie. He'd told her that he thought the new sled he'd gotten for Christmas was the fastest around.

"We'll see about that," Rachel murmured as she slipped her nightgown over her head. "I'll bet my trusty old sled will go faster than Orlie's shiny new one. He just likes to brag."

She opened her closet door and took out a long-sleeved dress. "I'd better dress warmly today if I'm going to race my sled during recess."

After dressing, Rachel hurried downstairs to the kitchen. Mom was in front of their gas-operated stove, stirring a pot of oatmeal. The spicy aroma of cinnamon tickled Rachel's nose and made her stomach rumble.

"*Guder mariye* [good morning], Rachel," Mom said with a cheery smile.

"Good morning, Mom."

"Did you sleep well last night?"

"The wind kept me awake at first, and then after I brought—" Rachel clamped her hand over her mouth. She had almost blurted out that she'd let Cuddles into her room.

"What's the matter?" Mom asked, squinting her blue eyes. "Why are you covering your mouth?"

Rachel dropped her hand. "Nothing's wrong. I slept okay. How about you, Mom?"

"Except for your *daed's* [dad's] snoring, I slept fairly well, too." Mom touched her stomach and smiled. "I guess I should get used to not sleeping so much. When the *boppli* [baby] is born in July, I'll be up several times during the night to feed the little one."

Rachel grimaced. She wasn't sure she wanted a new baby in the house. What if Mom and Pap loved the baby more than they loved her? What if she had to do more chores after the baby came?

"Would you please set the table?" Mom asked, touching Rachel's arm.

"*Jah* [yes], okay." Rachel reached into the cupboard to get the glasses, but her elbow bumped the box of brown sugar on the cupboard. The box tumbled to the floor, and—*splat!*—brown sugar spilled everywhere.

"Always trouble somewhere," Rachel muttered. "I'll clean it up right away, Mom." She hurried to the cleaning closet for the broom and dustpan.

Swish! Swish! She swept sugar into the dustpan. *Swish! Swish!* Just a few more sweeps and it would be done.

Rachel bent over to pick up the dustpan, when—*woosh!*—a gray-and-white ball of fur streaked into the room. The dustpan flew out of Rachel's hand, and brown sugar flew everywhere. Some even landed on Cuddles's head.

"Oh no," Rachel said with a groan.

"What's that cat doing in the house?" Mom rubbed the spot on her nose where her metal-framed glasses should have been. Instead, they had slipped to the end of her nose. "I wonder if one of the men left the back door open when they went to do their chores," she said, pushing her glasses back in place.

Rachel frowned. Come to think of it, she hadn't seen Cuddles on her bed this morning. The silly kitten must have hidden so she wouldn't be put out in the cold.

Rachel knew Mom didn't like Cuddles to be in her room—especially not on the bed. She wondered what she could tell Mom that wouldn't be a lie. Should she admit that she'd let Cuddles into her room last night, or should she let Mom think the cat had entered through an open door this morning? Maybe it would be best if she just kept quiet.

"However the cat got in," Mom said, "she's caused a mess. The troublesome creature needs to go back outside, *schnell* [quickly]."

"I'll put her out." Rachel scooped Cuddles into her arms, opened the back door, and set the cat on the porch. "You'd better go out to the barn now." She shook her finger. "And if you don't stop getting into trouble, Mom might not let you in the house anymore."

"Why didn't you bring your sled this morning?" Rachel asked her brother Jacob as she trudged through the snow, pulling her sled toward the schoolhouse.

"Don't feel like sledding." Jacob kicked at a clump of snow with the toe of his boot.

"Are you afraid my sled might beat yours in a race? Is that why you left it in the barn?"

Jacob shook his head.

"Then why didn't you bring it?"

"I just told you. . .I don't feel like sledding today."

"How come?"

"You ask too many questions, little *bensel* [silly child]."

"I'm not a silly child. Will you ever stop calling me that?"

"Maybe someday. . .when we're both old and gray."

Rachel frowned. "Very funny."

Jacob reached down and scooped up a handful of snow. He waited until Rachel walked past him, then *splat!*—the cold, wet snow hit the collar of Rachel's coat. Some ran down her neck.

Rachel shivered and glared at Jacob. "I think someone ought to wash your face in the snow!"

"Who's gonna do it?" Jacob taunted. "*You*, little bensel?"

Rachel was tempted to say something mean to her brother but figured he would say something even meaner.

You're the silly child, she thought as she hurried along. *Someday you'll be sorry you teased me so much, and I hope it's before we're both old and gray.*

When Rachel arrived at school, she spotted several sleds lined up near the porch. Orlie Troyer stood nearby talking with another boy.

"Guder mariye, Rachel," he said. "I see you brought your sled with you today."

"Good morning." Rachel leaned her sled against the building. "I can hardly wait for recess. It will be so much fun to go sledding."

Orlie motioned to his sled. "I'm sure I'll have more fun than anyone else, since I've got the fastest sled here."

"I'll bet my sled's faster," Rachel said.

Orlie wrinkled his freckled nose. "Bet it's not."

Before Rachel could respond, Orlie said, "How about if I race you at recess and we'll see who has the fastest sled?"

Rachel nodded. "I'd be happy to race you. I was going to suggest that."

Just then their teacher, Elizabeth Miller, rang the school bell. Jacob nudged Rachel's arm. "We'd better get inside."

"Jah, okay." Rachel hurried into the room with the rest of the children who'd been in the snowy schoolyard.

Rachel hung her coat on a wall peg near the door and placed her black outer bonnet and lunch pail on the shelf above. Then she went to her desk.

Elizabeth tapped her desk bell, signaling for everyone to get quiet. "Good morning, boys and girls."

"Good morning, Elizabeth," the children said.

Rachel was happy that Elizabeth was back from her trip to Tennessee. She'd gone there shortly before Christmas to see her grandmother. Rachel had missed Elizabeth.

Elizabeth opened her Bible and read from Proverbs 14:5: "A truthful witness does not deceive, but a false witness pours out lies."

Rachel cringed as she thought about this morning

when Mom had wondered how Cuddles had gotten in the house.

As soon as I get home I'd better tell Mom the truth about letting Cuddles into my room last night, Rachel decided.

"*Psst.* . .Rachel, stand for prayer." Mary nudged Rachel's arm from across the aisle.

Rachel jumped to her feet and bowed her head as she and the other children said the Lord's Prayer.

After the prayer, everyone filed to the front of the room and sang one song in English and one in German.

When the children returned to their seats, classes began.

For the next hour, Rachel concentrated on her schoolwork. When it was time for morning recess, Rachel hurried to the back of the room, slipped into her heavy wool cape and black bonnet, and rushed out the door.

"Can I take a quick ride?" Rachel's cousin Mary asked when Rachel grabbed hold of her sled.

Rachel's eyebrows furrowed. "Didn't you bring your sled today?"

Mary shook her head. "One of the runners is wobbly. Papa hasn't fixed it yet."

Rachel stared at her sled. Morning recess wasn't very long. If she let Mary borrow the sled, she might not have enough time to race Orlie. Still, Rachel didn't want to be selfish. "I'll let you use my sled after I race Orlie," she said.

"Please, Rachel." Mary pouted. "I'll just take one quick ride—I promise."

"Maybe Mary would like to race me," Orlie said, pulling his sled beside Rachel's.

Mary shook her head. "I just want a nice ride down the hill. I don't want to race anyone."

"That's okay. It's Rachel I promised to race anyway." Orlie gave Rachel his slanted grin. "We can have our race as soon as Mary brings your sled back up the hill."

Rachel nibbled on her lip. As much as she wanted to race Orlie right now, she wanted to please her cousin, too. Mary was Rachel's best friend, and if she didn't let Mary use the sled, Mary might think Rachel was selfish.

"Okay, Mary," Rachel said. "Just one ride, though. Remember, I'm supposed to race Orlie. He thinks he can beat me."

"Jah, okay." Mary grabbed the rope on Rachel's sled and pulled it to the hill behind the schoolhouse where the others were sledding.

Rachel followed. "Just one turn," she reminded her cousin.

Mary sat on the sled and grabbed the rope attached to the steering handles. "Would you please give me a push, Rachel?"

Rachel placed both hands on Mary's back. "One. . . two. . .three!" She pushed hard, but the sled only moved a few inches.

"Try it again, Rachel!" Mary directed over her shoulder. "You're not pushing hard enough."

Rachel gritted her teeth. "I did push hard. The sled doesn't want to move."

"If it won't move, then it sure won't beat my sled," Orlie said.

"Maybe some snow is stuck to the runners." Mary climbed off the sled and kicked at a clump of snow underneath the runners. Then she climbed back on. "Let's try it again."

"Ooph!" Rachel grunted as she gave Mary another hefty shove. This time the sled glided down the hill, but at a snail's pace.

Orlie snickered and nudged Rachel with his elbow. "You won't beat me on that slow sled!"

Rachel frowned. If her sled wouldn't go any faster than this, how could she beat Orlie?

"I think I'll take my sled for a trial run," Orlie said. "As fast as my sled goes, I should be back up here before Mary makes it to the bottom."

Rachel frowned again. Could Orlie's sled really be that fast?

Orlie jumped on his sled, pushed off with his feet, and—*zip!*—he sailed down the hill so fast it looked like he was flying.

"Oh great," she muttered. "Unless I can figure out some way to make my sled go faster than that, I'll never win a race against Orlie."

"That wasn't much of a ride, was it?" Rachel asked when Mary trudged up the hill several minutes later. Orlie was right behind her, wearing a triumphant smile.

Mary shrugged. "I thought the ride was okay."

"Maybe I need to wax the runners." Rachel wished she'd brought one of Mom's candles from home. Her brother Henry had told her once that candles worked well for waxing sled runners.

Orlie sauntered up to Rachel and shook his head. "Your sled is really slow. Are you sure you want to race me, Rachel?"

"Maybe you shouldn't race Orlie," Mary said. She leaned close to Rachel's ear. "His sled is really fast, and yours goes really slow. I don't see how you can win a race against him."

Rachel patted her cold cheeks to warm them as she pondered the problem. "I'll be right back."

"Where are you going?" Orlie called as Rachel hurried toward the schoolhouse.

She just kept trotting.

Rachel returned several minutes later with a candle she'd borrowed from their teacher. She smiled at Mary. "I'll take my sled now, please."

"What are you planning to do with that candle?" Mary asked.

"You'll see." Rachel squatted beside her sled, flipped it over, and rubbed the candle back and forth across the runners. "That should do the trick!" She turned the sled over again, grabbed the rope, and pulled it to the edge of the hill. "I'm ready when you are, Orlie!"

"Ready as I'll ever be!" Orlie looked at Rachel and winked. "This will be a piece of cake."

Rachel nodded. "I'm sure it will, only it will be *my* piece of cake."

"We'll see about that," Orlie grunted.

"Want me to say when to start?" Mary asked.

Rachel nodded. So did Orlie. All the other children lined up at the top of the hill to watch.

Mary cupped her hands around her mouth. "Get ready. . . Get set. . . Go!"

Everyone cheered as Rachel and Orlie pushed off with their feet. Orlie's sled whooshed ahead of Rachel's, but Rachel's sled picked up speed as it zoomed down the hill. It went so fast she could barely hold the rope. "Yippee!" she hollered. "I'm going to win this race!"

Whap!—the rope snapped in two. Rachel could no longer control which way she was going. "Oh no!" she cried. Rachel's sled was out of control—she headed straight for the creek!

Chapter 2

A Troublesome Day

Rachel rose out of the water sputtering and mumbling, "Always trouble somewhere."

A hand reached out to Rachel. Orlie stood in the water beside her sled. "What happened, Rachel? Are you okay?"

"I–I'm not hurt. I'm sure I'll be fine once my clothes are dry." Rachel tried to get up on her own, but fell back in the water with a *splash!*

"Here, let me help you," Orlie offered, extending his hand again.

Rachel took Orlie's hand, clambered to her feet, and plodded out of the water, pulling her sled along.

Mary stepped up to Rachel. "You shouldn't have waxed those runners so much. What were you thinking?"

"I thought if I waxed the runners it would make my sled go faster so I could win the race," Rachel explained.

"My sled did go faster. If the rope hadn't broken, I would have won."

"Jah, right," Orlie said, shaking his head.

Mary grabbed one end of the broken rope while Rachel grabbed the other. As they sloshed back up the hill, Rachel grumbled. She didn't like being wet and cold, and she didn't like losing the race. She wished she hadn't raced Orlie at all. She wished it was summer!

When Rachel entered the classroom, Elizabeth exclaimed, "Rachel, your clothes are wet! What happened?"

Rachel explained about the race and the broken rope that caused her to lose control of her sled.

"You shouldn't have waxed those runners," Mary put in.

"I—I know. You s–said that already." Rachel's teeth chattered so much she could barely talk. "If the r–rope hadn't broken, and the cr–creek hadn't b–been in the way, I would have w–won that race."

"You don't always have to win, Rachel," Mary said.

Rachel just rubbed her hands briskly over her cold arms.

"Rachel and Orlie, you both need to stand in front of the woodstove until your clothes are dry," Elizabeth instructed. "Otherwise, you might catch a cold."

"I'm not that wet, Teacher," Orlie said. "Just my boots and the bottom of my pants got wet when I went to help Rachel."

Elizabeth nodded. "Then take off your boots and socks and set them by the stove."

Orlie did as their teacher said then sat at his desk.

"What about my schoolwork?" Rachel asked. "How can I do that if I'm standing in front of the stove?"

"Maybe we could move your desk closer to the stove," Elizabeth suggested.

Rachel opened her mouth to reply, but all that came out was a big *ah-choo!*

Elizabeth's forehead wrinkled. "I think it will take too long for your clothes to dry with you still wearing them. You probably need to go home for the rest of the day."

"What about the spelling test tomorrow?" Spelling was Rachel's best subject, and she didn't want to miss studying for it.

"I'll give you the list of words," Elizabeth said. "You can practice them at home." She motioned to her helper, Sharon Smucker, who was helping the younger children with their coats. "Sharon, would you please get your horse and buggy ready and take Rachel home?"

"Of course I'll take her home." Sharon smiled at Rachel. "I should have the horse and buggy ready to go in a few minutes, so you stay here where it's warm. I'll pull up out front when I'm ready."

"*Danki* [thank you]." Rachel moved closer to the stove, and Sharon hurried out the door.

When Rachel arrived home from school, she found

Mom sitting at the kitchen table, reading the newspaper. The fire in the woodstove crackled and snapped, spilling its warmth into the room.

Mom looked up as Rachel stepped in. "Rachel, what are you doing home from school so soon?" She glanced at the clock on the far wall. "It's not even noon yet."

Rachel explained about the sled going out of control, and how she'd landed in the creek.

Mom squinted. "*Ach* [oh], Rachel, you're right—you are soaking wet!"

Rachel sneezed. "That's why Elizabeth sent me home. She didn't think my clothes would dry fast enough in front of the woodstove at school."

"You could go back to school after you change clothes," Mom suggested, "but I'm worried you might catch a cold."

"Elizabeth said I could stay home the rest of the day." Rachel lifted her backpack. "She gave me a list of spelling words to study."

"That's good," Mom said with a smile. "While you're getting out of those wet clothes, I'll run warm water in the tub so you can take a bath. After you finish your homework, you can help me bake a shoofly pie."

Rachel licked her lips. "Yum." She always enjoyed eating one of Mom's delicious molasses-filled pies.

After Rachel had gone over her spelling lesson, Mom set out a glass pie pan. "After the pie is done, I'll whip some cream, so we can have it with our pie tonight." Her glasses had slipped to the middle of her nose, and she pushed them back in place.

"That sounds *gut* [good]," Rachel said as she put her choring apron over her dress. "Mom, I've been wondering about something."

"What's that?"

"Since your glasses never seem to stay in place, why you don't get some new ones."

"New glasses wouldn't do me any good," Mom said.

"Why not?"

Mom reached under her glasses and rubbed the skinniest part of her nose. "The bridge of my nose is very narrow. I've always had trouble keeping my glasses in place."

Rachel touched the bridge of her own nose and frowned. She hoped she never had to wear glasses.

"Why don't you get out the pie ingredients while I roll the dough?" Mom motioned to the cupboard across the room.

"What do I need?"

"You'll need molasses, baking soda, brown sugar, eggs, and hot water for the filling. For the crumb part, you'll need flour, brown sugar, butter, nutmeg, and cinnamon," Mom said. "Oh, and would you please get some salt? I'll need to fill the salt shaker on the table before we have supper."

Rachel hurried to the cupboard where Mom kept

baking supplies. She set out each item while repeating it to Mom so she wouldn't forget anything. She didn't want the shoofly pie to turn out terrible, like the cookies she made last summer when she used baking soda instead of baking powder and didn't put in enough sugar.

Mom watched Rachel measure the ingredients. When the filling and crumbs had been mixed in a bowl and put into the pie shell, Mom smiled at Rachel and said, "It looks like I have enough dough left over for another pie. Why don't you make the second pie? Then you can put both pies in the oven."

"Will you watch me make the second pie?" Rachel asked.

Mom covered her mouth and yawned. "I'm feeling kind of tired, so I thought I'd lie on the sofa awhile."

"Are you okay, Mom?"

"I'm fine—just tired," Mom said as she turned on the oven. "I'm sure you'll do okay, but if you need any help, follow the recipe in the cookbook on the counter."

Mom sure is tired a lot lately. I guess it's because she'll soon have a baby. Rachel looked at the pie she'd put together with Mom. *I did all right when Mom was here. I hope I don't mess things up on my own.*

Rachel propped the toe of her right foot on the heel of her left foot as she stared at the ingredients on the counter. "Everything's here. I just need to make sure I put the right amount of each ingredient in the pie."

As Rachel added a cup of molasses to the bowl, she

thought about the spelling test they would have at school tomorrow. Even though spelling was her best subject and she'd already read through the list, she wanted to study more so she'd get a perfect score.

She glanced at her backpack, hanging from a wall peg near the back door. Maybe she could study for the spelling test while she made the pie. *Jah, that's just what I'll do!*

Rachel placed her spelling words on the counter next to the cookbook. As she added another ingredient to the bowl, she said the first spelling word: "Celebrate. C-e-l-e-b-r-a-t-e."

She stirred the filling with a wooden spoon as she said the next word. "Mediate. M-e-d-i-t-a-t-e." She shook her head. "No, it's mediate, not meditate. M-e-d-i-a-t-e." Rachel moved to the next word. "Selection. S-e-l-e-c-t-i-o-n. These words are so easy—a piece of cake," she said with a giggle. "No, make that a piece of pie."

Rachel continued to repeat the spelling words as she added the rest of the ingredients and poured half the filling into the pie crust. Next, she sprinkled half the crumb mixture over the filling then added more filling and the rest of the crumbs. Carefully, she carried the pie to the oven and set it on the rack. Then she did the same with the pie she and Mom had made together. She closed the oven door and set the timer for ten minutes.

Rachel grabbed her spelling words and sat at the

table. Soon the kitchen was filled with warmth from the stove and a delicious aroma of pies baking in the oven.

Ding! Ding! Ding!—the timer went off. Rachel turned the heat down to 350 degrees and set the timer for fifty more minutes. Rachel set two cooling racks on the counter and went back to the table to study her list of spelling words.

Ding! Ding! Ding!—the timer went off again.

When Rachel opened the oven door this time, the sweet smell of molasses rose with the steam. The edges of both pies were lightly brown—just perfect. She removed the pies and set them on the cooling racks then headed back to the table. If she studied her spelling words until Mom came back to the kitchen, she was sure to get a good grade on the test.

After supper that evening, Mom announced that she and Rachel had made shoofly pie for dessert.

"Yum." Jacob smacked his lips. "Is there any whipping cream to go with it?"

"Jah, there is," Mom said as she set one of the pies on the table. She smiled at Rachel. "I put the second pie shell in an aluminum pan, so this I know is the one you baked yourself. Would you like to cut and serve it for us?"

Rachel nodded, feeling pleased with herself. The pie she had baked looked as good as the one in the glass pan that she'd helped Mom make. She was sure her pie would taste delicious.

Rachel hurried across the room, took out six plates, and placed them on the table—one each for Grandpa Schrock, Pap, Henry, Jacob, Mom, and one for herself. Next, she got out a knife and cut the pie into six hefty pieces. She lifted out the first one and placed it on Grandpa's plate. Since he was the oldest member of their family, she thought he should be the first to taste her delicious pie.

While Rachel was serving the others, Grandpa dipped a spoon into the bowl of whipping cream Mom had set on the table. He winked at Rachel and forked a piece of pie into his mouth. As he began to chew, a strange look came over his face. His bushy gray eyebrows pulled together. His nose twitched. His lips curled up at the corners.

Rachel figured Mom probably hadn't put enough sugar in the whipping cream.

Pap took a bite of his pie and quickly reached for his glass of water.

"This pie sure looks good," Henry said. He took a bite, dashed across the room, and spit the pie into the sink. "Ugh! That tastes *baremlich* [terrible]! What did you do to this pie, Rachel?"

"I—I don't know. I thought I did everything Mom told me to do with the first pie." Rachel's throat felt clogged and tears sprang to her eyes. First the mishap with her sled at school and now a ruined pie!

Couldn't she do anything right? This had sure been a troublesome day!

Jacob tasted his pie then, and quickly dumped it in the garbage can. "This is the worst shoofly pie I've ever tasted! It's not even fit for a fly." He squinted at Rachel. "We'll probably all get the fly flu after eating this, and then our faces will turn blue."

"Jacob Yoder, that's a terrible thing to say," Mom said, shaking her head. "I'm sure Rachel didn't ruin the pie." She poked her fork into her piece and took a bite. Her lips curled, the way Grandpa's had, and she reached for her glass of water. "Ach, Rachel, the pie's not sweet enough, and it tastes salty."

Jacob placed his plate in the sink next to Henry's. "Maybe Rachel ruined the pie on purpose so we'd all get the fly flu and our faces would turn blue."

Rachel's chin quivered. *I won't cry in front of Jacob. I won't give him the satisfaction.*

"Stop teasing your sister, Jacob," Pap scolded. "I'm sure you couldn't bake a pie any better than hers."

"Bet I could."

Rachel was on the verge of telling Jacob that he could help Mom do the baking from now on, but Mom spoke first. "How much *melassich* [molasses] did you use, Rachel?"

"One cup," Rachel replied.

"How much brown sugar did you put in the filling?"

"Brown sugar?" Rachel stared at a stain on the

tablecloth. "I—uh—think maybe I forgot the brown sugar."

"Did you put brown sugar in the crumb mixture?" Grandpa asked, his bushy gray eyebrows lifting high on his forehead.

Rachel pursed her lips. "I'm not sure. I was studying my spelling words while I mixed the ingredients. That must be why I forgot the brown sugar."

"Did you use any salt?" Mom asked.

Rachel thought hard. "Jah, I think I did. It was sitting on the cupboard, so—"

Mom shook her head as she clucked her tongue. "The recipe I use calls for cinnamon and nutmeg in the crumb mixture, but no salt."

"But a box of salt was on the cupboard," Rachel sputtered.

"I asked you to set that out so I could fill the salt shaker on the table, remember?"

Rachel nodded slowly.

"No wonder Rachel's pie tastes so baremlich," Jacob said when he returned to the table. "Can I have a piece of the pie you made, Mom?"

Mom shook her head. "Not until you apologize to your sister for saying her pie is baremlich."

"But it is terrible," Jacob insisted. "In fact, it's the worst shoofly pie I've ever tasted!"

Rachel couldn't stand anymore. Sniffling, she ran out of the kitchen and up the stairs two at a time. She flew into her room and flopped onto her bed. She lay there staring at the ceiling. "I am a little bensel!"

A few minutes later, the door creaked open, and Mom stepped into the room. She sat beside Rachel and took her hand. "A ruined pie isn't the end of the world."

"Jacob and Henry think it is. They always make fun of me when I mess up." *Sniff! Sniff!* "I can never do anything right."

"That's not true." Mom pointed across the room to the collection of rocks Rachel had painted. "You made those look like ladybugs and turtles. Not everyone can paint as well as you do, daughter."

Rachel swiped at the tears rolling down her cheeks. "I thought I might try painting a rock to look like Cuddles sometime."

"That's a fine idea," Mom said with a nod.

Rachel remembered that she hadn't told Mom the truth about the cat in the house last night. She swallowed hard and sat up. "I—I need to tell you something, Mom."

"What's that?"

"When Cuddles bumped into the dustpan this morning, and you said you wondered how she'd gotten inside, I should have told you the truth."

"What truth?"

"I heard scratching at my window last night. When I opened it, Cuddles was in the tree, begging to get in." Rachel drew in a quick breath. "The wind was howling, and it was cold out there in the snow, so I—"

"Let the cat come into your room," Mom said, finishing Rachel's sentence.

Rachel nodded.

"Was Cuddles on your bed?"

"Jah."

"You know I don't mind the cat being inside as long as she's wearing a flea collar, but I don't approve of her being on your bed."

"I'm sorry for letting Cuddles sleep on my bed," Rachel said. "And I'm sorrier for not telling you sooner."

Mom gave Rachel a hug. "I accept your apology, and I'm glad you told the truth. Confession's always good for the soul."

Rachel nodded and nestled against Mom's chest. At least the troublesome day had ended on a good note.

Chapter 3

True or False

"Wheeee!" Rachel stretched out her legs as she hung onto the rope dangling from the hayloft in their barn. "This is fun!" she shouted to Jacob, who was cleaning one of the horse stalls. "Do you want to take a turn?"

Jacob held up the shovel in his hands. "I'd like to, but I've got work to do." He squinted at Rachel. "If I'm not mistaken, you're supposed to be in the house, studying for tomorrow's history test."

Rachel let go of the rope and dropped into the mound of hay below. "I'll study later. Right now I think I'll visit old Tom," she said, scrambling to her feet.

Jacob frowned. "You'll be sorry if you flunk that test."

"I passed my spelling test last week."

"That's different; you like spelling."

It was true—spelling came easy to Rachel. History was harder for her, and she didn't enjoy it nearly as much as she did spelling.

"I'll study later." Rachel headed for the stall where Pap's old buggy horse was kept when he wasn't in the pasture. Old Tom couldn't pull their buggy anymore, so Rachel visited him as often as she could.

As Rachel stepped into Tom's stall, the sweet smell of fresh hay tickled her nose.

She was glad Tom had a nice warm place to stay during the cold winter months. She was glad Pap had kept the horse even though he was getting old and couldn't do much.

"How are you doing, Tom?"

Tom dropped his head, and Rachel stroked his silky brown mane. "Are you warm enough here in the barn?"

Tom whinnied and nuzzled Rachel's hand with his warm nose.

"Sorry, but I didn't bring you a treat today," Rachel said. "If Mom has any apples, I'll bring you one tomorrow."

Tom lifted his head and snorted. He moved away from Rachel and found a spot to lie down in the hay.

Rachel figured Tom wanted to take a nap, so she left the stall and went to look for a ball of string, hoping to play with Cuddles. She found some string on a shelf where Pap kept his tools. She hurried toward a pile of straw on the other side of the barn, where Cuddles liked to sleep.

"What are you up to now?" Jacob asked as Rachel passed him.

"I'm going to play with Cuddles."

"I thought you were gonna study for the history test."

"You're not my boss," she mumbled. "I said I would study later."

Who did Jacob think he was, trying to tell her what to do?

"Never said I was." Jacob leaned the shovel against the wall. "I'm done cleaning, so I'm gonna do my homework. Are you sure you don't want to do yours now, too?"

She shook her head. "I can study after supper."

"Suit yourself." Jacob shrugged and headed out the door.

Rachel hurried over to the pile of straw, but Cuddles wasn't there. "Where are you, Cuddles? Come, kitty, kitty," she called.

She spotted Cuddles in the far corner of the barn, chasing a tiny gray mouse. "Stop it!" she scolded. "Leave that poor *maus* [mouse] alone."

Cuddles paid no attention to Rachel and continued the chase. Round and round the barn she went—leaping in the air, swiping with her paws, and meowing for all she was worth.

Rachel hollered for Cuddles to stop, but her yelling made no difference. "If you hurt that maus, you'll get no supper tonight." She shook her finger as the cat and mouse whizzed past again. "I won't let you chase my bubbles anymore!"

The mouse darted into a hole near one of the cow's stalls. Cuddles slammed into the wall. *Meow!* She shook her furry head and looked up at Rachel as if to say, *"Don't you feel sorry for me?"*

Rachel clucked her tongue, the way Mom often did. "That wouldn't have happened if you had listened to me."

Cuddles swiped a paw across Rachel's shoe. *Meow! Meow!*

Rachel thought about how sad she felt whenever she got in trouble. Maybe Cuddles felt that way, too. She bent down and scooped the cat into her arms. "I love you, Cuddles, but you must learn to listen."

Cuddles responded with a sandpapery kiss on Rachel's chin and began to purr.

Rachel found a seat on a bale of straw and placed Cuddles on her lap. It felt nice to sit in the warm barn and stroke her silky cat. It was a lot more fun than sitting at the kitchen table, studying for a history test she didn't want to take.

Rachel leaned her head against the wall and closed her eyes. *It's supposed to be a true or false test, so it might not be too hard. Maybe I can guess at which answers are right and which are wrong.*

During supper that evening, Rachel told her family about Cuddles and the mouse. "I hollered at Cuddles," she said, reaching for a pickle, "but the cat kept chasing that poor little maus."

"There are some things we just can't control," Grandpa said. "Stopping a cat from chasing a mouse is one of those things."

"That's right," Pap said with a nod. "Cuddles was doing what comes naturally for a cat, and it wasn't something you could control."

Rachel bit into the pickle and puckered her lips. She loved dill pickles, even if they were a bit tangy.

"Did you get all your homework done?" Mom asked, turning to Rachel.

Rachel opened her mouth to reply, but Jacob spoke first. "She never even opened her books." He stared at Rachel. "All she's done since she got home from school is play in the barn, dangle from the rope, pet Old Tom, and chase Cuddles."

Pap's eyebrows drew together as he frowned at Rachel. "Don't you have a history test in the morning?"

"Jah. I'll study after supper," she said.

Pap nodded and reached for the platter of roast beef. "I hope you do well on the test."

Rachel hoped that, too.

When supper was over and the dishes were done, Rachel headed for the stairs leading to her room.

"Don't forget your schoolbooks," Mom called. "You left them on the counter near the back door."

Rachel turned back and scooped up the books. When she entered her room, she placed the books on her dresser and sat on the end of her bed. *"Brrr."* She rubbed her hands briskly over her arms. "It sure is cold up here."

She reached for the extra quilt at the foot of her bed and wrapped it around her shoulders. Then she moved to the window and lifted the shade. The moon shone brightly, making the snow-covered yard glisten like a blanket of twinkling fireflies. It was a perfect night for sledding.

Rachel shivered as she thought about her recent sledding experience when she ended up in the creek. She would have to be more careful the next time she took her sled to school.

She leaned close to the frosty window and blew on it. A circle formed on the glass where her hot breath made contact. Using her finger, she drew her name. She blew again, and the clock by her bed kept time with her breathing. *Tick-tock. Tick-tock. Breathe in. . .blow out.*

Rachel stretched her arms over her head and yawned. She felt so sleepy. Maybe she would stretch out on the bed and rest awhile before she studied.

Cock-a-doodle-do! Cock-a-doodle-do!

Rachel sat up with a start. Was that the rooster crowing? Their old red rooster had never crowed in the middle of the night before.

She rolled over and stared at the clock by her bed. It was 6 a.m.!

Rachel glanced down at her wrinkled dress and

gasped. *I must have fallen asleep last night and never got ready for bed!*

She scrambled out of bed and hurried to her dresser. When she opened a drawer and took out a pair of clean socks, she spotted her schoolbooks on top of the dresser. "Oh no! I didn't study for the history test!"

Rachel glanced at the clock. It was too late to study now. She needed to get washed, dressed, and hurry downstairs to help Mom with breakfast. *Maybe I can study on the way to school. Jah, that's what I'll do.*

As Rachel trudged through the slippery snow toward the schoolhouse, she found it hard to hold her history book, which she had taken out of her backpack. Each time she took a step, the book shifted in her hands.

"Always trouble somewhere," Rachel grumbled as the book snapped shut.

"If you weren't trying to study while you walk, you wouldn't have so much trouble." Jacob snickered. "My silly *schweschder* [sister], the little bensel."

Rachel glared at Jacob. "I am not a silly child!"

"Jah, you are."

"Am not."

"Are so."

And so it went until Rachel and Jacob reached the schoolhouse. Between trying to keep her history book open and arguing with Jacob, Rachel hadn't studied at all. If she didn't think of some way to control this situation, she would probably fail her history test.

Rachel stomped the snow off her boots and was about to enter the schoolhouse when someone tapped her shoulder. She whirled around. There stood freckle-faced Orlie, wearing his usual crooked grin.

"Are you ready for another sled race during recess?" he asked.

Rachel shook her head. "I didn't bring my sled with me today."

"Maybe you can borrow your cousin Mary's sled." Orlie nudged Rachel's arm. "Mary said her daed fixed her wobbly runner last night, so she brought the sled with her today."

"No thanks. I'm not interested in racing you again."

"You don't feel like taking another swim in the creek, huh?"

Rachel ground her teeth together. Orlie teased as much as Jacob. Did he enjoy making fun of her?

She pushed past Orlie and stepped into the schoolhouse, where a burst of toasty air greeted her. Elizabeth had stoked the woodstove so the scholars would be warm and snug.

Rachel hoped to have time to study for the history test during the morning, but Elizabeth kept everyone busy with arithmetic problems.

Rachel had a hard time concentrating on arithmetic when she only wanted to open her history book and study for the test they'd take after their noon recess.

When Elizabeth announced that it was time for

morning recess, Rachel thought she might have time to look at her history book. But Mary insisted that Rachel join her and the other girls in a snowball fight against the boys.

"Oh, all right," Rachel finally agreed. She didn't want to disappoint Mary.

Everyone put on their coats, gloves, and hats, and hurried outside.

"Let's wait until each team has one hundred snowballs made before we start," Phoebe Byler suggested.

Aaron King grunted. "If we took the time to make that many snowballs, recess would be over before the snowball fight began."

"Aaron's right," Orlie put in. "Let's have each girl make three snowballs, and each boy make five snowballs."

"That's not right," Rachel spoke up. "Why should the boys get to make more snowballs than the girls?"

"Because there are eighteen girls and only twelve boys." Orlie planted his hands on his hips like he was the boss. "That will give the girls fifty-four snowballs and the boys will have—"

"Sixty!" Mary shouted. "That's not right!"

Jacob stepped forward. "Jah, it is. Since there are fewer boys than girls, we need an advantage."

"No, you don't," Becky Esh said with a shake of her head.

"Do so." Orlie insisted.

"Do not."

"Do so."

"Do not."

Rachel threw a snowball. *Splat!* It hit Orlie's cheek and ran down his neck.

"Hey, that was not fair! I wasn't ready! " He bent down, scooped a handful of snow, and threw it at Rachel.

She ducked, and the snowball whizzed over her head. "Ha! You missed me!" she shouted as she ran away.

Orlie chased Rachel, and everyone started making snowballs fast and flinging them at whoever got in their way. So much for a snowball fight with the girls against the boys!

Soon Elizabeth called to the children. A group of laughing red-nosed, rosy-cheeked scholars returned to the schoolhouse and hung up their coats, hats, and gloves. After everyone was seated at their desks, the curtain dividing the room was drawn, and grades three through eight were given a reading lesson, followed by a time of questions from the teacher about what they had learned.

At eleven thirty, the children were dismissed by rows to wash their hands, get their lunch boxes, and return to their seats. It was too cold to eat outside like they did on warmer days. After eating their lunches, the children were allowed to play outside until twelve thirty.

I have plenty of time to study for the test now, Rachel

thought as the other children donned their coats and filed out the door.

Rachel remained in her seat. She was reaching for her history book when Elizabeth asked, "Aren't you going outside to play with the others?"

"Not this time." Rachel shook her head. "It's too cold out, and I thought I would—"

"If you're not going outside, would you like to help me cut out some paper stars?"

"What are they for?" Rachel asked.

"Each time someone gets a perfect score on a lesson, he or she will get to pick out a star and write his or her name on it," Elizabeth replied. "A perfect score on a test will get the scholar two paper stars."

"Oh, I see."

"We'll put the stars around the schoolhouse and see if we can get so many that they go up to the ceiling." Elizabeth patted Rachel's head. "If you and I get some stars cut out now, we'll have enough to give everyone who gets a perfect score on the history test this afternoon."

Rachel knew if she spent the next half hour cutting out paper stars, she would have no time to study for the test. She couldn't tell Elizabeth she didn't want to help because she hadn't studied.

"Won't Sharon help you with the stars?" Rachel asked.

Elizabeth shook her head. "I asked her to go outside

with the scholars." She frowned. "After the snowball fight during morning recess, I figured either Sharon or I should be outside to be sure everything goes well."

Forcing a smile, Rachel nodded and said, "Okay, I'll help you cut out the stars."

Elizabeth gave Rachel a stack of colored paper, a pattern to trace the stars, and a pair of scissors; then she returned to her own desk and cut out stars, too.

Rachel hummed as she traced the first star onto a sheet of bright yellow paper. This was a lot more fun than studying for the history test would have been.

Lunch recess was over sooner than Rachel had hoped, and when everyone took their seats, Elizabeth said it was time for the middle-grade scholars to take their history test.

As Rachel stared at the true and false questions on the paper she'd been given, a knot formed in her stomach. She didn't know any of the answers. She could only guess.

What if my guesses are wrong? she fretted. *How can I face Mom and Pap if I fail this test?*

Rachel tapped her pencil along the edge of her desk. *Tap-tappety-tap-tap.*

She set the pencil down and placed her arms on top of the desk. Still, no answers came. She looked at the front of the room and stared at the letters and numbers on a wide strip of paper above the blackboard. *Think, Rachel. . .think hard. True or false? False or true?*

Suddenly, an idea popped into Rachel's head. She knew how she might be able to pass the test!

Orlie's desk used to be behind Rachel's, but last week Elizabeth had moved him in front of Rachel, because he kept whispering and tapping Rachel's shoulder. If Rachel craned her neck a bit, she had the perfect view of Orlie's desk.

In that moment, Rachel made a hasty decision. She would copy the answers from Orlie's paper.

Chapter 4

Buddy

Rachel Yoder, I'd like to speak to you," Elizabeth said when class was over for the day. "Orlie Troyer. . .I need to see you as well."

Rachel glanced over her shoulder. Everyone but Jacob had put on his or her coat and was heading out the door. Jacob stood at the back of the room with his arms folded and a scowl on his face.

"Jacob, you may wait outside for your sister." Elizabeth motioned Rachel and Orlie to the front of the room. "*Kumme* [come] now."

Rachel's heart hammered as she shuffled behind Orlie to their teacher's desk. The frown on Elizabeth's face let Rachel know that she'd probably done something wrong.

"I've been going over the true and false answers you both gave on the history test. Neither of you will get a star, because almost every one of your answers was wrong." Elizabeth paused and pointed to the stack of papers on her desk. "The strange thing is that each of you had exactly the same answers." She looked at Orlie. She looked at Rachel. "Which of you copied from the other person's paper?"

Rachel lowered her gaze and scuffed the toe of her shoe against the wooden floor.

"I don't know what you're talking about, Teacher," Orlie said. "I never copied anyone's paper."

Elizabeth touched Rachel's arm. "True or false, Rachel? Did you copy Orlie's paper?"

Rachel forced herself to look at the teacher. "True."

Elizabeth's forehead wrinkled. "Why would you do something like that?"

"I—I didn't know the answers," Rachel mumbled. "I was afraid to guess."

"You shouldn't have had to guess. Didn't you study?" Elizabeth questioned.

Rachel slowly shook her head. "I was going to study last night, but I fell asleep on my bed with my clothes on and didn't wake up until this morning." She drew in a quick breath. "I tried to study on the way to school, but my history book kept flopping shut. I figured I could study during morning recess, but Mary wanted me to join her and the others in the snow. Then after lunch, you asked me to cut out the stars, so—"

"No excuses, Rachel. I'm sure you could have made time to study yesterday if you'd wanted to." Elizabeth looked over at Orlie. "What about you? How much did you study for the test?"

Orlie's face turned red as a radish. "I tried to study, but I felt so bad when my *mamm* [mom] said I'd have to get rid of Buddy that I couldn't think about anything else."

"Who's Buddy?" Rachel asked, hoping the change of subject might take Elizabeth's mind off the history test.

"Buddy's my dog. Mama's been havin' sneezing fits lately and the doctor thinks she's allergic to Buddy." Orlie blinked his eyes and sniffed a couple of times. "Last night my daed said I'd have to find Buddy a new home."

"I'm sorry about that," Elizabeth said, "but it doesn't excuse you from studying." She leveled Rachel with a serious look. "And there's no excuse for cheating!"

Rachel cringed. When she'd copied Orlie's answers, she knew it was wrong. But she did it anyway. "I–I'm sorry, Teacher. I promise I'll never cheat on another test."

"I certainly hope not." Elizabeth motioned to Orlie. "Don't you think you owe him an apology, too?"

Rachel turned to face Orlie. "I'm sorry for copying your paper."

Elizabeth glanced out the window. "It's beginning to snow pretty hard, so you'd both better go home. For the rest of this week, Rachel will stay after school for one hour and do extra work." She reached for a sheet of paper, scribbled a note, and handed it to Rachel. "This is for your parents, letting them know that you cheated on the history test and what your punishment will be here at school."

Rachel swallowed hard. No doubt she would be punished at home, too.

"Are you gonna punish me, Teacher?" Orlie asked.

Elizabeth shook her head. "You didn't cheat, but you do need to study when you have a test."

He nodded. "From now on, I will."

"That will be all," Elizabeth said. "I'll see you both in the morning."

Rachel shuffled toward the door.

"Say, Rachel," Orlie said, as he, Jacob, and Rachel left the schoolyard together, "would you like to have a big shaggy dog named Buddy?"

"No thanks," she said with a shake of her head. "All the big shaggy dogs I've met like to bark and jump up on people."

"Buddy doesn't bark much," Orlie said. "And he only jumps up when he gets excited."

"No thanks," Rachel said again. "I've got a cat. Cats and dogs don't get along very well."

"They can learn to get along, just like people." Orlie stepped in front of Rachel. "Please say you'll take Buddy. I need to find him a good home."

"Sorry, but it won't be at *our* home." Rachel pushed past Orlie. She used to think Orlie was her friend, but why would a friend try to shove his mutt off onto someone who didn't want a dog?

"I'll take him," Jacob announced. "I asked for a puppy for my birthday a few years ago, but Mom said no to that because puppies make too many messes." His face broke into a wide smile. "Since Buddy's a full-grown dog, I don't think Mom will mind!"

"Well, I mind." Rachel's eyes narrowed. "Cuddles wouldn't like to have a big dog chasing her all the time."

"I'll train him to not chase the cat," Jacob said.

"How will you do that?"

Jacob shrugged. "I'll figure out something."

"Why don't you stop by my house on your way home?" Orlie suggested. "Then you can meet Buddy and decide if you'd like to take him home."

"No!" Rachel shouted.

"Yes!" Jacob hollered. "Orlie's place is right on the way, so we'll stop there now and meet Buddy."

When they arrived at Orlie's place, Rachel spotted Orlie's little sisters playing in the snow. She was tempted to join them, but Orlie nudged her arm and said, "Buddy's probably in the barn. I'll get him."

A few minutes later, Orlie returned from the barn with a big, red, shaggy dog.

Woof! The dog wagged his tail, jumped up, and licked Rachel's face.

"Ha ha! He likes you," Jacob said with a chuckle.

"Ha ha, yourself." Rachel wrinkled her nose and

crossed her eyes at Jacob. Then she pushed the dog away.

"Come on, Rachel. Don't give me that look. You know you like Buddy."

"I do not like him. He's big and hairy, and his tongue's wet and slimy!"

Orlie patted the dog's head. "He was only trying to be friendly." He looked at Jacob with a hopeful expression. "Do you like him?"

"Oh jah, I sure do!" Jacob said with a vigorous nod.

"Then why don't you take him home and see if your folks will let you keep him?"

"No!" Rachel shouted.

"Yes!" Jacob hollered.

"Danki," said Orlie. "It will make me feel much better if Buddy has a good home."

"Mom and Pap haven't said you could keep him yet," Rachel reminded her brother.

"I know," Jacob said, "but I'm hoping they'll say yes when they see how *wunderbaar* [wonderful] he is."

"I don't think he's wonderful, and I'm hoping they say no," Rachel mumbled.

"I'll get Buddy's leash so you can walk him home." Orlie dashed back to the barn. When he returned, he clipped a brown leather leash to Buddy's collar and patted the dog's head. "Good-bye, boy. Be good for Jacob. I'll come see you whenever I can."

Woof! Buddy wagged his tail and licked Orlie's hand.

"I guess we'd better go," Jacob said.

Rachel and Jacob had just started walking down the driveway when Orlie called, "Wait! I forgot to give you something!" He dashed to Jacob, reached into his pants pocket, and pulled out a plastic whistle. "Here, this is for you!"

"What's it for?" Jacob questioned.

"I trained Buddy with it. He comes when I blow it." Orlie placed the whistle in Jacob's hand. "It will also make him stop if he's running away from you."

"Danki, Orlie." Jacob smiled and put the whistle in his jacket pocket.

"You're welcome."

"See you at school." Jacob started walking again, with Buddy plodding beside him on the leash. Rachel walked on the other side of Jacob, wishing she could say something to make Jacob give up on the idea of taking Buddy home.

"See how nicely Buddy walks for me?" Jacob said. "I think he and I are gonna be real good friends. He seems to like you, too, Rachel."

Rachel only shrugged as Buddy nudged her hand with his cold nose. She trudged through the snow, gritting her teeth. Not only did she have a note in her backpack letting Mom and Pap know she'd been caught cheating, but a gross dog would probably live at their place from now on!

When Rachel and Jacob entered their yard, Jacob took Buddy to the barn. "I don't want him running back to Orlie's before I talk to Mom and Pap about letting me keep him," Jacob said to Rachel. "Don't say anything to Mom until I've talked to Pap," he added.

Rachel just grunted and headed for the house. She found Mom in the kitchen, baking chocolate chip cookies. They sure smelled good, but Rachel knew she wouldn't be able to eat any until she confessed that she cheated on the history test and had given Elizabeth's note to Mom.

"Hello, Rachel," Mom said as she put a tray of cookies into the oven. "Are you late getting home from school because of the snow?"

"Not really." Rachel dropped her backpack to the floor, slipped out of her coat and bonnet, and hung them on a wall peg near the back door. Then she picked up the backpack and walked across the room. "I did something today that I'm ashamed of," she said, sitting at the table.

Mom turned and wiped her floury hands on her apron. "What was that?"

"I—I cheated on my history test, and here's a note from Elizabeth." Rachel reached into her backpack, retrieved the note, and placed it on the table.

Mom sat across from Rachel and picked up the note. "Hmm. . .I see." She squinted and pushed her glasses to the bridge of her nose.

"Am I going to get a *bletsching* [spanking]?" Rachel asked.

"No," Mom said. "A spanking would be over with quickly and soon forgotten."

Rachel breathed a sigh of relief. Maybe she wouldn't be punished. Maybe Mom would just give her a lecture or quote a few scriptures from the Bible about cheating.

Mom dropped the note to the table and stared at Rachel. "Besides staying after school for the next week, when you come home you will have no playtime, and you'll do extra chores and studying."

"But, Mom," Rachel argued, "I'll be studying at school, and I already have so many chores."

"Then you shall have a few more." Mom pursed her lips and gave Rachel her "I mean what I say" look. "What you did was wrong. You need to learn a lesson."

"I know it was wrong to cheat, and I promised Elizabeth I would never do it again."

"Even so," Mom said, "You will be punished."

"What about Jacob?" Rachel asked. "Shouldn't he be punished for bringing home a big hairy mutt without asking?"

Mom's eyebrows squeezed together, making a deep wrinkle above her nose. "What are you talking about, Rachel?"

"Orlie Troyer's mutt. Orlie can't keep the dog anymore." Rachel could see by Mom's bewildered expression that she didn't quite believe her. "It's true.

Jacob's in the barn right now with Buddy."

"Buddy?"

"Orlie's dog."

Mom stood and pushed back her chair with such force that it toppled. Without bothering to pick it up, she grabbed her shawl off the wall peg and rushed out the door. Rachel followed.

They found Jacob in the barn, kneeling next to Buddy. Jacob jumped up. "I was going to find Pap soon, and then after I spoke with him, I was going to see if you—"

"I already know about the dog," Mom interrupted.

Jacob glared at Rachel. "You weren't supposed to tell. You're nothing but a *retschbeddi* [tattletale]."

"I never promised not to tell Mom." Rachel wrinkled her nose. "And I'm not a tattletale!"

"Jah, you are."

"No, I'm—"

"That will be enough, you two." Mom planted both hands on her hips. "Jacob, why did you bring the dog home without our permission?"

Jacob's chin quivered, and Rachel wondered if he might cry. "Orlie's mamm is allergic to the dog, and Orlie needs to find him a good home. I thought if I brought Buddy home, and you and Pap saw how nice he was, you'd let me keep him."

Mom's expression softened some as she knelt beside Jacob and stroked Buddy's floppy ear. "He does seem to be a nice *hund* [dog]."

Jacob nodded. "Oh jah, I think he's a wunderbaar hund."

"Even so, you should have asked before you brought the dog home," Mom said.

Jacob hung his head. "Sorry."

"I didn't want you to have a puppy before because they make so many messes, but since Buddy's a grown dog, puppy messes won't be a problem." Mom touched Jacob's shoulder. "If it's all right with your daed, you can keep the big fluffy dog."

Rachel flopped onto a bale of straw. "No, no," she moaned. She figured Mom had only given in to Jacob's request because he looked like he might cry.

"What's the matter with you, Rachel?" Mom asked. "You have a cat. Why shouldn't Jacob have a pet, too?"

"Because Buddy will chase Cuddles, and he might hurt her."

"He won't," Jacob insisted. "I'll teach him to get along with the cat."

"Humph!" Rachel frowned. "You can't make Buddy be nice to Cuddles any more than I can make Cuddles stop chasing mice."

"I'll bet I can. Buddy's real *schmaert* [smart]. I know he can be trained."

"I don't care how smart he is. He's a dog, and dogs don't like cats!"

Mom stepped between Rachel and Jacob. "Let's end

this discussion and wait and see what your daed says about you keeping Buddy."

"Where is Pap? He's not in the barn," Jacob said. "Is he in the house?"

Mom shook her head. "He, Grandpa, and Henry went to town. They said they'd be back in time for supper, but it's probably taking them longer because of the snow. I'm sure they'll be here soon, though."

Rachel squeezed her eyes shut. *I hope when Pap gets home he tells Jacob he can't keep Buddy.*

Chapter 5

More Troubles

For the rest of that week, Rachel had to stay after school every day. She cleaned the blackboards, swept the floor, and did extra reading from her history book. Knowing she had more studying and chores waiting at home made her feel cranky. The only good thing about staying after school was that Henry would pick her up every day with his horse and buggy. Since Jacob had chores to do at home, Mom didn't think it was fair to ask him to wait around the schoolyard until Rachel was ready to go home. Rachel liked that arrangement. Riding in the buggy was warmer than trudging through the cold snow. Besides, she didn't have to put up with Jacob's teasing.

"Are you glad the school week is over?" Henry asked on Friday afternoon when Rachel climbed into his buggy.

She nodded. "I'm happy the weekend is finally here.

At least I won't have any more school chores or lessons at the schoolhouse."

"You'll still have chores at home," Henry reminded her.

"Jah, I know—every day but Sunday." Sundays were for rest. All Rachel had to do on Sunday was help Mom serve a light breakfast and get ready for church. This Sunday, church would be held in the main section of Pap's barn. That meant they didn't have to travel to someone else's house for the service.

"From the looks of that sky, I'm guessing we might get more snow," Henry commented as he directed his horse onto the main road.

Rachel looked at the cloudy gray sky. "Maybe it will snow so hard the school board will decide to close the schoolhouse on Monday."

"The weather would have to get pretty bad before they did that." Henry snapped the reins to get his horse, Thunder, moving faster. Thunder turned his head and blew a puff of steam from his mouth. "Besides, think how bored you would be if you had to stay in the house all day."

"I would think of something fun to do," Rachel replied.

"More than likely Mom would think up something for you to do, and it would probably involve work."

Rachel didn't reply. She'd done so many chores this week, she didn't even want to think about work.

When Henry guided his horse and buggy up their

driveway, Rachel jumped down. She spotted Cuddles sitting on the porch railing. Had the cat been watching for Rachel? Or maybe she was looking for a mouse.

Rachel sloshed through the snow and stepped onto the porch. She dropped her schoolbooks onto the small table near the door and lifted the cat into her arms. "Did you miss me while I was at school?"

The cat purred and nuzzled Rachel's neck with her cold nose.

"I thought so. I missed you, too, Cuddles."

Rachel was about to bring Cuddles into the house when a furry red blob streaked across the porch. Cuddles hissed and jumped out of Rachel's arms. *Meow!*—she leaped off the porch!

Jacob's dog was right behind Cuddles, barking and swiping the poor cat's tail with his big pink tongue. Rachel wished Pap had said no when Jacob asked if he could keep Buddy. But Pap had seemed almost as eager to have the dog as Jacob had been.

"Halt ei, sell geht zu weit! [Stop, that's going too far!]" Rachel shouted. Where was Jacob, so he could blow that whistle? "Leave my cat alone, you big hairy mutt! Pick on someone your own size!"

Buddy skidded to a stop, whipped around, and raced back to the porch. Cuddles made a beeline for the barn. Rachel released a sigh of relief.

"You're a bad dog," Rachel said, shaking her finger at Buddy.

Slurp! Buddy swiped his tongue across Rachel's finger.

"Yuck! Why do you always lick me?" she grumbled.

Woof! Buddy wagged his tail, tipped his head to one side, and grabbed Rachel's history book in his slobbery mouth. Before Rachel could say a word, Buddy bounded off the porch and headed for the barn.

"Come back here you furry hund!" Rachel slid through the icy snow all the way to the barn. Just inside the door, she spotted Buddy scratching at a pile of straw. She looked around. There was no sign of Cuddles.

Rachel hurried over to Buddy. "What are you up to?"

Woof!

"Did you bury my book in the straw?"

Buddy cocked his head. *Woof! Woof!*

Rachel grunted. "Get out of my way!"

Buddy jumped up, put his huge paws on Rachel's chest, and swiped his slimy tongue across her cheek.

Rachel wrinkled her nose. "*Eww*. . .I think you need a minty doggie bone, because you have bad breath!" She pushed Buddy down with her knee then headed for the pile of straw to look for her book.

Buddy bounded over to Rachel and positioned his bulky body between her and the straw.

"You'd better move," Rachel threatened.

Buddy didn't budge. He just stood there with his tail waging and his tongue hanging out of his mouth.

"I'm warning you. . ."

Woof! Woof! Woof!

"What's the problem?" Henry asked, as he popped his head over one of the horse's stalls to look at Rachel.

She pointed at Buddy. "*He's* the problem!"

"What's Jacob's dog done now?"

"He chased my cat, stole my history book, and licked my face with his germy tongue." Rachel motioned to the pile of straw behind Buddy. "I think he buried the book in there."

Henry left the stall and grabbed Buddy's collar. "I'll hold the dog while you search for your book."

Rachel knelt in front of the straw and felt all around. "Here it is!" She withdrew the book, dusted it off with her hand, and turned it over. "There are no teeth marks." She glared at Buddy. "It's lucky for you that my book's not ruined."

"I'm glad you found it," Henry said. "I'll put Buddy back in his stall so he won't cause you any more trouble."

"Good idea." Rachel scrambled to her feet. She was almost to the door when she whirled around. "If you see Jacob, would you give him a message?"

"Jah, sure. What would you like me to tell him?"

"Tell him he'd better keep his promise and teach his dog to be nice to my cat!"

The following day when Rachel entered the barn, she was pleased to discover that the bales of hay that usually sat there had been removed. The floor was clean, too. It was ready for the backless wooden benches they would use for church tomorrow. She noticed that the benches were stacked along one wall. They would probably be set in place sometime later today. In the meantime, Rachel thought the barn was the perfect place to skateboard.

She glanced around. She saw no sign of Cuddles. No sign of Buddy, either. He must be in the empty horse stall where Jacob put him during the night.

Rachel cupped her hands around her mouth and called, "Here, Cuddles! Come kitty, kitty!"

All Rachel heard was the soft nicker of the buggy horses in their stalls at the other end of the barn.

"Cuddles! Where are you, Cuddles?" Rachel moved slowly around the barn, looking in every nook and cranny.

She was ready to give up and return to the house when she heard a faint, *meow*.

Rachel tipped her head and listened.

Meow! Meow! The sound grew louder.

Rachel followed the meowing sound, until she came to the ladder leading to the hayloft. She looked up. Cuddles sat in the hayloft, staring down at her.

Meow!

Rachel clapped her hands. "Here, kitty, kitty."

Cuddles didn't budge.

Rachel started up the ladder. "What a boppli you

are, Cuddles." As she picked up Cuddles, the cat dug her claws into Rachel's jacket and meowed louder.

"You're okay," Rachel whispered. "We're almost down."

When Rachel stepped off the ladder, she placed Cuddles on the floor and hurried to the shelf where she kept her skateboard. When she returned, Cuddles was lying on a straw bale, licking her paws.

Rachel picked up the cat and stepped onto the skateboard, holding Cuddles against her chest. "Here we go, now. This will be fun."

She pushed off with one foot, and the skateboard glided across the barn. She was about to turn and start for the other side of the barn, when Jacob's dog bounded in—*Woof! Woof!* Cuddles shrieked and tried to wriggle free, but Rachel held on tightly.

Woof! Buddy's tail flipped the hem of Rachel's long dress. With another loud bark, Buddy jumped up and swiped his big red tongue across Cuddles's head.

Yeow! Cuddles stuck out her claws and scratched Buddy's nose.

Woof! Woof! Buddy barked, and Cuddles leaped into the air. The skateboard wobbled, and Rachel toppled to the floor. "Trouble seems to follow everywhere I go," she muttered as she clambered to her feet.

Yeow!

Woof!

Rachel turned in time to see Cuddles race out

through the barn door with Buddy right behind her. Rachel rushed after them, hollering and waving her arms.

Cuddles and Buddy darted across the yard, zipped around trees, leaped over piles of snow, and slid across the icy lawn.

"Come back here, you two!" Rachel shouted. "Enough is enough!"

Cuddles's hair stood on the back of her neck. Buddy's tail swished. They both kept running.

Since Jacob wasn't there to blow the whistle Orlie had given him, Rachel knew she must do something to stop Jacob's dog from chasing her cat. Cuddles might get hurt!

When the animals raced past again, Rachel grabbed Buddy's collar. Cuddles meowed and leaped over the fence. Buddy let out a howl and tore across the yard, dragging Rachel facedown in the snow.

Jacob stepped into the yard, "Stop, Buddy! Stop!" He skidded across the yard and helped Rachel to her feet. "Are you all right? Why were you hanging onto Buddy's collar?"

"I was trying to save my cat!"

Jacob shook his head. "Don't you think you're overreacting? Buddy may like to chase Cuddles, but he hasn't hurt her, has he?"

"Well, no, but—"

"I think he only chases her because he wants to play."

"I don't think so." Rachel swiped her hand across her face, sending powdery snow all over Jacob.

He jumped back. "Watch what you're doing! I had a bath last night; I don't need a snow shower today!"

"Very funny." Rachel motioned to Buddy, who was across the yard, digging in the snow. "I thought you were going to teach him to behave. Where's that whistle Orlie gave you?"

"It's right here in my jacket." Jacob reached into his pocket, but pulled out an empty hand. "Oh no," he mumbled.

"What?"

"There's a hole in my pocket." Jacob's face turned red as a tomato. "I'm afraid I've lost the whistle."

"You lost it?" Rachel stared at Buddy, who was wagging his tail. "How can you train that mutt not to chase my cat if you don't have the whistle?"

Jacob rubbed his chin. "I don't know when the whistle fell out of my pocket, so I don't know where to look."

Rachel frowned. "I think the dog needs to go back to Orlie. He's out of control."

Jacob's eyes started to water. Rachel didn't know if it was due to the cold or if Jacob was getting teary-eyed because he didn't want to get rid of Buddy.

"I know what I'll do." Jacob moved to Buddy and patted his head. "The next time I go to town, I'll buy Buddy a new whistle!"

Chapter 6

Lots of Snow

Rachel pressed her nose against the living room window. Huge snowflakes drifted past the glass, whirling, swirling, spiraling toward the ground. More snowflakes piled on top of them. In some places the heavy snow had already made snowdrifts.

"I think we might be in for a blizzard," Mom said, stepping beside Rachel.

A few months ago, Rachel remembered seeing a wooly worm, more brown than black, crawling on the fence. Grandpa had said seeing a worm that color meant heavy snow would come soon. Rachel had never heard that about a wooly worm before, but she figured Grandpa must know what he was talking about because he had lived many years.

"Do you really think we'll have a blizzard?" Rachel asked her mother.

Mom nodded. "The way the snow's falling so fast,

and the wind's blowing with such powerful gusts, I'd say we're in for a good winter storm." She moved away from the window and stood with her back to the stone fireplace, where a cozy fire lapped at the logs and spilled warmth into the room. "If the weather gets bad enough, school might close until it improves."

Rachel joined Mom in front of the fireplace. If school closed, she wouldn't have any homework to do. Maybe she could sleep in every morning and spend her days playing with Cuddles or painting animal bodies on some of the rocks she found last summer.

"We can't do anything about the weather right now," Mom said, squeezing Rachel's shoulder. "Rudy and Esther are joining us for supper tonight, so I need your help in the kitchen."

Rachel sighed. It seemed like all she did was work, work, work. But she *was* glad to hear that Esther and her husband would come over tonight. Esther had missed their last church service because she was sick, and Rachel looked forward to spending time with her older sister. Esther had always listened to Rachel. She didn't call her "little bensel" the way Jacob often did, either.

"Wash your hands and set the table while I start cooking the noodles," Mom said when she and Rachel entered the kitchen.

Rachel went to the sink. "What else are we having besides noodles?"

"There's a ham in the oven, and we'll have boiled peas, tossed green salad, and hot rolls," Mom replied.

Rachel licked her lips as she lathered her hands with soap and water. "Just thinking about all that good food makes my stomach hungry."

Mom chuckled. "It seems you're always hungry, Rachel."

"Not when I'm *grank* [sick]."

"That's true," Mom agreed. "Most people aren't in the mood for food when they feel sick."

Rachel remembered when Mom first found out she was going to have a baby. Mom had often felt sick to her stomach. She'd called it "the morning sickness," and said she wasn't in the mood for food.

Mom stirred the boiling noodles on the stove then faced Rachel. "When your grandpa went to take a nap earlier this afternoon, he said I should wake him before Rudy and Esther arrive." She handed the wooden spoon to Rachel. "Would you please watch the noodles while I see if he's awake?"

"How about if I wake Grandpa?" Rachel didn't want to watch the noodles. What if she did something wrong? She didn't look forward to more of Jacob's teasing.

"When I was making the salad earlier, I smeared some tomato juice on my dress," Mom said. "I need to change before our company arrives, and since Grandpa's room is just down the hall from mine, it's easy for me to stop and wake him up."

"Okay, but what should I do if the noodles get done before you get back?" Rachel asked.

"Do you remember how I told you to tell if the noodles are done?"

Rachel nodded. "If I can cut them easily with the spoon, they're tender enough."

"That's right," said Mom. "If they get done before I come back, drain the water into the sink, put the noodles into a bowl, and mix them with a little butter and cheese."

"I think I can do that." Rachel decided the procedure didn't sound too hard. Besides, it shouldn't take Mom long to change her dress and wake Grandpa. She was sure Mom would return before the noodles were done.

"You'll do fine, Rachel." Mom said as she hurried from the room.

Rachel moved to the stove and watched the boiling noodles. Every few seconds she poked the spoon inside and stirred the noodles to keep them from sticking. Mom still wasn't back, so when the noodles felt tender, Rachel removed the kettle from the stove. Then she took out the strainer, placed it in the sink, and poured the noodles in.

"Oops!" Most of the noodles missed the strainer and landed in the sink.

"*Sis nau futsch*! [It's all ruined now!]" Rachel muttered

as she stared at the noodles. "What should I do?"

Suddenly, an idea popped into Rachel's head. She scooped up the noodles, put them back into the strainer, and turned on the faucet and rinsed them. Next, she took a clean bowl from the cupboard, and poured the noodles into it.

Rachel didn't want anyone to know what had happened. The sink was clean, she had rinsed the noodles—they shouldn't have any germs on them now.

When Rachel and her family gathered around the kitchen table that evening, Rudy commented on how good everything smelled.

"I agree," Esther put in. "It looks and smells *appeditlich* [delicious]. Mom outdid herself on this meal."

Mom smiled at Rachel. "I can't take all the credit. Rachel cooked the noodles."

"I love hot buttered noodles with plenty of cheese," Rudy said as he forked some into his mouth. He chewed the noodles a couple of times, and a strange expression crossed his face.

"Rudy, what's wrong?" Esther asked. "I thought you liked noodles."

Rudy opened his mouth and pulled out something that didn't look anything like a noodle. It was yellow and square.

"What in all the world?" Mom's glasses slipped to

the end of her nose as she studied the small object in Rudy's hand. "Why, that looks like part of the sponge I use for washing dishes!"

Grandpa nodded. "That's what it looks like to me."

Pap turned to Rachel and frowned. "Do you know how part of a sponge got in with the noodles?"

Rachel's face heated. She wished she could crawl under the table and hide. "Well, I—"

"I'll bet she dumped the noodles on the floor and was trying to wash them with the sponge," Jacob said.

"Please say that's not what happened." Mom's forehead wrinkled as she stared at Rachel. "If you dropped the noodles on the floor, then you should have thrown them out and started over with a new batch."

Rachel shook her head. "I didn't drop them on the floor."

"Then what happened?" Henry wanted to know.

"I was draining the water from the noodles into the strainer." Rachel drew in a quick breath. "But the noodles fell into the sink instead."

"Then what did you do?" Pap questioned.

"I scooped up the noodles, put them back in the strainer, and rinsed them off. Then I took a clean bowl from the cupboard and poured the noodles in." Rachel's ears burned with embarrassment, and her throat felt so tight she could barely swallow. Why was it that every time she tried to do something grownup she made a mess of things?

"I guess you didn't rinse the noodles well enough. Maybe you should have thrown them out and started over," Esther said gently.

"I didn't want to waste them or cause dinner to be late." Rachel shrugged. "I was afraid Mom would be mad if I threw them out."

Grandpa's bushy gray eyebrows lifted high on his forehead. "Maybe you should have waited until your mamm came back to the kitchen to tell you what to do."

Rachel lowered her head and mumbled, "Jah."

Jacob nudged Rachel's arm with his elbow. "And you wonder why I call you a little bensel?"

"Jacob, that's all we need to hear from you on the subject," Pap said. "Rachel feels bad enough about Rudy nearly eating a piece of sponge. You don't have to make her feel any worse."

"If she didn't think she had to be in control of everything. . ."

"Jacob. . ." Pap leaned closer to Jacob and squinted his eyes. "Do you want extra chores to do?"

"No, Pap."

"Then eat your meal and be quiet."

Any other time, Rachel might have found satisfaction in Jacob being scolded for teasing her. Not this time, though. She only wanted to find a place to hide and forget she'd ever been asked to watch the boiling noodles.

"May I be excused?" she asked.

"If you don't finish your supper, you can have no dessert," Mom said.

Rachel shrugged. "I don't care. I'm not hungry."

"Suit yourself; but remember, breakfast is a long time off," Pap said.

Rachel pushed back her chair and stood. Then she turned to Rudy. "I–I'm sorry about the sponge you almost ate." Without waiting for a reply, Rachel rushed out of the room. When she reached the hallway she grabbed her jacket and hurried out the back door.

As Rachel stepped into the snowy yard, her feet went numb from the cold. She should have put on her boots.

"I'll be okay if I hurry," Rachel muttered as she crunched through the snow and headed for the barn. If she found Cuddles there, maybe the two of them could stay warm together by burrowing in a clump of hay.

But she didn't see Cuddles—just Jacob's sleeping dog in the empty horse stall where Jacob was told to keep him until Pap found the time to build a dog house. Rachel was glad Buddy was sleeping. She didn't want to deal with him barking, jumping, or licking her face.

She sat on a bale of hay and closed her jacket tightly. "Sometimes I wish I wasn't me," she mumbled. "Sometimes I wish—"

The barn door swung open, and Esther stepped in. "I thought I might find you here."

Rachel only nodded.

"I came to tell you good-bye," Esther said.

"You're leaving already?"

"Jah. It's snowing much harder now, and Rudy thinks we should head for home before the roads get too bad."

"That's probably a good idea," Rachel agreed.

Esther sat beside Rachel. "I wanted to tell you one more thing."

"What's that?" Rachel asked.

"Don't let Jacob get under your skin. He just likes to tease."

"Jah, I know."

Esther slipped her arm around Rachel's shoulders. "I love you, little sister."

"I love you, too."

When Rachel woke up the following morning, she hurried to the window and lifted the shade. Everything in the yard was white, and the heavy swirling snowflakes kept her from seeing the barn.

Rachel rushed from her room and scrambled down the stairs in her bare feet. "It looks like we got that blizzard you said was coming!" she hollered as she darted into the kitchen and found Mom scrambling some eggs.

"Quiet down, Rachel." Mom put a finger to her lips. "Grandpa's still sleeping."

"Sorry." Rachel peered out the kitchen window.

"The snow is so deep I can't even see the path leading from the house to the barn."

"I know," said Mom. "Deacon Byler stopped by a few minutes ago and said they've decided to close the school until the weather improves."

Rachel jumped up and down; then she did a half-spin. "Yippee! That means I have the whole day to play in the snow!"

Mom shook her head. "It's much too cold to play outside."

"But what will I do all day?" Rachel hoped Mom didn't give her more chores. She'd had enough of those.

"Maybe after breakfast you and Jacob can play table games," Mom suggested.

"Let's play checkers," Jacob said as he stepped into the room.

Rachel frowned. "I don't like playing checkers."

"That's because you always lose."

Rachel squinted at Jacob. "I do not."

Jacob folded his arms. "Okay then. Prove it, right after breakfast!"

"It's nice to stay home from school today," Jacob said as he placed the checkerboard on the folding table in the living room. "This will be *snow* much fun!"

"Ha!" Rachel wrinkled her nose. "Very funny."

Jacob handed her the red checker pieces, and he took the black ones. "You can go first."

"Really?"

He nodded. "Said so, didn't I?"

Rachel made her first move and leaned back in her chair as she waited for Jacob to take his turn. "I hope the storm doesn't last too long. It's fun to be out of school for a day, but I wouldn't want to be cooped up in the house for too long."

"I'm sure the storm won't last forever." Jacob moved his checker piece. "You need to learn to be more patient."

Rachel didn't answer. Her mind was on the game, and how she hoped to win this time. She slid a red checker to the next square. "Your turn, Jacob."

"I know it's my turn. I'm thinking."

"Well, don't think too long. I don't have all day."

"Are you going somewhere?"

"No, I'm not." Rachel shivered and rubbed her hands over her arms. "*Brr*. . .even with a fire in the fireplace, this room seems awfully chilly."

"That's because it's cold outside." Jacob moved his checker piece. "Your turn."

"If it weren't for snow, I wouldn't have landed in the creek when I went sledding a few weeks ago," Rachel grumbled as she moved another checker piece. "I hate the snow!"

"You hate the snow? Since when?"

"I hate it when I have to stay inside and can't play in it."

"Mom says we should never hate anything," Jacob said.

"We're not supposed to hate *anyone*, not *anything*," Rachel corrected.

Jacob stared at Rachel. "Now how did the girl who flunked her history test a few weeks ago get to be so schmaert?"

"I've always been smart. I just don't like history."

"Are you saying you hate history?"

"No, I'm saying I don't *like* history."

"Whatever." Jacob gestured to the checkerboard. "Are you gonna move or not?"

"It's not my turn—it's yours."

A blank expression crossed Jacob's face, and Rachel gritted her teeth. Finally, Jacob picked up a black checker piece and—*click, click, click*—he jumped three of Rachel's red pieces.

"Now who likes to be in control?" she muttered as she took her turn.

"What was that?"

"Oh nothing."

"The only bad part about this blizzard," Jacob said, changing the subject back to the weather, "is that I won't be able to go to town and buy a new whistle for Buddy."

Buddy. Rachel frowned. Did they have to spoil the day by talking about that mutt?

"You still don't like Buddy, do you?" Jacob asked.

She shrugged. "He never listens to me, and he always chases my cat."

"I'll train him—you'll see. As soon as the snow lets up and Pap goes to town, I'll get that whistle. Then once I train Buddy, I'm sure he'll stop chasing Cuddles."

Rachel wasn't convinced that blowing a whistle could make a dog come to someone or stop running. "We'll have to wait and see how it goes," she muttered.

As the game continued, Rachel became more agitated and impatient with Jacob. He took forever to make a move, and since he was obviously winning, she wanted the game to be over. With an exasperated sigh, she reached across the board, picked up one of Jacob's black checker pieces and jumped four of her red pieces. "There!" she announced. "You win the game!"

Chapter 7
Grandpa's Secret

I am so bored. There's nothing fun to do," Rachel complained as she and Jacob sat at the kitchen table drinking the hot chocolate Mom fixed before she went to her room to take a nap. Grandpa was in his room resting, too. Pap and Henry had gone to the buggy shed to repair a broken wheel.

Jacob wrinkled his forehead. "I can't believe school's already been closed for three days on account of the snow."

"The last time I looked out the window, the snow had stopped and the wind wasn't howling so much," Rachel said. "Maybe tomorrow school will be open again."

"I hope so." Jacob poked at the marshmallow floating on top of his cup. "Maybe we could play a game."

Rachel groaned. "Not checkers, please!"

He shook his head. "We could work on a puzzle."

"That takes too much time, and I never can find any

of the end pieces."

"Then let's play hide-and-seek."

Rachel blew on her hot chocolate. "That would mean we'd have to run around the house looking for hiding places, which is not a good idea." She glanced at Grandpa's bedroom door down the hall. "We'll be in trouble if we wake Grandpa. We wouldn't want to wake Mom, either."

"That's true," Jacob agreed. "Mom needs her rest because she's expecting a boppli. Grandpa's old, so he needs his rest, too."

"Grandpa's not old," Rachel said with a shake of her head. "And don't you go saying he's going to die soon, either, because—"

Jacob held up his hand. "Who said anything about dying? I was only saying that Grandpa needs more rest because he's. . . Oh, never mind."

Rachel figured Jacob was just looking for an argument, so she changed the subject. "What other games could we play?"

Jacob tapped his fingers on the edge of the table. "Let's see. . . We could play Sorry."

Rachel shook her head. "You always cheat."

"Do not."

"Do so."

"All right," Jacob said, "you choose a game."

"How about Scrabble?" Rachel suggested.

"No way! You always win!"

"That's because I'm a good speller."

"Jah, you're one of the best spellers in our school. Not like me," Jacob mumbled. "I can barely spell my name."

Rachel poked Jacob's arm. "That's not so, and you know it."

He scooted his chair away from the table. "I still think we should play hide-and-seek."

"I told you before, we can't play that in the house." Rachel shook her head. "And we can't play it outside because it's too cold."

"How about the barn?" Jacob asked hopefully. "There are lots of good places to hide in Pap's barn."

"You're right!" Rachel jumped up and grabbed her jacket from the wall peg. "The barn will be a great place to play hide-and-seek!"

"Do you want to hide first or should I?" Jacob asked Rachel when they entered the barn.

"I guess I will." Rachel glanced around. "Where's Buddy? I don't want to hide near him."

"Buddy's a nice dog," Jacob said. "And he really does like you, Rachel."

"No, he doesn't."

"Jah, he does. Why do you think he likes to jump up and lick your face?"

Rachel scrunched up her nose. "It's so *ekelhaft* [disgusting] when he does that!"

"I've been working with him, and I think he's getting better."

"Humph! He still chases Cuddles."

Jacob heaved a sigh. "I know. I've tried feeding them together, but Buddy eats Cuddles's food, and then she hisses and swipes at his tail."

"That's because she doesn't like him."

"She will someday—hopefully after I buy Buddy a new whistle and train him."

Rachel grunted. "We'll see about that."

"So, are we gonna play hide-and-seek or not?" Jacob asked.

"I suppose so. . . As long as your dog doesn't bark and give away my hiding place."

"I put Buddy in the empty horse stall after I took him for a walk this morning."

"I'll bet it was hard trying to walk him in the snow." Rachel thought about the day Buddy had dragged her facedown in the freezing snow.

"It wasn't so bad." Jacob motioned to the rope hanging from the loft overhead. "I think I'll see if I can hang upside down on that while I count to one hundred and you look for a good place to hide."

Rachel looked up at the rope. Then she looked at Jacob and shook her head. "You're kidding, right?"

"No, I'm not." Jacob scampered up the ladder leading to the hayloft, grabbed the rope, and swung out over the pile of hay near Rachel. "Yippee! This is *snow* much fun!" he shouted. "Maybe I'll forget about playing hide-and-seek and swing on the rope."

Rachel planted her hands on her hips and scowled. "What am I supposed to do while you're swinging?"

"You can play with your cat." Jacob made another pass near Rachel, and as his feet touched the hayloft again, he called, "But that might be hard to do because she's up here sleeping!"

Rachel grunted. "Jacob Yoder, come down here right now! You promised we could play hide-and-seek, and you should never go back on a promise."

"I didn't promise; I just suggested it." He peered at her with a silly grin.

"Fine then—don't play!" Rachel folded her arms and stuck out her lower lip. "See if I care."

"Oh, all right, but I'm going to start counting from here." Still clinging to the rope, Jacob flipped upside down. His face turned crimson from the blood that had rushed to his head.

Rachel rolled her eyes toward the roof of the barn. "Now who's a bensel?"

"You are, little sister!" Jacob closed his eyes. "I'm starting to count now, so you'd better get going. One. . . two. . .three. . ."

Rachel scampered off in search of the best place to hide. *Should I hide in the loft? No, Jacob will hear me climb the ladder. Should I hide in the empty stall? No way! Buddy's in there, and he'll bark and give me away.*

Rachel spotted several bales of hay stacked in one corner. *That looks like a good place to hide!* She tiptoed across the floor and slipped behind them. Now she only had to wait for Jacob to find her.

Jacob finally quit counting, and Rachel tried to be as still as possible. She wondered how long it would take him to discover her hiding place.

Several minutes went by but no sign of Jacob. She didn't hear him walking anywhere, either.

More time passed. Still no Jacob.

Rachel tapped her foot impatiently. *What could be keeping him?*

She twirled her finger around the ties on her *kapp* [cap] and yawned. *Why hasn't he found me yet? What is taking him so long?*

Rachel bit the end of her nail. *If he doesn't find me soon, I won't play this game anymore.*

Several more minutes passed, and Rachel decided she had waited long enough. She slipped out from behind the bales of hay and stood in the middle of the room.

Whoosh! Jacob swept past her, still hanging onto the rope. This time he was right side up.

"Rachel! What are you doing out here?" he hollered. "You're supposed to be hiding."

"I was hiding, but I got tired of waiting." She clucked her tongue, the way Mom often did. "You're slower than sticky melassich, and you were supposed to be looking for me, not swinging on that rope!"

"I'm not slower than molasses. I just wanted to give you plenty of time to hide." Jacob let go of the rope and dropped into the mound of hay below. "*You*, little bensel, are just too impatient!"

Rachel opened her mouth to defend herself, but Pap stepped into the barn and asked Jacob to help him and Henry clean the horses' stalls.

With shoulders slumped and head down, Jacob headed for the stalls.

I guess Jacob's not having such a good time being out of school, either, Rachel thought as she sat on a stool near the woodstove. She sat with her chin cupped in her hand, thinking about how bored she was and how much she missed school.

Rachel swiveled on the stool and looked at the rope hanging from the rafters. *Maybe I should hang upside down like Jacob did.* She shook her head. *I guess that wouldn't be a good idea since I'm wearing a dress.*

Whoosh! A rush of cold air whipped against Rachel's legs as the barn door opened and Grandpa stepped in.

"What are you doing out here?" he asked, joining Rachel in front of the stove.

"Sitting. Thinking." She folded her arms so she wouldn't be tempted to bite another fingernail. It was a bad habit, Mom had told her often. "Trying to not be bored."

"I have an idea." Grandpa's bushy gray eyebrows

jiggled as he rubbed his hands.

"What's that?"

"Why don't we blow some bubbles?"

Rachel made a sweeping gesture of the barn with her hand. "Here?"

He nodded. "When I was a *buwe* [boy] and wanted something fun to do, I got out my bubble wand and made some remarkable bubbles."

"What's so remarkable about blowing bubbles?" Rachel had a bubble wand Pap had made for her birthday last year, but none of her bubbles had been remarkable.

Grandpa patted Rachel's arm. "I'll be right back with my surprise."

Rachel drummed her fingers along the edge of her stool as she waited for Grandpa to return.

A short time later, Grandpa returned carrying two bubble wands and a bottle of bubble solution. He set the jar on a shelf and opened the lid. He dipped one wand into the liquid and then the other. Slowly, he blew on the first wand until a bubble formed. Then he blew on the other wand, and another bubble formed. Next, he connected the two bubbles and made two more. By the time he was done, he had a chain of bubbles that looked like a worm.

Rachel clapped her hands. "Grandpa, you've made a wooly worm!"

Grandpa laughed from deep in his throat. "You're

right, Rachel—just like the wooly worms you took to school last fall."

Rachel nodded. "I still can't believe the way Orlie tried to win the race by pushing his wooly worm up the string with his tongue. That was so ekelhaft."

"It was a disgusting thing to do," Grandpa said with a nod. "You know, Rachel, it's not good for people to take control of things just to get their way."

Rachel stared at the floor as heat erupted on her cheeks. Was Grandpa talking about her? Did he think she liked to take control?

"Speaking of Orlie," she said, deciding it might be best to change the subject, "his birthday's coming soon. I need to think of something to give him for a present."

Grandpa blew on the bubbles and sent them sailing across the barn. "Maybe you should pray about it."

"I doubt that God would care about something like that."

"Nothing is too small for God to care about," Grandpa said. "You know, there's something I've been praying about, too."

"Have you been praying that God will melt the snow?"

He chuckled. "No, but maybe I should, so you and Jacob can go back to school."

"I was hoping it would snow really hard so school would be closed, but now I'm ready to go back," Rachel admitted.

"I understand." Grandpa handed Rachel one of the bubble wands. "Can you keep a secret?"

She nodded. She felt grown up to know Grandpa would trust her with his secret.

"The thing that I've been praying about is. . ." Grandpa leaned close to Rachel's ear and whispered, "I'm thinking about opening a greenhouse in the spring."

Rachel's eyes widened. "Really?"

"Jah. I've enjoyed working with flowers ever since I was a boy. Now that I'm older and retired from farming, I want to do something useful with the time I have left on this earth."

"I hope you have lots of time left," Rachel said as a lump formed in her throat. She couldn't imagine not having Grandpa around.

He leaned over and hugged Rachel. "Don't worry. If I take care of myself, I think I'll be with you a long time."

"I like flowers, too, Grandpa. I wish I could own a greenhouse some day." Rachel sighed. "But I guess that will never happen."

"Maybe when you're older and out of school," Grandpa said.

Rachel shook her head. "I doubt I'll ever get to do any of the things I really want to do."

"Besides owning a greenhouse, what else would you like to do?" he asked.

"I'd like to go for a ride in a car that has no top. When I told Jacob that, he said the idea was foolishness."

"You really want to ride in a convertible?"

She nodded.

"Why?"

"I think it would be fun to be in a car with the top down, going really fast." Rachel scrunched her nose. "But I don't know if it'll ever happen, and I'm getting tired of waiting."

"The Bible says in Proverbs 19:11: 'A man's wisdom gives him patience.'" Grandpa patted Rachel's head. "You need more patience, but you also need good judgment."

Rachel tipped her head. "What do you mean?"

"I had an experience once that taught me a lesson I'll never forget," he replied.

"What experience was that?"

Grandpa leaned his head back and closed his eyes. Rachel wondered if he had fallen asleep.

"It was a long time ago. . ." Grandpa said. "I was a teenage boy, like Henry."

Rachel realized now why Grandpa had closed his eyes. He was remembering.

"I wanted to ride a motorcycle. Wanted it more than anything." Grandpa paused, and his lips twitched. "Our English neighbor, Robert, got a motorcycle for his birthday one year, and Robert promised me a ride." He paused again.

Rachel fidgeted with the strings on her kapp. She was anxious for Grandpa to finish his story. "Did you get to take that ride, Grandpa?"

He opened his eyes and blinked. "I took it all right. Robert gave me the ride of my life."

"Did you go really fast?"

Grandpa nodded. "It was the fastest ride I've ever had."

Rachel's eyes widened, and her heart pounded. "Was it fun?"

"It was, until we skidded on some gravel and the motorcycle tipped over." Grandpa's forehead wrinkled. "Robert broke his leg, but I ended up with some nasty cuts and scrapes." He pulled up his pant leg and pointed to a finger-length scar.

Rachel's mouth fell open. "Grandpa, I never knew you did anything like that."

Grandpa nodded soberly. "You have to be careful about the choices you make, Rachel. Don't be in a hurry to experience all the things the world has to offer. Some things aren't as fun as you think they will be." He reached for Rachel's hand and gently squeezed her fingers.

Rachel nestled against Grandpa's shoulder. "I'm glad you came to live with us."

He smiled. "Me, too."

Chapter 8

Always in a Hurry

What are you making?" Jacob asked on Thursday morning when he entered the kitchen, where Rachel sat at the table.

Rachel turned in her chair. "I'm getting ready to paint a ladybug rock for Orlie, and I need to hurry so I can get it done on time."

"*Dummel dich net!* [Take your time, don't hurry!]" Jacob said, shaking his head.

Rachel frowned. "Why do you always tell me what to do?"

"Because you're a little bensel and need someone to tell you what to do."

"I don't need *you* telling me what to do." Rachel flapped her hand at him. "Go away. . .shoo. . .don't bother me."

"No problem. The roads are better today, so Pap hitched one of our buggy horses to the sleigh. I'm going to town with him and Grandpa." Jacob leaned close to Rachel's ear. "You won't have to put up with me for the rest of the morning, little bensel."

"If you're heading to town, don't forget to buy a whistle so you can train Buddy."

"I won't; that's why I decided to go along." Jacob peered over Rachel's shoulder. "Why are you making a painted rock for Orlie? I thought you didn't like him."

Rachel's cheeks burned. Would Jacob tease her about Orlie now? "I don't like some of the things Orlie does," she said, "but I don't dislike him. Right before Christmas I promised to make something for his birthday, so I'm trying to keep that promise."

Jacob's forehead wrinkled. "You still don't like the fact that Orlie gave me his dog, do you?"

"I don't like Buddy, but I'm not mad at Orlie." Rachel shrugged. "Besides, he had to give the mutt to someone."

Jacob nodded. "Well, I'd better go. I don't want to keep Pap and Grandpa waiting in the cold." *Bam!* Jacob slammed the back door.

Rachel picked up the small paintbrush lying on the table. If she hurried, she might have time to play in the snow.

She dipped her paintbrush in the bottle of black paint and painted the entire rock for the ladybug's body. Then she dipped the brush into the white paint to make the ladybug's eyes and antenna.

"Ach!" Rachel cried when she realized that the white paint had turned gray. "I should have cleaned the black paint off the brush before dipping it into the white paint."

Rachel rushed to the sink and washed out the brush then hurried back to the table. She dipped the brush into the white paint again and drew a circle for each eye and thin lines for the ladybug's antenna. Now it only needed some red circles on its body for wings, two black dots in the white circles for the eyes, and a red line for the mouth. Then the ladybug rock would be finished.

This time Rachel remembered to wash the brush before she dipped it into the red paint. But she didn't remember to wait until the black paint had dried before adding the red dots to the body.

"Ugh!" she moaned. The red paint had run into the black paint! Now she had to start over again.

Rachel was glad Jacob wasn't there to see her mistake. He probably would have teased her about it and called her a bensel.

Rachel took the rock to the sink and turned on the faucet. Black, red, and white paint dribbled off the rock and ran down the drain. "What a waste," she muttered.

"Rachel, please go outside and give the chickens food and water," Mom said as she stepped into the kitchen.

"Now?"

Mom nodded.

"Can't it wait until I finish painting Orlie's ladybug rock?"

Mom shook her head. "The chickens need to be cared for."

"Okay." Rachel placed the rock on the edge of the sink and dried her hands on a towel. At this rate, she would never get to play in the snow.

She slipped into her jacket and was almost to the back door when Mom called, "While you're outside, you'd better go to the barn and give Jacob's dog some food and water."

Rachel frowned. "Didn't Jacob do that before he left for town?"

Mom shook her head. "Your daed was in a hurry so Jacob asked Henry to give food and water to Buddy."

"Then why are you asking me to do it?"

"Because I asked Henry to chop wood for the stove, and he'll be busy with that for quite a while," Mom said. "Since you're going outside, I figured you could tend to Buddy."

Rachel wasn't happy about doing anything for Buddy, but she knew better than to argue. "Okay," she mumbled.

"And don't forget to take a bucket of hot water with you, because the water dishes in the chicken coop are probably frozen."

Rachel found a bucket in the utility room, filled it with hot water from the sink, and headed out the door. She walked carefully through the snow so she wouldn't spill any water. Besides the fact that it was hot, Rachel knew if she got any on her clothes, it could freeze right on the spot. The last thing she needed was to burn herself, or end up with a cold, frozen dress!

When Rachel entered the chicken coop, she discovered that the water in all the dishes was frozen, just as Mom had said. Carefully, she poured hot water over the ice. When it melted enough for the chickens to drink, she opened the bag of chicken feed and put some in each food dish.

When that was done, Rachel picked up the empty bucket and turned to go. She'd only taken a few steps, when—*whack!*—she was hit in the leg by the wing of a squawking chicken. Another hen squawked and soon the whole chicken coop became a whirl of noisy, flapping chickens.

Gripping the empty bucket, Rachel dashed for the door. She didn't look forward to returning to the chicken coop, but knew she would be expected to feed and water the chickens again tomorrow.

Rachel stepped outside and walked slowly across the yard. When she entered the barn she heard a whistling, snorting sound coming from the stall where Buddy slept. She set the bucket on the floor, hurried to the other side of the barn, and slowly opened the stall door. The last thing she needed was for Buddy to see her and get all excited.

As soon as Rachel saw Buddy, curled up in a mound of straw, she recognized the whistling, snorting sound.

Buddy was snoring!

She held her breath and tiptoed across the floor, careful not to wake the sleeping dog. Then she picked up Buddy's empty water dish and left the stall.

When Rachel reached the other side of the barn, she set the dish on the floor and grabbed the hose Pap used to clean things in the barn. The hose was connected to a water pipe, and during the cold winter months, Pap kept a lantern lit above the pipe so it wouldn't freeze.

Rachel leaned over, and was about to turn on the faucet, when—*fump!*—two big paws landed on her back and nearly pushed her over.

Rachel whirled around and shook her finger at Buddy. "Stay down! You almost knocked me down, you big, hairy mutt!" She would be glad when Jacob got home with a new whistle.

Buddy tipped his head to one side and whined.

"You should be ashamed of yourself, Buddy," she muttered.

The dog nudged Rachel with his cold, wet nose, the way he did when he wanted to play. She wished she'd remembered to close the stall door, but she hadn't expected Buddy to wake up while she was filling his water dish.

"I don't have time to play now." Rachel grunted. "I only came here to give you some food and water."

Buddy's tongue shot out, and he licked Rachel's hand.

"Stop that!" She wiped her hand on her jacket and

turned on the hose. When Buddy's dish was full of water, she carried it carefully back to his stall. Buddy followed and lapped at the water as soon as she set the dish on the floor.

Rachel put food in Buddy's dish; then she closed the stall door and headed out of the barn.

She tromped through the snow toward the house but halted when several snowflakes brushed her cheeks. "I hope we don't have another snowstorm," Rachel said with a groan. She needed to get Orlie's rock painted, and then she hoped to build a snowman.

The snow stopped as quickly as it had started, and when Rachel looked up, she realized the flakes of snow she'd felt had dropped from the tree overhead, not from the sky.

Rachel stared longingly at the ground, glistening with tiny ice crystals. It would be so much fun to make a pretty snow angel. If she was going to get Orlie's rock done today, she shouldn't take the time to play in the snow, but—well, maybe she could make just one snow angel.

Rachel dropped to the ground, spread her arms back and forth, and stared at the hazy sky. Of all the seasons, she liked summer the best, but there were some fun things to do in the winter.

Yip! Yip! Yip! Rachel's thoughts were interrupted as Buddy carried on in the barn.

She moaned and clambered to her feet. "Now what

is that dog's problem? He's been fed and watered; I thought he might go back to sleep."

Rachel glanced at the barn and gasped. Water ran out from under the barn door and formed a puddle in the yard!

"Oh no," she moaned. "I must have left the hose running!"

Stepping around the water, which seemed to freeze right before Rachel's eyes, she rushed into the barn. Sure enough, the hose was still running, and water ran everywhere.

"The hurrier I go, the behinder I get," Rachel mumbled. That was one of Grandma Yoder's favorite sayings. "Why, oh why, did I leave that hose running?"

Rachel sloshed her way over to the sink and turned off the water. Then, being careful to stay away from the frozen puddle outside, she started for the house.

Woof! Woof! Buddy bounded up to her, barking and wagging his tail.

"How did you get out?" Rachel scolded. She'd thought she had closed both the stall door and the barn door. She shook her head slowly and frowned. "Everything's so *verhuddelt* [mixed up] today."

As Rachel stepped forward, her foot slipped on the ice, and she grabbed Buddy's collar to keep from falling.

Buddy must have thought she wanted to play because he took off like a shot. Slipping and sliding over the frozen water and into the snowy yard, he pulled Rachel along.

"Stop, Buddy!" she hollered. But Buddy kept going. Around and around in circles he went, like an ice skater. Rachel's stomach flew up and her head spun like a top. This was not the kind of fun she'd planned to have today!

Buddy screeched to a stop, and Rachel plopped into a mound of snow.

Slurp! Slurp! The unruly dog licked her face with his big red tongue.

Rachel scrambled to her feet. "Bad dog! Jacob needs to teach you some manners!"

Buddy whimpered and lowered his head.

Rachel clomped up the stairs and rushed into the kitchen.

"Slow down, Rachel," Mom said. "What's your hurry?"

Before Rachel could reply, Buddy bolted into the room, circled Rachel, and crashed into the table. Rachel's jars of paint toppled over, and a pool of red, black, and white paint dripped onto the floor.

"Oh no!" Rachel wailed. "Now I can't paint a ladybug rock for Orlie's birthday!"

Mom grabbed Buddy's collar and ushered him out the door; then she turned to Rachel. "Why did you let Jacob's dog in the house?"

"I—I didn't. He followed me up to the house after I—" Tears sprang to Rachel's eyes. "Oh, Mom, everything I've tried to do this morning has gone wrong!"

"Besides this mess, what else has gone wrong?"

Mom asked, motioning to the paint.

Rachel grabbed a mop to clean the paint, while she told Mom about the trouble in the chicken coop, the barn, and then outside with the ice and Buddy dragging her across the slippery yard.

"It sounds to me like you could have avoided at least some of that trouble if you hadn't been in such a hurry." Mom clucked her tongue. "It doesn't pay to be impatient or to try to do things too quickly."

"I wanted to hurry so I could paint Orlie's rock, and then I hoped I could play in the snow." Rachel drew in a quick breath. "Now I have no paint left, so I can't give Orlie a rock for his birthday."

"Why don't you give Orlie one of your own painted rocks?" Mom suggested.

Rachel sniffed. "I—I do have that ladybug rock in my room. I guess I could give it to Orlie and make a new one for myself when I get more paint."

Mom smiled and patted Rachel's head. "That would be a nice thing to do."

Just then, the back door opened, and Jacob stepped into the house. "Whew! It was sure cold riding in that sleigh!" he said, rubbing his hands together.

"Where's your daed and Grandpa?" Mom questioned.

"In the barn, putting the horse away."

"Would you like some hot chocolate?" Mom asked.

Jacob nodded. "That sounds good."

Mom scurried to the stove. "I'd better put some

coffee on for the menfolk. It'll warm them when they come inside."

Rachel stepped up to Jacob. "Did you get the whistle for Buddy?"

He reached into his jacket pocket and withdrew a shiny plastic whistle. "Sure did. And this time I didn't lose it, because Mom patched the hole in my pocket."

"When are you going to try it out on Buddy?" Rachel asked.

"I'll probably wait until Saturday."

"Why not now?" she asked.

He slipped out of his jacket and rubbed his hands over his arms. "I'm too cold to work with Buddy right now, and later today I'm supposed to go to Grandma and Grandpa Yoder's to help Grandpa clean his barn."

"What about tomorrow?" she asked.

Jacob shook his head. "We saw Deacon Byler in town, and he said the schoolhouse will be open again tomorrow."

Rachel smiled. "Oh, that's good. I'm more than ready to go back to school."

"Jah, me, too."

"So can't you work with Buddy tomorrow after school?"

"I don't think so. Pap said something about my helping Henry groom the horses."

Rachel's smile turned to a frown. At this rate, Buddy would never be trained!

As Rachel headed to school the next day, she felt good about what she had in her coat pocket.

"Why are you wearing such a silly grin?" Jacob asked. "Are you glad we're going to school?"

She nodded and quickened her steps, careful not to step on any icy patches. When she entered the schoolyard, she spotted Orlie by the swings, building a snowman.

She pulled the ladybug rock out of her pocket and hoped no one would see her give the rock to Orlie. She was almost there when her foot slipped on a patch of ice. The rock flew out of Rachel's hand, and she landed face-down in a pile of snow.

"What happened?" Orlie asked, pulling Rachel to her feet.

"I was coming to give you—" She clamped her hand over her mouth. "Oh no—I lost it!"

Orlie's eyebrows drew together. "What did you lose?"

"Your birthday present. I dropped it in the *schnee* [snow]."

"You brought me a birthday present?"

She nodded. "It's one of my painted ladybug rocks."

"Let's look for it." Orlie dropped to his knees and pawed through the snow, like a dog trying to cover a bone. Rachel did the same. Snow flew to the left. Snow flew to the right. No ladybug rock was in sight.

"I think it's lost," Rachel mumbled.

Orlie grinned at Rachel as he helped her to her feet.

"It's okay. When the snow melts, I'm sure we'll find my birthday present."

Rachel smiled. She was glad Orlie was so understanding.

"How's Buddy getting along?" Orlie asked as they walked toward the schoolhouse.

"Well, he's—"

"I've been meaning to get over to your place to see him," Orlie interrupted, "but something's always prevented me from coming."

"Like what?" Rachel wanted to know.

"First my daed came down with the flu, so I had twice as many chores. Then it was the bad weather." Orlie's forehead wrinkled. "Maybe it's best if I don't see Buddy. It might make me miss him more than I already do."

"If you miss the dog so much, maybe you should take him back," Rachel said as she and Orlie stepped onto the schoolhouse porch.

"I can't. My mamm's allergic to Buddy, remember?"

Rachel nodded.

"So, how is Buddy doing? Is he happy living at your place?"

"He seems happy enough, but he chases my cat and won't come when he's called."

Orlie's eyebrows drew together. "Isn't Jacob using the whistle I gave him?"

Rachel explained how Jacob had lost the whistle but had bought a new one for Buddy yesterday. "Jacob thinks he can train Buddy better now that he has a new whistle," she added.

"I think he's right," Orlie said, nodding. "Using a whistle with Buddy always worked for me."

Rachel opened her lunch pail, pulled out a plump winter pear, and handed it to him. "This isn't the present I'd planned to give you today, but happy birthday, Orlie!"

Chapter 9

A *Dappich* [Clumsy] Day

Are you sure you don't want to go shopping with me and your daed?" Mom asked Rachel as she wrapped a large woolen shawl around her shoulders.

"Why are you going shopping? I thought Pap, Grandpa, and Jacob went shopping on Thursday."

Mom shook her head. "Not exactly. They went to town to pick up a new harness your daed ordered. Today we'll shop for groceries."

"I see."

"So do you want to go along?"

Rachel shook her head. "Since today's Saturday and there's still plenty of snow, I thought it would be fun to build a snowman."

"You could do that after we get home from town."

"I'd rather play in the snow than shop."

"Very well." Mom smiled. "Grandpa and Jacob are staying home, so if you need anything while we're gone, you can ask them."

"Where will Henry be?" Rachel questioned. "Is he going shopping with you?"

"Henry left awhile ago," Mom said. "He went to see his *aldi* [girlfriend], Nancy."

Rachel wrinkled her nose. "I hope Henry doesn't get married and leave us, the way Esther did last fall."

Mom shook her head. "Henry's only seventeen—too young for marriage. Besides, it's not like we never see Esther. She and Rudy only live a few miles away."

"Jah, I know."

"I'd better get outside. I'm sure your daed has the horse and buggy ready to go by now." Mom opened the back door. "Be good while we're gone, Rachel."

"I will." Rachel closed the door behind her mother and hurried to the utility room to put on her boots. She could hardly wait to get outside!

"Would you like to help me build a snowman?" Rachel called to Jacob when she stepped outside and saw him walking toward the barn.

"Maybe later. I'm going to train Buddy right now. I want to try the whistle I bought him the other day."

"Okay, but please don't let him out of the barn," Rachel hollered. "I don't want that mutt running all over the place. He might wreck my snowman."

"What snowman? I don't see a snowman." Jacob cupped his hands around his eyes, like he was looking through binoculars. "But I do see a *schneeballe* [snowball] coming." He scooped up a handful of snow and flung it at Rachel.

Whizz!—the white sphere hit Rachel's arm with a *splat!*

Jacob leaned his head back and laughed.

"Very funny!" Rachel grabbed some snow. She packed it into a snowball, and was ready to hurl it at Jacob, when he disappeared into the barn.

"That figures," Rachel mumbled as she squatted, ready to make the lower half of her snowman.

By the time Rachel had made a good-sized snowball and rolled it big enough for the bottom of the snowman's body, she was out of breath. "Whew! This is hard work," she panted. "I wish someone would help me."

Rachel thought about asking Grandpa, but knew he was taking a nap. Besides, the cold air would probably bother his arthritis.

She stood there until her toes throbbed. "I'd better keep moving," she told herself.

Rachel grabbed a wad of snow in her hands. Even through her woolen gloves, she could feel the biting cold as she packed it into a ball. *Push. Roll. Push. Roll.* Rachel pushed and rolled the snowball around the yard until it was the size she needed.

"Umph!" Rachel grunted as she tried to lift the snowball and set it on the lower half of the body. She'd made it too big. Now she couldn't even pick it up.

"Now what?" Rachel glanced at the barn. No sign of Jacob. *He must still be trying to train that troublesome dog. Guess I'll have to go ask him to help me.*

Rachel trudged through the snow, opened the barn door, and called, "Jacob, where are you?"

"I'm in here, working with Buddy," he said from the empty stall.

When Rachel stepped into the stall, she found Jacob kneeling on the floor beside Buddy. "How's it going?"

He shook his head. "Not so good. Look what happens when I blow on the whistle." Jacob led Buddy to one side of the barn, and then he went to the other side and blew the whistle. "Come, Buddy, come!"

Buddy didn't budge. He tipped his head back and howled. *Aw-oo-oo!*

"I didn't think a silly old whistle would make Buddy listen," Rachel said.

"He needs more time." Jacob held up the whistle. "This probably has a different sound than the whistle Orlie gave me. I'm sure sooner or later Buddy will get used to it and do what he's supposed to do."

"It will probably be later," Rachel muttered.

"Why did you come to the barn?" Jacob asked. "Did you give up on your snowman?"

"No, but I need your help putting the middle section of the snowman in place."

"Can't you do it?"

She shook her head. "I made it too big, and it's too

heavy for me to pick up."

"Don't go anywhere, Buddy; I'll be right back." Jacob patted Buddy's head and stood. "Let's go, Rachel."

Soon Rachel and Jacob had the body of the snowman set in place. "Now I only need to make the head," she said.

"The head won't need to be as big, so you won't need help for that," Jacob said. "I have to finish training Buddy."

Rachel smiled. "Danki for your help."

"*Gern gschehne.* [You are welcome.]" He trudged through the snowy path toward the barn.

Rachel's excitement mounted as she rolled the ball that would become the snowman's head.

Finally, Rachel had the snowman's head just the right size. She grunted as she lifted it and stood on her tiptoes to set it in place. She couldn't reach. She'd made the snowman's body too tall!

Rachel plodded back to the barn. "Jacob, I need your help again!"

"What now, Rachel?"

"My snowman's body is too tall. I can't reach high enough to set the head in place. Can you help me?"

Jacob groaned. "Can't you see that I'm busy? If you don't stop bothering me, I'll never finish training Buddy."

"Please, Jacob," Rachel pleaded. "I really do need your help."

"Okay. I'll be there as soon as I'm done."

"Danki."

Rachel left the barn and returned to her unfinished snowman. Her nose and toes grew colder as she waited . . .waited. . .waited. The longer she waited, the more impatient she became. With an exasperated sigh, she finally headed for the house. She returned a few minutes later carrying a small wooden stool. Lifting the snowman's head into her arms, she climbed onto the stool. Then she raised her arms, and—*oof!*—the head slipped out of her hands, landed in the snow, and rolled away.

Rachel hopped off the stool and tromped after the rolling snowball. But it was too late—it had rolled to the edge of the hill behind the house—and down it went!

"My snowman's head!" Rachel shrieked.

Rachel slipped and slid down the snowy hill. When she reached the bottom, she was relieved that the snowman's head hadn't broken. But it had rolled through so much snow it was twice as big as before!

Rachel knew she would never be able to carry the snowman's head back up the hill. Maybe she could roll it.

She groaned. "But if I roll it up the hill, it will make the head grow larger."

"Hey, little bensel! What are you doing down there?"

Rachel looked up. Jacob stood at the top of the hill, staring at her.

"When I tried to put the snowman's head on its body, it slipped off and rolled down the hill," she hollered at him. "Now the head's so big I can't get it back up the hill."

Jacob slid down the hill until he stood beside Rachel. "I said I would help you when I finished working with Buddy. Why didn't you wait?"

"I got tired of waiting," she replied. "You took too long."

Jacob nudged Rachel with his elbow. "You're just an *ungeduldich* [impatient] little bensel."

"I'm not impatient."

"Jah, you're impatient, and you try to control everything."

"I do not!"

Jacob nodded. "Want me to give you some examples?"

Rachel shook her head. Then she crouched down and started rolling the snowman's head in the snow.

"What are you doing?" Jacob questioned.

"I've decided to turn the snowman's head into a snowman's body here. When I'm done making this snowman, I'll make another head for the snowman in our yard."

"Do you want some help?"

"Jah, sure, but what about Buddy?"

Jacob chuckled. "I don't think he wants to help us build a snowman."

Rachel groaned and rolled her eyes. "I meant, don't you need to keep working with him?"

"Nope. I've given up for the day." Jacob scooped up some snow and started rolling it into a ball. He glanced over his shoulder. "Well, don't just stand there, Rachel. Get another snowball going!"

Rachel was on the verge of telling Jacob that he wasn't her boss, but she decided to keep quiet. If she said anything, they'd end up arguing, and then Jacob would walk away and leave her to build the snowmen by herself.

Rachel worked silently with Jacob as they made a plump snowman at the bottom of the hill. By the time they were finished, her nose and toes were so cold she could barely feel them.

"It looks pretty good, don't you think?" Jacob folded his arms and stared at the snowman. "All it needs now is a mouth, nose, and eyes."

"And d–don't forget a h–hat." Rachel shivered. She was so cold she was sure her lips were blue.

"You look cold. Should we finish the other snowman tomorrow?" Jacob asked.

"No, I'll be f–fine." Rachel plodded up the hill behind Jacob, huffing and puffing.

"Why don't you go in the house and get carrots for our snowmen's noses?" Jacob suggested. "While you're doing that, I'll make the second snowman's head."

Rachel nodded and hurried to the house. If she stood by the woodstove in the kitchen a few minutes, she might warm up enough to help Jacob finish their snowmen.

She went to the refrigerator and took out two long,

skinny carrots. Next, she removed four black buttons from Mom's sewing basket and placed them on the table. Then she removed her gloves and scurried to the woodstove. "Ah, that feels better," she said, holding her hands out to the warmth. She was tempted to take off her boots and thaw out her toes but figured that would take too much time.

Once the numbness in Rachel's fingers went away, she slipped on her gloves and headed for the door. On her way out, she grabbed two straw hats. One was Henry's and one was Pap's. Since it was winter, and the men wouldn't wear their straw hats until spring, Rachel thought it would be okay to use them for the snowmen.

"What took you so long?" Jacob asked when Rachel returned.

"I had to gather things we needed, and I stood by the stove a few minutes."

"Figured as much." He motioned to the snowman. "I put the head on while you were gone, so now we only need to give the icy fellow a face."

Rachel handed Jacob one of the carrots, two buttons, and Pap's straw hat. "Why don't you do the snowman at the bottom of the hill, and I'll do the one here in the yard?"

Jacob squinted at her. "Who put you in charge?"

"No one, but it was my idea to build the snowmen, so—"

"Never mind," he interrupted. "Let's just get this

job done before we both freeze." He took the carrot, buttons, and hat from Rachel, and then disappeared over the hill.

Rachel faced the snowman. With the head in place it was taller than she was, but if she used the stool she'd brought out earlier she should be able to reach high enough.

Soon Rachel had the buttons in place for the snowman's eyes, and the carrot for its nose. Then she plunked the straw hat on its head. She climbed down from the stool and stepped back to admire her work. It looked good, but something was missing. The snowman needed a mouth!

Rachel glanced around the yard, wondering what she could use. Maybe a small branch from a tree would work. She reached up to grab a smaller one, but her fingers were too cold to break it.

"What's the matter? Do you have a problem?"

Rachel whirled around at the sound of Jacob's voice. "Don't scare me like that! I thought you were still at the bottom of the hill."

He shook his head. "Nope. That snowman's done. I'm ready to go inside and warm up. How about you?"

"I'll be ready as soon as I give my snowman a mouth." She tugged on the tree branch and frowned. "If I can ever break it, that is."

"Step aside and I'll see what I can do."

Rachel did as Jacob said, and with one quick snap,

he broke off a small piece of the branch. "Here you go," he said, handing it to Rachel.

Rachel smiled as she put the snowman's mouth in place. "Danki for your help, Jacob."

"Sure, no problem," he said with a nod. "Are you ready to go inside now?"

"I'm more than ready."

When Rachel and Jacob stepped into the house, they hung their coats, gloves, and hats on a wall peg then slipped out of their boots. Rachel was glad her long stockings had stayed dry, but her feet felt so cold she could barely walk.

She plodded to the warm kitchen and sat at the table. "That feels so good," she said as she rested her feet on the chair closest to the woodstove. "Should we have some hot chocolate and cookies?"

Jacob nodded, rubbing his hands briskly together. "Jah, sure. Hot chocolate sounds wunderbaar!"

"Good. Why don't you fix the hot chocolate? I'll get out the cookies as soon as my toes thaw out."

"All right, little bensel," Jacob said, scrunching up his nose, "but I'm only doing it because I'm such a nice *bruder* [brother]."

Rachel was tempted to remind Jacob that he wasn't always nice, but he had helped her build the two snowmen, so she decided to keep quiet.

Soon the two sat across from each other enjoying steaming mugs of hot chocolate and some of Mom's fresh ginger cookies. Rachel listened to the steady *tick-tick-tick* of the kitchen clock. "I wonder what I can do until Mom and Pap get home from town."

"Maybe you should take a nap like Grandpa's doing," Jacob suggested.

She shook her head. "That wouldn't be any fun."

"Maybe you'd like to sit in front of the window and look out at our big, fat snowman."

"That might be fun, but it would soon become boring."

Jacob snapped his fingers. "I know. . .you could go out to the barn and play with your cat." Before Rachel could response, he added, "Oh, you'd better not. Buddy's in the barn, and if he sees you, he'll jump up and lick your face."

Rachel wrinkled her nose. "I hate it when Buddy does that."

"I've told you, he only does it because he likes you."

"Jah, well, I don't care much for him, and I'm not going to the barn right now," Rachel said with a shake of her head. "I'm staying in here where it's warm."

Jacob pushed away from the table and stood. "I think I'll go back to the barn and work with Buddy some more."

After Jacob left the house, Rachel sat there, staring at her empty cup. Suddenly, an idea popped into her head. "I'll paint a ladybug rock to replace the one I gave Orlie last week!" A few days earlier, Esther had given

Rachel some paint, so all Rachel needed was a flat, round rock.

She hurried to her room and searched through the box of rocks in her closet. Sure enough, one was shaped exactly right for a ladybug.

Rachel picked up the paint, a brush, and the rock; then she returned to the kitchen. She covered the table with some old newspapers she'd found in the utility room and removed the lids from the paint jars. She dipped her brush into the jar of black paint and painted the entire rock. While the paint dried, Rachel washed the brush and ate a few more ginger cookies. Now it was time to paint the ladybug's eyes and antenna.

Rachel picked up the jar of white paint, dipped the brush in, and painted a small circle for the first eye. She was about to dip the brush in again, to do the second eye, when—*blurp!*—she hiccupped. A blob of white paint shot up and landed on the front of her dress.

"Oh no!" Rachel jumped up and raced to the sink. She grabbed the wet sponge and blotted the white splotch on her dress, but that only smeared the paint.

"I'd better wash this dress before Mom gets home." Rachel scurried up the stairs to her room, changed into a clean dress, and rushed back to the kitchen. Then she ran warm water into the sink, added some detergent, and dropped the dress in.

Swish! Swish! Swish!—she dipped the dress up and down and swirled it around in the soapy water.

When she was sure the paint was out, she drained the soapy water and ran cold water into the sink. *Swish! Swish! Swish!*—she dipped the dress up and down then wrung it out. She carried it across the room and hung it over the back of a chair to dry by the stove.

Rachel glanced at the clock. Mom had said she and Pap should be home in time for lunch and it was eleven thirty. If the dress wasn't dry when they got home, Mom would know Rachel had slopped paint on her dress.

"I've got to think of something." Rachel scratched the side of her head. "I need to figure out how to dry my dress quickly."

Another idea popped into Rachel's head. *I know! I'll iron the water out of my dress!*

Rachel hurried to the utility closet and removed the ironing board. She knew it would be too dangerous for her to use the small propane torch to light the wick on the bottom of the iron Mom normally used, so she decided to heat Mom's old flat iron on the stove.

Rachel turned on the gas, and set the iron on the front burner. While the iron heated, she ate another cookie and drank a glass of milk. Then she peeked out the kitchen window. No sign of Pap's buggy. That was good. She glanced down the hall and saw that Grandpa's bedroom door was still closed. He must still be asleep.

Rachel removed the dress from the chair and placed it over the ironing board. When she lifted the iron from the stove and placed it on the dress, it sizzled.

"It's working!" she exclaimed. Rachel held the iron there until the spot was dry. She smiled. "At this rate the dress will be dry in no time at all."

Thump! Thump! Rachel tipped her head and listened. It sounded like someone was tromping down the stairs. But that was impossible. Mom, Pap, and Henry weren't home; Grandpa was asleep in his room; and Jacob was in the barn.

Thump! Thump! Thump! There it was again.

Rachel let go of the iron, raced into the hallway, and screeched to a halt. *Thump-thumpety-thump*—Rachel's cat was dragging a shoe down the stairs.

"Cuddles! Who let you in the house?" Rachel shook her finger at the cat. "And what are you doing with my shoe?"

Meow! Cuddles dropped the shoe and pawed at Rachel's leg.

"Don't 'meow' me," Rachel scolded. "You know better than to play with my shoes. I'll bet you snuck into the house when Jacob went to the barn, didn't you?"

Rachel picked up the cat. "I don't have time to play with you now, so out you go." She opened the back door and set Cuddles on the porch. "Find a warm place in the barn and take a nap." *Bam!* She quickly shut the door.

When Rachel returned to the kitchen, she gasped. A curl of smelly, gray smoke rose from her dress. "Ach!" she screamed. "My dress is burning!"

Rachel lifted the iron and stared in horror at an ugly brown scorch mark. She realized that when she'd gone to see what the *thump-thump-thump* on the stairs was, she'd left the iron on top of her dress.

A horse whinnied outside, and Rachel jumped. Mom and Pap must be home!

Rachel knew it would be impossible to cover the smoke or hide the scorch mark on her dress, so she stood in front of the ironing board and waited.

Mom entered the house. "What's that horrible smell?" she asked, sniffing the air.

Rachel pointed to her ruined dress and burst into tears. "I—I dribbled some paint on the front of my dress." *Sniff.* "Then I washed it in the sink." *Sniff. Sniff.* "I knew it would take too long to dry, so I tried to iron it." *Sniff.* "I heard a noise on the steps." *Sniff. Sniff.* "And when I came back to the kitchen, I'd left the iron on my dress. Now it's ruined!"

Mom slowly shook her head. "Oh, Rachel, don't you know how dangerous it was for you to leave the iron on your dress when you left the room?"

"I know, and I'm so sorry. I was afraid you'd be mad at me for spilling the paint, so I wanted to dry the dress before you got home." Rachel stared at the floor as tears blurred her vision. "Now you're mad at me for scorching the dress." She gulped a sob. "I'm having such a dappich day! I can't do anything right."

"You did the right thing by washing the paint out

of the dress so quickly," Mom said, her voice softening. "You just should have been more patient in letting it dry on its own."

Rachel nodded. "I'll save my money to buy material for a new dress."

"That won't be necessary. You can sew a patch over the scorch mark and wear the dress for doing your chores."

Rachel frowned. Even though Mom had given her a sewing kit for her birthday last year, she still couldn't sew very well.

Mom hugged Rachel. "You need to remember we can't always fix things or make them come out the way we would like. But you can always count on the knowledge that God loves you, and so do I."

Rachel smiled and hugged Mom back. "I love you, too."

Chapter 10

Chicken Pox and Chicken Soup

One morning in early February, Rachel came down to breakfast scratching her arms. "I think there might be bugs in my bed," she complained.

Mom placed a kettle of water on the back of the stove and turned to face Rachel. "What makes you think that?"

Rachel pulled the sleeve of her nightgown up and held out her arm. "I have little bumps all over my arms, and they itch something awful!"

"Ach, my!" Mom exclaimed. "Those bumps aren't from any bugs, Rachel. I'm afraid you've got *wasserpareble* [chicken pox]."

"Wasserpareble?" Rachel repeated.

Mom nodded. "That's what it looks like."

"If you've got chicken pox, you'd better stay away from me," Jacob said as he entered the room. "I sure don't want them."

"I'll hold my breath so I won't blow any germs on you," Rachel said.

Mom patted Rachel's shoulder. "It's okay. Jacob had the chicken pox before you were born."

Jacob's eyebrows lifted. "I did?"

Mom nodded. "You, Henry, and Esther had them at the same time."

"Why didn't I get them?" Rachel wanted to know.

"You weren't born yet," Mom replied. "In fact, Jacob was just a boppli when they all came down with the chicken pox."

"What about you and Pap?" Rachel asked. "Have you had the chicken pox?"

Mom nodded. "Your daed and I had them when we were *kinner* [children]."

"What about Grandpa? I wouldn't want him to get sick because of me," Rachel said, shaking her head.

"Why would I get sick?" Grandpa asked as he entered the kitchen.

Rachel moved to the other side of the room. "I've got the wasserpareble, Grandpa. So if you haven't had them, don't get close to me."

Grandpa chuckled. "No worries, Rachel. I had chicken pox when I was a boy."

Rachel breathed a sigh of relief. At least she didn't have to worry about spreading any chicken pox germs to her family.

Mom looked at Jacob, and then at Rachel. "Has

anyone at school had the chicken pox lately?"

Jacob shrugged. "Not that I know of."

"No one in class has been sick for several weeks," Rachel put in.

Mom peered at Rachel over the top of her glasses. "How do you feel? Does your throat hurt? Do you ache anywhere?"

"No, but I feel warm—and very itchy," Rachel said.

Mom touched Rachel's forehead. "I think you're running a fever." She turned back to the stove. "I'll fix some tea and toast and bring it to your room on a tray."

"Why can't I eat breakfast down here?"

"Because you're sick and need to be in bed where you can rest." Mom shook her head. "No school for you today, Rachel. Not until you're completely well."

"I don't want to miss school," Rachel wailed. "We're supposed to work on our valentines today. The school party is next week, you know."

"I'm afraid you'll have to work on yours at home," Mom said. "Now, scoot upstairs and get into bed. I'll bring your breakfast tray up soon."

Rachel swallowed around the lump in her throat and shuffled out of the kitchen. She didn't want to be sick. She wanted to go to school.

Fighting tears of frustration, Rachel climbed the stairs to her room and crawled into bed. She lay there, staring at the ceiling and wishing she could bring

Cuddles into her room to comfort her.

"How do you feel, Rachel?" Mom asked when she entered Rachel's bedroom.

"I feel awful." Rachel tried to sit up, but her head started to pound. She sank back into the pillow with a moan. "Now I've got a *koppweh* [headache], and my arms itch terribly."

"Try not to scratch. That will leave scars." Mom set the tray she carried on the small table beside Rachel's bed and moved to Rachel's dresser. "These should help," she said as she removed a pair of dark stockings.

"What are those for?" Rachel asked. "If I can't go to school and have to stay in bed, why do I need to wear stockings?"

"They're not for your feet. They're to put over your hands so you won't scratch the pox marks." Mom slipped one stocking over Rachel's right hand and one over her left hand. "That should help. Now I'm going back downstairs to make some comfrey tea to put on your pox."

Rachel squinted. "Why would you put tea on my pox?"

"The tea is supposed to help them not itch so much." Mom patted Rachel's hand. "As soon as the tea is cool, I'll be back."

When Mom left the room, Rachel rolled onto her side. Tears trickled down her cheeks. *Why do I always have so much trouble?*

Rachel spent the next several days in bed, trying not to scratch, and feeling sorry for herself. Besides the fact that she would miss the valentine party at school on Friday, she would also miss the spelling bee. Since spelling was Rachel's favorite subject, she felt grouchy about having to stay home from school. Mom had reminded Rachel several times that she needed to learn more patience and that some things weren't in her control. However, Rachel was determined to get out of bed and prove she was doing better.

Screetch. . .screetch. A scratching sound at the window drew Rachel's attention. It had to be Cuddles, begging to get in.

Rachel pushed her covers aside and crawled out of bed. Her body ached, and her muscles felt like limp, wet noodles. With a shaky hand she lifted the window shade. Sure enough, Cuddles was perched on a tree branch outside Rachel's window.

As soon as Rachel opened the window, Cuddles leaped into her arms.

Rachel smiled. It was comforting to hold Cuddles and listen to her purr. Rachel knew Mom didn't like the cat on her bed, but she couldn't resist lying down with Cuddles in her arms. After a while, the cat crawled to the bottom of the bed and fell asleep.

Maybe if I go downstairs and find something to do, I'll feel better, Rachel thought. She slipped into her robe and slippers then tiptoed out of the room, so she wouldn't disturb Cuddles.

When Rachel entered the kitchen, the delicious aroma of chicken soup tickled her nose, and made her stomach rumble.

"Rachel, what are you doing out of bed?" Mom asked.

"I thought I should make some valentine hearts—in case I'm well enough to go to school on Friday."

Mom shook her head. "You won't be well enough. You should be back in bed."

"Oh, please, Mom. I promise I'll sit quietly at the table and work on my valentines. If I get tired, I'll go straight back to bed."

"Oh, all right," Mom finally agreed. "But you won't be up to going back to school on Friday. Jacob can take the valentines you make for the scholars, and then bring the ones home that they've made for you."

Rachel found some red and white paper, scissors, glue, and a black marking pen in Mom's craft drawer. She carried them to the table and sat down. She wouldn't admit it to Mom, but she was already tired.

She sat there several minutes, breathing slowly and rubbing her forehead.

"Does your head hurt?" Mom asked.

"Just a bit."

"Maybe you should go back up to bed and forget the valentines for now."

"I'll be all right." Rachel picked up the scissors and a piece of red paper; then she cut out a heart.

Mom went back to stirring the pot of soup. "I think this is done. Would you like a bowl of chicken soup, Rachel?"

"Jah, I would," Rachel replied.

Mom ladled some soup into a bowl and set it on the table. "Be careful not to spill soup on your valentines," she said.

"Aren't you going to have some?" Rachel asked.

"I was planning to eat lunch after your daed and grandpa get back from town, but the soup smells so good, I think I'll join you." Mom ladled some soup into another bowl and started across the room. She was almost to the table when Cuddles streaked into the kitchen and zipped over Mom's foot. Mom stumbled, bumped into a chair, and—*splat!*—her bowl of soup splattered all over the table!

Rachel jumped up. "My valentines—they're ruined!"

Mom pointed to Cuddles, who sat on the floor licking some of the spilled soup. "I didn't let the cat in the house. How do you suppose she got in?"

"I—I brought her inside," Rachel admitted. "She was in the tree outside my window, scratching to get in."

"Please don't tell me she was on your bed again."

Rachel nodded slowly as her head began to pound, and the room started to spin.

"Rachel, how many times have I told you—"

"I—I feel so dizzy." Rachel reached for the back of the chair, and Mom grabbed her arm.

"I knew you shouldn't have gotten up so soon." Mom guided Rachel toward the steps. "Back to bed with you now."

"What about my soggy valentine hearts?"

"I'll clean up the mess after I tuck you into bed."

Rachel spent the rest of the afternoon feeling sorry for herself. Not only had she disobeyed Mom and let Cuddles sleep on her bed, but now all her valentines were ruined. She wouldn't have any to send to school with Jacob.

Tap-tap-tap. Someone knocked on Rachel's bedroom door.

"Come in," she said with a sigh.

Esther poked her head inside the door. "Would you like some company?"

Rachel shrugged. "I suppose."

Esther sat in the chair by Rachel's bed. "I went to town this morning and decided to drop by on my way home to see how you feel."

Rachel scrunched up her nose. "I feel baremlich."

"That's understandable," Esther said with a nod. "Everyone feels terrible when they're grank."

"I'm not feeling terrible because I'm sick." Rachel pushed herself to a sitting position and leaned against the pillows. "I feel terrible because Mom spilled soup on my valentine hearts, and now they're ruined." She sniffed. "And I feel terrible because I can't go to school on Friday."

"If you went to school you might expose everyone to the chicken pox," Esther said.

"I know, but if I stay home I'll miss the spelling bee and the Valentine's Day party." Tears welled in Rachel's eyes, and she blinked to keep them from spilling over.

Esther patted Rachel's hand. "You'll have other spelling bees, and I'm sure Jacob will bring your valentines home."

Rachel's chin quivered. "I wish I could do something to get well quicker."

"Just rest in bed, and do everything Mom says. Be patient and you'll be well before you know it."

"But not before Friday." Rachel nearly choked on the words.

"You need to relax and put your hope in the Lord, like the Bible says we should do," Esther said.

"Where does it say that?"

"In Isaiah 40:31, it says: 'But those who hope in the Lord will renew their strength. They will soar on wings like eagles; they will run and not grow weary, they will walk and not be faint.' "

"I almost fainted when I was in the kitchen," Rachel said.

"That's because you should have been in bed resting. You're not ready to be up for a long time yet." Esther gently squeezed Rachel's arm. "I'm going downstairs to help Mom make some pretty valentine hearts so Jacob can take them to school for you on Friday."

Rachel smiled. "Danki, Esther."

"Gern gschehne," Esther replied before she slipped out the door.

Rachel pulled the covers under her chin. It was nice to have a kind, helpful sister.

Chapter 11

Worst Day Ever

Slow down, Rachel. If you're not careful, you'll slip and fall," Jacob called as Rachel hurried on the snowy path leading to the schoolhouse. "What's the rush?"

"I'm anxious to get to school so I can get my valentines." Rachel turned to face Jacob. "The ones *you* forgot to bring home for me."

Jacob scrunched up his nose. "You should be glad I remembered to take the valentines to school that Mom and Esther made for you to give the others."

"Well," Rachel said, lifting her chin, "that was only because on the day of the party, Mom put them in a plastic bag and handed them to you on your way out the door."

Jacob shrugged. "At least they got there."

"But I still don't have *my* valentines."

"You'll get them when you get to school!" Jacob tromped past Rachel, kicking powdery snow all over her dress. "Hurry up, slowpoke. You'll make me late."

Rachel gritted her teeth. She wondered if Jacob would ever stop making fun of her. When they were both old and gray, would he still tease and call her names?

"Have you had any luck training Buddy?" Rachel asked, deciding they needed to change the subject.

Jacob shook his head. "Not yet. I think I may give up on the whistle and try to train Buddy on my own."

"I don't care how you train him, but you'd better think of something before my cat gets hurt."

"Buddy hasn't hurt Cuddles yet, Rachel. I've told you before, Buddy just wants to play."

"Even if that's true, I don't like it when he chases Cuddles, and neither does she!"

Jacob nudged Rachel's arm. "You worry too much, little bensel."

Ignoring Jacob's teasing, Rachel trudged on. When she entered the schoolhouse, she was surprised to see that no valentines were inside her desk.

She glanced around the room. Maybe Orlie or one of the other boys had hidden her valentines. If she'd had time, she would have asked some of the scholars if they knew anything about the valentines. But Elizabeth had already opened her Bible to read the morning scripture.

When the Bible reading was over, the children stood and repeated the Lord's Prayer and then sang. As soon as they returned to their seats, Rachel raised her hand.

Elizabeth and her helper didn't seem to notice; they were busy handing out everyone's arithmetic papers.

Rachel hoped she could ask about the valentines when Sharon came by her desk, but when Sharon handed Rachel her arithmetic lesson, she hurried up the aisle before Rachel could speak.

Tap-tap-tap. Rachel tapped her pencil on the edge of her desk and stared at the arithmetic problems. Thanks to the itchy chicken pox, she'd been out of school almost two weeks. Even though she'd done some schoolwork at home, she hadn't spent much time on arithmetic. She hoped she could do all the problems.

"Psst. . ."

Rachel glanced across the aisle at her cousin Mary.

"You'd better get your lesson done," Mary whispered. "If you don't, you won't get to go outside for morning recess."

Rachel nodded. Mary was right. If she didn't finish her assignment before ten o'clock, she would probably have to skip recess in order to finish it.

Rachel picked up her pencil again. Between every problem she glanced at the clock on the wall. It was hard to be patient when she wanted to see her valentines.

Rachel finished the last problem just as Elizabeth announced that it was time to turn in their papers. Rachel handed her arithmetic paper to Sharon. She was getting ready to ask about her valentines when Sharon hurried off.

Maybe I won't go outside for recess, Rachel decided. *While others are playing in the snow, I'll look through everyone's desk for my valentines.*

After the children's papers were collected, Elizabeth said it was time for recess.

Everyone scurried to the back of the room to get their coats, gloves, and hats, but Rachel stayed at her desk.

"Aren't you going outside?" Mary asked, coming to stand beside Rachel.

Rachel shook her head. "I'd rather stay in here, where it's warm."

"Are you feeling all right? You're not still feeling grank, are you?"

"I'm not sick. I just want to stay inside."

Mary shrugged and rushed out the door.

Rachel waited until Elizabeth and Sharon went outside; then she hurried to the first desk on the right side of the room and lifted the lid. There were several books, a shriveled apple, and two pencils, but no sign of her valentine cards.

Rachel moved on. She found no valentines in the next desk, either. She went up the row, lifting lids and looking inside every desk. She was ready to move to the next row, when the door swung open.

"Rachel, what are you doing?"

Bam! Rachel slammed the lid on the desk and faced her teacher. "I—I was looking for my valentines."

"In someone else's desk?"

Rachel nodded. "When I didn't find the valentines in my desk, I thought maybe someone had taken the valentines and hidden them."

Elizabeth shook her head. "I put your valentines in my desk."

"That's good to hear," Rachel said with a smile. "Can I please have them?"

"Sorry, Rachel," Elizabeth said, "but I won't give them to you until school ends this afternoon."

Rachel's smile turned to a frown. "How come?"

"For one thing, there's some candy in your sack of cards. I don't want you to be tempted to eat any now and spoil your lunch."

Rachel smiled. She hadn't even realized she might get candy with her valentines. "I won't eat too many," she said.

Elizabeth shook her head. "You'll have to wait until after school."

Rachel knew better than to argue. She didn't want to stay after school or have to take another note home to Mom and Pap. "Guess I'll go outside and play," she said with a sigh.

Elizabeth pointed to the clock. "We only have a few minutes left of recess—not enough time for you to go outside." She started to walk away, but turned back around. "One more thing, Rachel. . .no more snooping in other people's desks."

"I won't, Teacher; I promise."

As Rachel and Jacob walked home from school, Rachel stopped every few feet, reached into her sack of valentines, and pulled out a piece of candy.

"You're gonna be too full for supper if you keep eating like that," Jacob said.

"No, I won't." Rachel popped a piece of taffy into her mouth. "Ouch! I bit my tongue!"

"That's what you get for trying to eat so much candy at once." Jacob shook his finger at her. "Why don't you slow down and quit being so ungeduldich?"

"I'm not impatient."

"Jah, you are."

Rachel decided not to argue. It was more fun to eat her candy.

By the time they reached home, most of Rachel's candy was gone. "I don't feel well," she complained as they stepped onto the porch.

"What's wrong?" Jacob asked.

She held her stomach and groaned. "I've got a *bauchweh* [stomachache]."

The skin around Jacob's blue eyes crinkled when he frowned at her. "After all that candy you ate, I'm not surprised that your stomach hurts."

"You don't have to be mean."

"I'm not. I'm just stating facts."

Rachel was getting ready to respond, when—*zip!*—her cat raced past. *Zip! Zip!* Jacob's dog was on the cat's tail.

"Buddy, stop!" Rachel shouted. "Leave my cat alone!"

Whoof! Buddy lunged for Cuddles. *Whish!*—Cuddles scurried up the nearest tree.

Buddy pawed at the trunk of the tree. *Woof! Woof!*

"Get your *dumm* [dumb] dog!" Rachel shouted. She'd forgotten all about her stomachache. Her only concern was for Cuddles.

"Buddy's not dumb. He's a very schmaert dog." Jacob reached into his jacket pocket and pulled out the whistle. "Maybe he'll respond this time." He blew on the whistle. "Come here, Buddy!"

Buddy tipped his head back and howled. *Aw-oo-oo!*

"Jah, Buddy's schmaert all right—schmaert and dumm at the same time. He's smart enough to chase my cat up a tree and too dumb to know what to do when you blow that whistle." Rachel frowned. "If Cuddles gets stuck up there, it'll be your fault, Jacob!"

"She's not going to get stuck."

"How do you know?"

"Because she's a cat, and cats climb trees."

"I don't see what that proves."

Jacob grunted. "If the cat went up the tree, she'll come back down."

Rachel looked up. Cuddles sat on one of the highest branches. The poor thing looked so pathetic.

Woof! Woof! Woof! Buddy continued to bark while he pawed at the tree.

"Get down, Buddy! Go away!" Rachel scolded.

"I'll take him to the barn," Jacob said. He grabbed Buddy's collar and led him away.

"Here, Cuddles. Come, kitty, kitty," Rachel begged her frightened cat. "That mean old dog is gone now. It's safe for you to come down."

Meow! Cuddles trembled.

Rachel shivered. It was cold outside and she wanted to go into the house where it was toasty. She thought Cuddles needed to go inside, too. "Please, Cuddles, come to me."

Meow! Meow!

"I know what I'll do!" Rachel set her backpack and sack full of valentines on the porch. Then she hurried to the barn.

"Did your cat come out of the tree?" Jacob asked as he closed the door to the stall where he kept Buddy.

She shook her head. "Not yet. I came in here to get Cuddles's food dish."

"Why?"

"To coax her down."

Jacob frowned. "If you leave her alone, she'll come down on her own."

"What if she doesn't?"

"She will."

"But she may not, so I'm going to help her." Rachel picked up Cuddles's dish and started for the barn door.

"Why do you have to be so impatient?" Jacob called.

"You can't control every situation, you know!"

Rachel ignored Jacob and kept walking. When she came to the tree where Buddy had chased Cuddles, she looked up. The cat still sat there, looking more frightened than before.

"This is my worst day ever," Rachel mumbled.

"You say that every day," Jacob said, joining her in front of the tree.

"Do not."

"Do so."

Rachel didn't feel like arguing. She had more important things on her mind. "Maybe I should climb the tree and bring Cuddles down," she said.

Jacob shook his head. "Don't be silly. That tree is too high for you to climb, and it could be dangerous."

"I'm not afraid."

"You should be."

Mom came out of the house. "I thought I heard voices." She looked at Rachel. "What's going on?"

"Jacob's dog chased my cat up the tree." Rachel pointed upwards. "Now Cuddles can't get down."

"She *can* get down," Jacob said.

"No, she can't."

"Can, too."

"I'm sure Cuddles will come down when she's ready." Mom stepped off the porch and touched Rachel's shoulder. "Why don't you and Jacob come inside and have hot chocolate and cookies?"

"That sounds good," Jacob quickly replied.

"What about you, Rachel?" Mom asked. "Are you hungry for peanut butter cookies?"

"Rachel's not hungry for anything," Jacob said. "She's got a bauchweh from eating too much candy."

Rachel squinted at Jacob. *"Blappermaul* [blabbermouth]."

"Where did you get candy, Rachel?" Mom questioned.

"From school. It was in the sack with my valentines Jacob kept forgetting to bring home."

"She got so impatient that she ate all the candy on the walk home," Jacob said.

"I didn't eat it all." Rachel pointed to the sack on the porch. "I still have a few pieces left."

Mom clucked her tongue. "You know better than to eat too much candy, Rachel."

"I tried not to, Mom, but it tasted so good."

"If you've got a bauchweh, then you don't need any cookies," Mom said. "But you should get inside out of this cold."

"I'll be there in a few minutes." Rachel lifted the bowl of cat food and pointed to the tree. "I'm hoping Cuddles will get hungry. I want to see if she'll come down when she sees this food."

Mom nodded. "All right, but don't stay out here too long."

Jacob nudged Rachel with his elbow. "Only a little bensel would stand out here in the cold, staring at a cat in a tree." He snickered and followed Mom into the house.

Rachel ground her teeth together. *A lot Jacob knows. He can't even train his dog. I'll show him I'm not a silly child!*

Rachel set the cat food on the ground and rushed back to the barn. From behind Buddy's stall she heard, *Arf! Arf!*

Rachel held her hands over her ears. "Be quiet, Buddy!" She was glad the door to the stall was closed. The last thing she needed was Buddy jumping on her.

Buddy kept barking and scratched the stall door.

"You're not coming out," Rachel shouted as she spotted the small stepladder.

With a joyous bark, Buddy leaped over the stall door and bounded up to Rachel. "Bad dog! I hope Pap builds a doghouse and pen for you soon." She grunted. "Better yet, I hope Jacob decides to find you another home!"

Buddy wriggled and wagged his tail. Apparently he didn't realize she was irritated with him.

Rachel grabbed Buddy's collar and led him back to the stall. "Stay in here!" She slammed the door. Then she left the barn, dragging the ladder behind her.

When Rachel reached the tree, she positioned the ladder below one of the branches and put her foot on the first rung. One. . .two. . .three steps. . .she began to climb the ladder. When she reached the top rung, she stepped onto the branch. "I'm coming, Cuddles!"

Chapter 12
Self-Control

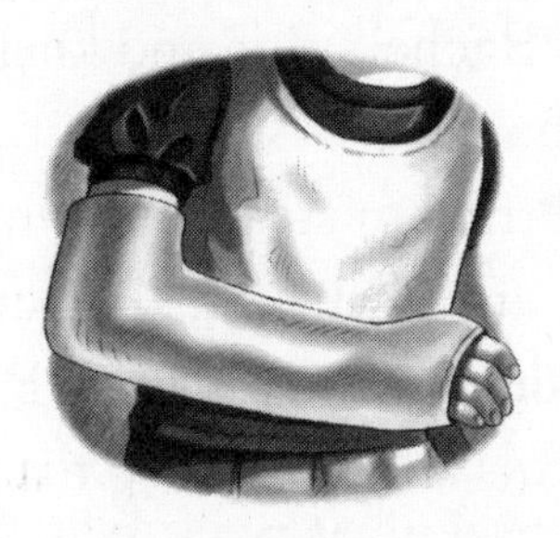

The wind whistled through the tree as Rachel stepped from one branch to the other, until she was right under Cuddles. She reached out her hand. "Here, Cuddles. Come, kitty, kitty."

"Rachel Yoder, what do you think you're doing?"

Rachel jumped at the sound of Pap's deep voice.

Meow! Rachel's cat shrieked and leaped from the tree.

"Cuddles!" Quickly, Rachel started back down the tree. As she took her first step, her dress snagged on a branch. She reached down to pull it loose, but lost her footing.

Rachel wobbled back and forth and grabbed the branch overhead, her heart pounding so hard she could hear it roar in her ears. Her fingers were cold and stiff, and it was hard to hold the branch. Suddenly, her hand slipped and her knees buckled. "Heeelp!" Rachel tumbled toward the ground.

Oomph! Rachel's arm smacked into the wooden ladder. Her lungs felt like all the air had been squeezed out as she dropped into a mound of snow.

Pap rushed to Rachel's side and knelt beside her. "Rachel, are you hurt?"

When Rachel tried to stand a searing pain shot through her right arm. "My arm—it hurts so much!"

"Let's get inside where it's warm." Pap scooped Rachel into his arms and started up the porch steps.

"What about Cuddles?" Rachel's eyes had teared up so much she couldn't see a thing. "Is—is Cuddles hurt?"

"Your cat's fine," Pap said. "When she fell from the tree, she landed on her feet. Then she took off for the barn."

Mom greeted them at the door. "What happened to Rachel?"

"She fell from the maple tree. I think she may have broken her arm," Pap said as he placed Rachel on the living room sofa.

Mom gasped. "What were you doing in the tree, Rachel?"

"I—I was trying to get Cuddles, but then she jumped, and—" Rachel's voice broke on a sob.

When Pap examined Rachel's arm, she tried not to cry. It wasn't easy to be brave when she hurt so badly.

"It's starting to swell, and I'm pretty sure Rachel's arm is broken," Pap said, looking up at Mom. "We'll need to call one of our English neighbors for a ride to the hospital."

Mom nodded.

"I don't want to go to the hospital!" Rachel wailed. She didn't care about being brave anymore. She was worried about what they might do to her at the hospital.

Mom put her hand on Rachel's shoulder. "Calm down, daughter. If your arm is broken, you'll need to have it set and put in a cast."

Grandpa stepped into the room, followed by Jacob and Henry. They all crowded around the sofa and stared at Rachel.

"What happened?" Henry asked.

"She fell from the maple tree," Pap explained.

Jacob grunted. "I told you not to climb up there, Rachel."

Rachel cried harder. She felt bad enough; did Jacob have to make her feel worse?

"Henry, run to the Johnsons' and see if they can take us to the hospital," Pap said. "Rachel will need her arm X-rayed to see if it's broken."

"I—I don't want to go," Rachel cried.

"It'll be all right," Mom quietly said. "The doctors and nurses will take care of you. Everything will be just fine."

Later that day, Rachel and her parents returned from

the hospital. Rachel wore a pink cast on her arm, and Mom and Pap wore relief on their faces.

"How'd things go at the hospital?" Jacob asked as he sat on the sofa beside Rachel.

"Everything went fine, but I'll have to wear my cast for six whole weeks," she replied. "I also have to be careful not to get it wet."

Jacob patted Rachel's left arm. "Six weeks isn't so bad. The time will go quicker than you think."

"There are so many things I can't do with only one arm—especially since I'm right-handed." Rachel frowned. "If I had to break an arm, why couldn't it have been the left one?"

"There are still many things you can do." Mom handed Rachel a pain pill the doctor had given her. "The more you use your left hand, the better you'll get at it."

Rachel popped the pill in her mouth and gulped some water. Then she turned to Jacob and said, "If that *mupsich* [stupid] dog of yours hadn't chased my cat up the tree, I wouldn't have a broken arm."

Jacob grunted. "Buddy's not stupid, and if you hadn't climbed the tree, you wouldn't have fallen. And if you hadn't fallen, you wouldn't have—"

"Your brother's right, Rachel," Pap interrupted. "You should have waited for Cuddles to come down on her own."

Rachel sniffed. "I never seem to do anything right."

"That's not true, Rachel," Grandpa said as he sat in the rocking chair and propped his feet on a footstool near the fireplace. "You do lots of good things, but you need to learn to have more patience and self-control."

She nodded as tears filled her eyes.

Mom handed Rachel a tissue. "Now dry your eyes and get ready for a surprise."

"Surprise?" Rachel loved surprises. "What's the surprise, Mom?"

Mom smiled and motioned to Pap. "Your daed's decided to make homemade ice cream for dessert tonight."

Rachel's eyebrows shot up. "Homemade ice cream in the middle of winter?"

"Jah, sure," Pap said with a chuckle. "Cold, creamy, vanilla ice cream tastes wunderbaar any time of the year."

Rachel nodded. "I love homemade ice cream!"

"And eating ice cream is something you can do with one arm," Henry added as he entered the room from the kitchen.

"While you and your mamm were in seeing the doctor, I called Esther and Rudy and told them what happened," Pap said. "I also invited them to join us for ice cream tonight."

"I'm glad you did. It's always nice to see Esther and Rudy," Rachel said with a smile. "Will Grandma and Grandpa Yoder come over, too?"

Pap shook his head. "Grandma came down with a bad cold yesterday, so she doesn't feel like going anywhere."

"I'm sure they'll come visit you as soon as Grandma feels better." Mom motioned to the sofa. "Do you want to stretch out here and rest until supper? Or would you rather go to your room?"

"If I stay here, can I have Cuddles with me?"

Mom hesitated but nodded. "I'll have Jacob bring her in."

Jacob frowned. "Why do I have to do it?"

"Because Rachel's not going out to the barn to look for the cat," Pap said.

"She might slip and fall on the ice," Grandpa added. "You wouldn't want that to happen, would you, Jacob?"

"No, of course not." Jacob started for the door, but turned back around. "Can I bring Buddy in the house, too?"

"No!" everyone shouted.

"Just thought I'd ask." Jacob shrugged and hurried out the door.

"I think Henry and I had better head outside, too," Pap said. "We have some chores to do." He smiled at Mom. "We'll be back in plenty of time for supper."

Mom smiled. "Since we got home from the hospital so late, we'll just have soup and sandwiches for supper."

When Pap and Henry headed outside, Grandpa left

his rocking chair and picked up a paper sack that had been lying on the table near the sofa. "After you left for the hospital, I found this on the porch." He placed the sack in Rachel's lap. "I believe your valentine cards from school are inside."

Rachel peered into the sack and nodded. She'd forgotten about her valentine cards. "Can I have a piece of candy?" she asked.

Mom shook her head. "I think you had enough candy earlier, don't you?"

"I guess I did." Rachel thought about the stomachache she'd had after eating too much candy. As bad as her stomach had hurt, it didn't compare to the pain she'd felt when she'd hit the ladder and broken her arm. She wouldn't have had that stomachache if she hadn't eaten too much candy, and she wouldn't have broken her arm if she hadn't climbed the tree.

Mom kissed Rachel's forehead. "I'll let you look at your valentines while I go to the kitchen and heat some soup."

"Okay, Mom."

Grandpa sat at the end of the sofa. "Would you like me to rub your feet while you read your valentines, Rachel?"

"Jah, sure. That would feel good." Rachel nestled against the sofa cushions and took a drink of water. It was nice to be treated special. Maybe the next six weeks wouldn't be so bad after all.

That evening after supper, Rudy and Esther showed up.

"You're right on time," Pap said, winking at Rudy. "I was about to begin cranking the ice cream."

Rudy chuckled. "Then you'll need another pair of strong arms to help."

Pap nodded. "Usually Rachel gets the first chance to crank, but since she only has one good arm and needs to rest, we men will have to do the cranking ourselves." He smiled at Rachel, who sat on the sofa with Cuddles draped across her lap.

"How do you feel?" Esther asked. "Does your arm hurt much?"

"A little, but the medicine the doctor gave me for pain helps." Rachel yawned. "It also makes me sleepy."

"Don't fall asleep yet," Mom said. "The ice cream will be ready to eat soon." She motioned to the kitchen. "That is, if our men ever start cranking."

"I guess we've had our orders." Grandpa smiled at Pap. "If you don't mind, Levi, I'd like to be the first one to crank."

"Don't mind at all." Pap patted Rachel's knee. "Don't fall asleep now, you hear?"

She grinned. "I won't, Pap."

When the men left the room, Mom sat in the rocking chair, and Esther sat on the couch beside Rachel. She touched Rachel's cast. "Rudy and I were sorry to hear about your accident. It's a good thing this happened to you during the winter."

"Why's that?" Rachel asked.

"If it had happened during spring, summer, or autumn, you wouldn't have had the snow to break your fall." Esther's forehead wrinkled. "You could have been hurt worse."

"I guess that's true." Rachel glanced at her cast and sighed. "I wish I hadn't been foolish enough to climb that tree. I guess that's what I get for being so impatient."

"Sometimes we learn lessons the hard way," Mom said.

Rachel nodded. "Grandpa says I should practice *self-control* instead of trying to *be in control*."

"Grandpa's right," Mom agreed.

"Changing the subject," Esther said with a smile. "I have some good news for you, Rachel."

"What's that?" Rachel was always eager to hear good news.

"Rudy and I are going to have a boppli."

Rachel's mouth dropped open. "Really? When will the baby be born?"

"Early October."

"That's just a few months after Mom's supposed to have her boppli." Rachel looked at Mom. "Did you know Esther was expecting a baby?"

"Jah. Esther told me a few days ago, but she asked

me not to say anything, because she wanted to tell you."

Esther smiled. "Are you happy about becoming an aunt, Rachel?"

"I'm happy if you are," Rachel replied.

"I truly am, and so is Rudy. He hopes it will be a buwe, but I'm hoping for a *maedel* [girl]." Esther continued to talk about how she couldn't wait to become a mother, and how much fun it would be when her baby and Mom's baby were old enough to play together.

Mom's voice blended with Esther's, and soon Rachel noisily yawned as her head lulled against the pillows. *In a few months, I'm going to be a big sister and an aunt.* Her eyes shut. *I wonder if the babies will be boys or girls.*

"Wake up, Rachel! The ice cream is ready!"

Rachel's eyes snapped open, and she sat up with a start. Jacob's face was a few inches from hers. "Don't scare me like that," she said.

"I wanted you to know the ice cream's ready."

"You didn't have to yell."

"How else could I wake you?"

Mom nodded toward the kitchen. "Jacob, why don't you help Pap dish up the ice cream? Then you can bring it in here for us."

"Jah, okay." Jacob scurried out of the room.

A few minutes later, he returned with two bowls of ice cream. He handed one to Rachel and gave one to

Mom. Rudy came in next, with two bowls—one for him and one for Esther. Then Pap and Henry arrived, each carrying their bowls of ice cream. Finally, Grandpa showed up with two bowls. He gave one to Jacob and kept one for himself.

"This looks appeditlich," Rachel said, smacking her lips. She placed the bowl on her lap, and using her left arm, dipped the spoon into the creamy ice cream. "Yum. It *is* delicious!" She took another bite, and then another. The ice cream tasted so good, she couldn't eat it fast enough.

Zing! Rachel dropped the spoon into the bowl and gasped as she grabbed her forehead.

"What's wrong?" Mom rushed over to Rachel. "Does your arm hurt again?"

Rachel drew in a deep breath and shook her head. "It's not my arm. I—I had a brain freeze."

"That's because you were eating too fast," Henry said. "I always get that when I eat ice cream too quickly."

"I'll take smaller bites," Rachel said.

When Rachel finished her ice cream, she was going to ask for a second bowl, but changed her mind. She remembered how her stomach had hurt after she'd eaten too much candy, so she knew it would be better if she stopped eating before she made herself sick.

"This has been nice," Rudy said, "but it's getting late, and it's time for Esther and me to head home."

Esther nodded. "I'm sure Rachel is ready to go to bed."

Rachel yawned. She could barely keep her eyes open.

Rudy and Esther gathered their coats and said good-bye.

"Is it all right if I go to the barn and say goodnight to Buddy?" Jacob asked as Mom gathered everyone's empty bowls.

"You'll need to go to bed soon, but I guess you can go to the barn for a few minutes," Mom replied.

Jacob raced for the door, and just as his fingers touched the knob, Mom called, "Before you go to the barn, please go to the chicken coop and see if there are any eggs."

Jacob's forehead wrinkled. "How come?"

"Your daed used the last of our eggs to make the ice cream," Mom said. "I'll need more for breakfast."

Rachel listened to see what Jacob would say. She knew he didn't like to collect eggs.

To Rachel's surprise, Jacob smiled and said, "Sure, Mom, I'll get those eggs right away." He rushed out the door.

Mom turned to Rachel and said, "It's been a long day, hasn't it?"

Rachel nodded and pointed to her cast. "A long and painful day."

"Things will get better as your arm begins to heal." Mom stroked Rachel's cheek. "And the medicine the doctor gave you will help with the pain."

Rachel stared at the fireplace across the room. Orange and red flames lapped at the logs as they crackled and popped. Her eyelids grew heavy again, and she started to doze.

"Let's go upstairs, and I'll help you get ready for bed," Mom said, tapping Rachel's shoulder.

Rachel nodded and stood. She and Mom were almost to the stairs when the back door opened, and Jacob burst into the hallway. His face was red as a cherry, and gooey, broken eggshells covered his jacket.

Mom's mouth dropped open. "Ach, Jacob! What happened?"

"I was in such a hurry to gather the eggs so I could get to the barn to see Buddy that I forgot to carry an egg basket to the chicken coop." Jacob drew in a breath and blew it out quickly. "I tried to carry the eggs inside my coat, but then I slipped on a patch of ice and all the eggs broke."

"Are you hurt?" Mom asked with concern.

Jacob shook his head. "Just the eggs."

Rachel chuckled. "Guess I'm not the only one in the family who gets in a hurry to do things."

Jacob turned to Mom and said, "I'm sorry. Maybe I can find more eggs in the morning."

Mom nodded and pushed her glasses to the bridge of her nose. "This has been quite a day. I hope both of my kinner have learned a good lesson."

"I have," Rachel and Jacob said at the same time.

"Jacob, you'd better clean up while I help Rachel get ready for bed," Mom said.

Jacob scurried to the bathroom as Rachel and Mom headed upstairs. A short time later, Rachel snuggled beneath the cozy quilt on her bed. She was almost asleep when the bedroom door opened and Grandpa poked his head into her room. "May I come in?"

"Of course," Rachel replied.

"I wanted to say goodnight." Grandpa stepped into the room, bent down, and kissed Rachel's forehead.

She smiled up at him. "I love you, Grandpa."

"I love you, too, Rachel." Grandpa moved to the window and lifted the shade. "It's snowing again. If we get another blizzard, you may not be able to go school tomorrow."

"That's okay." Rachel smiled. "I guess I can't do anything about it. I think I'm learning my lesson, Grandpa. When I try to be in control, I mess things up. The weather is out of my control. And so are many other things."

Rachel yawned and closed her eyes. "I'm thankful that God's in control of everything."

Recipe for Mrs. Yoder's Shoofly Pie

2 (8 inch) unbaked pie shells

Filling:
1 cup molasses
1 cup hot water
1 teaspoon baking soda
2 eggs, beaten
½ cup brown sugar

Crumb Mixture:
2 cups flour
¾ cup brown sugar
⅓ cup butter
½ teaspoon nutmeg
½ teaspoon cinnamon

Preheat oven to 400 degrees. Combine molasses, hot water, and baking soda in bowl. Add eggs and brown sugar. Divide half the mixture equally into the unbaked pie shells. Mix the ingredients for the crumb mixture in a separate bowl. Sprinkle half of crumb mixture over filling in each pie. Add second half of filling to pies, and sprinkle last half of crumb mixture over top. Bake for 10 minutes at 400 degrees, then reduce heat to 350 for 50 minutes. Recipe makes two 8-inch pies.

New Beginnings

Dedication

To the students and teachers at the Pleasant Ridge School in Shipshewana, Indiana. Thanks for letting me visit with you!

Glossary

ach—oh
bensel—silly child
boppli—baby
bruder—brother
danki—thank you
daed—dad
dochder—daughter
dumm—dumb
gaul—horse
gemmummelt—mumbling
grossdaadi—grandfather
grossmudder—grandmother
gut nacht—good night
hochmut—pride
jah—yes
kapp—cap
kichlin—cookies
kinner—children
kumme—come
lecherich—ridiculous
mamm—mom
midder—mothers
millich—milk
mudich—spirited
mupsich—stupid
naas—nose
naerfich—nervous
narrisch—crazy
reider—rider
rutschich—squirming
schmaert—smart
schnell—quickly
schpeckmaus—bat
schweschder—sister
verhuddelt—mixed up
wunderbaar—wonderful

Duh die katz naus.—Put the cat out.
En aldi grauns—An old grumbler
Es dutt mir leed.—I am sorry.
Fege.—Run about.
Kanscht seller gaul reide?—Are you able to ride that horse?
Schpiele gern—Like to play
Was fehlt dir denn?—What's the matter with you?
Was is do uff?—What's the matter here?
Wie geht's?—How are you?

Chapter 1

Saying Good-bye

Plunk! Plunk! Plunk! Plunk! Ten-year-old Rachel Yoder dropped four dirty spoons into the sink full of soapy water. Mom had gone outside to hang some laundry on the clothesline and left Rachel to wash the dishes. Doing dishes was not one of Rachel's favorite things to do on a sunny spring morning. She'd much rather be outside playing with her cat, Cuddles; riding on her skateboard in the barn; petting their old horse, Tom; or looking at the colorful flowers blooming in Mom's flowerbeds.

Rachel looked out the kitchen window and spotted Grandpa Schrock working in the garden. Even pulling weeds would be better than doing dishes!

At least I have two hands I can use to do the dishes, Rachel thought. When she'd broken her arm a few months ago, she'd learned to do some things using only one hand. She was glad her arm had healed and she didn't have to wear the uncomfortable cast anymore. And she was glad this was Saturday and she could go outside to play after the dishes were done.

On the other side of the yard she saw Pap and her seventeen-year-old brother, Henry. They were building a dog run for her brother Jacob's dog. Jacob was twelve years old and was sometimes nice to Rachel, but most of the time he just picked on her. Now that spring was here and the snow had melted, Pap decided it was time to get Buddy out of the empty stall in the barn. The big, shaggy, red dog had slept there since Orlie Troyer gave him to Jacob a few months ago.

Buddy had been nothing but trouble ever since he'd come to live at their place. Rachel thought he deserved to be locked up. During the winter, when Jacob kept Buddy in the empty stall, Buddy jumped over the door and escaped several times. Rachel was glad the hairy mutt wouldn't be able to escape from his new dog run with a sturdy wire fence around it.

Rachel washed all the silverware and looked out the window again. She saw Jacob step out of the barn. Buddy was at his side, wagging his tail and nudging Jacob's hand with his nose.

Rachel frowned as she thought of all the times Buddy had licked her hand or face with his big slimy tongue.

Swish! Swish! Rachel ran the sponge over one of their breakfast plates as she continued to stare out the window, where she saw Buddy and Jacob in the backyard, playing with a ball.

Jacob tossed the ball across the yard, and Buddy raced after it. Jacob clapped his hands to call Buddy back, but Buddy didn't come. Instead he rolled the ball with his nose, and then he took off in the opposite direction. Jacob sprinted after the dog, hollering and waving his hands.

Rachel grunted. "*Mupsich* [stupid] dog never does come when you call him." She thought about the whistle Jacob bought so he could train Buddy. But blowing the whistle never made the dog come when he was called. Buddy had a mind of his own. Rachel didn't think he could ever be trained.

She sloshed another dish around in the soapy water, rinsed it, and placed it in the dish drainer. *I hope Cuddles isn't in the yard right now. If Buddy sees my cat, he'll probably forget about the ball and start chasing after her.*

Rachel grabbed the frying pan Mom had used to make scrambled eggs for breakfast and dropped it into the soapy water. *Woosh!*—several bubbles floated into the air. One landed on Rachel's nose. *Pop!* She giggled and wiped it away then started scrubbing the frying pan.

The rumble of buggy wheels and the *clip-clop* of a horse's hooves pulled Rachel's gaze back to the window. When the horse and buggy came to a stop near the barn, Uncle Ben stepped down, followed by Aunt Irma, and Rachel's cousins—Mary, Nancy, Abe, and Sam.

Rachel saw Mom drop a towel into the laundry basket and hurry over to greet them. Grandpa set his shovel aside and headed toward Uncle Ben's buggy. Pap and Henry put their tools down and joined them. Jacob stopped chasing after Buddy and headed that way, too.

Rachel scoured the frying pan once more and

quickly dried it and her hands before putting it away. Then she flung open the back door and raced outside. "What a surprise! I didn't know you were coming over today!" she called to Mary.

Woof! Woof! Buddy raced around the side of the house, leaped into the air, and slurped his wet tongue across Rachel's chin.

"Yuck! Your breath is bad!" She pushed Buddy down with her knee. "Get away from me, bad breath Buddy."

Buddy whimpered and slunk toward the barn with his tail between his legs.

Rachel hurried over to Mary, but when Mary turned to face her, she wasn't smiling. "We—we came to give you some news," she said.

Rachel looked over at her cousins, Nancy, Abe, and Sam. They weren't smiling, either. Only Uncle Ben and Aunt Irma were smiling.

"What's going on?" Rachel asked. "What news do you have?"

Mary's chin trembled, and tears gathered in her eyes. "We're gonna move away."

"Moving where?" Pap asked before Rachel could voice the question.

"To Indiana," Uncle Ben said.

Rachel looked back at Mary, and Mary gave a slow nod. "It's true."

Everyone began to talk at once.

"Why are you going to Indiana?"

"How soon do you plan to move?"

"Is your place up for sale?"

"We'll surely miss you."

Rachel stood there, too numb to say a word. Mary couldn't be moving. She had been Rachel's friend since they were little. *Oh, what will I do without Mary?* she silently moaned.

Pap held up his hand. "We can't all talk at once. Let's ask one question at a time, and then my *bruder* [brother], Ben, can answer our questions."

"Why are you moving to Indiana?" Mom asked.

"As I'm sure you all know," Uncle Ben looked at Aunt Irma, "my wife's bruder, Noah, and his family moved there last year, and Noah bought a dairy farm."

Everyone nodded.

Uncle Ben smiled. "Noah's dairy business is doing real well, and he asked me to move to Indiana and be his partner."

"But you started working at the buggy shop not long ago," Henry said. "Why would you want to quit your new job and move to Indiana?"

"I like my job at the buggy shop, but as I'm sure you know, your *daed* [dad] and I grew up on a dairy farm. I'm sure I'll enjoy working with the cows on Noah's farm even more," Uncle Ben replied.

Hearing that Mary and her family would be leaving was the worst possible news! Rachel bit off the end of her thumbnail and spit it on the ground. She'd been trying to give up her nervous habit of nail biting, but it was hard not to feel anxious about her best friend moving away. "Can't you start a dairy farm right here?" she asked.

"Our place here is too small for that," Uncle Ben said.

"Can't you buy more land?" Rachel asked.

Uncle Ben shook his head. "I'm afraid not. Land here in Lancaster County is getting too expensive, and there's not a lot of land available to buy anymore."

Rachel looked up at Aunt Irma with tears blurring her vision. "Can't Mary stay with us?"

Aunt Irma shook her head. "We could never leave any of our *kinner* [children] here. They will come to Indiana with us."

Grandpa, who stood beside Rachel, patted the top of her head. "If your folks moved somewhere else, wouldn't you want to go with them?"

Rachel looked at Mom, Pap, Jacob, Henry, and Grandpa. As much as she liked her home here, she knew if Mom and Pap decided to move, she'd want to go with them. "*Jah* [yes]," she said in a near whisper, "I'd want to move, too."

"What about Grandpa and Grandma Yoder?" Jacob asked. "Who's gonna look after them if you move away?"

Uncle Ben looked over at Pap. "As you know, our sister, Karen, and her husband, Amos, have been renting a place in Tennessee."

Pap nodded.

"Amos and Karen have decided to move to Pennsylvania and buy our house. That means they'll be living next door to our folks, same as we have been for the past twelve years."

Rachel swallowed around the lump in her throat.

She didn't like the idea of someone else living in Uncle Ben and Aunt Irma's house—especially someone she didn't know very well. She'd only seen Uncle Amos and Aunt Karen a few times, and the last time she'd seen them she was seven years old. Aunt Karen had given birth to a baby boy named Gerald three years ago, but Rachel hadn't met him yet. *If only I could do something to keep Mary's family from moving,* she thought.

"When do you plan to move?" Pap asked Uncle Ben.

"Two weeks from today."

"Two weeks?" Rachel's mouth fell open.

"Why so soon?" Mom asked.

"Noah just bought fifty more cows, and now he's busier than ever," Uncle Ben replied. "He needs me there as soon as possible."

"Let us know when you're ready to start packing," Pap said. "We'll be there to help."

With tears clinging to her eyelashes, Rachel turned to Mary and gave her a hug. "I'm going to miss you so much!"

The day before Mary's family was supposed to move, Mary came over to Rachel's to spend the night.

"I can't believe this is the last time we'll ever have a sleepover," Rachel said as the girls climbed the steps to her room.

Mary clasped Rachel's hand. "Don't say that. We'll have more sleepovers. My family will come back to Pennsylvania to visit, and your family can come see our new home in Indiana."

Rachel shook her head as tears gathered in her eyes. "It won't be the same. We won't be best friends anymore."

"We'll always be best friends," Mary said. "My moving away won't change that."

When they entered Rachel's room, Rachel flopped onto her bed with a groan. "I wish you didn't have to go. Can't you talk your folks out of moving?"

"Papa has already made up his mind." Mary set her overnight bag on the floor and joined Rachel on the bed. "Besides, the house we've lived in since before I was a baby won't be ours after Saturday. Uncle Amos and Aunt Karen are moving from Tennessee soon, and then they'll be living in our old house."

"I know." Rachel sniffed. "I just wish things could stay the same as they are right now." She touched Mary's hand. "I'm going to miss you so much, and I–I'm afraid you'll forget about me."

"Never!" Mary reached down and opened the canvas satchel she'd brought along. "I have something for you." She handed Rachel a little faceless doll with brown hair just like Mary's. "I asked my *mamm* [mom] if I could give you my doll so you would have something to remember me by."

Rachel hugged the doll close to her chest. "*Danki* [thank you], Mary. I'll think of you every time I play with this doll." She hopped off the bed and hurried across the room. "I have something to give you, too."

"What is it?"

Rachel opened the bottom drawer of her dresser and

took out a rock she'd painted to look like a ladybug. "I signed my name on the bottom," she said, handing the rock to Mary. "That way you won't forget who gave it to you."

"I'll never forget you, Rachel. Thank you."

"I wish you could have brought Stripes over tonight, so he could say good-bye to Cuddles," Rachel said as she and Mary put their nightgowns on and got ready for bed.

"Mama didn't think it was a good idea," Mary said. "Stripes isn't good about staying in the yard, and if I'd brought him over to play with Cuddles, he could've run off. Since Mama and Papa are busy packing our things, they wouldn't want to be bothered with having to hunt for my cat."

"Maybe I can bring Cuddles over to your house to say good-bye," Rachel said as they crawled into bed. "I can't believe you're moving tomorrow."

Mary nodded and fluffed up her pillow.

Rachel stared at the ceiling. Even if they stayed awake all night there wouldn't be enough time to say all the things she wanted to say to Mary. Writing letters and a visit once in a while wouldn't be the same as spending the night at one another's house, playing in the haylofts in their barns, or eating lunch at school together. Tears trickled down Rachel's cheeks. After Mary moved away, nothing would ever be the same.

"Can you please open the window, Rachel?" Mary asked. "It's kind of stuffy in here."

"I suppose I could, but I have to be careful not to let

Cuddles in. Mom doesn't like it when Cuddles sneaks into my room and gets up on the bed."

"We could just open it enough so some fresh air gets in."

Rachel pushed the covers aside, turned on the flashlight by her bed, and padded across the room. She'd no more than opened the window, when—*meow!*—Cuddles leaped from the tree right into her arms.

"Oh no!" Rachel exclaimed.

"Is that Cuddles?" Mary asked as she sat up in bed.

"Jah. She must have been sitting in the tree hoping I would open the window."

"Bring her over here so I can pet her."

Rachel shook her head. "No, Mary. . .Mom doesn't like me to have Cuddles on the bed. She has to go back outside."

"Don't put her out just yet. I'll come over there so I can pet Cuddles." Mary scrambled out of bed and hurried across the room.

Rachel handed the cat to Mary, and Cuddles purred loudly while Mary petted the top of her head. "She sure is soft and silky, isn't she?"

"Jah, but she'd better go back out now." Rachel opened the window wider, and was about to take the cat from Mary, when—*flap! flap!*—something flew into the room.

"What was that?" Mary squealed.

"I—I don't know. I think it might have been a bird." Rachel shined her flashlight around the room. *Woosh! Woosh!* The creature flew so fast she could barely follow it with the light.

"It's a *schpeckmaus* [bat]!" Mary dropped to the floor and dove under Rachel's bed, with Cuddles still in her arms.

Woosh! Woosh! Rachel dropped to her knees and shined the light again. Sure enough, there was a little brown bat flying around her room. "Yeow!" Rachel hollered as it swooped past her head. She ducked lower and scurried under the bed to join Mary and Cuddles.

"Wh–what are we gonna do?" Mary's voice quivered. "How are we gonna get that bat out of your room?"

"Let's lie here real quiet. Maybe it'll fly out the open window." Rachel reached over and stroked Cuddles's head for comfort.

"You don't suppose it will fly under the bed and bite us, do you?"

"I don't think so. Pap told me once that the bats we have around here aren't dangerous."

Mary giggled. "Then what are we doing under the bed?"

Rachel laughed, too. "Do you want to crawl out and see if the bat's still there?"

"No way! Do you?"

"Nope."

"Let's close our eyes and go to sleep," Mary suggested. "When we wake up in the morning, maybe the bat will be gone."

Rachel didn't think she would sleep very comfortably on the hard floor underneath the bed, but she wasn't going to crawl out if Mary wasn't. "*Gut nacht* [good night], Mary," she said.

"Good night, Rachel."

Cock-a-doodle-do! Cock-a-doodle-do!

Rachel groaned and released a noisy yawn. The rooster was crowing; it must be morning. *Thwack!*—she bumped her head as she tried to sit up. Then she remembered—she, Mary, and Cuddles had slept under her bed to get away from the bat that flew into her room last night.

Rachel glanced over at Mary, still asleep with Cuddles in her arms. "Wake up. . .it's morning," she whispered, nudging Mary's arm.

Mary's eyes snapped open. "Is—is the bat gone?"

"I don't know. I don't hear it flying around." Rachel started to crawl out from under her bed when the bedroom door opened and Mom stepped in.

"What in the world are you doing, Rachel? And where is Mary?"

Before Rachel could respond, Mom knelt down and peered under the bed. "What are you two doing under there, and what's Cuddles doing in your room?"

"It was stuffy in here last night," Rachel explained. "Cuddles came in when I opened the window. Then a bat flew in, and Mary and I were kind of scared, so we slept under my bed."

Mom's forehead wrinkled, and Rachel thought for sure she was in for a lecture. But then Mom's lips lifted into a smile and her eyes twinkled. "A bat got into my room once when I was a girl."

"What did you do?" asked Rachel.

"I hid under the bed." Mom held onto the bedpost and laughed so hard tears streamed down her cheeks. Rachel joined Mom's laughter, and Mary crawled out from the under the bed and started laughing, too.

Finally Mom stopped laughing. She used the corner of her apron to dry her eyes, and she looked around the room. "There's no sign of a bat in here now. It must have flown out the window."

Rachel took Cuddles from Mary. "I'll put her back in the tree."

Mom nodded. "Then we need to hurry and eat breakfast so we can take Mary home. Today's the big move, and we need to be there to help them pack."

Rachel frowned. With all the laughter going on in her room, she'd almost forgotten that Mary would be moving today.

As if she could read her thoughts, Mom patted Rachel's arm and said, "I'm glad you and Mary were able to spend the night together—even if you had to sleep under your bed."

Rachel managed a weak smile. Maybe when they got to Uncle Ben and Aunt Irma's house, she could talk them out of moving.

When Pap guided their horse and buggy onto Uncle Ben's driveway, Rachel thought she was going to break down and sob. Two big moving trucks were parked near the barn. Several people rushed around the yard, hauling boxes and furniture out of the house and into the trucks.

Pap halted the horse near the hitching rail, and Mom, Mary, Grandpa, and Rachel climbed down from the buggy. Henry pulled his horse and buggy in next to Pap's, and he and Jacob climbed down from it, too.

"What can we do to help?" Pap called to Uncle Ben, who was carrying a large box out to the truck.

Uncle Ben motioned to the house with his head. "There are more boxes and furniture in there that need to be put in the trucks."

For the next few hours everyone scurried about, loading the trucks, cleaning the house, and fixing snacks for those who had come to help. By noon the house was empty and both trucks were full and ready to go.

As Rachel and Mary walked through the house together, their footsteps and voices echoed in the bare rooms. There wasn't a stick of furniture or anything else left to remind Rachel that this had been Mary and her family's home. It didn't look right to see everything gone. It wasn't right for Mary to move to Indiana.

"Mary, Nancy, Abe, and Sam. . .it's time for us to head out. Our drivers are ready to go," Uncle Ben called.

A lump formed in Rachel's throat as she looked at Mary. "I wish you didn't have to go."

"Me neither," Mary said as tears filled her eyes.

Rachel rushed over to Uncle Ben and grabbed hold of his arm. "Won't you change your mind and stay here in Pennsylvania?"

He slowly shook his head. "I'm sorry, Rachel, but our plans have been made and my bruder is expecting us to arrive at his place in a few days."

Mom hugged Aunt Irma then turned to Rachel and said, "Say good-bye to your cousins." She nodded at Jacob and Henry. "You boys need to say good-bye, too."

Mary grabbed Rachel and gave her a hug. "I'll write to you soon, I promise."

Rachel could only nod in reply. Her throat felt like it was clogged with a glob of peanut butter. No matter how much she wanted, she knew she wasn't in control of this situation. She'd learned that lesson all too well when she broke her arm a few months ago.

"We'll try to visit you soon after our *boppli* [baby] is born," Pap said as Mary's family climbed into the trucks with their drivers.

"We'll look forward to that," Aunt Irma called.

As the trucks pulled out of the driveway, Rachel thought her heart was breaking in two. She wasn't sure if she would ever see Mary again.

"You and Mary can still be friends even though you won't see each other as often as before," Mom said gently. "But you're a friendly girl, and I'm sure it won't be long until you make another best friend." She placed her hand on Rachel's slumped shoulder. "There's a little song I learned about friendship when I was a girl. Would you like me to sing it to you?"

"I guess so."

"Make new friends but keep the old," Mom sang in a clear voice. "One is silver the other is gold."

Rachel sniffed. "I—I don't want a new friend. I just want my best friend, Mary!"

Chapter 2

Verhuddelt

As Rachel walked behind Jacob on their way to school Monday morning, her heart ached. With each step she took she felt more and more depressed. Mary had moved on Saturday. Their house was empty, their barn was empty, and even Mary's desk would be empty—forever.

Rachel kicked a rock with the toe of her sneaker. "It's Uncle Ben's fault," she mumbled under her breath. "He shouldn't have taken Mary away."

Jacob nudged Rachel's arm. "*Was fehlt dir denn?* [What's the matter with you?] What are you *gemmummelt* [mumbling] about?"

"I wasn't mumbling."

"Jah, you were."

"I was just thinking about Mary moving and how much I'm going to miss her."

"They said they'd come to visit," Jacob reminded her. "And after Mom has the boppli, maybe we can make a trip to Indiana and visit them, too."

"But it could be a long time before they come back here for a visit. Mom might not feel up to traveling with the baby for a long time, either." Rachel swallowed hard, hoping she wouldn't cry in front of Jacob. If she did, he would probably call her a little *bensel* [silly child].

"I'm going to miss everyone in Mary's family, too," Jacob said, "but I won't go around all droopy because they're gone."

"I'm not droopy," Rachel said, frowning.

"Jah, you are."

Rachel clamped her mouth shut and hurried ahead, refusing to argue with Jacob anymore. They walked on in silence—Jacob whistling, Rachel kicking stones as she thought about how much she already missed Mary.

When they arrived at the schoolhouse, Rachel spotted Orlie down on his knees, staring at something in the grass. Curious as to what it might be, Rachel hurried over to Orlie.

"Look what I found!" he said excitedly.

"What is it?"

"It's a painted ladybug rock. It must be the one you made for my birthday in February." He grinned and held the rock out to her. "Now that it's spring and the snow's melted, it was easy to find the rock!"

"That's nice." Rachel had almost forgotten about the painted rock she'd made for Orlie's birthday and had accidentally dropped in the snow.

"You don't seem very excited about the rock. Isn't it amazing that I found it?" Orlie asked.

She only shrugged in reply.

"What's wrong? Why do you look so sad?"

The mysterious glob of peanut butter clogged Rachel's throat again and she swallowed a couple of times. "Mary and her family moved to Indiana on Saturday."

"I probably would have known that if we'd had church yesterday," Orlie said.

Rachel nodded. The Amish church they belonged to had church every other Sunday, and they took turns having it in one another's homes.

"How come Mary's family moved to Indiana?" Orlie asked.

"Her daed's going to help run a dairy farm." Rachel frowned. "It won't be the same with Mary gone."

Just then an Amish girl who looked to be about Rachel's age walked across the yard toward them. She had dark brown hair and matching eyes, and a deep dimple in each cheek. Rachel had never seen the girl before and figured she must be new. "What have you got there?" the girl asked, pointing at the rock in Orlie's hand.

Orlie smiled. "It's a ladybug rock."

She wrinkled her nose. "I don't like bugs!"

"Not even ladybugs?" Orlie asked.

She shook her head. "I don't like any kind of bugs."

Orlie looked at Rachel and said, "Have you met Audra Burkholder yet?"

Rachel shook her head.

"Audra and her family moved to the farm next to our place on Saturday." Orlie grinned. "Guess Saturday must have been moving day here in Lancaster County."

Rachel gritted her teeth. Was Orlie trying to make her feel worse about Mary moving?

"We used to live in Ohio, but we moved here to be closer to my *grossdaadi* [grandfather] and *grossmudder* [grandmother]." Audra looked at Rachel. "What's your name?"

"Rachel Yoder."

"Rachel's grandpa used to live in Ohio. Isn't that right, Rachel?" Orlie asked.

Rachel only nodded in reply. She didn't want to talk to Orlie or the new girl named Audra right now. "I think I'd better get inside," she said as she started walking toward the schoolhouse.

"What's the hurry?" Orlie called. "Elizabeth hasn't rung the bell yet."

Rachel ignored him and hurried up the schoolhouse stairs. After she put her lunch pail on the shelf just inside the door, she trudged over to her desk and sat down. She glanced at Mary's old desk and blinked back tears. For the rest of this school year Rachel would have to look at the empty desk across from her and be reminded that her best friend moved away.

A few minutes later, Elizabeth rang the school bell. *Clang! Clang! Clang!*

The children filed into the room and took their seats. Audra stood up front by the teacher's desk, red-faced and staring at the floor.

"Good morning, boys and girls," Elizabeth said.

"Good morning, Elizabeth," the scholars replied in unison.

"We have a new girl with us today. Her name is Audra Burkholder. Audra and her family moved here from Ohio." Elizabeth nudged Audra's arm. "Would you like to tell the class something about yourself?"

Audra's face turned even redder as she raised her head and looked at the class. "Well, uh—my mamm and daed are Andy and Naomi, and I have four older brothers. Walter and Perry are married. Jared's sixteen, so he's out of school already. Brian, my youngest brother, is twelve. Brian's not here today because he has a bad cold." Audra looked at the teacher. "Oh, and starting today, my daed and Jared will be working at the buggy shop."

Rachel cringed. Uncle Ben used to work at the buggy shop, until he decided he'd rather be milking cows. *I wish Uncle Ben still worked at the buggy shop, not Audra's daed and bruder.*

"We're happy to have you in our class, Audra." Elizabeth looked at the scholars and smiled. "During recess you'll have a chance to get to know Audra better. Please make her feel welcome." She pointed to Mary's empty desk. Rachel's heart skipped a beat. "That desk will be yours, Audra."

No! No! No! Rachel silently screamed. Tears burned in her eyes as she watched Audra sit at Mary's desk. Audra opened her backpack, took out a writing tablet and some books, and lifted the lid of the desk to put them inside.

When Rachel realized her mouth was hanging open, she snapped her jaw shut. *Mary's things should be in there—not Audra's,* she thought. *This isn't right. It's not right at all!*

Elizabeth picked up her Bible. "I'll be reading from Ecclesiastes 4:9–10: 'Two are better than one, because they have a good return for their work: If one falls down, his friend can help him up. But pity the man who falls and has no one to help him up!' "

Rachel's heart clenched. Mary had been that kind of friend. Whenever Rachel felt sad, Mary cheered her up. Now Rachel had no best friend, except maybe Orlie. After he'd helped Rachel with her lines in the Christmas program last year, they'd had a secret friendship. Even so, she didn't think of him as a "best friend."

Orlie's sharp whisper jolted Rachel out of her thoughts. "We're supposed to stand. It's time to repeat the Lord's Prayer."

Rachel stood and recited the prayer with the others, even though her heart wasn't in it. When she filed to the front of the room with the rest of the children to sing a few songs, her throat felt swollen. She moved to stand next to Orlie, but Audra squeezed in where Rachel wanted to stand. She sighed, slumped her shoulders, and found a spot at the end of the line.

Rachel glanced at the clock on the far wall. She would be glad when it was time for morning recess and she could go outside to play. Maybe she and Orlie could talk about the ladybug rock she'd painted for him. She might also ask if he could come over to their place and help Jacob train Buddy.

The next hour ticked by slowly as Rachel worked on her arithmetic lesson. Every few minutes she glanced at the clock. Finally, Elizabeth announced that it was time for recess.

Rachel hurried outside and was happy to see that the sun shone brightly. It had been hiding behind the clouds on the walk to school. She spotted Orlie standing near the teeter-totter. She was about to head that way when she saw Audra walk up to him. No way was she going over there now!

Rachel moved over to the swings and sat down. She let her feet dangle but didn't pump her legs. It didn't feel right to swing without Mary.

Phoebe Wagler took the other swing and started pumping her legs. *Pump, pump, swing. Pump, pump, swing.* The swing moved back and forth, and Phoebe giggled excitedly. "This is so much fun! I love to swing!"

Rachel stared at the ground.

"When's your mamm due to have her boppli, Rachel?" Phoebe asked.

"This summer—probably July." Rachel decided to get her swing moving, too. Maybe then Phoebe would stop talking to her. *Pump, pump, swing. Pump, pump, swing.*

"My baby sister, Darlene, is ten weeks old." Phoebe grinned. "It's so cute when she gurgles and coos. I don't think there's anything sweeter than a boppli."

Rachel hoped her baby sister or brother would be cute and sweet. She didn't like the idea of having a fussy baby in the house.

The bell rang, calling everyone back inside. Rachel

left the swing and hurried into the schoolhouse. She'd just taken her seat when Orlie turned in his chair and said, "Audra told me her daed might let her visit the buggy shop on Saturday. She invited me to go along. How about you, Rachel? Would you like to see the buggy shop, too?"

Rachel shook her head. "I've seen it already—when my uncle Ben worked there."

"Oh." Orlie turned around before Rachel could say anything more. So much for asking if Orlie might come over to their place on Saturday. He obviously had other plans.

At eleven thirty, Elizabeth dismissed the classroom by rows to get their lunch pails. Rachel frowned when Audra's row was dismissed first.

When Rachel reached up to take her lunch pail down from the shelf, Jacob took his down at the same time. "Are you in a better mood now, Rachel?" he asked.

She narrowed her eyes at him. "What do you think?"

"I think you're an old sourpuss today. If Mom packed a bottle of Pap's homemade root beer in your lunch pail, maybe you'll be sweeter after you drink it."

"It would take more than a bottle of root beer to make *you* sweeter," Rachel muttered as she headed out to the porch to eat her lunch. She took a seat on the top step, opened her lunch pail, and took out her sandwich. Her stomach rumbled as she removed the plastic wrapping. Peanut butter and jelly was her favorite kind. She lifted it to her mouth and was about to take a bite, when a fishy smell wafted up to her nose.

"Eww. . .tuna!"

But how could that be? Rachel wondered. She'd watched Mom make her sandwich this morning, and it had been peanut butter and jelly—not tuna fish!

She looked in the lunch pail and saw an orange, two cookies, and a bottle of milk. *This isn't the lunch Mom made for me!*

Rachel looked across the porch, where several other girls sat, and spotted Audra—eating a peanut butter and jelly sandwich!

Rachel tossed the tuna sandwich in the lunch pail and slammed the lid. Then she marched over to Audra and said, "I believe that's my sandwich you're eating!"

Audra looked up at Rachel and wrinkled her forehead. "What makes you think that?"

Rachel handed the lunch pail to Audra. "There's a tuna fish sandwich in here, and it's not mine. You're eating *my* peanut butter and jelly sandwich." She pointed to the lunch pail sitting on the porch beside Audra. "And that's *my* lunch pail!"

Audra's eyes widened as she looked at one lunch pail and then the other. "I think I made a mistake," she said. "Our lunch pails look almost alike. They must have gotten *verhuddelt* [mixed up]. Since I've already eaten part of your sandwich, why don't you go ahead and eat my lunch?"

Rachel shook her head so hard the ties on her *kapp* [cap] flipped around her face. "No way! I hate the taste of tuna!"

Audra shrugged and handed the half-eaten peanut butter and jelly sandwich to Rachel. "All right then.

Here you go."

Rachel nearly gagged. "No thanks!" She wasn't about to eat that peanut butter and jelly sandwich now. Not with Audra's germs on it! "I'll bet you took my lunch pail on purpose!"

Audra shook her head. "Why would I do that? I didn't know the lunch pail I took was yours. I thought it was mine."

Rachel bent down, snatched her lunch pail, and shoved Audra's lunch pail in its place. At least she could eat the apple and banana bread Mom had packed.

She plopped down on her seat across the porch step and opened the lid. Sure enough, there was a big red apple and two slices of banana bread.

Rachel unwrapped the banana bread and was about to take a bite when she remembered that Mary liked banana bread, too. Rachel's eyes filled with tears. She tossed the banana bread into the lunch pail and shut the lid with a *snap!* She wasn't hungry anymore.

"Aren't you gonna eat your banana bread?" Jacob asked, taking a seat beside Rachel.

She shook her head. "I can't."

"Why not?"

"It reminds me of Mary."

The skin around Jacob's blue eyes wrinkled. "Huh?"

"Banana bread was one of Mary's favorites." Rachel sighed. "Now that Mary's gone, every time I see a piece of banana bread, I'll think of her."

"That's *lecherich* [ridiculous], Rachel." Jacob grabbed her lunch pail, flipped open the lid, and helped himself to the pieces of banana bread.

"Hey!" Rachel frowned at him. "What do you think you're doing?"

He shrugged. "Figured if you're not gonna eat the banana bread then I will."

Rachel was about to say something mean to Jacob when she noticed several children staring at her. "Fine then, I hope you enjoy every bite!" She jumped up, raced down the steps, and ran all the way to the swings.

As Rachel walked home from school that afternoon, she kept thinking about the lunch pail mix up and how happy Audra had looked eating Rachel's peanut butter and jelly sandwich. "I'll do something to make sure that doesn't happen again," Rachel muttered under her breath.

Jacob nudged Rachel's arm. "You're mumbling again, just like you did this morning. What's wrong now?"

As they continued walking, Rachel told Jacob about Audra eating her peanut butter and jelly sandwich. "I think she took my lunch pail on purpose because she doesn't like me," she grumbled.

"Audra's new at our school," Jacob said. "She doesn't know you well enough to decide whether she likes you or not."

"Humph!" Rachel grunted. "I could tell by the way she looked at me that she doesn't like me."

"You're lecherich, little bensel." Jacob shook his head and kept walking.

"I'm not ridiculous, and I wish you would stop calling me a silly child!"

"When you stop acting like a silly child, I'll stop calling you one."

As Rachel hurried on, an idea popped into her head. *When I get home, I'm going to paint a picture of a ladybug on my lunch pail. That should keep Audra from thinking it's hers!*

When Rachel and Jacob arrived home, Jacob went out to the dog run to see Buddy, and Rachel hurried to the house. She set her lunch pail on the kitchen counter and went upstairs to her room to get out her paints. When she returned to the kitchen, she spread some newspaper on the table, placed her lunch pail on it, and opened a bottle of black paint. She had just finished painting the body of the ladybug on one side of her lunch pail when Mom entered the kitchen.

"What are you doing, Rachel?"

"I'm painting a ladybug on both sides of my lunch pail."

Mom squinted over the top of her metal-framed glasses. "Why would you want to do something like that?"

"Because there's a new girl at school named Audra Burkholder, and our lunch pails got verhuddelt because she took mine instead of hers. The sandwich in the lunch pail I opened was tuna fish—not peanut butter and jelly." Rachel frowned. "I think Audra took my lunch on purpose."

"Do your lunch pails look alike?" Mom asked.

"Jah."

"Then I'm sure Audra took your lunch pail by mistake."

Rachel stared at her lunch pail and heaved a big sigh. "Elizabeth gave Mary's old desk to Audra, and now every time I look over there I'll be reminded that Mary's gone and I lost my best friend."

Mom clucked her tongue. "I don't think you're being fair, Rachel. Audra's new at your school, and I'm sure she needs a friend. You should give her a chance, don't you think?"

Rachel shrugged.

"Why don't you invite Audra over to play after school? You might become good friends."

"I don't need a friend. Not a friend like Audra, anyway." Rachel thought about Sherry, the English girl she'd met at the farmer's market last summer, and wondered if she would make a good friend. Sherry had let Rachel walk her dog, even though they'd just met. The only problem was, Rachel didn't know where Sherry lived, and she hadn't seen her since that day at the market. Rachel needed a friend now. She needed Mary!

Mom moved over to the cupboard and took out a glass. "Sometimes the very thing we think we don't want is exactly what we need," she said as she filled her glass with water.

I don't need Audra, Rachel thought. *And I don't want her, either.* Rachel dipped a clean brush into the jar of white paint so she could paint the ladybug's eyes and antennas. She was sure of one thing—she could never be Audra Burkholder's friend!

Chapter 3

Raining Sideways

It's raining pretty hard. You'd better wear your boots to school this morning," Mom said as she handed Rachel her lunch pail with a ladybug painted on both sides.

Rachel peeked out the kitchen window and wrinkled her nose. Not a speck of sun. "I hate the rain!"

Mom looked at Rachel over the top of her glasses. "You know how I feel about that word *hate*."

"I know, but I just don't like walking to school in the rain." Rachel set the lunch pail on the floor, slipped her feet into her rubber boots, and put on her raincoat. "If it keeps raining, we probably won't get to play outside during recess today."

"It's been a dry spring so far and we need a good soaking," Mom said. "If you can't play outside during recess, I'm sure you'll find something fun to do indoors."

"Maybe you can sit at your desk and draw a picture, little bensel," Jacob said as he joined Rachel in the utility room.

"Stop calling your sister that name," Mom said before Rachel could respond. "She is not a silly child."

Rachel smiled to herself. At least she wasn't the only one being scolded by Mom this morning.

"We'd better get going or we're gonna be late for school," Jacob said, nudging Rachel's arm.

"Just let me get my umbrella." Rachel opened the closet door, but her umbrella wasn't there. "Has anyone seen my umbrella?"

"Where did you put it?" Mom asked.

"I thought it was in here." Rachel squinted at Jacob. "Did you take my umbrella?"

He grunted. "Why would I want your *dumm* [dumb] old umbrella?"

"It's not dumb and it's not old," Rachel said. "Esther gave it to me for Christmas." Rachel's older sister always gave Rachel nice presents for her birthday and Christmas, and Rachel would feel bad if she lost the umbrella.

Jacob opened the back door. "Let's go, Rachel."

"I'm not going without my umbrella."

"Aw, come on. You won't melt from a little bit of rain." Jacob snickered and shook his head.

Rachel looked out the door. "That's more than a little rain. It's coming down by the buckets. The drainage ditch out by the road is so full, it's starting to overflow. If the rain doesn't stop soon, Pap's fields will flood and turn into ponds."

"I can't believe the way you exaggerate." Jacob stepped onto the porch. "Are you coming or not?"

Rachel frowned. "It's raining too hard to walk without an umbrella."

Mom went to the kitchen and returned with a large black umbrella. "You may borrow my umbrella today," she said, handing it to Rachel.

"Danki, Mom." Rachel picked up her lunch pail and slipped it into her backpack.

Mom bent down and gave Rachel a hug. Then she patted Jacob's shoulder. "Have a good day."

"You, too, Mom," Rachel and Jacob said at the same time.

Rachel opened the umbrella and sloshed down the muddy driveway behind Jacob. When they reached the edge of the road she noticed there were puddles everywhere.

Rachel walked carefully, stepping around the puddles. Any other time she would have enjoyed plodding through the puddles, but not today. She dreaded going to school—dreaded seeing Audra sitting at Mary's desk—dreaded having to stay indoors for recess.

Woosh! The wind picked up and whipped against Rachel's legs, making it hard for her to walk. *Splat! Splat! Splat!* The rain splattered on her umbrella and splashed against the part of her dress that hung below her raincoat.

"Hurry up, slowpoke," Jacob called over his shoulder. "You're walking too slow."

"I can't walk any faster because it's raining sideways and the wind's slowing me down," Rachel complained. Her day was off to a very bad start.

"It's not raining sideways. The wind's just blowing the rain, that's all. What a bensel you are."

"Mom said you're not supposed to call me a silly child anymore."

Jacob grunted and kept walking.

Rachel gripped the umbrella tighter. Deep down she sometimes wished she could do something so Jacob would get in trouble.

Woosh! Another gust of wind came up, and—*floop!*—Rachel's umbrella turned inside out. "No, no, no," she groaned. "Always trouble somewhere!"

Struggling against the blustery wind and drenching rain, Rachel tried to pull the umbrella right side out. It didn't budge. The wind was too strong, and the rain poured down so hard she could barely see.

"Would it help if I walked slower and closer to you so I can block the wind?" Jacob asked.

Rachel wasn't sure why Jacob was being so nice all of a sudden, but she really didn't think him walking closer to her would help that much. "Danki anyway," she said, "but you'd better keep moving. If we walk any slower we'll be late to school."

Jacob shrugged and continued on. Rachel trudged wearily behind.

By the time they arrived at the schoolhouse Rachel was wet and cold. As she stepped onto the porch, she looked up at the sky and spotted a ray of sun peeking through the clouds. She hoped this was the end of her troubles for today.

Elizabeth rang the bell, and Rachel followed Jacob

inside. She'd just slipped out of her raincoat and boots when Orlie walked up and pointed at her umbrella. "What happened to that?" he asked with a snicker.

"It turned inside out because of the wind."

"It sure looks funny." He laughed some more. "I'll bet you had a hard time staying dry under that, huh?"

"Very funny!" Rachel struggled with the umbrella but finally got it turned right side out again. Next she took her lunch pail out of her backpack and was about to place it on the shelf near the door when Phoebe tapped her on the shoulder. "Did you get a new lunch pail? I like those cute little ladybugs."

"This is my old lunch pail. I painted lady bugs on both sides so no one would think the lunch pail was hers." Rachel glanced over at Audra, who sat on the floor struggling to take off her boots.

Audra wrinkled her nose and turned her back to Rachel.

"I wish I had a ladybug painted on my lunch pail," Phoebe said. "You're really good at art, Rachel."

Rachel felt pleased knowing someone thought she could paint well. "Would you like me to paint something on your lunch pail?" she asked Phoebe.

"Oh, jah. Could you do a ladybug like yours?"

Rachel shook her head. "If I put a ladybug on your lunch pail, then it will look like my lunch pail and we might get them verhuddelt."

"How about a butterfly or a turtle?" Phoebe suggested. "Could you paint one of those?"

"Jah, sure, if it's all right with your mamm." Phoebe

was two years younger than Rachel, and Rachel didn't think it would be right to paint anything on Phoebe's lunch pail unless Phoebe's mother gave her permission.

"I'll ask Mama when I get home." Phoebe smiled. "Can you bring your paints to school tomorrow?"

Rachel nodded. "If your mamm says it's okay, maybe I can paint something on your lunch pail during our lunch recess."

"That'd be good." Phoebe scurried off to her desk, and Rachel did the same. Maybe this wouldn't be such a bad day after all.

Elizabeth opened her Bible and had just started reading from Matthew 5:22, when Aaron King, the boy who sat behind Rachel, tapped her on the shoulder. "*Psst*. . .Rachel. . .I heard about the ladybugs you painted on your lunch pail," he whispered.

Rachel only nodded in reply. She knew everyone was expected to be quiet during the time of scripture reading.

Aaron tapped her shoulder again. "I also heard you're gonna bring your paints to school tomorrow. Could you paint a frog on my lunch pail?"

Rachel smiled. It was nice to know someone else appreciated her artwork.

"*Psst*. . .Rachel, did you hear what I said?"

Rachel turned around. "Jah, Aaron," she said, forgetting to whisper. "If your folks don't mind, I'd be happy to paint something on your lunch pail."

"Rachel Yoder, stop talking and turn around. You know better than to do that when I'm reading from the Bible."

Rachel jumped at the sound of her teacher's voice. Her face heated up as she turned toward the front of the room. She raised her hand.

"What is it, Rachel?"

"Aaron was asking if I could—"

Elizabeth shook her head. "You're the one who was turned around, and your voice was the only one I heard. Make sure it doesn't happen again."

Rachel's face grew hotter. *It's Aaron's fault I got in trouble. He should be in trouble with Elizabeth, too.* She tried to concentrate on the verse of scripture Elizabeth was reading about not being angry with others, but all she could think about was how the teacher had embarrassed her in front of the class and how Aaron had gotten her in trouble. She squeezed her eyes shut to keep tears from falling. *I'm not going to paint anything on Aaron's lunch pail now!*

When the scripture, prayer, and songs were done, it was time for arithmetic. Rachel had just opened her math book, when—*bzzz. . .bzzz*—a pesky fly flew past her nose. *Bzzz. . .bzzz. . .bzzz.*

Rachel swatted at the fly, but it buzzed past her again. Maybe, if she was real fast, she could catch that irritating fly in her hand. It couldn't be that hard; she'd seen her brother Henry do it many times.

Rachel kept a close watch on the fly as it zipped over Orlie's head, flew around Audra's desk, and zoomed back to her own desk.

When the fly buzzed in front of Rachel's face, she reached out, and—*woosh!*—trapped the fly in her hand.

R-r-zzz. . .r-r-zzz. . . Rachel felt the vibration of the fly's wings flapping against her fingers and palm.

With a satisfied smile, Rachel held her hand up to her ear. *R-r-zzz. . .r-r-zzz. . .* She heard the fly buzzing.

Elizabeth left her desk and headed down the center aisle. "What have you got in your hand?" she asked, stopping in front of Rachel's desk.

Everyone in the room stopped what they were doing and turned to look at Rachel. Rachel's face heated up. "There's—uh—a fly in my hand."

Elizabeth's forehead wrinkled. "A fly?"

Rachel nodded.

"What are you doing with a fly in your hand?"

"It was bothering me, so I caught it."

"Well, please let it go and finish your arithmetic lesson."

Rachel opened her hand, and—*zip!*—the fly flew straight up and landed on Elizabeth's nose. The children all laughed, but Elizabeth frowned. She swatted at the fly as it buzzed across the room. Then it circled Sharon Smucker, the teacher's helper, darted over Aaron's head, and flew toward Rachel's desk. Rachel reached out, and—*woosh!*—the fly was trapped in her hand again.

Elizabeth's mouth dropped open, and the children all clapped.

Rachel smiled. "Would you like me to put the fly outside?"

Elizabeth nodded. "Please do. And be sure to wash your hands once you've let the fly go."

Rachel headed to the back of the room, opened the door, and released the pesky fly. Then she hurried to the outdoor pump, washed her hands, and raced back inside.

When she returned to her seat, Elizabeth told the class to turn in their papers. "It's not raining anymore and the sun is beginning to shine, so you may go outside for recess," she said.

Rachel didn't bother to put on her coat or boots before hurrying out the door.

"That was sure something the way you caught that fly in your hand," Orlie said when he caught up to Rachel near the swings. "How'd you learn to do that anyway?"

She smiled, noticing that Orlie didn't smell like garlic today. Maybe his mother had quit making him eat a piece of garlic every day like she'd done last winter. "I learned to catch flies by watching my brother Henry," she said. "He does it all the time."

"Do you think you can teach me how to catch a fly?" Orlie asked.

"I suppose I could."

"*Eww*. . .I'd never want to touch a dirty old fly. I don't like bugs at all," Audra said, stepping between Rachel and Orlie. She looked at Rachel and wrinkled her nose. "How could you stand touching that filthy fly? Aren't you worried about getting germs?"

"My little sister's not worried about that at all," Jacob said before Rachel could respond. "She's already got the fly flu."

Audra's eyes widened. "The fly flu?"

Jacob nodded. "That's right."

"How did you get the fly flu?" Audra asked Rachel.

Rachel was about to tell Audra that she'd better stay away from her, because the fly flu was contagious, when Orlie said, "There's no such thing as the fly flu. Rachel's bruder just likes to tease."

Jacob snorted a laugh and slapped his knee. "Once, when Rachel made a shoofly pie, it turned out so bad we all thought we were gonna come down with the fly flu."

Rachel poked Jacob's arm. "If you don't stop saying mean things, when we get home I'll tell Mom you were teasing me again."

"You do and I'll tell Mom that you were showing off in class today."

"I was not."

"Were so."

"Was not."

"I don't know about you, Orlie," Audra spoke up, "but I'm not going to stay here and listen to these two argue."

"Me neither," said Orlie. "Let's head over to the swings."

As Audra tromped past Rachel, she stepped in a mud puddle, and—*splat!*—a wave of mud splashed up and all over Rachel's new dress!

Rachel groaned. "What'd you do that for, Audra?"

Audra's face turned red. "I–I'm sorry."

Rachel looked down at her dress and clenched her fists. "My mamm's not going to be happy when she sees that I've got mud all over my new dress."

"I didn't do it on purpose," Audra said. "It was just an accident."

Rachel whirled around and headed back to the schoolhouse. *I don't care what Audra says. I'll bet she stepped in that mud puddle on purpose because she doesn't like me. Well, I don't like her either.*

As Rachel and Jacob walked home from school that afternoon, it started to rain.

"Oh, great," Rachel complained. "I hope it doesn't rain sideways again."

Jacob ignored her and kept walking.

Rachel looked down at her dirty dress. "I'm mad at Audra for splattering mud all over my dress," she grumbled. "I'm sure she did it on purpose, too."

Jacob shook his head. "I doubt it, Rachel."

"Humph! A lot you know."

"I heard Audra and Orlie talking during recess, and Audra seemed nice enough to me. Maybe you need to give her a chance."

"I wouldn't be surprised if Mom makes me wash my dress, the way she did last summer when I fell in the pond during our end-of-the-school-year picnic," Rachel said, ignoring Jacob's comment about Audra.

Jacob halted and turned to face Rachel. "If you're so upset about the mud, why don't you hold out your skirt and the let rain wash it off?"

Rachel grunted. "That's a crazy idea, Jacob."

"No it's not. Just hold out the side of your skirt and

let the rain wash it clean."

"But then my dress will be sopping wet."

"Would you rather that it be wet or dirty?"

"Neither."

"Then quit complaining."

"I'm not."

"Jah, you are. You've had a bad attitude ever since Mary moved away."

Rachel swallowed around the lump in her throat. She didn't need Jacob to remind her of how miserable she felt without Mary. And she didn't like him sticking up for Audra. Rain splattered Rachel's cheeks, mixing with her tears. She felt like she'd been rained on all day.

By the time Rachel's house came into view, her legs were so wet they felt like two limp noodles. She trudged up the back steps behind Jacob and followed him into the house.

Rachel's teeth chattered as she slipped out of her raincoat and boots. She opened Mom's umbrella and set it on the floor in the corner of the utility room so it could dry.

"Mmm. . .I smell something good." Jacob's nose twitched as he hung his coat on a wall peg near the door. "I'll bet Mom made a batch of cookies today."

The sweet smell of cinnamon and molasses drew Rachel into the kitchen where she saw Mom removing a tray of cookies from the oven.

"I knew it. . .cookies!" Jacob smacked his lips.

"Oh, Rachel, I found your umbrella after you left for school this morning. It was under your bed." Mom turned with a smile on her face, but when she looked at Rachel, her smile disappeared. "*Ach* [oh], Rachel, what happened to your dress?"

"That new girl, Audra, stepped in a puddle during recess and splattered mud all over me," Rachel said. "I think she did it on purpose because she doesn't like me."

"What makes you so sure she doesn't like you?" Mom asked.

"I think it's Rachel who doesn't like Audra," Jacob said before Rachel could reply. "She's still mad at Audra for eating her peanut butter sandwich yesterday."

Mom looked at Rachel over the top of her glasses. "Is that so, Rachel?"

Rachel nodded. "Audra didn't take my lunch pail today, though. Everyone knew it was mine since I painted ladybugs on both sides of it. In fact, two of the kinner asked if I'd paint something on their lunch pails."

"You paint very well, so I'm sure you'll do a nice job."

"Is it all right if I take my paints and brushes tomorrow so I can paint something on Phoebe's and Aaron's lunch pails?" Rachel asked.

"I suppose it would be all right." Mom pointed to Rachel's dress. "In the meantime, run upstairs and get changed out of that dress. When you come back down I'll have some cookies and hot chocolate waiting."

"Danki, Mom." Rachel hurried up the stairs, smiling to herself. Mom hadn't seemed that upset about the mud-splattered dress. Maybe she wouldn't make Rachel wash it after all.

When Rachel returned to the kitchen, she took a seat at the table across from Jacob. Mom placed a plate of ginger cookies in the middle of the table and gave Rachel and Jacob mugs of hot chocolate. "Would either of you like some marshmallows to go in your hot chocolate?"

Jacob nodded eagerly and so did Rachel. Mom took a bag of marshmallows from the cupboard and handed it to Jacob. He took three, gave the bag to Rachel, and she took four. She popped one in her mouth and dropped the other three in her mug.

Mom poured herself a cup of hot chocolate and took a seat beside Rachel. "Did you put your dirty dress in the laundry basket?"

Rachel nodded. "I put my wet stockings in there, too."

"I'll wash clothes tomorrow." Mom glanced at the raindrops splattered against the kitchen window. "If it continues to rain, I'll have to hang the clean clothes in the cellar."

"I hope Buddy stayed dry in his doghouse today," Jacob said. "When I'm done with my hot chocolate I think I'll go outside and check on him."

"I'm going out to the barn to see Cuddles," Rachel said. "After that, I may write Mary a letter."

"Speaking of Mary. . ." Mom smiled at Rachel. "When I checked the answering machine in our phone shed this morning, there was a message from your aunt Irma."

Rachel's eyes widened. "What'd she say?"

"Just that they'd made it to Indiana and will call

again or write a letter after they get settled in."

"Was there a message for me from Mary?"

Mom shook her head. "I'm afraid not, but I'm sure Mary will write to you soon."

A lump formed in Rachel's throat and she swallowed hard. If Mary hadn't cared enough to give her mamm a message for Rachel then maybe Rachel wouldn't bother to write Mary a letter after all.

"I—I think I'll go out to the barn and see Cuddles," she mumbled.

"Mom pointed to Rachel's mug. "You haven't finished drinking your hot chocolate yet."

"I'll finish it when I come back inside."

Jacob rolled his eyes. "It'll be cold by then, little bensel."

"Jacob Yoder, what have I told you about calling your sister a silly child?" Mom squinted at Jacob over the top of her glasses.

"Sorry," he mumbled.

Mom patted Rachel's hand. "Go on out to the barn. When you come back to the house I'll heat your hot chocolate for you."

"Danki." Rachel pushed away from the table, grabbed her raincoat, and rushed out the door.

"Cuddles. . .where are you Cuddles?" Rachel panted as she raced into the barn.

"Rachel, is that you?"

Rachel glanced around. That was Grandpa's voice, but she saw no sign of him.

"Where are you, Grandpa?"

"I–I'm over here behind the hay."

Rachel hurried over to the bales of hay piled in one corner of the barn and found Grandpa down on his knees. "What's wrong, Grandpa? How come your face is all red, and why are you on your knees?"

"I was moving some bales, and I pulled a muscle in my back. It hurts something awful, and I don't think I can't get up on my own." He moaned. "Can you get me some help?"

"Jah, Grandpa. I'll be right back." Rachel dashed out of the barn and hurried into the house. She found Mom and Jacob still in the kitchen.

"Grandpa's in the barn and he hurt his back. He says he can't get up, so he sent me to get help."

Mom jumped up from her chair. "Jacob, your daed and Henry are fixing some fences on the other side of the pasture. Run out there and get them right away!"

Jacob grabbed his jacket and rushed out the door.

"I'm going out to the barn to be with my daed," Mom said to Rachel. "You can either wait here or come along."

"I'll come with you." Rachel followed Mom out the door, praying that Grandpa would be okay.

Chapter 4
Unexpected Company

Rachel did what she could to help Grandpa Schrock feel better, like playing games with him and bringing him water and special treats like Mom's ginger cookies while he rested in bed. The doctor said Grandpa pulled a muscle in his lower back and gave Grandpa some medicine for the pain. The doctor also told Grandpa to rest his back until the swelling went down. So every day after school, Rachel sat next to Grandpa's bed and listened as he told her about the greenhouse he wanted to build in the spring. He hadn't told Pap about the idea yet, and said he figured until his back got better, there was no point in mentioning it. Right now the best thing he could do was rest.

Helping Mom take care of Grandpa made Rachel feel a little less lonely for Mary, and things were somewhat better at school now, too. Rachel took her paints to school the day after she'd taken her ladybug lunch pail. She painted a turtle on Aaron's lunch pail and a butterfly on Phoebe's lunch pail. When the others saw what a good job she could do, several asked her to paint their lunch pails, too.

On Saturday, Rachel decided she would spend the morning visiting with Grandpa.

Tap. . .tap. . .tap. She knocked on his bedroom door.

No answer.

"Grandpa, are you awake?"

Still no answer.

Rachel pressed her ear against the door. *Zzzzzz. . .* Soft snoring sounds came from Grandpa's room. He was obviously taking a nap.

Rachel headed to the kitchen, where Mom was busy making a shoofly pie. At least she hadn't asked Rachel to help make it. The last time Rachel had made a shoofly pie she left out the sugar and put in too much salt. It tasted awful, and Jacob made sure Rachel knew about it.

"Is it all right if I go over to Grandma and Grandpa Yoder's house?" Rachel asked Mom. "I haven't visited with them in a while."

Mom nodded as she rolled out the pie dough. "I'm sure they would like that. Why don't you take some of the ginger cookies I made the other day? Those are Grandpa Yoder's favorite kind of cookies, you know."

"I'd be happy to take some cookies along." Rachel smiled. She knew Grandpa Yoder liked to dunk them in milk just like she did.

A short time later, Rachel headed across the field toward her grandparents' house, carrying a paper sack full of ginger cookies. She'd thought about bringing

Cuddles along, but since Mary's cat, Stripes, wasn't there for Cuddles to play with, she decided it would be best to leave Cuddles at home.

Rachel hadn't been over to Grandma and Grandpa Yoder's place since Mary and her family moved away. Aunt Karen, Uncle Amos, and their little boy, Gerald, lived next door to Grandma and Grandpa Yoder now. Rachel had avoided going over there. She didn't want to be reminded that Mary lived in Indiana now, where Rachel would probably never get to go. It was hard not to be angry with Uncle Ben for taking Mary away. It was hard not to be upset with Mary for not writing Rachel any letters. Of course, Rachel hadn't written to Mary yet either. She'd been waiting for Mary to write to her first.

Maybe I'll write Mary a letter when I get home today, Rachel decided as her grandparents' house came into view. *Then I can tell her about Grandpa Schrock's sore back and my visit with Grandma and Grandpa Yoder.* Since Mary and her family had lived next door to Grandma and Grandpa Yoder for several years, Mary would probably want to know how they were doing.

Rachel stepped onto Grandma and Grandpa's back porch and knocked on the door. *Tap. . .tap. . .tap.* When no one answered, she knocked again.

Still no answer. Maybe they'd gone next door to Aunt Karen's.

Rachel frowned. She didn't want to go over there, but she didn't want to miss the chance of seeing Grandma and Grandpa, either.

With a sense of dread, she stepped onto the porch of Mary's old house and knocked on the door. *Tap. . .tap. . .* The door opened after the second knock.

"Rachel, what a surprise! We weren't expecting any visitors today," Aunt Karen said with a friendly smile.

"I came to see Grandma and Grandpa, but they didn't answer my knock. Are they here?"

Aunt Karen shook her head. "They're not home. Grandpa took Grandma to town to do some shopping today. I don't expect they'll be home until late this afternoon."

Struggling with the urge to nibble on a fingernail, Rachel fidgeted with the ties on her kapp. "Oh, I see. Guess I'll head back home then."

Rachel turned and started for the stairs, but Aunt Karen called out to her. "Won't you come in and visit? I'm sure Gerald would love to see you."

Before Rachel could reply, Gerald stuck his head out the door. When he saw Rachel, his face broke into a wide smile. "*Kumme* [come]," he said, reaching his hand out to her.

Rachel couldn't say no to the cute little blond-haired boy with eyes as blue as a summer sky. She glanced at the sack of cookies in her hand and knew it wouldn't be right if she didn't share a few with her little cousin. "Jah, okay. I'll come inside, but only for a little while."

Rachel looked at Aunt Karen and lifted the sack. "I brought some ginger cookies for Grandma and Grandpa Yoder. Maybe you and Gerald would like a few, too."

Aunt Karen smiled. "That's very nice of you, Rachel." She opened the door wider. "Let's go to the kitchen and I'll pour us some milk to go with the cookies."

"We'll need to save some for Grandma and Grandpa, though," Rachel added quickly as she followed Aunt Karen to the kitchen. "Ginger cookies are Grandpa's favorite kind."

"Of course," Aunt Karen said with a nod. "When they get home I'll see that they get the cookies."

Gerald reached up and grabbed Rachel's hand. "Kumme." He pointed to the sack. *"Kichlin* [cookies]." Then he pointed to the refrigerator. *"Millich* [milk]."

"All right, let's have some cookies." Rachel let Gerald lead her to the table. Once they were seated, she opened the sack and placed two cookies on a napkin in front of him. She gave Aunt Karen two cookies, and helped herself to two as well.

Aunt Karen poured three glasses of milk and set them on the table. Then she took a seat in the chair next to Rachel.

Rachel glanced around the room and noticed the way Aunt Karen had placed all her things. Even the battery-operated clock on the wall that made bird sounds every half hour made the kitchen look different. It was strange how much a house could change by having different people living in it. *At least there aren't strangers living in Mary's old house,* Rachel thought.

"You'll have to come back soon and bring your mamm along," Aunt Karen said.

Rachel nodded. "When she's not busy or taking a nap."

"Your mamm's expecting a boppli soon, isn't she?"

"Jah. It's supposed to be born sometime in July," Rachel said as she dunked a cookie in her glass of milk.

"I imagine you're looking forward to being a big sister."

Rachel only shrugged in reply.

"Are you hoping the baby will be a boy or a girl?" Aunt Karen asked.

"I guess it would be nice to have a little sister," Rachel said.

Aunt Karen smiled. "I'm hoping the next boppli we have will be a boy so Gerald will have a brother."

Rachel glanced over at Gerald. There was a dribble of milk running down his chin, and the floor underneath him was littered with cookie crumbs.

I suppose that's what I have to look forward to after our boppli's born and is old enough to eat by herself, Rachel thought. *I just hope I'm not expected to clean up the mess.*

When they were finished eating, Gerald hopped off his chair, grabbed Rachel's hand and said, "Gerald *schpiele gern* [like to play]."

"I'll be the *gaul* [horse] and you can be the *reider* [rider]." Rachel spoke to her cousin in Pennsylvania Dutch. Gerald only knew a few words in English and wouldn't learn to speak it well until he attended school in the first grade.

The toddler nodded enthusiastically, and Rachel squatted down so he could climb on her back. As she crawled around the kitchen on her hands and knees, Gerald hollered, "*Fege* [run about], gaul!"

"*Kanscht seller gaul reide* [Are you able to ride that horse], Gerald?" Aunt Karen asked with a chuckle. "She looks pretty *mudich* [spirited] to me."

Gerald thumped Rachel's side with his knee and kept hollering, "Fege, gaul!"

Rachel was getting tired, and her knees started to hurt. She turned her head and was about to tell Gerald he had to get off when, *whack!*—his fist came up and punched her right in the eye!

"Ach, my eye!" Rachel cried as she pushed Gerald off and clambered to her feet.

Aunt Karen rushed forward. "Rachel, are you all right?"

Rachel blinked against stinging tears. "My eye hurts!"

"Let me take a look." Aunt Karen's forehead wrinkled. "It's watering quite a bit, and the skin around your eye is starting to swell. You'd better take a seat at the table and let me put some ice on it."

Rachel sat down, and Aunt Karen scurried over to the refrigerator.

Gerald plodded over to Rachel and reached out his hand. "Fege, gaul?"

She pushed his hand aside. "Go away. It's your fault my eye's sore and swollen."

"I'm sure Gerald didn't do it on purpose," Aunt Karen said as she handed Rachel a small bag of ice. "Gerald, tell Cousin Rachel you're sorry."

"*Es dutt mir leed* [I am sorry]," he said.

Rachel held the ice against her eye as she clamped her lips together. She didn't think Gerald was one bit sorry. He'd only said he was sorry because Aunt Karen had told him to.

Gerald grunted then he let lose with a loud, "*Wa-a-a!*"

Rachel ignored him.

Aunt Karen peeked under the ice bag. "It looks like your eye is going to be okay, Rachel, and Gerald really wants you to forgive him."

Rachel knew what she had to do. Even though in her heart she hadn't forgiven Gerald, she nodded and said, "I forgive you."

By the time Rachel returned home, her eye felt pretty much back to normal. As she rounded the corner of the house, she was surprised to see a horse and buggy tied to their hitching rail. Had Mom gotten some unexpected company?

Rachel hurried into the house. When she stepped into the kitchen, she halted, horrified at what she saw. Audra's mother, Naomi, sat at the table drinking a cup of tea, and Audra sat on the floor holding Cuddles!

Mom turned to Rachel and smiled. "Audra and her mamm stopped by for a visit."

Rachel was frozen in shock. She just stood there staring at Cuddles, who purred loudly as Audra stroked her ear. *Traitor!* she thought. *How could you cozy up to someone who doesn't even like me?*

"Audra's brother, Brian, is upstairs with Jacob. Rachel, why don't you take Audra up to your room so you can play and get better acquainted?" Mom suggested.

Playing with Audra was the last thing Rachel wanted to do, but she knew better than to argue with Mom—especially in front of guests.

Rachel looked at Audra and fought the urge to bite a fingernail. "*Duh die katz naus* [put the cat out]. Mom doesn't allow the cat to be in my room."

"How come?" Audra asked.

"She just doesn't, that's all." Rachel bent down and snatched Cuddles from Audra. Then she opened the back door and set the cat on the porch.

Audra picked up her backpack off the floor and followed Rachel upstairs.

When they entered Rachel's room, Rachel took a seat on the end of her bed. Audra set her backpack next to Rachel. "I brought some things for us to play with," she said.

Rachel tipped her head. "You knew you were coming over here today?"

Audra nodded. "Oh jah. Your mamm talked to my mamm when she saw her at the store last week. She invited us to come over and visit sometime soon. Mama thought today was as good a time as any, but then we got here and found out you weren't at home."

"I went to see my Grandma and Grandpa Yoder, but they weren't at home," Rachel said. "So I visited with my Aunt Karen and her little boy." Rachel chose not to mention that Gerald poked her in the eye. Audra might think it was funny or make fun of Rachel because she'd been down on her knees giving Gerald a horsey ride.

Audra opened the backpack and removed a yo-yo, a

set of jacks, some crayons, and a coloring book. "What should we do first?"

Rachel stared at the things Audra had laid out on her bed. She wasn't in the mood to play with any of them. "How about a game of Scrabble?" she suggested. Rachel was good at spelling and making big words. She figured she could win the game easily.

"Jah, okay," Audra said with a shrug.

Rachel went to her closet and got out the Scrabble board. She placed it on the bed, and then she and Audra took seats on either side of the board. Audra went first, spelling the word *flower*. Using the letter *F*, going up and down, Rachel spelled the word *farmer*.

They continued to play until Rachel spelled the word *zephyr*, using squares that awarded double points.

Audra squinted at the board. "There's no such word as *zephyr*. You cheated, Rachel."

"Did not."

"Did so."

"Did not, and I'll prove it to you." Rachel hopped off the bed and scurried over to her desk. She kept a dictionary in the bottom drawer and knew it would prove there was such a word as *zephyr*. She brought it back to the bed and opened it to the section for the letter Z. "See, it's right here," she said, pointing to the word. "Zephyr: The west wind. A soft, gentle breeze."

Audra pursed her lips.

Ha! Rachel knew her unexpected guest couldn't argue with the dictionary.

"I don't want to play this game anymore," Audra

said. "Let's do something else."

"Like what?"

Audra pointed to the dresser across the room where the faceless doll Mary had given Rachel sat. "I'd like to play with her."

"My best friend gave me that faceless doll before she moved away," Rachel said. "I won't let anyone play with it but me."

Audra thrust out her bottom lip. "Why not?"

"Because the doll is special, and I don't want it to get ruined."

"Please, Rachel. I just want to hold her," Audra pleaded.

Rachel shook her head.

"I think you're being selfish."

Rachel was about to respond, when Mom called from the foot of the stairs, "I've set some cookies and milk on the kitchen table. Anyone who would like some, come on down!"

"Do you want some milk and cookies?" Rachel asked Audra.

Audra nodded. "That's sounds good."

"Then let's go."

"You go ahead," Audra said. "I'll be down as soon as I put my toys in my backpack."

"See you downstairs then." Rachel skipped out of the room and knocked on Jacob's bedroom door.

"Who is it?" he called.

"It's me, Rachel. Did you hear Mom say there are cookies and milk downstairs?"

"Jah, I did. Brian and I will be down in a minute."

"Okay." Rachel tromped down the stairs. She wished she didn't have to sit in the kitchen and eat cookies with Audra. She wished Audra's mother would say it was time for her, Audra, and Brian to go home.

Rachel flopped into a chair.

"Where are Audra and the boys?" Mom asked.

"They'll be down soon," Rachel replied.

A few moments later Audra took a seat at the table, hooking the straps of her backpack around the back of her chair.

Mom passed Audra the plate of cookies, and then she handed it to Rachel.

S-c-r-e-e-c-h. The back door creaked open.

"Levi, is that you?" Mom called over her shoulder.

"No, it's Jacob. Brian and I are going outside for a minute," Jacob said, poking his head inside the kitchen door.

"Don't you want some cookies and milk?"

"We'll have some when we come back in. I want Brian to meet Buddy." Jacob disappeared and the back door slammed shut.

Mom and Naomi visited while they sipped tea and ate cookies. Audra dunked a cookie in her glass of milk and looked at the door. "Can we go home now?" she asked her mother.

Naomi shook her head. "Not until Brian comes inside and has some cookies."

Audra fidgeted in her chair. *She seems kind of nervous,* Rachel thought. *Maybe she wants to go home just as much as I want her to leave.*

Rachel kept looking at the clock. Five minutes passed. Then ten more minutes went by. Finally, the boys entered the kitchen and took seats at the table. They each ate five cookies and drank two glasses of milk.

"I think it's time for us to go," Naomi said.

Rachel breathed a sigh of relief. *Finally.*

Audra's mother gave Mom a hug and said Mom should come visit her soon. It was obvious that she and Mom were already becoming friends.

It's fine with me if Mom wants to have Naomi as a friend, Rachel thought as she watched the Burkholders drive away in their buggy. *I just hope she doesn't expect me to be Audra's friend. I could never be friends with someone who accuses me of cheating at Scrabble.*

Rachel set her empty glass in the sink and walked up the steps to her room. She decided she would get her book on flowers and take it to Grandpa's room so they could talk about the things he wanted to grow in his greenhouse.

When Rachel entered her room, she opened the bottom drawer of her dresser and removed the book. As she shut the drawer, she glanced at the top of the dresser and blinked. Something was wrong. Something was missing.

Rachel's heart pounded like a galloping horse, and she pressed the palm of her hand to her forehead. "My faceless doll is missing!" she gasped. "I'll bet anything that Audra took it!"

Chapter 5

A Shocking Discovery

"Audra took my doll!" Rachel wailed when she ran into the kitchen where Mom was slicing some apples at the table.

Mom's glasses had slipped to the end of her nose, like they often did because the bridge of her nose was too narrow. She pushed them back in place and stared at Rachel like she'd lost her mind. "What are you talking about?"

"The faceless doll Mary gave me—it's missing." Rachel sniffed and swallowed around the lump clogging her throat. "When I came downstairs earlier for cookies and milk I left Audra alone in my room so she could pick up her toys. The—the doll was there before, but now it's gone, and I'm sure Audra took it!"

"Calm down, Rachel, and come have a seat." Mom motioned to the chair beside her. "You do tend to be kind of forgetful sometimes. You probably misplaced the doll."

Rachel shook her head. "No, no—I didn't! The doll

was sitting on top of my dresser. That's where I put it after Mary gave it to me."

"Have you taken the doll down to play with it since Mary left?" Mom asked.

"I—I held it a few times, but I always put it right back on the dresser." Rachel frowned. "Audra saw it there and asked if she could play with it."

"Did she play with it?"

Rachel flopped into the chair. "No way! I told her it was a gift from my best friend and that I wouldn't let anyone play with it but me."

"That was rather selfish, don't you think?"

Rachel stared at the table as her eyes filled with tears. "The doll is all I have to remember Mary. I was afraid Audra might ruin it."

"I'm sure she wouldn't have ruined it with you sitting right there." Mom patted Rachel's arm. "Maybe Audra decided to play with the doll for a few minutes before she came downstairs for cookies and milk. She could have put the doll somewhere else in your room."

Rachel sniffed. "I looked everywhere. I'll bet Audra stuffed my doll into her backpack with the toys she brought so no one would see her sneak it out of the house."

"What reason would Audra have for taking your doll?"

"Because she doesn't like me. I told you that before."

"She brought her toys over here so she could play with you today," Mom reminded Rachel. "I don't think she would have done that if she didn't like you."

"Audra's mamm probably told her to bring some toys." Rachel frowned and crossed her arms. "Besides, Audra accused me of cheating at Scrabble, and she's been mean to me at school."

Mom reached for an apple from the bowl sitting in the center of the table. "I think you're being unfair to Audra. You're not giving yourself a chance to like her, and you're not giving her a chance to be your friend."

"I don't want Audra to be my friend. I want Mary back—and that's it!" Rachel jumped up and raced out the back door. Mom didn't understand the way she felt; no one did. Grownups often forgot what it was like to be a kid.

Rachel ran to the barn to look for Cuddles. Maybe if she held the cat and petted her it would make her feel better. When Rachel was trapped in their neighbors' cellar last summer, Cuddles had comforted her, even though she was only a tiny kitten then.

When Rachel entered the barn, she was greeted by a musty odor coming from the leftover winter hay stacked against one wall. She didn't mind the smell, though. She liked being in the barn where the horses and cows were kept.

Rachel found Cuddles lying on a bale of hay, purring and licking her paws. She took a seat beside the cat so she could think. "You don't have a care in the world, Cuddles. It's me who has all the troubles." Rachel picked up the cat and held it in her lap. "What I'd like to know is how you could let Audra hold you and pet you? Don't you care that she's not my friend?"

Cuddles responded with a lazy, *meow!* Then she licked Rachel's hand with her warm, sandpapery tongue.

Rachel rubbed Cuddles behind one ear as she leaned her head against the wall and closed her eyes. She wanted to go over to Audra's house right now and ask for her doll back. She knew where Audra lived, too, because Audra had mentioned what road their house was on.

Maybe I'll go inside and ask Mom if I can go for a walk, Rachel thought. *Jah, that's just what I need to do.*

Rachel opened her eyes, set Cuddles on the hay next to her, and was about to get up when she spotted something dangling from the hayloft overhead. She gasped. "Ach! That's my faceless doll hanging by one arm!"

"Heh. . .heh. . .heh." Rachel heard snickering coming from somewhere high up in the barn. "Jacob Yoder is that you up there?"

Jacob poked his head out from behind a mound of hay in the loft and grinned. "How'd you like my little surprise, Rachel?"

She shook her finger at him and scowled. "I don't think your *little surprise* is one bit funny! You'd better get my doll down from there, *schnell* [quickly]!"

"Jah, okay. You don't have to get so worked up about it." Jacob untied the rope and let the doll loose.

Rachel held her breath as the doll dropped from the hayloft. She reached for it but missed. The poor little doll landed facedown on the floor!

"My faceless doll had better not be ruined!" Rachel shouted. She scooped the doll into her arms and checked it over, front and back. Lucky for Jacob there were no rips in the cloth body or the doll's clothes. Since the doll had landed in a clump of hay, it wasn't even dirty.

"How did you get my doll?" Rachel called up to Jacob. "And why'd you hang it in the hayloft like that?"

Jacob scrambled down the ladder and marched up to Rachel. "I took it from your room after you and Audra went downstairs for cookies and milk." He wrinkled his nose and squinted at her. "Figured I'd teach you a lesson for being so moody and grumpy lately."

Rachel's chin trembled and tears stung the backs of her eyes. "You'd be grumpy and moody, too, if your best friend moved away." She held the doll close and sniffed a couple of times. "This little faceless doll is all I have to remember Mary by."

"Aw, come on, Rachel. You're not going to cry, are you?" Jacob touched her arm. "I'm sorry for hanging your doll in the hayloft. I was only teasing. I didn't think you'd get so upset."

"I don't think you're really sorry, Jacob. All you ever do is tease and make fun of me. I'm getting sick and tired of it!" Rachel pushed Jacob's hand away and rushed out of the barn.

When Rachel entered the house a few moments later, she held her doll out to Mom and said, "I found it!"

Mom smiled. "Was it in your room?"

Rachel shook her head. "It was in the barn—

hanging by one arm from the hayloft!"

Mom's eyebrows furrowed. "How did it get up there?"

"Jacob did it!"

"Why would Jacob take your doll?"

"He said it was to teach me a lesson because I've been moody and grumpy lately."

"Jacob shouldn't have taken your doll," Mom said with a shake of her head, "but he's right about you acting moody and grumpy. You've been that way ever since Mary and her family moved to Indiana."

Rachel stared at the floor as her eyes flooded with tears. "I can't help it. I miss Mary something awful." *Sniff. Sniff.* "I don't think I'll ever forgive Uncle Ben for taking her away."

"I know you miss your cousin, but that's no reason to be grumpy or unforgiving with others. Mary's daed did what he thought was best for him and his family, and he has a new job that he really enjoys." Mom pulled Rachel to her side and gave her a hug. "I'll have a talk with Jacob about what he did to your doll, but I want you to think about the things I've said and what you might do to improve your attitude."

Rachel nodded slowly. "All right, Mom."

Rachel spent the next hour lying on her bed, holding her faceless doll in her arms, tears trickling down her cheeks. Having the doll close made her feel a little closer to Mary.

She squeezed her eyes shut, trying to stop the flow

of tears. *I wonder why Mary hasn't written to me yet. Has she forgotten about me? Has she found another friend she likes better? Maybe I should write a letter to her now and find out why she hasn't written.*

Rachel heard laughter coming from the backyard, and her eyes popped open. She dried her eyes with the back of her hand, climbed off the bed, and hurried over to the window. Orlie stood beside Jacob in front of Buddy's new dog run, pointing at Buddy. He said something to Jacob that Rachel couldn't understand, even though her window was slightly open.

Rachel rolled her eyes. That smelly mutt was lying on top of his dog house with his head between his dirty paws!

Orlie looked up toward Rachel's open window and waved at her. Jacob looked up and waved, too. "Come out and join us, Rachel!" Orlie shouted with his hands cupped around his mouth.

Rachel blew out a big puff of air. The last thing she wanted to do was be with Orlie or Jacob right now. But if she didn't go outside, Jacob would probably tell Mom she was being moody and grumpy again.

Rachel set the faceless doll on her dresser and headed downstairs.

"*Wie geht's?* [How are you?]" Orlie asked when Rachel joined him and Jacob in front of the dog run a few minutes later.

"I've been better," she said, squinting at Jacob.

Jacob squinted right back at her and said, "I was just telling Orlie that ever since Pap built the doghouse,

Buddy won't sleep in it. Instead, he sleeps on the roof."

Rachel snickered as she shook her head. "That dog of yours is so dumm."

"He's not dumb." Jacob motioned to Buddy, who was now snoring and grunting in his sleep. "He's just different, that's all."

Rachel looked over at Orlie. "Did Buddy do weird things when he lived with you?"

Orlie shrugged. "Sometimes, but I guess all dogs do some weird things."

"Just like people," Jacob muttered under his breath.

Rachel bumped Jacob's arm. "What was that?"

"Oh, nothing."

"So, Jacob, how is Buddy's training coming along?" Orlie asked.

"Not so well," Jacob replied. "He doesn't respond to the new whistle I bought him. In fact, whenever I blow it, all he does is howl."

"Why don't I try the whistle and see if it works for me?" Orlie suggested.

"Okay. Let me get Buddy out of the pen." Jacob opened the door of the dog run and called, "Here, Buddy. Come on out and see Orlie."

Buddy's eyes opened and his head snapped up in attention. His ears flicked forward. His tail wagged. He leaped off the doghouse and raced toward Rachel.

"Ach!" Rachel jumped back, but it was too late. *Slurp, slurp, slurp.* Buddy swiped his long pink tongue across Rachel's arm.

"Yuck!" She pushed the dog away and scowled at

Jacob. “That dog of yours has horrible breath!”

“He’s a dog. What do you expect?”

“Maybe you should brush his teeth.”

Jacob ignored Rachel’s last comment and reached into his pants pocket. He pulled out the plastic whistle he’d been using to train Buddy and handed it to Orlie. “Here you go.”

Orlie put the whistle between his lips and blew. *Whee. . .whee. . .whee.*

Rachel gritted her teeth and covered her ears, knowing what would come next.

Buddy leaned his head way back and howled.

Orlie stood there with a confused look on his face. “This isn’t the right kind of whistle. The whistle I had for Buddy was a silent whistle—the kind only a dog can hear.”

Jacob rubbed his chin. “Hmm. . .guess I’ll have to save up my money so I can buy one of those silent whistles.”

“Either that or you can keep working with Buddy on your own.” Orlie patted Buddy’s head. “If you work with him long enough, I’m sure he’ll begin to understand and start obeying your commands.”

Rachel grunted. “I don’t think Jacob could say or do anything that would make Buddy mind. That dog’s just a dumm mutt.”

“No he’s not.” Jacob shook his head. “He’s a good dog—a smart dog, and I’m sure he can be trained.”

“I’ll believe it when I see it.” Rachel motioned to the house. “I’m going to the kitchen to see if there’s anything good to eat. Are you two coming?"

"I think we'll work with Buddy awhile," Jacob said. "We'll be up in a little bit."

"Suit yourself." Rachel sprinted across the lawn, anxious to get to the house before Buddy decided to give her more kisses with his slimy tongue.

When Rachel entered the kitchen, she was pleased to see Grandpa sitting at the table reading a magazine.

"How's your back doing today, Grandpa?" she asked. "Are you feeling any better?"

He nodded. "At least I can stand up straight when I walk now. Of course, it'll be some time before I'm able to work in the garden or do any lifting."

"You shouldn't lift anything heavy," Mom said as she set a plate of ginger cookies on the table. She smiled at Rachel. "I did more baking today. Would you like to join Grandpa and me for cookies and milk?"

Rachel nodded. "That sounds good."

Mom motioned to the window. "I see Orlie Troyer out there with Jacob. Why don't you call them inside for some cookies, Rachel?"

"They're playing with Buddy. Jacob said they might be in later." Rachel pulled out the chair beside Grandpa and sat down. "Orlie told Jacob that the whistle he's been using to train Buddy is the wrong kind. He should have been using a silent whistle, not a whistle that blows so loudly it hurts people's ears."

"It probably hurts Buddy's ears, too." Grandpa reached for a cookie. "No wonder that poor dog howls so much."

"I wish Jacob would get rid of Buddy." Rachel frowned. "He's nothing but trouble."

"I think the dog's doing better now that he has his own dog run." Mom set some glasses on the table, along with a jug of cold milk. "With a little more work, I'm sure Buddy will be just fine."

"Humph!" Rachel folded her arms. "He'll probably never stop chasing Cuddles."

Mom poured milk into the glasses and clucked her tongue. "I wish you wouldn't be so negative, Rachel."

Rachel grabbed a cookie and dunked it in her milk. It was easy for Mom to be positive about Buddy. The beast never tried to kiss Mom. He saved his slurpy kisses just for Rachel!

After Rachel ate three cookies and finished her milk, Mom looked at her and said, "Since the boys haven't come in yet, why don't you take a tray of cookies and milk out to the porch for them?"

Rachel wrinkled her nose. "Do I have to?"

Mom nodded. "I think it would be a nice thing to do."

Rachel didn't feel like doing anything nice for Jacob, but she knew better than to argue with Mom. "Okay," she said, rising from her seat.

Mom put two glasses of milk and a plate of cookies on a tray and handed it to Rachel. Then she pushed the screen door open and held it while Rachel stepped outside.

Rachel was about to the set the tray on the small table on the porch when—*whack!*—Orlie dashed onto the porch right behind Buddy and bumped Rachel's arm. The tray slipped out of her hands and crashed to the floor, spilling milk and cookies all over Rachel's dress and her sneakers.

"Look what you did!" Rachel shouted.

"I–I'm sorry," Orlie stammered.

"You bumped into me on purpose!"

"I was chasing after Buddy and didn't see you—"

Without waiting for Orlie to finish his sentence, Rachel jerked open the screen door and dashed into the house. "Always trouble somewhere," she grumbled.

Chapter 6

Another Rotten Day

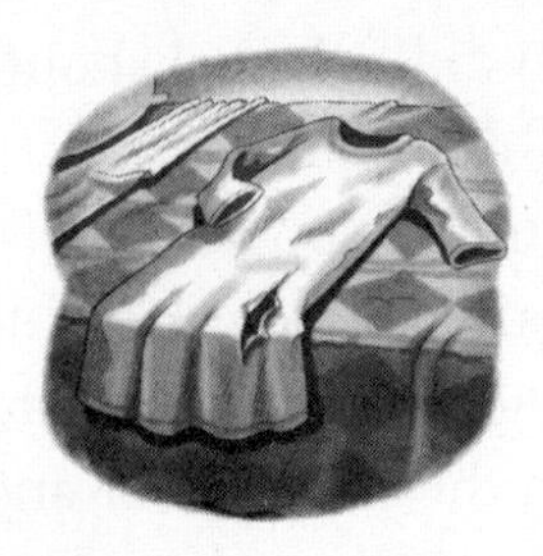

When Rachel arrived at school on Monday morning, she spotted Orlie standing near the swings—talking to Audra!

Rachel frowned. She still hadn't forgiven Orlie for bumping into her on Saturday and spilling milk all over her dress and sneakers. Even though Rachel knew Audra hadn't taken her doll, she was still angry with Audra for accusing her of cheating at Scrabble, for splattering mud on her dress, and for eating her peanut butter and jelly sandwich.

Rachel crossed her arms when she saw Orlie hand Audra an apple. She thought of the day Orlie gave her an apple with a big fat worm inside. He claimed he didn't know the worm was there, but she was sure he'd given her that wormy apple on purpose.

She clenched her hands into tight little balls. *I'll bet the apple he gave Audra doesn't have a worm in it. I'll bet Orlie likes Audra more than he likes me.*

"What are you looking at, and how come you're

wearing such a sour look on your face?" Jacob asked, nudging Rachel with his elbow.

"I'm not looking at anything important." Rachel stretched her lips into a wide, fake smile. "And I was not wearing a sour look."

"Jah, you were." Jacob nudged her again. "And take that silly grin off your face. It doesn't look real."

"Just leave me alone," Rachel grumbled as she started up the schoolhouse stairs.

"Elizabeth hasn't rung the bell yet," Jacob called after her.

"I don't care." Rachel opened the door and went inside. She had just put her lunch pail on the shelf when Elizabeth walked by and said, "Couldn't wait for the bell, huh, Rachel?"

Rachel only shrugged in reply.

"Go ahead and take your seat," Elizabeth said. "I'm sure the others will be in as soon as I ring the bell."

Rachel flopped into the chair at her desk. She took out her pencil and paper when Orlie entered and took a seat at the desk in front of her. "Was your mamm mad about the milk you got on your dress the other day?" he asked.

She frowned. "*I* didn't get the milk on my dress. *You* bumped into me, so it was *your* fault my dress and sneakers got covered with milk."

"It was an accident. I told you I was sorry."

Rachel placed her hands on her desk and stared straight ahead. She wasn't interested in anything Orlie had to say.

"Good morning boys and girls," Elizabeth said as she took a seat at her desk.

"Good morning, Elizabeth," Rachel said along with the other children.

"I'll be reading Matthew 18:21–22," Elizabeth said as she opened her Bible. "Then Peter came to Jesus and asked, 'Lord, how many times shall I forgive my brother when he sins against me? Up to seven times?' Jesus answered, 'I tell you, not seven times, but seventy-seven times.' "

Rachel was tempted to bite off a fingernail, but she picked up her pencil and stuck it between her teeth instead. Seventy-seven times? That seemed impossible! Maybe the verse was talking about good friends, like Mary. If Mary had said or done something to hurt Rachel, it would be easy to forgive her—but not Orlie or Audra, who weren't even her friends.

As Rachel stood with the other children to recite the Lord's Prayer, she glanced across the aisle at Audra's desk. There sat the big red apple Orlie had given her.

Rachel barely heard the words being recited by her classmates. All she could think about was how miserable she felt without Mary. During singing time, Rachel struggled to sing along.

When the children finished the last song and were about to return to their seats—*whoosh!*—a sparrow swooped into the room through an open window.

Some of the children screamed and ran to hide under their desks. Others darted around the room, laughing and trying to catch the little bird. Rachel just stood there, wishing there was something she could do to rescue the poor creature.

Aaron and Orlie bumped heads as they lunged for the sparrow at the same time.

The bird swooped past Jacob. He raced after it, tripped on Phoebe's foot, and fell flat on his face.

"Scholars, back to your desks, schnell!" Elizabeth clapped her hands, and everyone raced to their seats.

Rachel had just sat down when—*floop*—the little bird landed right on her head! She sat there a few seconds to see what the bird would do and was surprised when it didn't fly away. Maybe it needed a friend as much as she did.

The room got quiet as everyone stared at Rachel. Slowly she raised her hands and lifted the sparrow off her head. Then she walked to the back of the room, opened the door, and stepped onto the porch to let the bird go.

Rachel smiled as she watched the sparrow fly up to a tree. *At least I know someone likes me today.*

Rachel was in a better mood by the time she got home from school that afternoon. After the sparrow landed on her head and she set him free outdoors, the rest of the day had gone better. Everyone said how special they thought it was that the little bird landed on her head. Everyone but Audra, that is. She hadn't said a word to Rachel all day. Well, that was fine with Rachel. She didn't like talking to Audra anyway.

"I think I'll ride my skateboard in the barn," Rachel

told Jacob as they entered their yard. "I checked there last night, and the floor in the main part of the barn is clear of hay."

Jacob shook his head. "As many times as you've fallen on that skateboard, I'm surprised you still ride it."

"As our teacher always says, 'Practice makes perfect.' "

"Jah, well, you can practice riding your skateboard if you want to, but I'm going to work with Buddy."

Rachel put her hands on her hips and squinted at Jacob. "You'd better not let that mutt in the barn while I'm skateboarding."

Jacob shook his head. "Don't worry. We'll stay in the yard."

"Good." Rachel tromped up the steps and entered the house. She glanced in the kitchen, but there was no sign of Mom. Maybe she was in the living room.

Rachel looked in the living room, but Mom wasn't there, either. She was probably in her room taking a nap. Mom took lots of naps now that she was expecting a baby.

Rachel hurried upstairs and changed out of her school dress into one of the dresses she wore for playing and doing chores. Then she rushed downstairs and out the door.

When Rachel entered the barn, she headed straight for the shelf where she kept her skateboard. She carried it to the part of the barn where the hay had been cleared. Buddy was nowhere to be seen, so Rachel thought it'd be fun to give Cuddles a ride on her skateboard.

Rachel cupped her hands around her mouth and called, "Here, Cuddles! Come, kitty, kitty."

Cuddles stuck her head out from behind a bale of hay. *Meow!*

Rachel clapped her hands. "Come here, Cuddles. Let's go for a ride on my skateboard."

Meow! Meow! Cuddles darted behind the bale of hay.

"All right then," Rachel said with a shrug, "if you don't want to go for a ride, I'll have all the fun myself." She stepped onto her skateboard with her right foot, pushed off with her left foot, and sailed across the barn floor. "*Whee*. . .this is so much fun! You don't know what you're missing, Cuddles."

Rachel turned and headed back across the barn on her skateboard. The barn door opened and Henry stepped in. At the same time, Cuddles darted out from behind the bale of hay and zipped right in front of Henry.

"Look out for my cat!" Rachel shouted. It was too late—Henry stepped right on Cuddles's tail!

Mee-ow! Cuddles screeched, and her ears went straight back. Then she darted across the floor in front of Rachel.

Rachel swerved to miss hitting the cat, but her skateboard tipped and fell to the floor with a crash.

"Ouch! Ouch! Ouch!" Rachel tried not to cry, but her knees started to bleed and they hurt something awful.

"Rachel, are you hurt?" Henry asked, rushing to her side.

She nodded and touched her skinned knees. "You should have watched where you were going."

"I'm sorry," said Henry as he helped Rachel to her feet. "I never expected your cat to run in front of me like that."

Rachel's chin trembled and her eyes filled with tears. "Look at my dress!" she wailed, pointing to an ugly tear in the skirt. "Mom's gonna be awful mad when she sees this. If you hadn't stepped on Cuddles's tail, it wouldn't have happened."

"How do you know that?" Henry motioned to Cuddles, who lay curled on a patch of straw, licking her paws. "That *narrisch* [crazy] cat of yours could have raced in front of your skateboard and caused you to fall even if I hadn't stepped on her tail."

Rachel frowned. "You're not sorry for making me fall. You're trying to put the blame on Cuddles." She whirled around and raced out of the barn.

When Rachel stepped into the kitchen a few moments later, she found Mom sitting at the table drinking a cup of tea.

"Rachel, your dress—and your knees!" Mom exclaimed. "What in the world happened?"

Rachel told Mom what happened, and she ended it by saying, "I'm really mad at Henry for what he did!"

"Did Henry apologize?" Mom asked.

Rachel nodded. "But I don't think he meant it."

"I'm sure Henry didn't purposely step on the cat's tail. You need to forgive your brother."

Rachel stared at the floor.

Mom left her seat, opened a cupboard door, and took out a box of bandages and some antiseptic. Rachel took a seat at the table and stuck out both legs.

"Does it hurt much?" Mom asked as she dabbed some of the medicine on Rachel's knees.

"A little."

When Mom finished bandaging Rachel's knees she said, "Run upstairs now and change out of your dress. When you come down, you can mend your dress."

Rachel swallowed around the lump in her throat. "I don't see why I have to fix the hole in my dress. It was Henry's fault that it tore."

Mom squinted at Rachel over the top of her glasses. "As I said before, I don't think Henry stepped on Cuddles's tail on purpose. Now do as I say and run upstairs to change your dress."

Rachel trudged up the stairs, mumbling, "I don't think anyone likes me."

Rachel changed into a clean dress and was walking down the stairs when—*whack!*—she heard something hit the living room window. Rachel raced into the room and looked out the window. Lying in the flowerbed was a baby robin with its feet in the air. Rachel dropped her torn dress on a chair and raced outside. She had reached the spot where the bird lay, when Cuddles streaked across the yard, heading straight for the helpless little bird.

"No, Cuddles!" Rachel quickly picked up the bird. Relieved to see that it was still breathing, she set it on one of their bird feeders. "Don't worry, little birdie," she said. "You'll be okay. I'm sure you'll be able to fly again."

Rachel dashed into the house. "Mom, Mom!" she shouted as she raced into the kitchen. "A baby robin hit the living room window, and it was lying in the flowerbed with its feet in the air. I rescued the poor thing and put it on one of our bird feeders."

"Are you sure the bird wasn't dead?" Mom asked. "Hitting the window like that could have done in a baby bird."

Rachel shook her head. "No, no, I'm sure it was still breathing. I'm going back outside to check on it." She ran back outside and over to the feeder. She was happy to see that the little bird was still there, and it was breathing!

"Come on, little birdie, fly away, fly away." Rachel stared at the bird, hoping it would fly.

Suddenly, the bird opened its eyes, looked right at Rachel, and flew high into the tree.

Rachel smiled. This was the second time today that she'd rescued a bird, and she felt really good about that. In fact, helping her little bird friends had made her feel better about her otherwise rotten day.

She wished she could tell Mary about the two birds she had helped. Maybe this was a good time to write that letter to Mary she'd been meaning to write.

Rachel hurried into the house and went straight to her room. She took a seat at her desk and got out a piece of paper and a pencil. Then she began writing the letter.

Dear Mary,

I've been waiting to hear from you ever since you moved, and I don't understand why I haven't gotten a letter yet.

Have you been busy unpacking? I've been busy here, too. Grandpa hurt his back the other day, but he's doing better now.

There's a new girl at school. Her name is Audra, and Elizabeth gave her your desk. Audra's been mean to me, and it doesn't seem right for her to be sitting in your desk.

Something good happened today, though. A bird got into the schoolhouse and no one could catch it. Then the bird landed on my head, and everyone was surprised when I picked it up and took it outside.

When I got home from school today, a bird hit our window and landed in the flowerbed. I thought it might be dead, but I set it on a bird feeder, and when I checked on it again, it was okay and flew into the tree.

Rachel stopped writing for a moment when a lump formed in her throat. She should have been telling Mary all these things in person—not writing them in a letter.

"Oh, Mary, I miss you so much. Please write back to me."

Chapter 7

Chain of Events

As Rachel entered the schoolyard the following morning, she spotted Orlie talking with Audra again. They were grinning like a couple of little kids with a sack full of candy. Rachel noticed that Orlie held Audra's backpack, as well as his own.

Rachel kicked at a stone with the toe of her sneaker. *I knew it. Orlie does like Audra better than me. He probably walked her to school this morning.*

Rachel wasn't sure why she cared so much. It wasn't as if she and Orlie were best friends or anything. Only Mary had been Rachel's best friend, but now Rachel had no friends at all.

"I don't care," she mumbled under her breath. "I don't need any friends."

"What was that, Rachel?" Jacob asked.

"Nothing."

"You said something. I heard you."

"It was nothing important, and I wasn't talking to you, anyway."

"Who were you talking to, little bensel?"

"I was talking to myself." Rachel whirled around. "And stop calling me that! I'm getting tired of you picking on me all the time."

"I'm just teasing." Jacob wrinkled his nose. "Can't you even take a joke?"

Rachel didn't answer. Instead, she plodded up the schoolhouse steps and hurried inside.

"You're the first one in class again," Elizabeth said when Rachel took a seat behind her desk a few minutes later. "You must really like being in school. Maybe you'll grow up to be a teacher like me someday."

Rachel pursed her lips. She hadn't even thought of what she'd like to do when she grew up. Maybe becoming a schoolteacher wouldn't be a bad idea. It would be better than getting married like her sister Esther had done. On the other hand, Esther seemed really happy being married to Rudy. Now that they were expecting a baby, Esther had a smile on her face all the time.

"So what do you think, Rachel?" Elizabeth asked. "Would you like to be a schoolteacher someday?"

Rachel shrugged. "Maybe."

Elizabeth smiled and patted Rachel's shoulder. "I guess I'd better ring the school bell now."

"I want everyone to play baseball," Elizabeth announced before dismissing the class for their noontime recess. "It's a beautiful spring day, and the fresh air and exercise will be good for us all."

Rachel frowned. She wanted to swing—not play baseball during recess.

Even though she enjoyed doing lots of outdoor games, playing baseball was not one of her favorite things to do.

"Let's play the boys against the girls!" Aaron shouted.

"No way," said Phoebe. "There are too many good boy players, so it wouldn't be fair if all the boys were on one team."

"I agree," Audra spoke up.

"I'll decide who will be on each team," Elizabeth said. "I'll also play on one of the teams, and my helper, Sharon, will be on the other."

Elizabeth soon had the children divided into two teams, and everyone took their place. Rachel was glad she wasn't on Orlie's team, but it didn't make her happy to see that Audra was on his team.

Rachel's team was up first, with Rachel first in line to bat. With a sense of determination, she stepped up to the plate. Gripping the bat and clenching her teeth, she waited for Orlie to pitch the ball.

He smiled at Rachel, gave a quick nod, and—*whizz!*—the ball zipped over home plate. Rachel swung hard but missed.

"Strike one!" Elizabeth hollered.

Orlie pitched another ball to Rachel, and she missed again, the weight of the bat spinning her around in a circle.

"Strike two!"

Rachel knew she only had one more strike left, and then she'd be out. She couldn't let that happen. She had to hit the ball and make it to first base—maybe two or three bases—maybe even make a homerun!

She took her stance, holding the bat firm and steady. The pitch came fast, and—*whack!*—she smacked it out into left field!

Rachel dropped the bat to the ground and took off running. She ran so fast her kapp strings waved behind her like streamers. She sprinted to first base and kept on running.

She heard Orlie holler, "Catch that ball, Audra! Tag Rachel out!"

Rachel kept running—past second base and heading for third. She was going to make it—maybe all the way home!

Rachel saw a white blur out of the corner of her eye, and then Audra leaping into the air. *Thwack!* The ball thunked Rachel right on the nose!

"Ach, my *naas* [nose]!" Rachel nearly gagged when she felt something drip down her throat—a strange, metallic taste. She touched the end of her nose, and when she looked at her fingers, there was blood on them.

Orlie rushed forward. "I'm sorry, Rachel. I thought Audra was gonna catch the ball."

"I tried to catch the ball, but it came too fast." Audra stared at Rachel and squinted. "I hope your naas isn't broken. It looks kind of swollen."

Elizabeth rushed up to Rachel and covered her nose

with a tissue. "You'd better come inside with me so I can get the bleeding stopped."

With tears stinging her eyes and her nose throbbing like crazy, Rachel followed her teacher into the schoolhouse.

"Take a seat at your desk, and I'll get some cold water and a clean cloth," Elizabeth instructed. "In the meantime, keep that tissue over your nose."

Rachel did as her teacher said, trying not to give in to the threatening tears pushing against her eyelids. *I'll bet Orlie threw that ball so it would hit me in the nose,* she fumed. *Audra probably missed it on purpose, too.*

Elizabeth returned to Rachel's desk and placed a cold cloth on Rachel's nose and one on the back of her neck. "Let's see if that stops the bleeding," she said. "If it doesn't, I'll try some vinegar."

"Vinegar?" Rachel had never heard of anyone with a nosebleed having to drink vinegar.

"It's an old-time remedy," Elizabeth explained. "You put a little vinegar on the end of a tissue and stick it up your nostril to stop the bleeding."

"That sounds awful." Rachel hoped her nose would stop bleeding on its own. It was one thing to eat something that had vinegar in it, like pickled beets or dill pickles, but putting vinegar up her nose didn't sound fun at all. She was sure it would sting.

A few minutes later, Elizabeth came to check her nose. When she pulled the cloth aside, she smiled and said, "The bleeding has slowed. It should stop soon, I think."

Rachel breathed a sigh of relief. *No vinegar for me.*

By the time the others had come inside from recess, Rachel's nose had stopped bleeding.

"Are you all right?" Orlie asked as he took his seat in front of Rachel.

"My nose has stopped bleeding, but it still hurts," she said.

"You're not mad at me, I hope."

Rachel gave no reply.

Orlie shrugged and turned to face the front of the room.

Rachel took out her spelling book. Spelling was her favorite subject, and since she was the best speller in the third and fourth grades, she hoped she would feel better after they'd had their spelling bee.

While Rachel waited for the teacher to get things ready, she studied the list of spelling words: *address, blister, cavity, disturb, entry, faithful, gelatin*. . . She knew how to spell every word on the page and should be able to easily win the class spelling bee.

She glanced across the aisle. Audra was studying her spelling words, too. Could Audra spell well? She didn't like bugs and couldn't play baseball very well. Maybe Audra liked spelling and would be hard to beat. She'd played Scrabble fairly well—until she'd accused Rachel of cheating. Maybe. . .

"All right, scholars," Elizabeth said, rising from her desk, "this is how we're going to do our spelling bee today." She motioned to the front of the room. "Those of you in grades one and two will line up to receive your words first. When we have a winner from that group, the third and fourth graders will come up front, followed by the fifth and sixth graders. Our seventh and eighth graders will go last."

Rachel was glad the first and second graders were going first. That gave her more time to study her list of spelling words. Of course, she didn't know which of the words on the list Elizabeth would ask, but she wasn't worried. In fact, she figured the spelling bee would be the best part of her day.

It didn't take long until the first and second graders were done. Danny Fisher was the last scholar standing, and he got to put a yellow star on the first and second grader's section of the wall. Then he got to choose one of the new fiction books Elizabeth had brought to school today. Sharon gave all the first and second graders a piece of candy from a basket on her desk.

"Now it's time for the third and fourth graders to take their places," Elizabeth said.

Rachel hopped up from her desk and made her way to the front of the room. She squeezed into a spot between Orlie and Audra. *At least they aren't standing together this time.*

Elizabeth started at the end of the line, giving the first word, *street*, to Nona Lapp.

That's an easy word, Rachel thought. *I could spell "street" when I was in the first grade.*

Nona spelled the word correctly, and Elizabeth continued down the line. When she came to Orlie she gave him the word *walnut*. Orlie rubbed his chin and squinted his eyes. "Hmm. . .let me think."

"The word is *walnut*," Elizabeth repeated. "Can you spell it, Orlie?"

Orlie blinked a couple of times, and a silly grin came over his face. "Sure, I can spell *it*. *I-T*."

Everyone laughed—except Elizabeth and Sharon.

Elizabeth frowned and said, "Orlie Troyer, do you want to stay after school today?"

He shook his head and stared at the floor. "No, Elizabeth."

"Then stop fooling around and spell the word *walnut* for us."

Orlie shifted from his right foot to his left foot and bit his lip nervously. Rachel could tell he was struggling and didn't know how to spell the word. She was tempted to whisper it to him but knew that would be cheating. Once, she cheated on a history test, and after that she promised never to cheat again.

Elizabeth tapped her foot against the hardwood floor. "We're waiting for your answer, Orlie."

Orlie cleared his throat a couple of times and finally lifted his head. "W-a-l-l-n-u-t. Walnut."

Rachel groaned inwardly, and Elizabeth shook her head. "That's incorrect. I'm sorry, Orlie, you'll have to take your seat."

With a bright smile, Orlie dashed back to his desk. It seemed as if he was glad he had missed the word. Rachel knew spelling wasn't one of Orlie's best subjects. Maybe he was relieved that he didn't have to stand in front of the class and be embarrassed any longer. Now he could sit in his desk and wait for someone else to mess up.

I hope it's not me, Rachel thought. *I don't want to miss one single word. I want to win this spelling bee.*

"Rachel, did you hear what I said?"

Rachel jerked her head toward Elizabeth. She'd been so busy thinking about Orlie and how much she wanted to win that she hadn't heard what her teacher said.

"Uh. . .what was that?" she mumbled.

Everyone laughed, and Rachel's face heated up.

Elizabeth clucked her tongue. "Please spell the word *walnut.*"

Rachel nodded. "Walnut. W-a-l-n-u-t. Walnut."

"That's correct," Elizabeth said.

Rachel smiled, feeling quite pleased with herself.

Elizabeth faced Audra. "Your word is *windmill.*"

Rachel held her breath and waited to see if Audra could spell the word.

Audra smiled and said, "Windmill. W-i-n-d-m-i-l-l. Windmill."

"Correct."

I guess Audra's a good speller, Rachel thought. *Either that or it was a lucky guess.*

Elizabeth continued down the line, giving each of the students in the third and fourth grades a word. Some spelled their words correctly and others ended up taking their seats like Orlie. Elizabeth started at the beginning of the line again, and when it was Rachel's turn, she spelled her next word correctly. Audra spelled her word correctly, too.

On and on it went, until only two scholars were left standing—Rachel and Audra.

The next word went to Rachel. It was *harness*.

Rachel's heart went *thump. . .thump. . .thump.* "H-a-r-" She paused and drew in a quick breath. *I've got to get this right. I can't mess up now.*

"Do you know the word, Rachel?" Elizabeth asked.

Rachel started again. "H-a-r-n-e-s-s. Harness."

"That's correct."

Rachel breathed a sigh of relief.

Elizabeth faced Audra. "Your word is *oxygen*."

Audra scratched her head. "Let's see now. . ."

"We're waiting, Audra," Elizabeth said.

Audra's forehead wrinkled and she pursed her lips. "O-x-y— No, the correct spelling is. . .uh—o-x-e-g-e-n."

Elizabeth shook her head. "I'm sorry, Audra, that's wrong."

Audra's face turned bright red. With head down and shoulders slumped, she shuffled to her desk.

"Rachel, you're the winner of the third and fourth grade spelling bee." Elizabeth handed Rachel a star to put on the wall and motioned to the basket on Sharon's desk. "Help yourself to a piece of candy."

Rachel took a stick of licorice then went to hang up her star. She felt really good about herself—maybe even full of a little *hochmut* [pride]. She remembered hearing their bishop say during church one day that it was wrong to be full of hochmut. "*We should be humble, never boastful,*" he'd said.

As Rachel put her star in place, she thought about the bishop's words. It was hard not to feel prideful sometimes—especially when she'd done something that made her feel so good. Maybe it was all right to feel good when she'd done something well. She just needed to be careful not to brag about it.

Rachel headed back to her desk. She was almost there when Audra turned sideways in her desk, and—*thump!*—Rachel tripped on Audra's foot and landed face-down on the floor!

Blood spurted out of Rachel's nose. "No, no! Not again!" she moaned. Why was it that every time things seemed to be going well, something happened to bring more trouble?

"Are you all right?" Elizabeth asked as she helped Rachel to her feet.

"My naas—it's bleeding." Rachel struggled not to cry as Elizabeth led her to the back of the schoolhouse where she kept a basin of water. Rachel sat on a stool while Elizabeth put wet cloths on her nose and the back of her neck.

"Audra tripped me on purpose," Rachel whimpered.

"Now, Rachel, why would Audra do that?"

"She's probably jealous because I won the spelling bee."

"Audra shouldn't have had her feet in the aisle," Elizabeth said, "but I don't think she tripped you on purpose."

Rachel folded her arms and sat there feeling sorry for herself. Why did everyone think Audra was so nice?

Couldn't they see she was nothing but trouble?

Audra approached Rachel quietly, a worried expression on her face. "I'm sorry about your nose, Rachel," she said. "I turned in my seat so I could ask Orlie something and didn't see you coming down the aisle."

Rachel stared straight ahead.

Elizabeth touched Rachel's shoulder. "Aren't you going to accept Audra's apology?"

Rachel lifted her shoulders in a shrug.

"God tells us to forgive others when they apologize," Elizabeth said.

Rachel closed her eyes and prayed: *Lord, I still think Audra tripped me on purpose, but help me to forgive her and have a better attitude.*

She opened her eyes and mumbled, "I forgive you, Audra."

Elizabeth turned to Audra. "From now on, please keep your feet under your desk and not in the aisle."

"I will." Audra hurried back to her desk.

Rachel clenched her hands into fists to keep herself from biting a nail.

Chapter 8

Wishing Fishing

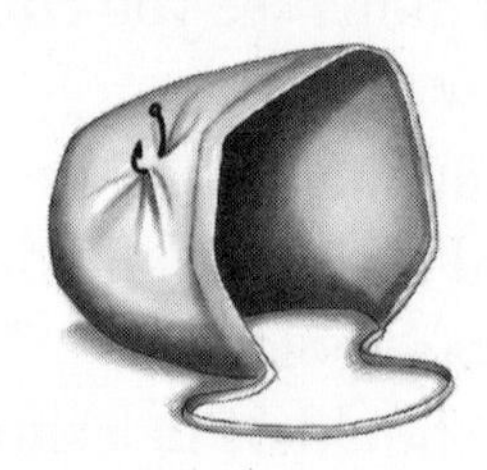

Would you like to do some wishing fishing with me today?" Grandpa asked Rachel on Saturday morning as she stood at the sink helping Mom do the dishes.

"What's wishing fishing?" Rachel asked, turning to face Grandpa.

He wiggled his bushy gray eyebrows. "Wishing fishing is when you drop your line into the water and sit there wishing you'll catch a big one."

Rachel giggled and dropped the sponge into the water, sending colorful bubbles to the ceiling. "Wishing fishing sounds like fun, Grandpa. Are you sure you're feeling up to it?"

"My back's doing better now. I think a day in the sunshine with my fishing pole is just what I need. Maybe it's what you need, too, Rachel."

"That's a good idea," said Mom as she reached into the drainer and plucked out a clean dish to dry. She looked at Rachel and smiled. "Your daed and Jacob left for town right after breakfast, and Henry's going over to see his girlfriend soon. You and Grandpa will have some time to be alone together today."

"What about you, Mom?" Rachel asked. "What are you going to do today?"

"I'm planning to sew some clothes for the boppli." Mom patted her round belly. "It won't be too many more months before our little one will be born, and he or she will need some clothes to wear."

Grandpa left the table and came to stand beside Rachel. "I'll bet you're getting excited about being a big *schweschder* [sister], jah?" he asked, squeezing her shoulder.

Rachel shrugged. She didn't want to think about becoming a big sister right now. She just wanted to think about going fishing with Grandpa.

Grandpa ambled across the room and plucked his straw hat from the wall peg where he'd hung it last night. "I'll go on out to the barn and get our fishing poles. Then I'll hitch a horse to one of your daed's buggies. When you're done with the dishes, come on out." He looked over his shoulder and winked at her. Then he plopped his straw hat on his head. "It won't be long until we'll be doing some wishing fishing!"

"Ah, the Lord is so good!" Grandpa said as he and Rachel sat on a grassy spot on the shoreline of the pond. "Can you smell that fresh spring air?"

Rachel's nose twitched as she inhaled deeply. "Jah, it does smell kind of nice."

"Pretty soon there'll be wild flowers growing all

around the pond." Grandpa smiled. "Those will smell nice, too."

Rachel nodded.

"Speaking of flowers," Grandpa said. "After you went to bed last night, I spoke with your daed about my greenhouse idea."

"What'd he say?"

"He agreed to help me build it near the front of his property."

"Oh, Grandpa, that's *wunderbaar* [wonderful]. When will it happen?"

"Probably sometime this spring." He patted her arm. "Maybe you'd like to help me in the greenhouse when you're not in school."

Rachel nodded happily. "I'd like that. I think being around all those flowers will be a lot of fun!" She removed her sneakers and wiggled her bare toes in the grass. It felt nice to be here with Grandpa, talking about his new greenhouse and getting ready to catch some fish. Today was turning out to be a pretty good day.

"Having a greenhouse will be fun," Grandpa said, "but it will also mean a lot of work."

"Working with flowers won't seem like work to me," Rachel said with a shake of her head.

Grandpa chuckled. "I guess we'll have to wait and see about that." He reached into his bag of fishing supplies and pulled out a can of worms. "Would you like me to bait your hook, Rachel?"

"That's all right. I can do it myself." Rachel reached into the can, plucked out a fat, wiggly worm, and baited her hook. Then she cast the line into the water.

Grandpa took a worm from the can and baited his hook. He drew his arm back, flicked his wrist, and—*swish*—Rachel's kapp lifted right off her head.

She looked up in shock at her hat as it dangled from the fishhook at the end of Grandpa's line. "Grandpa, what'd you do that for?"

"*Was is do uff?* [What's the matter here?]" His forehead wrinkled as he studied the kapp hanging in midair.

Rachel giggled as she watched the kapp sway in the gentle breeze. "It looks like you caught a big one, Grandpa!"

Grandpa's eyes twinkled and he laughed. "We won't be throwing this one back into the lake."

Rachel jumped up to retrieve her kapp. She worked to gently remove the hook, but the hook left a noticeable hole. "Oh no! You put a hole in my kapp! It's ruined now," she said with a frown.

Grandpa examined the damage to her kapp. "I'm sorry, Rachel. It was an accident. I sure didn't do it on purpose."

Rachel tossed her pole to the ground. "I don't feel like fishing anymore."

"Come on, Rachel," Grandpa said, placing a hand on her shoulder. "Let's not let a little accident ruin our wishing fishing trip."

She crossed her arms and stared straight ahead.

"Are you going to forgive me?"

Rachel shrugged. "Mom's gonna be mad when she

sees that my kapp is ruined."

"I'll explain things to your mamm."

"She'll probably make me wear the kapp with a hole in it because she doesn't have time to make me a new one. She's too busy making *baby clothes*." Rachel sniffed. "After the boppli's born, Mom will be even busier than she is now. She probably won't have time to sew anything for me."

"I'm sure she'll take the time to make you a new kapp," Grandpa said. "Either that or she'll fix the hole in this kapp." Grandpa motioned to Rachel's fishing pole. "Are you going to fish or not?"

She shook her head. "I'm out of the mood."

"Suit yourself." Grandpa cast his line into the water. Rachel sat staring at the trees on the other side of the pond. So much for a fun day of wishing fishing! The only thing she was wishing for now was a kapp that didn't have a hole in it. If she had to wear her kapp with a hole in it to school on Monday morning, Jacob, Orlie, and some of the other kids would probably make fun of her.

"You've been awfully grumpy and unforgiving lately," Grandpa said. "What's the problem?"

She shrugged.

"Does it have anything to do with Mary moving to Indiana?"

"Maybe."

Grandpa took one hand off his fishing pole and touched Rachel's arm. "I realize you're having a hard time adjusting, but you shouldn't take it out on everyone. If you're not careful, you won't have any friends at all."

She grunted. "I don't need any friends."

"Jah, you do. We all need a good friend or two." Grandpa plucked a blade of grass and put it between his teeth. "If your attitude doesn't change, you might lose the friends you do have, and you certainly won't make any new ones."

"Humph!" Rachel grunted. "I could never be Audra's friend."

"Audra?"

"She's that new girl at school." Rachel clucked her tongue, the way Mom often did. "Audra and I are as different as Cuddles and Buddy. I don't think we could ever get along."

"It doesn't matter whether you like the same things or not," Grandpa said. "You can still be Audra's friend if you want to be."

I don't want to be Audra's friend, Rachel thought, but she didn't tell Grandpa that. Instead, she picked up her pole and cast her line into the water. "I guess I will fish awhile," she said.

Grandpa smiled. "That's good to hear."

It wasn't long before Rachel had a bite on her line, and she quickly reeled in a nice big fish.

"Do you need help taking the fish off the hook?" Grandpa asked.

Rachel shook her head. "I can manage." Carefully, she removed the hook from the fish's mouth. Then she put the fish in the bucket Grandpa brought along. She baited her hook with another wiggly worm and cast her line into the water again.

In no time at all Rachel caught two more fish, but Grandpa had only caught one. He didn't seem to mind, though, as he leaned back on his elbows in the grass and lifted his face to the sun. "Ah, the Lord is good," he murmured.

Just then Rachel spotted a plump little frog leaping along the water's edge. It made her think of the day she caught two frogs in their backyard. She put them in a box and took them to church, hoping to race them after the service was over. But one of the frogs escaped from the box and made quite a scene during church. When Mom found out that Rachel was the one responsible for the leaping frog, she wasn't happy at all. In fact, she'd given Rachel extra chores to do. Right then and there Rachel had decided she would never catch another frog and bring it to church.

But I could catch a frog here at the pond and take it home with me, Rachel thought. She set her fishing pole aside and crawled slowly through the grass toward the frog.

"What are you doing, Rachel?" Grandpa asked.

"Shh. . .I'm getting ready to catch a frog." She reached out her hand, and—*flump!*—the frog leaped into the air and landed on a rock in the shallow water.

Rachel leaned out as far as she could, but she couldn't quite reach the frog.

Ribbet! Ribbet! Mr. Frog leaped onto another rock a short distance away.

Rachel knew there was only one way to catch that sneaky old frog, but she would have to move fast. She crouched down low and waited to see what the frog would do. It just sat there, still as could be.

In one quick movement, Rachel stepped into the water and thrust out her arm. Her fingers were just inches from the frog, but it leaped again. This time it landed back in the grass. *Ribbet! Ribbet!*

"I don't think that old frog wants to be caught," Grandpa said with a chuckle.

Rachel groaned and trudged through the water. She was getting ready to step out when her foot slipped on a slimy rock, and—*splash!*—into the water she went! She came up spitting and sputtering, "Trouble, trouble, trouble! All I ever have is trouble!"

Grandpa held his sides and rocked back and forth as he laughed. "Ach, Rachel, I thought you came here to fish, not take a dip in the pond."

"It's not funny, Grandpa," Rachel said as she sloshed out of the water. "My kapp's got a hole in it, and now my clothes are soaking wet. I'll be in trouble with Mom for sure."

Grandpa grabbed an old quilt from the back of his buggy and wrapped it around her shoulders. "I'm sure your mamm will understand once you explain what happened."

Rachel shook her head. "You don't know Mom like I do."

He laughed some more and slapped his knee. "She's my *dochder* [daughter], Rachel. I raised her for over nineteen years before she married your daed. I think I know her well enough."

Rachel thought about the day last summer when she fell in the pond while making a mud dam with Jacob. Mom called them out of the water, saying it was time to go home. Jacob went right away, but Rachel didn't come when she was called, choosing instead to work on her dam. Then she slipped on a slimy rock and fell into the water, just like she did today. As punishment for not coming when she was called, Rachel had to wash her dress when they got home from the picnic.

Mom will probably be mad when she sees my torn kapp and wet dress, Rachel thought as she grabbed her fishing pole and climbed into the buggy. *She'll probably give me more chores to do.*

When Rachel and Grandpa arrived home, she spotted Jacob in the yard, giving Buddy a ride in the wheelbarrow Mom used for gardening. "Jacob giving his dog a ride in the wheelbarrow is so lecherich," she said as Grandpa helped her down from the buggy.

Grandpa's forehead wrinkled. "It's no more ridiculous than you trying to catch a frog or giving Cuddles a ride on your skateboard."

I wonder if Grandpa's mad because I got three fish and he only got one, Rachel thought as she hurried across the lawn. *Maybe that's why he's sticking up for Jacob.*

When Rachel entered the house, she found Mom lying on the sofa reading a book. "I thought you were going to sew baby clothes today," Rachel said as she stood in the doorway.

"I did get some sewing done, but I got tired and decided to rest." Mom gave a noisy yawn. "How was the fishing? Did you catch any fish?"

Rachel nodded. "I got three and Grandpa got one."

Mom chuckled but didn't look up. "I'll bet he wasn't too happy about only getting one fish."

"He said he didn't mind."

Mom sat up and stretched. "Where is Grandpa now?"

"He's outside putting the horse in the barn." Rachel removed her kapp from her head. "Grandpa snagged my kapp with his fishing hook, and now there's a hole in it," she said with a frown. "Then I fell in the pond and got my dress all wet."

"It's too bad those things happened, but it's not the end of the world. I have some extra kapps put away in a drawer, so you can have one of those. You will need to get out of your wet clothes, though."

Rachel waited to see if Mom would say anything more.

"Is there something else?" Mom asked, giving Rachel a questioning look.

Rachel shook her head. "No, I—uh—just wondered if you wanted me to wash my dress."

Mom shook her head. "I'll wash clothes on Monday morning, so just put your dress and under things in the laundry basket. Then change into some clean clothes."

"Okay, Mom." Rachel looked at her kapp again. At least she wouldn't have to wear a kapp with a hole in it to school on Monday morning. And she couldn't get over how calm Mom had seemed when she'd told her what had happened at the pond. *Maybe Grandpa does know her better than me,* she thought. *Or maybe it's because I wasn't being disobedient when I fell in the pond this time.*

Rachel turned toward the door leading to the stairs, but she'd only taken a few steps when Mom called, "Oh, Rachel, I almost forgot. There's a surprise on the table for you."

"What surprise?" Rachel loved surprises.

"A letter came for you in today's mail."

"Is—is it from Mary?"

Mom nodded.

Well, it's about time Mary wrote to me, Rachel thought.

"I got a letter from Mary's mamm, too."

Rachel started for the kitchen but halted again when Mom said, "You can get the letter now, but then you'd better go right upstairs and change out of those wet clothes."

"Okay, Mom." Rachel raced into the kitchen. Sure enough, there was a letter lying on the table. She scooped it up and rushed upstairs to her room. She placed the letter on the bed and quickly changed into a clean dress. Then she picked up the letter and flopped onto the mattress.

Rachel's hands shook as she tore the envelope open and began to read.

Dear Rachel,

I'm sorry it's taken me so long to write, but I've been awful busy since we moved. There have been boxes to unpack, things to put away, and the house to help clean.

I like my new school. The teacher's name is Sadie, and she's real nice. Oh, and I've made a new friend. . .Betty Stutzman. She used to live in Missouri and moved here a few months before we did. Betty and I are going shopping with our midder *[mothers] this Saturday. We'll probably go out to lunch somewhere, too.*

How are things with you? Have you taken Cuddles for any more rides on your skateboard?

Write back soon.

Love,
Mary

Rachel let the letter fall to the bed. She felt like she'd been kicked in the stomach by a wild horse. It wasn't fair! Mary had a new friend—and she didn't. And Mary hadn't said a word about the letter Rachel had written her. Didn't Mary even care how miserable Rachel had felt since she'd moved away?

I'm not going to write Mary back, Rachel decided. Tears welled in her eyes, and she pulled the pillow over her head. "Oh, Mary, I miss you so much. I have no friends now, and I'm so lonely."

The bed squeaked, and Rachel felt someone touch her hand. "You have to be a friend if you want to have any friends," Mom said softly.

Rachel pulled the pillow aside and sniffed. "Mary doesn't need me anymore. She's found a new friend. I wish Mary would move back to Pennsylvania so things would be like they used to be."

"I know it's hard to have your best friend move away, but you shouldn't be mad at Mary for making a new friend." Mom handed Rachel a tissue. "Don't you think it's time for you to make a new friend, too?"

Rachel sniffled and blew her nose. "I'll think about it."

Chapter 9

Bubbles and Troubles

Rachel grunted as she carried a basket of clean clothes out to the clothesline and placed it on the ground. When she arrived home from school this afternoon, Mom said she hadn't felt well this morning, so it had taken her longer than normal to get their clothes washed, and she'd only hung a few things on the line. She asked Rachel to hang the rest of the things while she went back inside to rest before it was time to start supper.

Rachel glanced at the barn. She wished she was in there riding her skateboard or playing with Cuddles instead of hanging laundry out to dry. Maybe if she hurried and got it done, there would be time for her to play before she had to help Mom with supper.

Rachel bent down, picked up a pair of grandpa's trousers, and stepped onto the wooden stool she used to help her reach the clothesline. She had just clipped the trousers to the line when Buddy ambled across the yard toward her, an old bone hanging from his mouth.

She looked away in disgust, hoping the dog wouldn't notice her.

Disgusting mutt, Rachel thought as she pinned one of Mom's towels to the line. *He's nothing but trouble.*

Woof! Woof!

Rachel looked down just in time to see Buddy drop his bone at her feet, dip his head into the basket, and grab one of the towels in his mouth.

"Give me that!" she shouted.

Buddy flicked his ears, swished his tail, and darted away, dragging the towel across the grass.

Rachel hopped down from the stool and tore across the yard after him. "You come back with that towel, you bad breath, hairy beast!"

Buddy kept running—straight through the biggest patch of mud he could find!

Rachel gasped. "Look what you've done to Mom's clean towel! It's filthy!" Rachel grabbed one end of the towel and pulled.

Buddy's whole body shook as he growled and yanked on the towel.

"You'd better let go," Rachel said through gritted teeth.

Gr-r-r-r. . . Rip! The towel tore in two!

Rachel's whole body felt angry. She shook her fists and stamped her feet at Buddy and hollered, "Mom's not gonna be happy about this!"

Woof! Woof! Buddy wagged his tail, dropped his half of the towel, and bounded back to the laundry basket.

Rachel took off after him, waving her piece of towel

in the air. "Oh no, you don't!"

But she was too late. Buddy grabbed another towel, and he ran in circles, dragging the towel across the grass, through the dirt, and into the same mud.

Rachel knew better than to grab the towel this time. Buddy would probably tear it like the last one. She turned toward the house and cupped one hand around her mouth. "Jacob Yoder, you'd better come out here right now and get your dog!"

Jacob poked his head out the back door. "What's the trouble, Rachel? Why are you yelling?"

"Buddy's the trouble! *Your* dog took a clean towel from the laundry basket, dragged it through the mud, then ripped it in two when I tried to take it from him." Rachel pointed to Buddy, who lay under the clothesline with his head resting on the second towel he'd swiped from the basket. "Now he's got another towel and is using it for a pillow!"

Jacob sprinted across the yard, grabbed Buddy's collar, and pulled him away from the towel. "There, is that better?"

Rachel shook her head. "Nothing will be better until you get rid of that nuisance! He's been nothing but trouble ever since Orlie gave him to you!"

"I think you're exaggerating," Jacob said. "Buddy's a nice dog."

She held up the dirty piece of towel in her hand. "Do you call this *nice*?"

"I don't think Buddy ripped it on purpose. He probably thought you were playing."

"Jah, right! That dog needs to be trained, and you ought to know better than to let him run free on laundry day!"

Jacob scratched the side of his head. "I thought I had Buddy penned up. I wonder if I forgot to latch the gate on his pen."

"I'm going in the house right now to tell Mom what happened. If I get in trouble for this, it'll be your fault for not keeping Buddy penned up!"

Before Jacob had a chance to reply, Rachel raced across the yard toward the house. She'd just stepped into the kitchen when—*bam!*—she heard a loud crash followed by a rattling noise coming from the living room.

"Mom, are you okay?" Rachel hurried into the room where she found Mom on her hands and knees holding pieces of a broken jar. Dozens of marbles rolled all over the floor!

Rachel gasped. "Ach, Mom, what happened to my jar of marbles?"

Mom looked up and stared at Rachel over the top of her glasses. "I was dusting the end table and accidentally knocked the jar on the floor."

Rachel frowned. "I saved up my money to buy that special jar for my marbles and now it's broken. Why weren't you more careful when you were dusting, Mom?"

"I didn't do it on purpose," Mom said as she rose slowly to her feet. "I'm sorry your jar is broken, but if you'd put the jar of marbles away in your room like I asked you to do this morning, this would not have happened." She pointed to the piece of towel in Rachel's hands. "What happened to that towel?"

"It's Buddy's fault." Rachel sniffed a couple of times, trying to hold back the tears clogging her throat. "He got out of his dog run and took a towel from the basket of clean clothes. When I ran after him, he sloshed the towel through mud. Then when I tried to get the towel away from him, he ripped it in two." She gulped in a quick breath of air. "When I wasn't looking, Buddy pulled another towel from the basket and laid his dirty, smelly head on it like it was a pillow. I think you should make Jacob get rid of him!"

"Do I ask Mom to get rid of you every time you do something wrong?" Jacob said as he entered the room. He looked over at Mom. "I don't think Buddy meant to get those towels dirty. I'm sure he was only playing." He glared at Rachel. "And it's *her* fault one of the towels ripped in two!"

"Were you outside when this all happened?" Mom asked Jacob.

He shook his head. "I was in the kitchen having a snack."

"You know your dog's not supposed to be out of his pen unless you're there to watch him."

Jacob stared at the floor. "I know, but I didn't let Buddy out of his pen, honest."

"How did Buddy get out?" Mom asked.

Jacob shrugged. "I don't know. Maybe he unlatched the gate."

"Right!" Rachel grunted. "Like that dumm mutt's

smart enough to unlatch the gate himself."

"He's not a dumm mutt. He's very *schmaert* [smart]," Jacob said. "You're just *en aldi grauns* [an old grumbler] who likes to blame everyone for everything and doesn't know how to forgive."

Rachel's chin quivered as she glared at him. "You take that back, Jacob Yoder!"

"Why should I? It's the truth."

"A lot you know. For your information—"

Mom clapped her hands. "That's enough!" She motioned to the marbles on the floor. "Rachel, gather up all these marbles before one of us slips on them and gets hurt. After that, you can wash the towel Buddy laid his head on." She looked over at Jacob. "Go outside and make sure your dog is in his pen and that the gate's secured. I don't want any more dirty laundry to do today."

Jacob nodded and hurried out of the room. Rachel dropped to her knees and started gathering up marbles, grumbling as she put each one into an empty coffee can Mom gave her. By the time she finished, she was tired and cranky.

Maybe Jacob's right, Rachel thought as she lugged the marbles up the steps to her room. *I do feel like en aldi grauns today.*

Rachel put the marble-filled coffee can on the floor in her closet. She was tempted to sit on the bed and hold her faceless doll, but she knew Mom was waiting for her to wash the dirty towel. With a weary sigh she headed back downstairs.

When Rachel finished washing the towel in the

kitchen sink, Mom smiled and said, "You're free to play until it's time to help with supper. Why don't you find something fun to do?"

"Don't you want me to hang up the rest of the laundry that's still in the basket outside?" Rachel asked.

Mom shook her head. "I'll take care of that."

"But I thought you weren't feeling well today."

"I just had a queasy stomach this morning, but I'm feeling better this afternoon." She patted Rachel's head. "I think you've done enough work for now, so I'll take over your job of hanging the clothes."

"Danki, Mom." Rachel headed out to the barn, hoping to find Cuddles there. But when she entered the barn, she saw no sign of her cat. She took a seat on a bale of straw and looked around. It was quiet in the barn. Sunbeams streamed through the cracks in the ceiling, and a pigeon cooed from the loft overhead.

Rachel yawned and closed her eyes. She was too tired to skateboard or swing on the rope hanging from the hayloft. *Maybe I'll visit with old Tom,* she decided. *He probably needs cheering up as much as I do.*

Rachel walked to the part of the barn where the horses were kept. When she came to old Tom's stall, she opened the door and peeked in. She was disappointed to see that the old horse was lying in a pile of straw, fast asleep.

"Guess I'd better find something else to do," Rachel mumbled as she shut the stall door and headed back through the barn. She was almost to the door when she spotted a jar of bubbles on a shelf. *Maybe Grandpa would like to blow some bubbles with me,* she thought as she reached for the jar. *Grandpa makes bubbles better than anyone I know.*

Rachel hurried to the house. She found Mom in the kitchen, peeling potatoes over the kitchen sink. "Did you finish hanging the laundry already?" she asked.

Mom nodded. "Just got it done a few minutes ago."

"Is it time to start supper?" Rachel hoped she had time to play before she had to help Mom in the kitchen.

Mom pushed her glasses to the bridge of her nose and shook her head. "I'm just getting a head start on things. You go ahead and play some more if you want to."

"I'm going to sit on the back porch and blow some bubbles," Rachel said. "I came in the house to see if Grandpa wants to join me."

Mom motioned to the bedroom down the hall. "Grandpa's taking a nap right now. He spent most of the day working in the garden and said he was plumb tuckered out."

Rachel couldn't hide her disappointment as she frowned and said, "Maybe I won't blow any bubbles then."

Mom clucked her tongue noisily. "Don't martyr yourself, Rachel."

"What's 'martyr' mean?" Rachel asked.

"A martyr is a willing victim who suffers for a cause," Mom replied as she continued peeling potatoes. "People who martyr themselves often do it to make others feel sorry for them."

Rachel thought about that a few seconds. Was she

acting like a martyr by not wanting to blow bubbles by herself?

"You've been grumpy and out of sorts ever since Mary moved away," Mom said. "I think what you need to do is go out on the porch, blow a few bubbles, and thank God for all the good things He's given you."

"Jah, okay." Rachel went out the door, took a seat on the porch step, and opened the jar of bubbles. She dipped the bubble wand inside, pulled it back out, and blew. A colorful bubble formed. When she waved the wand, the bubble sailed across the yard.

Rachel made a couple more bubbles, and was about to put the lid back on the jar, when Cuddles darted out from under the porch and pounced on a bubble that hovered just above the ground.

Rachel blew another bubble—and then another. As fast as she made each bubble, Cuddles popped it. Rachel laughed.

This is kind of fun, Rachel thought. In fact, she was actually having a good time. She hadn't laughed this much since Mary moved away.

She closed her eyes. *Dear God: Thanks for Cuddles, and bubbles, and all the good things You've given me.*

Rachel's eyes snapped open when Cuddles bounded up the steps, pranced over to the bubble jar, and—*thunk!*—swatted at it with her right front paw. *Splat!*—the bubble liquid spilled out of the jar and all over the porch.

Rachel groaned. So much for a fun time of blowing bubbles!

She closed her eyes and thought about all her

troubles. She had trouble with Audra, trouble with Jacob, trouble with Buddy, and now trouble with Cuddles.

She sighed deeply. *I used to have some friends, but they seem to be disappearing as fast as Cuddles popped my bubbles. I wonder if I'll ever have any friends again. I wonder if my life will always be full of popping bubbles and all kinds of troubles.*

Chapter 10

In the Doghouse

The following Saturday morning, after Rachel finished feeding the chickens, she saw a big truck pull into their yard. She figured maybe Pap had ordered some farming supplies, so she walked past the truck without paying it much attention.

"Hey, little girl," the driver said as he and another man climbed out of the truck. "Do you know where we're supposed to put this trampoline?" He jabbed his thumb toward a large cardboard box in the back of the truck.

Rachel tipped her head and looked at the box. "Trampoline?"

He nodded. "That's right. I need to know where we should set it up."

"There must be some mistake." She shook her head. "I'm sure no one here ordered a trampoline. I think you must have come to the wrong address."

The man studied the piece of paper in his hands. "Is this the home of Levi Yoder?"

Rachel nodded.

"Then this is the right address."

Since it wasn't Christmas or anyone's birthday, Rachel was sure it was a mistake. She was about to head to the house to tell Mom about the delivery when Grandpa came out the back door, grinning from ear to ear.

"Is that the trampoline I ordered?" he asked, motioning to the back of the truck.

The deliveryman nodded. "Are you Levi Yoder?"

"No, I'm Noah Schrock. I'm the one who ordered the trampoline."

Rachel's mouth dropped open. "*You* ordered a trampoline?"

Grandpa nodded. "Sure did."

"Who–who's it for?" Rachel squeaked. "I mean, it's nobody's birthday, and it's not Christmas, so—"

"It doesn't have to be a special occasion for me to give a gift, and this gift is for everyone in the family." Grandpa pulled his fingers through his long beard and chuckled. "Well, anyone who's able to jump on the silly thing."

Rachel's heart went *thump-thump-thump!* "That would be me!" she said excitedly. "I'd love to jump on the trampoline!"

He smiled and patted the top of her head. "I figured you might."

The delivery man cleared his throat real loud. "Where do you want us to put the trampoline?"

Grandpa looked at Rachel, and Rachel shrugged. "Pap's out in the fields with Henry and Jacob. Should I go ask Mom?"

Grandpa nodded.

Rachel raced into the house. "Mom, guess what?" she hollered when she entered the kitchen where Mom sat at her sewing machine. "Grandpa bought us a trampoline!"

Mom looked up and smiled. "I knew he was going to. I just didn't know when it would arrive."

"How come you never said anything?" Rachel asked.

Mom rubbed the bridge of her nose, where her glasses were supposed to be, then she pushed them back in place. "He said he wanted it to be a surprise."

"It's a surprise, all right." Rachel's head bobbed up and down. "The deliverymen want to know where they should set up the trampoline."

Mom tapped her finger against her chin. "Let's see now. . . . Between the barn and the garden might be a good place."

"All right, I'll tell the men where you want it." Rachel raced for the door.

By the time the men had the trampoline set up, Jacob, Henry, and Pap had returned from the fields for lunch.

"Look what Grandpa bought for us." Rachel pointed to the trampoline. "I can hardly wait to try it out!"

"It's very nice," Pap said, "but you'll have to wait until after lunch to jump on it."

Rachel wished she could jump on it now, but she knew better than to argue with Pap. If she did, he might say she couldn't jump at all.

"I think I'm going to take my faceless doll to jump on

the trampoline," Rachel said to Mom when lunch was over and the dishes were done.

Mom squinted at Rachel over the top of her glasses. "Do you think that's a good idea? What if the doll falls off the trampoline and lands in the dirt?"

"That won't happen because I'll be holding onto her."

Mom shrugged. "All right then. But do be careful."

"I will, Mom."

As Rachel passed the living room, she spotted Grandpa sitting in the rocking chair. His eyes were closed and soft snores came from his slightly open mouth, letting her know he was asleep.

She scampered up the stairs to her room, hurried over to her dresser, picked up the doll, and raced out of the room.

"Where's Jacob? Is he going to jump on the trampoline with me?" Rachel asked Mom when she stepped into the kitchen.

"I'm not sure what Jacob plans to do," Mom replied as she picked up a broom and started sweeping the floor. "Your daed and Henry returned to work in the fields, but I think Jacob went out to the dog run to see Buddy."

Rachel wrinkled her nose. "If he'd rather spend time with that mutt than jump on the new trampoline, that's fine with me."

"Be careful," Mom called as Rachel scurried out the door.

"I will." Rachel hurried out to the trampoline.

Using the step stool Grandpa put there before

lunch, she set her doll on the trampoline and climbed up beside it. Her legs wobbled as she picked up the doll and stood. She sucked in a deep breath and held both arms out at her sides to keep her balance. She'd never been on a trampoline before, but she'd seen other children jumping on their trampolines. It didn't look so hard. She was sure she could do it.

Keeping both arms out at her sides as she held onto her doll, Rachel began to bounce slowly. Up. . .down. . . up. . .down. She picked up speed and jumped a little higher. Up. . .down. . .up. . .down. . . "*Whee*. . .this is sure fun!"

Woof! Woof! Woof!

Rachel glanced to the right and saw Jacob running across the yard with Buddy at his side. They were heading her way.

"Oh no," she mumbled. "Here comes trouble."

"Are you and your doll having fun up there, Rachel?" Jacob asked as he approached the trampoline.

She nodded and kept jumping.

Woof! Woof! Buddy stood beneath the trampoline with his mouth wide open.

"I hope you're not planning to let that dog of yours on the trampoline," Rachel said.

Jacob shook his head. "Of course not. We're just here to watch."

"Look how high I can go!" Rachel jumped so high her breath caught in her throat. Suddenly the doll snapped out of her hand. It flipped into the air, floated back down, and landed right in Buddy's mouth!

Rachel gasped.

Buddy pranced off toward his dog run with the faceless doll's body dangling from his mouth.

"Jacob, get your dog!" Rachel hollered. "He's got my doll!"

Jacob took off after Buddy, and Rachel jumped down from the trampoline and rushed after him. They found Buddy lying outside his doghouse with the doll between his paws.

Rachel gingerly picked up the doll and nearly choked on her words. "It–it's all chewed up!" She shook her finger at Buddy as tears clogged her throat. "You're a *bad dog*, and I'm very angry with you!"

Buddy looked up at her and whimpered.

"He didn't mean to do it," Jacob said. "When the doll flew off the trampoline, Buddy probably thought you were throwing him a toy to play with."

"I was *not* throwing him a toy!" Rachel scowled at Jacob and held up the mangled doll. "This is what happens when you let that flea-bitten animal run free!"

"I'm sorry," Jacob mumbled. "I didn't know Buddy would chew up your doll."

Rachel burst into tears. "Mary gave me this to remember her by, and—and now it's ruined!"

"I said I was sorry. What more can I do?"

"You can keep that dog in his pen where he belongs!"

"He can't be in there every minute of the day," Jacob said. "It wouldn't be fair."

"I suppose it's fair that my doll's chewed up?"

Jacob pointed to the doghouse and said, "In, Buddy."

Woof! Woof! Instead of going to the doghouse like he was supposed to do, Buddy jumped up and raced across the yard like his tail was on fire.

Jacob took off after the dog, waving his hands and hollering, "Come back here, Buddy! Come back here right now!"

Rachel groaned and stomped to the house. "Look what Jacob's dog did to my doll!" she wailed when she entered the kitchen and found Mom and Grandpa sitting at the table drinking tea.

Mom's mouth fell open, and Grandpa's bushy gray eyebrows shot up when they looked at the mangled doll Rachel held in her hands.

"How did Buddy get your doll?" Mom asked.

"The doll slipped when I was jumping on the trampoline, and Buddy was standing nearby with his mouth wide open." Rachel sniffed a couple of times. "The beautiful faceless doll Mary gave me landed in Buddy's mouth, and he chewed it all up! Now the doll is ruined!"

Mom pulled Rachel into her arms and gave her a hug. "As soon as I find the time, I'll make you another doll."

Rachel shook her head. "It wouldn't be the same. This doll was all I had to remember Mary. Now, thanks to Jacob's big hairy bad-breathed mutt, my doll is gone!"

"Sounds to me like Buddy's in the doghouse," said Grandpa with a shake of his head.

"No, he's not." Rachel motioned to the kitchen

window. "Look out there and you'll see—Buddy's running around the yard, and Jacob's chasing after him."

"When I said Buddy was in the doghouse, I meant that he's gotten himself in trouble." Grandpa's lips curved slightly upwards. "It's an old expression that people use, Rachel."

Rachel didn't like the fact that Grandpa thought this was funny. And she didn't like Buddy or what he'd done to her doll!

"You know, Rachel," Grandpa continued, "it was your choice to take the doll outside on the trampoline."

"That's right," Mom said. "So you can't put all the blame on Jacob or his dog. If the doll hadn't fallen off the trampoline, Buddy wouldn't have run away with it and chewed it up."

Rachel frowned. She didn't understand why everyone was taking Buddy's side. It wasn't fair!

With a strangled sob, she marched across the kitchen, threw the mangled doll into the garbage can, and rushed out of the room.

Rachel entered her bedroom, flopped onto the bed, and cried into her pillow until there were no tears left. Finally she sat up, dried her eyes on a tissue, and went over to her desk. She pulled open the drawer, took out some paper and a pen, and wrote Mary a letter.

Dear Mary,

Today started out pretty good. A delivery truck came with a new trampoline Grandpa ordered for us. I thought it would be fun to hold the faceless doll you gave me while I jumped on the trampoline, but a terrible thing happened. When I did a really high bounce, the doll slipped out of my hand and Jacob's dumm dog caught the doll in his mouth. Then Buddy ran across the yard, and by the time Jacob and I got to him, the hairy mutt had chewed up the doll! Now I have nothing to remember you by.

Rachel stopped writing long enough to blow her nose. Telling Mary about the doll made her feel even sadder, but she thought Mary had a right to know what had happened.

Swallowing against the lump in her throat, Rachel continued with the letter.

I wish Jacob would get rid of Buddy. That dog's been nothing but trouble since the first day he came to live here. He chases Cuddles, doesn't come when he's called, and he likes to jump up and lick my face!

Grandpa says that when someone's in trouble, they're in the doghouse. Well, I can tell you this much—Buddy's in the doghouse with me!

Chapter 11

Skateboard Mishap

Ach, Mom, do I have to go?" Rachel groaned when she came downstairs Saturday morning. Mom said they would be visiting Audra and her mother.

Mom glanced at Rachel over the top of her glasses. "I think you need to go and make peace with Audra, don't you?"

Rachel frowned. "I don't see why. Audra doesn't like me, and I don't like her."

"Be that as it may," Mom said as she moved to the stove, "when I met Naomi at the store the other day, she invited us to visit at their place today, so we're going."

Rachel was tempted to argue, but she knew once Mom had made up her mind about something, there was no changing it. Feeling like something heavy rested on her shoulders, she began setting the table for breakfast.

"How come you're wearing such a big frown on your face this morning, Rachel?" Jacob asked when he entered the kitchen a few minutes later.

"I'm not frowning," she mumbled as she placed the glasses on the table.

"Jah, you are."

"Am not."

He nudged her arm. "Then how come there's a row of tiny wrinkles on your forehead?"

Rachel reached up and touched her forehead. Jacob was right—there were some wrinkles there.

Jacob went to the sink and turned on the water to wash his hands. "So how come you're frowning, Rachel?"

"She's upset because she and I are going over to the Burkholders' house after breakfast," Mom said before Rachel could reply.

"Mom wants me to make peace with Audra," Rachel muttered.

"I think that's a good idea," Jacob said. "While you're at it, why don't you stop by Buddy's doghouse and make peace with him?"

Rachel whirled around and scowled at Jacob. "I'll never make peace with your dog. He's nothing but trouble!"

"You're nothing but trouble," Jacob shot back.

"No, you're bigger tr—"

Mom clapped her hands. "That's enough! I get tired of you two bickering all the time. It's certainly not pleasing to God."

Rachel's cheeks heated up. She didn't like it when Mom scolded her—even when she knew she was wrong.

"You're awfully quiet," Mom said as she and Rachel traveled down the road in one of Pap's buggies.

Rachel shrugged. "There's not much to say."

"What's new at school?"

"Nothing much. It's the same old thing day after day."

"Are you looking forward to summer break coming soon?"

"I guess so."

"Grandpa's looking forward to building his new greenhouse."

Rachel perked up at the mention of Grandpa's greenhouse. "Grandpa said I might be able to help in the greenhouse whenever I'm not in school."

"That would be nice." Mom reached across the seat and touched Rachel's arm. "Of course, you won't be able to work in the greenhouse all the time. There will be chores at the house to do, and after the boppli comes I'll need your help even more for a while."

Rachel frowned. She didn't like the idea of having more chores to do. She wasn't sure she liked the idea of Mom having a baby, either. But then, there wasn't much she could do about that. She just hoped she'd be able to spend plenty of time with Grandpa in his greenhouse. She was sure working around all those flowers would be a lot of fun.

"Here we are," Mom said as she guided their horse and buggy onto the Burkholders' driveway.

Rachel spotted Audra's mother sitting in a chair on the front porch, but there was no sign of Audra. *Good. Maybe Audra's not here today. Maybe she went to visit Orlie or something.*

Mom stopped the buggy in front of the hitching rail near the barn and climbed down. Rachel did the same.

"I'm glad you were able to come," Naomi said when Mom and Rachel joined her on the porch. She turned to Rachel and smiled. "Audra's in the barn playing. Would you like to join her?"

Rachel forced a smile to her lips and said what she knew Mom expected her to say: "Jah, sure." She left the porch and walked slowly to the barn.

She found Audra sitting on a bale of straw, fiddling with the string on a wooden yo-yo.

"Jacob has one of those," Rachel said, "but he doesn't play with it much anymore." She sighed. "He'd rather play with his dog."

Audra grunted. "My older bruder Jared made this for me, but I may never get to play with it if I can't get the string untangled."

"Want me to try?" Rachel offered.

"Jah, sure, if you think you can." Audra handed the yo-yo to Rachel.

As Rachel worked on untangling the string, Audra hummed and tapped her foot.

Rachel gritted her teeth as she struggled with the yo-yo string. It really was a mess!

"If you can't get it, that's okay," Audra said. "I don't need to play with the yo-yo right now."

"I'm sure I can get it. Just give me a few more minutes." Rachel fiddled with the string awhile longer and finally gave up. "Why don't we do something else?"

she suggested, setting the yo-yo aside. "I don't like to play with yo-yos that much anyway."

"Do you know how to skateboard?" Audra asked.

"Jah, sure," Rachel said with a nod.

"Maybe you'd like to try out the new skateboard ramp Jared made."

"You have your own skateboard ramp?"

"Actually, it belongs to both me and Brian. We take turns using it," Audra said.

"The only place I have to skateboard is the concrete floor of our barn—when it's not full of hay, that is," Rachel said. "It would be wunderbaar to have a ramp of my own to skateboard on."

Audra nodded. "Jared built the ramp at the back of the barn. Let's go there now, shall we?"

"Okay."

Audra led the way, and Rachel followed. They'd only gone a few steps, when Audra halted and shrieked. "Eeeeek!"

"What's the matter?" Rachel asked. "Why are you yelling?"

"I almost ran into that!" Audra pointed to a long-legged spider inside a lacy web. "I hate spiders!"

"It's not moving. Maybe it's dead." Rachel couldn't imagine why Audra would be scared of a little old spider.

Audra shivered. "I sure hope so."

"There's only one way to find out." Rachel grabbed a piece of straw and poked the spider gently. The spider wiggled its legs.

"It's definitely *not* dead," Rachel said.

"Yuck!" Audra scrunched up her nose. "How could you touch that horrible thing?"

"It was easy." Rachel shrugged. "Unless some dirty insect lands on my food, bugs don't bother me at all."

"I think all bugs are disgusting!" Audra ducked under the spider web. "That's where we skateboard." She pointed to the wooden ramp that had been set up near the back of the barn.

As Rachel stared at it, she felt envious. Why couldn't she have a ramp like that to skate on? Maybe she would ask Pap or Henry to build one for her next birthday.

"Here's my skateboard." Audra picked up the wooden skateboard sitting on the floor near the ramp. "Jared made this for me, too."

"If I'd known you had a place to skateboard, I would have brought my skateboard with me today," Rachel said. "My brothers gave me a skateboard for my birthday last year."

"We can take turns using mine," Audra said.

"Really? You'd let me use your skateboard?"

"Sure, why not?" Audra handed the skateboard to Rachel. "I'll even let you go first."

Rachel was surprised at how nice Audra was being. Maybe the two of them could be friends after all. She smiled and took the skateboard from Audra. "Danki."

Rachel stepped onto the skateboard and skated back and forth across the floor a few times. Then, pushing off as fast as she could, she headed for the ramp. "*Whee*. . . this is so much fun!" She skated up one side of the ramp and down the other.

"It's my turn now," Audra said.

"Just one more time." Rachel got the skateboard going good, and up the ramp she went. "Watch this, Audra." Leaning to one side, Rachel swerved back and forth, tipped the skateboard with the heel of her foot, and sailed down the other side.

She was almost to the bottom of the ramp when—*floop!*—the back wheel of the skateboard dropped off the edge of the ramp. Rachel's foot slipped, too, and the skateboard flew into the air and landed on the floor with a *thud*.

"Ach, my skateboard—you've ruined it!" Audra hollered.

Rachel went weak in the knees when she saw that the skateboard had broken into two pieces. "I'm sorry. I didn't expect that to happen," she stammered.

Audra's lower lip jutted out and she stamped her foot. "I think you did that on purpose."

Rachel shook her head. "Why would I do that?"

"Maybe to get even with me for mixing up our lunch pails at school. Or maybe you're still mad about the mud I splattered on your dress, or the baseball that hit you in the nose, or the nosebleed you got when I accidentally tripped you at school." Audra's forehead wrinkled as she squinted at Rachel. "You haven't liked me since my first day of school!"

"I wasn't trying to get even with you—honest." Rachel swallowed around the lump in her throat. It was bad enough that Audra wouldn't accept her apology, but she was also worried that she'd be in trouble with Mom for breaking Audra's skateboard.

"I still think you broke my skateboard on purpose." Audra's eyes filled with tears. "I'm glad you're not my friend, Rachel. I don't want a friend like you!"

"Fine. If you won't accept my apology, I'm going home!" Rachel rushed out of the barn and stomped onto the Burkholders' porch where Mom sat visiting with Naomi. "I want to go home," she announced.

"Naomi and I aren't done visiting yet," Mom said. "Why don't you go back to the barn and play?"

"I can't."

"Why not?"

"I accidentally broke Audra's skateboard, and—" Rachel blinked against stinging tears and sniffed a couple of times. "I apologized to Audra, but she refuses to forgive me. She thinks I broke her skateboard on purpose."

Before either Mom or Naomi could reply, Audra showed up, holding the two pieces of her skateboard. "Look what Rachel did!" She looked at Rachel and scowled. "I'm sure she did it on purpose because she doesn't like me."

"Is that true?" Mom asked, touching Rachel's shoulder.

Rachel shook her head. "No, it's not. Audra said I could use her skateboard. When I was skating down the ramp, one of the back wheels slipped off. Then my foot slipped and I—I lost my balance." She paused and swiped at the tears rolling down her cheeks. "The skateboard sailed out from under me, flipped into the air, and broke in two pieces when it landed on the floor."

"Sounds like an accident to me," Naomi said, looking at Audra.

"No, it wasn't. Rachel broke it on purpose!" Audra jerked open the screen door and dashed into the house.

"I'll see that Rachel saves up her money and buys Audra a new skateboard," Mom said.

Naomi shook her head. "That's not necessary. I'm sure Jared will make Audra another skateboard."

Mom looked back at Rachel, as though hoping she might say something, but Rachel turned away. "I'll be out in the buggy waiting for you," she mumbled.

"I'll be there as soon as I finish my tea," Mom said.

As Rachel walked away, she heard Mom say to Naomi, "I'm sorry this happened. I had hoped Audra and Rachel would become friends."

"Jah," Naomi replied. "Our move to Pennsylvania has been hard on Audra, and I was hoping she would make new friends right away."

"I wish our girls could see how much they need each other and that they could be good friends if they would only try," Mom said.

I could never be friends with someone who won't accept my apology, Rachel thought as she hurried toward the buggy.

Chapter 12

Change of Heart

As Rachel and Mom traveled home from the Burkholders', Rachel leaned back and closed her eyes. All she could think about was the skateboard she'd broken. It wasn't fair that Audra had refused to accept her apology, or that she'd thought Rachel had broken the skateboard on purpose.

"Are you sleeping, Rachel?" Mom asked.

Rachel's eyes snapped open. "No, I was just thinking."

"About Audra's skateboard?"

"Jah."

"Don't you think it would be nice if you bought her a new skateboard?"

"Audra's mamm said I didn't have to. She said Jared would make Audra another skateboard when he found the time."

"That's true, but Jared's very busy helping his daed in the buggy shop right now. It could be quite awhile before he has the time to make a skateboard for Audra," Mom said.

Rachel frowned. "New skateboards cost a lot of money, and I only have a few quarters in my piggy bank."

"Maybe you could do some odd jobs or paint more of your ladybug rocks to sell at Kauffman's store."

"Even if I did that, it would take a long time before I had enough money to buy a new skateboard." Rachel remembered how last year she put a skateboard in layaway at Kauffman's. She sold several painted rocks, hoping to get the skateboard out of layaway in time for her birthday, but didn't come up with enough money in time. After Jacob and Henry gave her a homemade skateboard, she took the fancy store-bought skateboard out of layaway and used the money she made on something else.

Mom reached across the seat and patted Rachel's hand. "You think about it, okay?"

Rachel nodded.

When they arrived home, Rachel spotted Jacob's dog chasing her cat across the front yard. "Oh no," she moaned. "It looks like Cuddles is in trouble again."

Rachel jumped out of the buggy and sprinted across the yard. "Stop, Buddy!" she shouted. "Stop chasing Cuddles!"

Woof! Woof! Buddy kept running as he nipped at Cuddles's tail.

Me-ow! Cuddles shrieked and tore off in the direction of the creek. Buddy followed, and Rachel raced after him.

Just as the water came into view, the unthinkable happened. *Splat!*—Rachel's cat jumped into the creek!

Rachel gasped. "Cuddles!"

Meow! Meow! Cuddles splashed around in the water, her little head bobbing up and down.

"Hang on, Cuddles! I'm coming!" Rachel raced for the creek, but before she could put one foot in the water, Buddy leaped in, grabbed Cuddles by the scruff of the neck, and hauled her out of the water. He set the cat on the ground, and—*slurp*, *slurp*—licked her waterlogged head with his big red tongue.

Meow! Cuddles swiped her little pink tongue across Buddy's paw and began to purr.

Rachel's jaw dropped. She could hardly believe what she was seeing. Even though Buddy and Cuddles were complete opposites, they'd actually become friends.

I wonder if there's a way Audra and I could become friends, Rachel thought. Audra's mother said that Audra needed a friend. The truth was Rachel needed a friend, too. But she knew in order for that to happen, she would have to do something to make Audra want to be her friend. She also knew she would never make any new friends or keep the ones she had if she didn't learn to forgive.

"I've been doing the same thing to everyone else as Audra did to me today," Rachel whispered as she bent to pick up her cat. "I've refused to accept anyone's apology. I've even held grudges against my friends and family for everything they've done to hurt me—even when it was an accident."

Rachel bowed her head and closed her eyes. *Dear God,* she silently prayed, *I've been angry with everyone because Mary moved away, and I didn't see that I could keep Mary as a friend and make new friends, too. Forgive me for not forgiving. Please show me what to do to make things better between Audra and me.*

Rachel had just opened her eyes when an idea popped into her head. She knew just what she needed to do!

She picked up her cat, called Buddy to follow, and started for home, singing the little song Mom taught her about making friends: "Make new friends but keep the old. One is silver and the other gold."

Rachel was halfway to the house when Jacob came running across the field. "Mom said Buddy was chasing Cuddles and you took off after them. Is everything all right?"

Rachel nodded. "It is now."

"What happened?"

"Cuddles got into the creek, and I was afraid she might drown." Rachel looked down at Jacob's dog and patted the top of his head. "Buddy jumped in the water and rescued Cuddles. I think they've become friends."

Jacob smiled and reached over to pet Cuddles behind her ear. "I'll bet they've been friends the whole time, Rachel. I think Buddy only chases after Cuddles because he likes her and wants to play."

Woof! Woof! Buddy jumped up, put his big paws on Rachel's chest, and—*slurp, slurp*—kissed her right on the nose.

"Get down, Buddy!" Rachel pushed him down with her knee. "I'm glad you saved Cuddles from drowning, and it's good that the two of you are friends, but I still don't appreciate your sloppy kisses."

Jacob chuckled. "I've told you before. . .Buddy licks your face because he likes you, Rachel."

Rachel wiped her nose with the back of her hand. "Jah, well, I might like him, too, if he would stop licking me."

Woof! Woof! Woof! Buddy looked up at Cuddles and wagged his tail.

Meow! Cuddles leaped from Rachel's arm and took off after Buddy.

"Now that's sure a switch. Instead of Buddy chasing Cuddles, she's chasing after him!" Jacob laughed so hard he doubled over and held his sides.

Rachel laughed, too. She ran the rest of the way home, singing at the top of her lungs, "Make new friends but keep the old. One is silver and the other gold!"

When Rachel sat around the table having lunch with her family that afternoon, she was so excited she could hardly stay in her chair. She'd come up with an idea and had gotten Mom's permission to go over to Audra's again after lunch. Henry had agreed to drive Rachel there, since he was going that way to see his girlfriend. Then Grandpa would pick Rachel up a few hours later.

Quit *rutschich* [squirming], and eat your lunch, Rachel," Mom said, pointing to the peanut butter and jelly sandwich on Rachel's plate.

"I'm sorry. I'm just anxious to go."

Henry chuckled. "You can't go until I'm ready, and

I'm not done eating yet."

Rachel picked up her sandwich and took a big bite. By the time she'd finished eating it, Henry was done with his sandwich, too.

"I'll be outside hitching my horse to the buggy," he said, pushing away from the table. "Come on out when you're ready, Rachel."

"Before you go, I'd like to say something—to you and the rest of the family."

"What is it, Rachel?" Mom asked.

"I—uh—" Rachel fiddled with the napkin in her lap. "I'm sorry for the way I've been acting since Mary moved away. I know it wasn't right to blame everyone for all the bad things that happened to me. I should have forgiven when someone said 'I'm sorry.' "

Grandpa reached over and took Rachel's hand. "I accept your apology."

"Me, too," said Mom, Pap, Henry, and Jacob.

Rachel was glad she had such a loving, forgiving family. She smiled at Henry.

"I'll come outside as soon as I've helped Mom with the dishes."

"I think Jacob can help me do the dishes today," Mom said as Henry went out the door.

"What?" Jacob's mouth dropped open. "Washing dishes is women's work!"

"No it's not," said Pap as he scooped up his plate. "Before you kinner came along I used to help your mamm do the dishes almost every night." He wiggled his eyebrows playfully. "I kind of liked sloshing those dishes around in the soapy water. Made me feel good to see them get nice and clean."

Mom looked over at Pap and smiled. "That's right, you sure did."

Pap grinned.

Jacob rolled his eyes, and Rachel snickered. Then she picked up her dishes and took them over to the sink. "I'm heading out to the barn to get what I need to take to Audra's house," she said. "Maybe by then Henry will have his horse and buggy ready to go."

"I'll come over to the Burkholders' to get you in two hours," Grandpa said.

"Danki," Rachel called as she raced out the door.

As Rachel sat beside Henry in his buggy, she squirmed and glanced at the box sitting at her feet. After she'd put her gift to Audra in the box, she taped it shut and tied a red bow on the top so it would look like a present. She hoped Audra would accept the gift.

"You look kind of *naerfich* [nervous], Rachel," Henry said. "Are you worried Audra won't like your present?"

"A little," she admitted.

He reached across the seat and touched her arm. "Don't worry. I'm sure she'll like it just fine."

Rachel remained quiet for the rest of the trip, listening to the steady *clip-clop* of the horse's hooves and the whir from the engines as cars whizzed by.

Finally Henry pulled on the reins and directed the horse up the Burkholders' driveway. He stopped the buggy when they reached the barn, and Rachel climbed down. She lifted out the box that had been sitting on the floor. "Danki for the ride, Henry."

"You're welcome. When you get back home, tell Mom I'll be there in time for supper. See you later, Rachel." Henry lifted his hand in a wave, turned the buggy around, and headed down the driveway.

Drawing in a deep breath for courage, Rachel headed for Audra's house. When she stepped onto the porch, she set the box on the floor and knocked on the door. A few seconds later, Audra's mother answered.

"Rachel, I'm surprised to see you here again today." Naomi looked around. "Is your mamm with you?"

Rachel shook her head. "My brother, Henry, gave me a ride, and Grandpa will pick me up in a couple hours. I came to see Audra." She motioned to the box. "I have something I want to give her."

Naomi opened the door and called, "Audra, someone's here to see you."

A few moments later, Audra peeked her head around the door. She frowned when she saw Rachel. "What's *she* doing here?"

"I brought you something," Rachel said.

Audra's forehead wrinkled and she stepped through the doorway. "What is it?"

Rachel picked up the box and handed it to Audra. "Why don't you open it and see for yourself?"

Audra placed the box on the small table near the door and removed the ribbon. Then she tore the tape off the box, lifted the flaps, and peered inside. "It's a skateboard!"

"It's the skateboard my brothers made for my birthday last year," Rachel explained. "It's to replace your broken skateboard."

"No, Rachel," Naomi said. "You can't give away one of your birthday presents. Especially since your brothers made it."

"It's okay," Rachel said. "I asked Henry and Jacob first, and they both said the skateboard is mine and I can do whatever I want with it." She smiled at Audra. "I want you to have it."

Audra's eyes widened as she lifted the skateboard out of the box. "Danki, Rachel."

"You're welcome."

"You can come over anytime you want and use the skateboard," Audra said.

Rachel smiled. "I'd like that, but there's something else I'd like even more."

"What's that?" Audra asked.

"I'd like you to be my friend."

"I'd like that, too." Audra motioned to the house. "Would you like to go up to my room and play?"

Rachel nodded.

Audra led the way, and Rachel followed her into the house.

When they entered Audra's room, Audra turned to Rachel and said, "Why don't you take a seat on the bed while I get something from my closet?"

"Okay."

When Audra returned, she held a faceless doll in her hands. "This is to replace the one Jacob's dog chewed up," she said, handing it to Rachel.

Rachel's mouth dropped open. "You—you know about that?"

Audra nodded. "I heard Jacob telling Orlie about it during recess one day."

Rachel hardly knew what to say. "Are you sure you want to give me your doll?"

"I'm very sure." Audra took a seat on the bed beside Rachel. "Whenever you come here to play we can take turns riding my new skateboard." She patted the top of the doll's head. "And when I come to your house, we can take turns playing with your new faceless doll."

"You can jump on our new trampoline when you come over to my house," Rachel said. "And I promise not to take my new faceless doll out to the trampoline when we jump."

Audra giggled. "No, that wouldn't be a good idea at all."

Rachel smiled as she thought about the verse of scripture from Ecclesiastes 4:9–10, about two being better than one. From then on, Rachel would try to remember to be kind and forgiving. She was glad she'd finally found a new friend, for she and Audra had both been given the chance for a new beginning.